PRAISE FOR *MILLICENT GLENN'S LAST WISH*

"A heartwarming and affecting novel centered around the love between mothers and daughters, of what we share and the secrets we keep . . . Whitaker brings us back to the 1950s, highlighting the old gender norms and the cost paid by those who tried to shake them . . . an engaging and illuminating walk through the not-so-distant past . . . with a worthy heroine to lead readers through a life full of loss, love, heartbreak, and, ultimately, forgiveness."

—Karen White, *New York Times* bestselling author of *A Long Time Gone* and the Tradd Street Series

"Tori Whitaker explores the depths of mother love with insight, care, and heart-wrenching honesty in this post–World War II story brimming with exceptional historical detail. A moving and emotionally charged debut by a writer to watch."

—Susan Meissner, bestselling author of *The Last Year of the War*

"A novel about the legacies women pass to their daughters—and the price of the secrets they keep. Millie is a heroine to cheer for as she makes her journey from . . . working wife and mom to grandmother seeking forgiveness for her decisions—made because of jaw-dropping challenges you will never forget. You'll miss her long after the book's cover is closed."

—Jenna Blum, *New York Times* bestselling author of *The Lost Family* and *Those Who Save Us*

"I loved this story. Tori Whitaker has created characters who are irresistibly real and hard to leave behind! A meticulously crafted debut."

—Lynn Cullen, bestselling author of *The Sisters of Summit Avenue* and *Mrs. Poe*

"Packed with midcentury nostalgia and Cincinnati local interest, Whitaker's dual-timeline debut walks a tightrope between a mother's yearning to be truly known and what makes her eminently unknowable: a desire to protect her daughter that was born of love. Mothers and daughters alike will not soon forget Millicent's last wish; they'll recognize it as their own."

—Kathryn Craft, award-winning author of *The Far End of Happy* and *The Art of Falling*

"Get ready to meet your new favorite author as Tori Whitaker moves deftly forward and back in time in a lyrical exploration of motherhood and longing, secrets and regrets, mistakes and, ultimately, absolution. This is an author with great insight into both history and the female heart, and I highly recommend this heartfelt, beautifully written debut."

—Joshilyn Jackson, *New York Times* and *USA Today* bestselling author of *Never Have I Ever* and *The Almost Sisters*

"Tenderly told and full of heart, *Millicent Glenn's Last Wish* is a deeply satisfying story that hooked me from the first page. Tori Whitaker's debut offers a fresh and poignant perspective on motherhood, loss, and, ultimately, forgiveness."

—Lynda Cohen Loigman, nationally bestselling author of *The Two-Family House* and *The Wartime Sisters*

"Attend the debut of a bright new talent . . . It's alternately joyous and sad, scary and hopeful, but always wise and warm and overflowing with the wonder of being human."

—William Martin, *New York Times* bestselling author of *Cape Cod* and *Bound for Gold*

"*Millicent Glenn's Last* Wish is a delight of a book that explores how one long-held secret can shape a family. Tori Whitaker's characters sparkle with warmth and humanity, especially ninety-year-old Mil, whose voice rings clear and true throughout these charming pages."

—Tara Conklin, *New York Times* bestselling author of
The Last Romantics

"A poignant and touching story of three generations of women and the secret family tragedy that unwittingly binds them. With rich settings and fully realized characters that you'll root for, this book broke my heart—and then stitched it back together again."

—Colleen Oakley, author of *You Were There Too*

"A page-turner . . . of the lives of three generations of women, spanning the post–World War II baby boom into the modern age. Each has experienced life at a different phase of emerging feminism. As the layered revelation of long-held secrets peels away, these women discover healing for years of misunderstanding, grief, and betrayal . . . a masterwork."

—Diane C. McPhail, author of *The Abolitionist's Daughter*

"Tori Whitaker's moving novel . . . offers a clear-eyed look at how 'the good old days' were not always so good, particularly when it came to women's reproductive health and autonomy. This well-researched and timely novel made me thankful for past generations of women, who, like the titular character, fought hard for the rights I hold so dear today. An impressive debut."

—Susan Rebecca White, author of *We Are All Good People Here*

"A beautifully told and astonishing tale of the mysterious ties that hold a family together . . . Rich in detail and imbued with compassion, these characters struggle toward necessary forgiveness of a shocking maternity ward tragedy that feels all too relevant, even today. Whitaker cuts close to the bone from page one!"

—Kimberly Brock, award-winning author of *The River Witch*

"Readers, meet Millicent Glenn, a tough, savvy lady who has survived many challenges in her ninety-one years. But now she's facing her biggest one yet . . . I rooted for Millicent and found the tenderness and complexity of the mother-daughter relationship so lovingly woven through this emotional and gripping story."

—Marybeth Mayhew Whalen, author of *This Secret Thing* and cofounder of She Reads

"Written with compassion and grace, Tori Whitaker's *Millicent Glenn's Last Wish* is a nuanced debut illuminating the multigenerational strength of love, loss, survival, and the limitless power of family. I dare you to read without shedding a tear. Readers will think on these characters long after turning the last page."

—Sarah McCoy, *New York Times* and international bestselling author of *Marilla of Green Gables*

Millicent Glenn's Last Wish

Millicent Glenn's Last Wish

TORI WHITAKER

LAKE UNION
PUBLISHING

Text copyright © 2020 by Tori Whitaker
All rights reserved.

Published by Lake Union Publishing, Seattle

www.apub.com

Amazon, the Amazon logo, and Lake Union Publishing are trademarks of Amazon.com, Inc., or its affiliates.

ISBN-13: 9781542023313
ISBN-10: 1542023319

Cover design by Black Kat Design

Printed in the United States of America

For her

Had I but known the cost of wisdom, might I have carried on in a state of folly?

—Anonymous

Baby boom: a temporary marked increase in the birth rate, especially the one following World War II.

2015

Cincinnati
September

They say we shouldn't ask a question if we can't handle the answer. So I almost hadn't asked mine. Almost. I'd been a young wife and willful, and I'd imagined how I would feel when I got old—ancient, maybe ninety years old—lying listless on a mattress in a nursing home, looking back on my life and lamenting: Why hadn't I placed the call?

No matter what I would learn by asking, I had reasoned, surely knowing would be better than not knowing.

Now here I was, Millicent Glenn, soon to be ninety-one and not in a nursing home after all—I had my own house in the suburbs and took care of my own self, too. I pulled on my garden gloves and bent over a pot on my stoop. Getting down in the border beds was hard on my knees these days. And my hands couldn't take digging up rocks and dry soil. Arthritis had won that battle. But I wasn't an invalid; I didn't do water aerobics twice a week for nothing. If it took me all day, I'd have the prettiest pots of mums on the block, yellow and purple and deep fall orange. Nourishing these plants was my way to keep something alive.

I dipped into a bag of potting mix, inhaling its clean, earthy smell of compost and peat. A car engine startled me, and I turned to see a white sedan rolling into my drive, one I didn't recognize. I squinted into the morning sun. A woman? I stepped off my stoop with my trowel in hand and onto my sidewalk's brick pavers. I patted my cell phone in the pocket of my smock, feeling safer as I watched the car door open. The woman climbed out. She waved.

"Surprise," she said, her longish, silver-streaked hair gently blowing across her forehead.

Jane? What was she doing here? I hadn't seen my daughter since Christmas the year before. I felt jittery all over—thrilled to see her and on guard both at once.

"Jane, my goodness," I called out as she came my way. Thankfully I had mind enough not to call her Janie, the nickname she'd hated since she turned seventeen. I wouldn't set things off on the wrong foot right from the get-go. If I'd known she was coming, I'd have worn the gold sweater she'd shipped up last Mother's Day. I stripped off my gloves and tossed them atop one of the inkberry shrubs.

"You're looking at a freshly minted retiree," she said.

"A retiree?" I tapped my left hearing aid. Had I heard her right?

"Back in Ohio to stay," she said, setting a covered basket down in the grass and giving me an awkward hug. Jane's greetings usually consisted of simple how-are-yous and quick pecks on the cheek.

"I can't believe it," I said. "It's wonderful news." My heart pounded so hard I pressed my hand to my chest to try to settle it. It wasn't the first time Jane had arrived home unannounced—she had done this once before more than thirty years ago. But I doubted we'd rehash that memory. So Jane had finally retired. She was sixty-five, after all. I glanced again at her car, empty of suitcases or boxes. Was she staying with Kelsey? Surely my granddaughter, Jane's only child, would've let me know. I stiffened.

"Does Kelsey know you're back?" I asked. "Why didn't you tell me you were coming? And when did you get that car?" Jane and I hadn't talked since August's once-a-month-whether-we-needed-it-or-not phone call.

"Glad to see you, too. Nothing like a Mommy interrogation to greet me," she said. Jane picked up the basket and handed it to me. I lifted the thick cotton toweling that covered it.

"Oranges," I said. My daughter remembered my childhood story of growing up in the tenements; a charity lady had delivered oranges to my family one Christmas, and I'd had a soft spot for them ever since. At this moment, my soft spot was all mushy. "Thank you, honey. What a kind thing to do."

"You're welcome," she said, and I thought I saw a note of sadness pass across her face. I hoped I was wrong. "Guess I'm just in time to help you plant?"

"Yes. But first come in, come in. Let me look at you." I opened my colonial-blue front door, and my security system tinkled its friendly hello.

"Something smells delicious," Jane said as she stepped into my small foyer.

"Just so happens I baked a batch of brownies." I'd stirred them up the night before and popped them in the oven that morning. I'd known I'd want a treat after working outside all day—and it was a good thing, too, given I now had company. I hung Jane's jean jacket in the closet of this house her late father had built.

"Not sure I'm ready for this glacial cold weather," Jane said, faking a shiver.

It was fifty-nine degrees, for Pete's sake, on its way to sixty-two. A perfectly sunny September day in Cincinnati. "You aren't a Georgia Peach anymore," I said.

"Like I was ever the eyelash-batting Southern belle type," she said. I was still getting used to her sporadic drawl, though.

She wore her Levi's with a Habitat for Humanity long-sleeved jersey. Jane had worked at Habitat's world headquarters a couple of hours from Atlanta in a town that held some charm. She'd been bitten by the home-building bug years ago, thanks to her father, but her journey in constructing homes had taken a very different course. I studied the face of my baby from across my kitchen island. Jane was tall and attractive in her seventh decade. She'd hardly ever needed a smidge of makeup. In her hippie youth, a crown of daisies had been adornment enough. Still, her pretty face revealed the deepening crevasses of age, or stress, or both—though nothing hid her small childhood scar. It'd marked its territory above her left brow so I would never forget.

I poured us mugs of milk and sliced the brownies. They were chewy with crispy edges, just the way Jane and her daddy had always liked them.

"Any marijuana in these?" she said, the word *marijuana* sounding long and slow off her tongue.

"If only I'd known you were coming," I quipped back.

I thought I saw a smile but couldn't be sure. Were we really ready to joke about her youthful rebellions? They hadn't been funny at the time.

"You bake the best brownies in the galaxy," Jane said, mimicking what she'd said as a kid. A memory flashed of her at age four, scooting a kitchen chair up to the counter, climbing atop, and helping me bake. We wore matching bibbed aprons I'd made myself, white with red rickrack sewn around the edges. I could still see Janie cracking the eggs and leveling the flour with the flat side of a knife. She'd been the cutest little thing.

Sitting in my breakfast bay lined with windows, her plate in hand, Jane surveyed the room. My cane rested against the wall for the occasional day when I needed it. I couldn't help suspecting that something besides retirement had brought Jane back to Ohio after twenty years away.

"I always adored these knotty pine cabinets," she said. "Did Daddy pick them out, or did you?"

"I did," I said with satisfaction. I'd helped Dennis in the home-building business once upon a time. Well, I'd more than helped him. I'd been his partner. "Honey, where are you going to be staying? With Kelsey?"

"Me and Kelsey and her husband in a loft? Huh. She offered, but three's a crowd. I rented a place over in Milford. The movers arrive tomorrow."

So Kelsey had known about Jane's move but not informed me. "Milford, oh good," I said, trying to mask my dismay. Kelsey and I talked three or four times a week. We enjoyed grandma-granddaughter days at least twice a month. I felt as if she and Jane had thrown a party and not invited me. Yet I was so glad to see my daughter home. "Milford's a great place," I said, managing a smile. "Nice and close."

We chatted for a while about safe topics: Kelsey's job at the museum, Jane's drive up from Georgia. Then, before we ever got back to my mums, Jane said she'd better go to her new place to prepare for the movers.

"I'll wrap up these brownies," I said. "You can take them with you."

"Let me help," she said.

"I can do this." I was frustrated that she'd caught me in one of my daily struggles. Tasks took me twice as long as before, but I'd get them done. Except for opening jars and fighting with plastic wrap.

"Just let me do it," she said, reaching in as I was trying to rip the plastic from its box.

"Ouch!" My thumb grated along the serrated metal lip and started to bleed.

"Oh my gosh," Jane said. "I'm sorry." She tore a paper towel off the roll and dabbed the cut.

"It's not your fault," I said. "These days my skin is as thin as that cellophane. Band-Aids are in the cabinet where I keep the measuring cups."

Would my child need to care for me one day? I still tidied my own house. I drove my own car. No one had taken my keys away yet, and they wouldn't if I had my say. I might not contribute to society the way I had when I worked—and I wasn't treasurer of the neighborhood association anymore—but I wasn't useless, was I? The baggers at the grocery loaded the bags for young mothers, too, not just me. And I wasn't the only resident on the street for whom the kind young man next door cleared the driveway with his snowblower each winter. But I was getting slower all the time, cautious and deliberate with each step. A simple slip in the tub could lead to a broken hip. For women my age that was a death sentence.

"Let me kiss your boo-boo," Jane said then, and she pressed her lips lightly to my bandaged thumb. "It'll make it all better." I had used those same words when she was seven. She'd fallen off her bike and scraped her shin on the greasy metal chain. Her words now sounded so touching and ridiculous and out of the blue, they made me laugh.

"Jane," I said, hoping I wouldn't put a damper on things, but I needed to know. "What's the real reason you're here?"

"What do you mean?" she said, frowning. "You and Kelsey have been hounding me to move home for years. I've retired. I'm here. It's a surprise that I'd hoped you'd be happy about."

"Of course I'm happy. I never wanted you to leave in the first place, remember?" I said. "It's just so . . . sudden."

"You don't have to read anything into this. I made a quick decision, and here I am. Period."

"But I just—"

"Maybe I shouldn't have come." Jane scowled and shook her head. "It's partly your worrywart ways that drove me off to start with."

6

One minute I was basking in memories of kissing her boo-boos—proof that I'd been a good mommy—and the next I was chided for being overprotective. My daughter had been home less than an hour and I'd already riled her up. "I apologize, Jane," I said. "I want to enjoy our time together now that you're home, I do."

She snorted. "Sorry for snapping. Old habit, I guess."

I touched the pocket of my smock, knowing I had stowed two tissues inside—I counted everything, from buttons on blouses to each egg in the fridge. But I didn't want to get weepy. My best friend, Pauline Irving, gone a year already, once jokingly called me the poster child for self-control. She was one of three people who'd truly known me, though, who'd known the pain I concealed from most.

Jane said, "Really, Mom—I never intended to hurt your feelings."

"Honey, we all do and say things that we regret. You. Me. Everyone." I could have added, *including your father.* But I was thinking, *especially me.*

It was eerie. Before she'd arrived, I'd been remembering that fateful phone call long ago, when I was a young wife. What my daughter didn't know was that when she was twenty-three, I'd tried to tell her what I'd learned on that call. I'd tried to explain about the woman with the beauty mark . . . and the album hidden in my basement. But our conversation had escalated into something else so ugly I was incapable of going on. That'd been the morning after news anchor Walter Cronkite said the Supreme Court had decided *Roe v. Wade.* Jane had been living in Arizona at the time and had come back to town for a wedding. I was standing in this very room, nervous as a kid sent to the principal, when I broached my subject with her—but before I could get to the point, Jane blew up. Out of nowhere she accused me of things I'd never done. One could argue, though, that what I'd tried to confess was far worse. There'd also been the time I'd tried sitting her down months after Dennis had passed, but Jane was hurting too much to listen. I may as well have been talking to the walls. Then I worked up the nerve once more when she came for my birthday five years back. That day she had told me she loved me for the first time in ages, and I couldn't go through with it. I hadn't wanted to sour the mood.

Our relationship was like that: forever one of polar extremes. And the only thing that I could predict was that I could never predict where we'd land next.

Now, as I approached what my granddaughter called my "big nine-one," if I could be granted my life's last wish, I knew what it would be. Not that I was the kind of girl, nor the kind of old lady, who put much stock in wishes. Never had. As a child, while I might've gotten a cake for my birthday, it never had candles to make a wish upon. Mama couldn't afford them. And never did I believe in genies in bottles. But perhaps with Jane home, I'd finally be able to tell her what had happened all those years ago. I'd get her to understand me better—why I am the way I am. And maybe I'd come to understand her.

If I could be granted my life's last wish, it would be that Jane would forgive me.

PART ONE

CHAPTER ONE

December 26, 1944

Mama had just finished curling my hair in the corner bedroom upstairs that had once belonged to my fiancé's sister. This room with the 1920s rose floral wallpaper had a slanted ceiling beneath the Glenns' farm-house roof and was to be my marital bedroom. Mama had styled my hair in a straight-back pomp, à la the Andrews Sisters. The curling iron's metal tongs, made hot from the stove in the kitchen, were now cooled and their scorched scent scarcely noticeable. Mama teased my hair above my forehead and smoothed it back high. Then she swept my sandy-colored, longish rolls up on both sides with pins.

"I love it, Mama," I said, and she smiled. "Will you bring me my veil?"

The veil of ivory netting hung in the bedroom where Mama would stay the night. Opa, my maternal grandfather, had a guest room, too. I'd lived with them both in a tiny two-room flat until that morning—when we'd awakened to the shouts of neighbors who had eight people residing in rooms the size of ours. Our home was only an hour away, but Mama and Opa had come early to help with the wedding and to meet my future in-laws.

I twirled around like the ballerina in a music box I'd seen on display at Pogue's, feeling lovely in my slim satin gown of ivory. Mama had said the fabric was cut across the grain, which was why its fluid drape clung to my body, its shiny folds falling gracefully from my knees until the hemline brushed the floor. Mine was not a secondhand gown; it was a thirdhand gown from a thrift shop, its style ten years old. But it was the dress of my dreams. I loved its slim sleeves that fitted close at my wrists and ended in sharp points near the knuckles of each hand. Mama had taken needle and thread to the cuffs' buttons, twelve in all, to ensure they wouldn't pop off. She'd spent her life sewing for herself and for me—and for others, too, to feed our family. Mama was wrapped in her purple rayon sheath she'd made two years before. It was the closest thing to a dressy-dress that she owned, but she carried herself like a woman of means.

The man I was to wed was the only Glenn kid left at home, and he was on a farmer's deferment from military service. Dennis and I would live with his folks until, as Papa Glenn put it, "the newlyweds got on their feet." We all knew that would wait until after the war was over— when farmers could cut back on raising crops for our troops. But no matter our accommodations, I couldn't wait to marry Dennis, to sleep every night with my one true love.

The wife of Dennis's brother slipped into the room with their one-year-old, Margaret, toddling beside her. "We're here," Abbie pronounced. "Your honorary flower girl is ready." Abbie had striking Irish eyes of hazel and a wide-set mouth, but her pretty face didn't warm to me. She gave my gown a once-over without so much as a smile. Abbie and my fiancé had grown up on neighboring farms, eating beefsteak tomatoes warm off the vine and sharing a shaker of salt, so I wanted her to see how happy I made him. I hoped Abbie would become my friend, too.

"Margaret is precious, Abbie," I said. The velvet of the child's emerald-green dress, which Abbie had fashioned from a length off an old gown, was as soft as the wings of a fairy. "I can't wait," I said, "to have lots of little girls of my own." I'd been an only child and had always wanted siblings like the other families I knew.

"Well, then, Millie Kraus," Abbie said, grinning and wrinkling her nose at the same time. "If you're to have a big family, I guess it's a good thing you're not a working girl anymore. Especially down in the city."

I winced. The way Abbie stressed *working girl* felt like a slap, and so that was a slap in my mama's face, too. Thank goodness Mama hadn't heard it.

Dennis's mother joined me as Abbie was leaving. I wiggled my fingers down low at my sides to shake off Abbie's air.

Mother Glenn's hair, piled into her usual bun, was so thick that her tresses, if freed from their bands and their pins, would fall in ropes down her back. She might have looked years younger were it not for that bun, though today she'd wound it with blue ribbons that matched her midnight-blue dress. She delivered my bouquet of fir branches and twigs with berries that she and Mama had gathered from trees on the grounds.

"It's gorgeous," I said. Abundant red ribbon wrapped the bunch, with strands that hung down long. The satin ribbon had been a splurge for my wedding. I'd paid for it myself with money I'd earned at Kroger before I'd quit to move here. That ribbon was more than an embellishment: it represented how productive I could be, how useful.

Mama stepped in and gingerly draped my veil atop the back of a chair.

"I'll leave you two for now," Dennis's mother said. "It's a big day in a mother's life, not just the bride's." She hugged us and added, "Sylvia, you raised a great girl. Smart. Kind. Pretty. Hard-working." Mama's face grew pink as she squeezed Mother Glenn's hands.

I felt myself turning pink, too. I wanted so badly to fit in.

Mama took my arm and guided me to the sleigh bed that was so high it required a stepstool to climb up—a far cry from the fold-out cot I grew up sleeping on. "You know, I've been fretting," she said, "that these people would be highfalutin."

My mother's apprehension was understandable. All my life we'd lived in two-room flats. The Glenns' house had four bedrooms upstairs and three large rooms down. The farm had 144 acres off old Reading Road, land Dennis's family had worked since before the Civil War. But neither of our families had reveled in the prosperity of what some already called the glorious Roaring Twenties. The men in my family had long been brewers of beer. Opa had once owned a home, and as a girl, Mama had worn new shoes and had her own room. But they'd lost their entire livelihoods during Prohibition. Dennis's family had suffered in a glutted farmer's market after the Great War, when prices on food plunged. Then came the Crash. Then the Depression. Then another war. Our families weren't so unalike after all.

"The Glenns are wonderful to you," Mama said. She slid her palm along my leg, savoring the smooth cloth of my gown. "They're good people, Mil. I can tell. But you'll always be my daughter."

I leaned and kissed her temple. "Of course I will."

A great ruckus emerged from down below. The remaining Glenn nieces and nephews had arrived. I could picture them dressed in their Sunday school finery as their high voices drifted through the cracks of the boards below Mama and me. "Uncle Dennis is getting hitched!" the children sang. Their little feet pounded across the wooden planks.

Then Mother Glenn's voice rang out above the clatter. "Children, children, *shhh*. We must prepare for the bride."

"Best be putting on your veil," Mama said.

Soon she was stepping back to appraise me, her expression filled with maternal pride. She fluffed the veil, making its scalloped edge dance about my elbows. "I'll go down and join the others. Opa will be along soon to escort you," she said. "I'm happy for you." Her voice weakened for the first time. "You will remember what I taught you?"

"Yes," I said, but she was compelled to tell me again all the same.

"You have to have a means of earning," she said, just as she had when I turned six, and had said in each of my fourteen years since, "lest you find yourself without a bed or a soupbone to your name."

I nodded agreement. "I love you, Mama."

"I love you, too, my daughter," she said, and she turned to leave.

I gazed into the oval mirror above the walnut dresser. I had something old, my gown; something new, the ribbon that tied my bouquet; something borrowed, a bottle of perfume; and something blue, my eyes. I applied a fresh coat of Tangee Red-Red lipstick, too. The tiny stone on my ring finger glinted as if it were a queen's jewel. Dennis had saved up his funds, and his father had loaned him the rest.

Dennis's great-aunt began playing "I'll Be Home for Christmas" on the upright piano downstairs. It was almost time. From the dresser, I picked up the fan-shaped bottle of Shalimar, the golden perfume Dennis's oldest sister had let me borrow. I removed its ornamental stopper and dabbed silky dots high on each end of my collarbone, left and right. I inhaled the Oriental notes of jasmine and musk. Then I bent to the mirror one last time to make sure my face was picture-perfect. And there in the mirror's reflection stood my grandfather. My beloved opa would give me away today. My father had died of rheumatic fever when I was less than a year old. Too young for me to remember him.

Despite Opa's bum leg that made him limp, he stood tall and proud, nearly filling the length of the open door. I swiveled around. I'd never seen him wear a tie before.

"Ready to marry your beau?" Opa said. He was smiling his classic closed-lip smile with its deep, crescent-shaped ruts. Opa's eyetooth had been missing since before I was born. When I was young, he'd said he could never see out of that tooth anyway. He stepped closer and took one of my hands in his rough ones. "You're the most beautiful bride I've ever seen," he said. It was a line that all grandfathers told all granddaughters on all wedding days, I was sure. But coming from my opa, I knew he believed the words to be true. I hoped my groom would agree.

Opa and I descended the narrow, enclosed stairs. His arm was looped tightly in mine, and I could feel him shaking. The melody of "Wedding March" made my skin tingle, and the room at the foot of the steps glowed as if it awaited us.

Downstairs, Opa walked me along the pretty little aisle the Glenn nieces and nephews had fashioned with sprigs of fragrant greenery. The women had lit votive candles, and the men had hung evergreen boughs across the mantel and windowsills. A fresh-cut tree glittered with hand-made ornaments, strings of popped corn, and the Glenns' few treasured glass bulbs. Family members and friends gathered around the room, straining to get a peek as Opa and I passed. I felt as if I were walking in a magical storybook tale.

Then I got my first glimpse of him. My Dennis. He was standing between the two high, paned windows darkened by dusk, hands folded together in front of him. He wore a two-piece pinstriped brown suit with crisp creases running up each leg. His gaze was intent upon me, and I felt our love in my heart and in my bones and in all my skin.

As I progressed slowly toward him in the candlelit room, Dennis smiled in his boyish way that said: *You're dazzling. And you're bowling me over, girl. Come. Let our lives together begin.*

When the time came to exchange our vows, I faced my man and repeated after the minister: "to love, cherish, and obey . . ." and the last word suddenly struck me as odd. I had grown up obeying Mama and Opa. I was a woman now and had someone else to obey? But Dennis's heavily lashed eyes were locked with mine, and one dimple peeped out just for me, and then my discomfort evaporated. This man loved me. He loved me for who I was—no matter that I had been an impoverished girl from the slums. And I loved him.

Then it was his turn to repeat his vows. Dennis would love and cherish me, too, and—as the traditional words went—in lieu of obeying me, he would endow me with all his worldly goods. Out of the periphery of my vision, I caught Mama's face flush. She raised her chin.

I would not forget her lessons; I would earn my own sum. It was important to me regardless of her opinion.

Dennis and I kissed beneath the mistletoe before the crackling hickory logs. And with Dennis's strong hands on my back and the spicy scent of his cologne, the sweet taste of his lips consumed me. I felt ecstatic. Charmed. We belonged together until death did us part.

Dennis's great-aunt commenced to playing a hymn I didn't know, but it sounded tinkling and joyous and bright. Dennis and I turned to face our loved ones, and given Mama's expression during the vows, I was relieved to see elation in her face. It matched my opa's. Dennis's parents, too, were grinning broadly for this happy occasion.

"Congratulations, baby brother. You're a lucky guy." Nathan slapped Dennis on the back and winked at me. "Try to keep this fella in line, will ya?"

I blushed. "I'll do my best." Nathan's wife, Abbie, forced a smile.

Mother Glenn led us to the refreshments. "Make way, please," she said to the well-wishers crowding around us. "The bride and groom must go first, so everyone else can dive in."

She'd set a long table in the parlor beneath the map of Europe with white and red pushpins showing where our troops were moving in the war. Lovely linens covered the table in what Dennis's younger sister had called a cloth of white damask. The two Glenn sisters ladled punch out of the largest clear glass bowl I'd ever seen. They'd soon slice our four-layer red velvet cake that they'd piped with white icing—a luxury, given they'd used more than a week's worth of sugar rations. The banquet included finger sandwiches with hand-cut biscuits, ham, turkey, and yellow cheese. Everything was arranged on plates of varying heights. There were plenty of relishes: home-canned pickles, pickled red beets, and deviled eggs served on glass plates with indented cups that cradled each half. Mother Glenn had brought out a tray of sliced breads, too— pumpkin bread, date nut bread, and bread with red and green cherries. She'd baked with honey from the farm when sugar supplies ran out.

And a ball of churned butter rested in an etched glass dish. There were two short-handled spreaders dunked into the center and tied with tiny red bows.

I'd come a long way since the days of my getting one orange for Christmas. I sometimes feared my good fortune could never last.

My husband—how strange it was to think of him as that—and I fed each other food and kissed between bites. We welcomed the guests with their hugs and kind words. Then the Glenn sisters started clapping their hands, getting everyone's attention. What was this? I held tight to my cup of punch. The Glenn grandchildren—two boys and three girls in all—squirmed and laughed as they gathered around their mothers' knees. They looked so sweet in their red-and-green sweaters and spit-shined shoes. And such rosy cheeks.

The room quieted to a murmur, and Mother Glenn stepped to the fore. "All right, children. Are you ready? One, two, three."

"We love you, Uncle Dennis and Aunt Millie," they said in unison. Tears welled in my eyes. It was official. I was now their aunt. I had never felt so honored.

"We love you, too, you precious little ones," I said, bending down to their height.

I saw my mother smiling at me. I wanted Dennis and me to have children like these. Four or more of our own at least—enough babies to fill a whole birthday party with ice cream and cake and lots of lit candles.

"Oh, Mama," I said, reaching for her elbow. The music resumed, and I spoke so that she could barely hear. "I can't wait to have a house full of little elves, just like them."

Her face shifted. "Not all women have babies the way alley cats squirt out kittens."

My vision darted side to side. My sister-in-law Abbie was frowning at us from about a yard away. Had she heard? I hoped not.

Mama had first used those words with me when I was a child, after I'd asked why I had no brothers or sisters. I'd wanted someone to play hide-and-seek with in the park or to curl up with under a tent made of blankets or to form a chorus of voices when my birthday song was sung. I wanted big birthday parties even if we had no candles on a cake at all. But there'd been an edge in Mama's voice that bade me never to speak again of having siblings.

"I'm sorry, Mama," I whispered. "I never meant to hurt your feelings."

I felt bad for her, but my life would be different. For one thing, my father had died too young. My handsome husband turned from a conversation with a friend and pressed a soft kiss to my cheek. Dennis and I would have the big, rowdy family of our dreams. And I would be the perfect mother.

There was nothing to stop us.

2015

I climbed out of Jane's white Taurus in front of Union Terminal. It was an art deco building with a great round clock on the front with red neon hands. The building awed me the same way it had in 1933. I'd been eight years old then and couldn't fathom why the clock had twelve dashes where real numbers should be. Before that I'd watched men erect this limestone structure with its massive steel beams, and I'd thought it was shaped like a rainbow. Opa had taken me here the first week it opened. We never rode the trains. We'd come to watch the people, to see the murals inside for free. Today the terminal also housed Cincinnati's multimuseum center, where my granddaughter was employed. This imposing place symbolized the passage of time in my life. Yet unlike me, this building got to go on reinventing itself, finding new purpose. It would remain standing long after I was buried.

Kelsey's job was not in the terminal's children's museum, which was filled with stations to learn and play. Nor was it in the museum where the bones of a dinosaur's tail stretched above a man's head. Kelsey was an archivist in the history library downstairs, and today she was getting off early.

"Kelsey said we should meet her in front of the OMNIMAX Theater," I said to Jane.

"We're early," Jane said, shooting me a sideways glance. She hadn't inherited my punctuality gene.

We stood among grade-schoolers, on a field trip I presumed, in the center of the grand rotunda with its towering arched ceiling. I was about their age the first time I beheld the murals in this rotunda. "The panoramic murals are made of mosaic glass tiles," a teacher was saying. "The one on the left shows the history of our country." She pointed to the Native Americans. "And the murals to the right depict the past of Cincinnati," she said. "See the river? The steamboats?"

Opa's face had wrinkled with anger when he'd told me how the city's great brewing industry was nowhere in the scene; the German artist had begun the designs when Prohibition still reigned.

When Kelsey arrived at our designated spot, she threw out her arms and said, "Hello, my two besties, my favorite women in the whole wide world." She always dropped her professional persona the minute she saw me—and I relished being at least one of her besties. She wore some kind of poncho or cape that draped over her shoulders and hung open in front. Her glasses had large, round frames in the primary blue of a color wheel, although her vision was twenty-twenty. Her flowing plaid skirt, purple flats, and loose top bearing John Lennon's face all spoke to how her mother had influenced her. Or it could be Kelsey's bohemian style was the latest rage.

Kelsey embraced me first. "You'll turn some heads today, Grandma, you senior sexpot, you."

"Hi, sweetie," I said, rolling my eyes in fun. All I wore was a pair of brown slacks and my gold cable-knit sweater—nothing with buttons or zippers or heels. I kissed Kelsey, leaving my trademark lipstick-print on her cheek. How I loved that girl. Imagine calling a thirty-eight-year-old married career woman a girl. But Kelsey would always be Grandma's little girl, my munchkin doing cartwheels in the yard.

"What about me?" Jane said, pretending to pout, and they hugged.

Watching them together warmed my heart. But something also niggled at me. Something foolish. With Jane back home, I didn't have Kelsey all to myself anymore.

"Let's do the whispering drinking fountains," I said, "before going to the Rookwood for malts."

"We absolutely have to do the fountains," Kelsey said as the students marched by, hand in hand in pairs. The buddy system.

"Really?" That was Jane. "Aren't we a bit too old for those?"

"Mom," Kelsey said. "I want to create some déjà vu."

I felt as if Kelsey had come to my rescue. My opa had taught me the trick of the terminal's whispering drinking fountains. The first time Dennis and I had performed the same experiment with Jane, she was five. Then she and I had passed the tradition down to Kelsey when she was a kid. Given my age, who knew if this time could be my last? Surely Jane wouldn't begrudge me that.

"You take the one at that end, Mom." Kelsey pointed Jane toward the drinking fountain in the far-right corner. My daughter didn't look thrilled to be the one going solo, but this required us to split up. "I'll text you when it's time," Kelsey said. "Grandma, you stick with me."

We headed to the fountain at the opposite end of the rotunda. We dodged more youngsters and passengers bound for the Amtrak rails until we were standing in line at the fountain. Jane was getting into position on the other side of one of the largest half domes in the world; this place spanned 180 feet. "That's as long as eighteen boxcars lined end to end," my opa had told me way back when.

"I've been so excited for today," Kelsey said, squeezing me with one arm.

"Me too." I hoped this day would go well.

Only one person in line separated us from the drinking fountain. Kelsey texted Jane.

We stepped up for our turn. "You first," Kelsey said, looking at her cell. "Go."

I bent over the dark marble fountain as if I were going to crank the knob and sip from a flowing arch of water. Instead, I spoke into it in a normal tone of voice: "Jane? Jane? Can you hear me?"

I listened carefully, the volume high on my hearing aids. I could feel my granddaughter breathing as she hovered over my shoulder to hear, too.

"I'm here." It was Jane's voice coming through the fountains, a scientific trick of the dome. She sounded faint, like an echo or the voice of God. "Can you hear me?" she said.

"We hear you," Kelsey and I said in unison.

"Has Kelsey told you yet, Mom?" Jane said.

"Told me what?" I said back, confused and oblivious as to whether anyone was waiting in line behind us.

Jane's whisper of a voice came through again clearly: "I'm going to be a grandma."

I pulled back, covered my mouth, and looked at Kelsey, thinking I was hearing Jane wrong.

"I'm going to have a baby, Grandma," she said with a flicker of panic, probably noting the mix of excitement and bewilderment on my face. This was how I would learn she was pregnant?

"I didn't expect Mom to blurt it out," Kelsey said, frowning. "I'd planned on telling you today myself. But she's gonna be Nana. And you're going to be Great-Grandmama."

My granddaughter's face lit up more than when she'd finally grown tall enough to ride The Beast roller coaster at Kings Island. My joy for her trumped all my misgivings.

We stepped aside, and I took hold of her arms. "That's the most wonderful news," I said. A knot formed in my throat. Kelsey was expecting after all these years. "I couldn't be happier for you. You and Aaron both," I said.

"I'm sixteen weeks along." She rubbed her tummy.

Four months along already? How could that be?

My daughter jogged up before I could confirm. Sounding a little winded, she said, "Now you know. My grandchild is the main reason I moved back to Ohio. Kelsey's been dying to tell you, but I insisted she wait. I wanted to see your face. Gotta say, it's priceless."

No wonder Jane had retired so suddenly. Now it made sense. She was going to be a grandmother.

But why had Kelsey waited this long to share her news with me? That, I could not believe. How had I missed all the signs? She looked the same. If my Kelsey was showing beneath all those layers of clothes, I couldn't tell it. Jane wasn't home a week, and already my relationship with my granddaughter was shifting. I had been first to hear when Aaron proposed to Kelsey, the first to learn when they purchased a condo. For the last thirteen years, since Kelsey got out of grad school, she and I had enjoyed outings a couple of times a month. Just us two. We'd go down to Mecklenburg's for sauerbraten or to a tiny Italian trattoria. We'd see art at the Taft or sit out a rainstorm playing checkers or chess.

I looked away to hide my reddening face. First, these two had kept to themselves Jane's return home. And now this. Jane had made sure I was last to know Kelsey's big news—and worse, she'd managed to tell it to me herself. Jane had struggled some over the years while away, knowing how close Kelsey and I were. Once my daughter had returned, I'd known our family dynamic would change. I just hadn't foreseen it would be so abrupt.

～

I sat across the square table from my daughter and granddaughter in Union Terminal's Rookwood Ice Cream Parlor, glancing from one to the other as they spoke and used lots of hand gestures. Originally a tearoom, this place maintained its whimsical, locally made tiles in the

Rookwood colors of mint green, pale gray, yellow, and pink. We sipped on chocolate malts from disposable cups with plastic lids.

"Any morning sickness?" I asked. With Kelsey into her second trimester, it had probably passed. I still couldn't get over how I'd missed her nausea or her fatigue, given how often we saw each other.

"I've been pretty lucky," Kelsey said. "Hardly any at all."

"You must take that from your great-grandma Glenn's side of the family," I said.

"Did you have morning sickness when you were pregnant, Mom?" Jane asked.

"This is Kelsey's day to shine," I said, still miffed that Jane had butted in with Kelsey's news. "As you know, I'm four months behind on hearing all the details."

"Kels didn't tell anyone she was pregnant," Jane said in a snappish way, "until her first trimester was done. Including me."

Well, at least there was that. But I didn't respond. Instead, I directed my next question to Kelsey. "Know what you're having? Boy? Girl?"

"Not yet. But we won't be hosting a gender-reveal party."

I frowned. "What in the world is a gender-reveal party?"

"It's when friends gather to celebrate whether a couple's having a boy or a girl. Could be they slice a big piece of cake, a cake baked with pink or blue batter. Some parties let guests smash plastic golf balls outside, and pink or blue powder sprays up in big clouds." Kelsey threw her hands in the air. "Personally, I think it's silly."

I shook my head in wonder. Kelsey might've thought a gender-reveal party crossed a line, but she'd created a spectacle or two herself. When she got engaged, Aaron popped the question at the Hauck Botanical Gardens—with a hired photographer and six friends coming out of the leaves to watch. Then there was the engagement party, and the bachelorettes "doing Nashville," and the kitchen shower and lingerie shower and "couple's shower." I'd never seen so many gifts. There was the bridal brunch and wedding spa treatments and custom-labeled bottles of wine.

Kelsey's generation craved more, more, more. They'd never really lived without. I'd been ecstatic just to wear a real gown and marry Dennis Glenn in a candlelit parlor.

"Everything has to be Instagram-worthy." That was Jane. "Young people these days."

My daughter and I exchanged glances; we could be comrades on this point. We were capable of a moment of unity today after all. My spirits lifted.

Kelsey went on about how much weight she was allowed to gain and how she and Aaron would turn their spare room into a nursery.

"The first night Janie was in our house," I said, "your papaw and I sat with the door cracked so the soft light of the hall filtered into the bedroom. We huddled over the cradle, watching her sleep for an hour."

Then I turned to Jane. "Your hair was thick as a baby goat's. If I had died right there on that day, I would've died a fulfilled woman."

"Aww," said Kelsey. "That's the sweetest thing I ever heard."

"I'm pretty sure I cried," Jane said, "and screamed and spat up and made messes of diapers."

"You were a perfect baby," I said. I watched my daughter's face register surprise. "Everything we'd wanted."

A sentimental wave flowed over me, washing away the petty, foolish jealousies of an old woman. Jane and I need not compete for Kelsey's affection. The three of us were together.

"Too bad I wasn't perfect in your eyes when I grew up," Jane said.

That yanked me right out of my peace. Tears stung my eyes. I loved that girl every day of her life. I don't know how I messed up by not letting her know it—and by letting the rifts between us drag on forever.

Kelsey tried to redirect us. "There's a chance Aaron and I will wait to be surprised with the baby's gender. As women did in your day, Grandma." She winked.

I shifted my gaze to Jane, already thinking of her as a Nana, but her eyes didn't meet mine. She was staring blankly out at the fanciful flowers and dragonfly tiles in the frieze.

I turned back to Kelsey. "When it comes to finding out the gender, as long as you and your husband agree on whether or not to be surprised, that's what's important."

Kelsey lifted her brows. "Well, I don't think that one will be an issue. We are still deciding, though, whether or not I'll continue to work. It's tough. I absolutely love what I do. And it's not as if my income goes to waste," she said.

Again my granddaughter evoked memories of my husband and me—and now, too, my work in the early days and reflections on how Mama had raised me. There would be time enough to discuss all this with Kelsey.

"Then there's the midwife-versus-hospital debate we're having," she said, and I stiffened.

The word *hospital* alone was enough to make me tense, but this was exacerbated by the fact that Kelsey and her husband were in disagreement. Spouses should be aligned on critical matters of family. Dennis and I had learned that the hard way.

"What do you mean by debate?" I asked.

Kelsey drummed her fingers on the table, stalling. "I suppose you guys will know sooner or later. I want to use a midwife. Actually, I want to give birth at home." She made a face that mimicked "Eek."

"Oh my," I said, before I'd thought better of it. Jane snapped out of her daze and faced me.

I fiddled nervously with the napkins on the table. Were home births as safe as hospitals? Not that hospitals were always safe. I knew that as well as anyone. I had tried throughout today's conversation to focus on Kelsey and her baby, and then I'd allowed myself to indulge in the joyous memories of bringing Janie home. But other memories were sealed inside of me, and I felt the lock on them cracking open.

I looked up to find Jane out-and-out glaring at me. She hadn't done that yet since her return. But I knew that glare. It warned, *Don't intrude here, Mother. Not with Kelsey.*

Jane's look left me feeling duly scolded. Yet I had to protect my granddaughter.

"What does Aaron think?" I said as nonchalantly as I could. It was hard, considering how my pulse spiked. "About a midwife at home versus the hospital."

"Daddy-to-be thinks I should deliver where there are machines and intercoms and drugs and doctors in case of trouble. It's the lawyer in him."

What if Aaron has a point? I thought but didn't say.

"This is my body, though, isn't it?" Kelsey said.

I shuddered. I'd said those very words myself . . . long, long ago.

"Don't even start," Jane said, picking up on the swelling sense of my alarm. "In my day women were trained on how to have natural births in hospitals—Lamaze classes and all that. Though I guess I proved a hospital wasn't necessary."

Jane had delivered Kelsey in a commune in the wilds of Arizona without a doctor—and without a husband. And she hadn't had the courtesy to let her father and me know until Kelsey was three months old. She'd simply arrived from Arizona unannounced (much the way she'd landed in my drive days before now). It'd been the end of summer when Dennis heard a car door shut and we moseyed from the kitchen to our front door stoop, both of us in our early fifties. There was our Jane, looking more beautiful than we'd seen her the year before: she was twenty-seven and carrying a baby. The two were both bare-legged and barefooted, wearing flimsy sleeveless tops and shorts. No one spoke. As Jane neared us, we could smell the sun and the heat and the dust of the West, and we could smell *baby*. One look at that tiny round face told us she was ours. That baby belonged to our Jane. And Jane had said nothing about her existence till then. I remember how blood rushed through every vein I had, and how salty tears clouded my eyes and I had to wipe them away with the pads of my fingers to get a clearer look, and how I reached out my empty arms—my sad and empty arms—and that baby girl snuggled into me as if she already knew who I was.

Regardless of the reasons why Jane had punished us—reasons I'd yet to decipher—she'd seen how we instantly loved Kelsey, and she never deprived us of her again. If only Jane and I had become closer in the process—truly close, that is. Not just close for outward appearances.

Yet today was about my granddaughter's baby. And though I was last to hear the news, we were still early in this wondrous phase. I had no idea which labor and delivery path was right for her in this day and age. All I knew was this: I needed Kelsey and her baby to be safe more than I needed to breathe in air.

"I'll let you guys know what I decide," Kelsey said. The firmness of her tone suggested she wasn't going to let this topic blossom into a tug-of-war between her mother and me. Always the peacemaker. She pulled her brown hair into a ponytail—hair almost as long as a real pony's tail—wrapping what she called a scrunchy around and around it.

"Besides, regardless of what route Aaron and I take," she said, "I'll create a formal birthing plan." Kelsey explained how such a plan would express in writing her desire not to have, for example, continuous fetal heart monitoring. "I won't lie confined to a machine for ten hours, that's for sure," she said. "Doesn't help a thing. Except put more dollars in hospital coffers."

She certainly was determined. She got that from her mother. Or maybe she got it from me—and I prickled with a mixed bag of pride and dread.

Then Jane surprised me by saying, "Kels, maybe Aaron's just being cautious, given your age. Have you—"

"*High risk* is practically an obsolete term, based on age alone," Kelsey said, detecting her own mother's protective streak. Was that a sheen of perspiration across Kelsey's forehead? "And trust me, I've had all the prenatal screenings and tests known to woman." She projected the confidence of the professional she was. She'd done her research. "Ensuring my baby and I are well is why I held off telling anyone my news early on. But the OB I saw and the midwives' group both agree: I'm the picture of health."

A voice—a deep male voice from decades before—echoed in my head, and I went weak: *Mrs. Glenn, you're a star patient.*

CHAPTER TWO

August 1945

We were soaked on our way to Cincinnati's downtown celebration, wet with sweat from trekking in eighty-five-degree heat and horrible humidity. But neither my husband nor I minded. Hitler had been dead since spring; now Japan had formally surrendered. Today was V-J Day. The war was over. Thousands of people, many more than when the Reds had won the World Series five years back, crowded the streets en route to Fountain Square. Train whistles blew and steeple bells tolled as if playing duets for our soldiers.

Today was a turning point for the country—and also for us. What better time was there to be newlyweds looking ahead to our future?

I crossed my fingers that I was expecting. My sister-in-law Abbie never failed to remind me that she'd gotten pregnant the first month she was married. Dennis's sister had also birthed a child by her first anniversary. I was three days late in my monthlies, but I'd been late before. I wouldn't get anyone's hopes up yet. At least not anyone else's. The last time I thought I might be pregnant, Dennis and I had gotten all excited. When it ended up I wasn't, I felt as if I'd done something wrong. He'd laughed and said we just needed to "practice more."

Tons of tiny paper scraps drifted in waves from windows high in the buildings on Vine. I'd never heard so much cheering. "No more rationing gasoline," someone yelled. "No more boys in body bags. Long live the USA." There was a buzz among the revelers, electricity carrying the current of prosperity to come.

Though my family was of German blood, we had been in Cincinnati for four generations. Mama had lost her brother in the Great War. She, Opa, and I had long despised what the Nazis were doing in Europe, and we had done our part for this country. I thought of the red, white, and blue poster that had hung in Mama's front window when I'd lived with them: THIS IS A V HOME. It meant the three of us had taken the Victory Home Pledge. We'd salvaged metal, like bottle caps and cans, so the military could make ammunition. We saved bacon and beef fat for glycerin for bombs. We scrimped to buy a war bond. So today's celebration was personal to me.

When Dennis and I first glimpsed the bronze lady atop the fountain that had stood in its spot since before Opa was born, he picked me up and swung me around, the heels of my shoes knocking into other couples doing the same. He set me down and looked into my eyes.

"You're the prettiest girl a guy ever got," he said, "not to mention the smartest."

I broke out in a huge grin. "And you're the most charming guy a girl ever snagged."

It was a wonder I'd met him at all—he, the boy from the farm, and I, the girl from the city. We might not have lasted to a second date had we not disclosed our difficult pasts on the first night we met.

We'd met in July of the year before. Girlfriends and I had giggled our way down the gangplank of the steamboat the *Island Queen* with its high-pitched calliope music. We had come by river to Coney Island, Cincinnati's amusement park. "I do adore a man in uniform," my friend Shirley had said, itching to find handsome men on furlough. We'd ambled through the park in our button-up shifts, rolled-down socks, and brown leather loafers. The boulevard had neatly trimmed grasses and great pom-poms of red geraniums. Shirley's cousin Ava's boyfriend and his buddies met up with us at the dodgems. They wore dungarees with crisp, collared shirts—not uniforms, because they were farmers on deferment.

"I'm Dennis," said the cute one with dimples that rivaled Tyrone Power's. He smelled of fresh air and clean laundry, and I imagined his farm with vast green pastures, crops of wheat made gold by the sun, and shady copses of trees. Given I was raised in the city's basin, the main wood that surrounded me was the clapboards of the tenements. Cars rumbled by where I lived and smokestacks smoked—very different from a farm, I was sure. Dennis's eyes crinkled as he smiled, blue as a noontime sky on a clear day. But what would he and I have in common? Probably nothing.

"I'm Millie Kraus," I said, since he'd introduced himself. No need to be impolite.

"Everyone's heading to the games," he said. His voice was deep, as if he could have been in radio. "Let me win you a prize?"

He was nice, but I didn't see the point in going on. Our worlds were too far apart. As the rest of the guys and gals headed off in packs, though, it looked as if I had no choice.

In the whirl of lights and blaring music and the smell of popping corn, Dennis and I came to the milk bottle game—three metal milk bottles stacked in a pyramid and one dirty softball. "Knock 'em all over, and your pretty little lady wins a prize," the barker said. Dennis reared back his arm and blasted the ball through the two bottom bottles, knocking over all three.

"We have a winner!" Red lights blinked. I squealed and found myself hopping up and down on my tiptoes.

"Pretty girl, claim your prize," the barker said. The manufacturer of stuffed monkey prizes had turned production over to army gear. So I won a pack of Orbit gum instead. It wasn't Juicy Fruit—Wrigley's shipped that favorite only to our troops. But Dennis and I each enjoyed a stick.

"How about riding the Ferris wheel?" he said. "It's beautiful at night, isn't it?"

"Perfect," I said. And it was. We soon climbed into a seat made for two.

"You're out of high school, right?" he asked on our way up as the seat bucket swayed to and fro.

"Yes," I said. I had graduated near the top of my class the year before. But what would this clean-cut country boy think of my being a working girl? I looked out over the park's lights, from the Flying Scooter to the Wildcat roller coaster. "I grew up in Over-the-Rhine," I said. Hearing me name my neighborhood, he would know I was poor. Things were a little better for my family now, but when I was a child, I'd once gone a whole winter with only two pairs of socks. I ate stale bread three times a day. But I wouldn't deny who I was then, nor who I was now. "I work the cash register at Kroger down on Pearl."

"Working girl, huh? My parents would like you," he said with a smile. "Farmers and their wives believe in hard work." What a kind thing to say.

"You're on military deferment?" I said. "If we're gonna win this war, our troops need the food."

Dennis looked into the darkness, not out over the lights of the rides and the river. Had I said something wrong?

"I went to enlist the year before last," he said as the Ferris wheel made another loop, "when I was eighteen."

"Oh," I said, puzzled.

"I wanted to serve my country overseas, not just with the crops. I went to the recruiting office, jumped through all the hoops." He laughed nervously, his eyes meeting mine. "I don't know why I'm telling anyone this, especially a girl. It doesn't affect me in the day-to-day, but apparently I have a high-frequency hearing loss."

I didn't understand the significance. But I let my face suggest he go on.

"The medical officer said, 'Scram, kid. The roar of bomber planes will turn ears like yours deaf. Go back to the farm. Help put fuel in men's bellies. They'll thank you for it later.'"

Had it been hard for Dennis to be called a kid, when the soldiers his age were called men? "Well, I can't help but think," I said, thoughtfully, "he did you a favor by turning you away."

"Maybe. But I'd wanted to go. It was hard feeling like I'd flunked the physical."

I could see from the tightness of Dennis's jaw, from his lips tucked in at the corners, that this was a difficult admission.

So we both had our histories. But we'd both been forthright. He held my hand then, and I melted from the snug, rugged warmth of it.

By the time we disembarked the *Island Queen* at Public Landing, Dennis and I had danced in the boat's ballroom to the big band tunes of the Clyde Trask Orchestra. Then we'd scurried hand in hand, weaving through the crowd to the tiny uppermost deck, the one known as the smoocher hideaway. We sat beneath a waning moon in the cooling midnight air, his arms around me. The *Queen*'s white glow was majestic against the water's dark depths with its splash of whitecaps. Dennis's lips came to mine with the taste of mint Orbit gum and a soft intensity that said hello and goodbye and I need to see you again and please don't make me wait, for waiting I can't possibly do.

Now Dennis looked around at the V-J celebration. We had moved to the outskirts of the crowd.

"Dennis Glenn," I said, "I can see the wheels in your head spinning."

He grinned. "Our success is so close, I can taste it," he said, his arms squeezing me tighter, smashing the pack of cigarettes in his shirt pocket.

"*Ahh*, and what exactly does it taste like?"

"Sweet, like Granddaddy's clover honey."

I laughed. "Tell me more," I said, hopeful that Dennis's new work would take us into the city. It wasn't that I was anxious to leave the farm. I'd come to love the peaceful, starry nights, playing with a litter of kittens in the haymow, bursting a ripe watermelon over my knee in the patch, and watching the children make diamond rings by pinching off the sticky lights of summer night fireflies. Mother Glenn had taught me to make noodles and to can tomatoes and to appreciate pink tulips and purple lilacs in the spring. I loved how useful she was, how the work she did mattered to the sustenance of the farm. I loved how the farmhouse had stood in its place for generations. I loved the stability that came with that.

The idea of leaving there scared me. I had moved seven times when I was young. That's what people in poverty did—and no way did I want to go back.

Yet if Dennis and I left the farm, I, too, could get a paying job again.

You have to have a means of earning, lest you find yourself without a bed or a soupbone to your name. It was Mama's voice in concert with my own.

I missed having my own money. When I was seventeen, I'd been waiting to buy bread at the original Super Market opened by Mr. Kroger decades before. The manager watched me helping shoppers in line—older people trying to figure out when butter rations kicked in and when coupons for beef would run out. It was confusing to many, but not to me. When the manager thanked me, I flat-out said, "Why not hire me? I'm good with numbers." My straight As in algebra convinced him to give me a shot as a cashier. I never lost him a cent. And Mama was so proud. More important, that job had given me a purpose. It had shown me I could make a useful contribution.

"I can construct houses," Dennis said, wiping sweat from his forehead with the back of his wrist. "Like Nathan's house—the prefabricated one he and I built from a Sears and Roebuck kit. Prefab houses are springing up all over."

"You mean you'd order the house kits from the Sears catalog, build them, and then sell them?"

He shook his head. "Not exactly. I'd like to become a dealer for a prefab manufacturer and earn a profit. Build the houses for other families who can't do it themselves."

"Oh," I said. This idea was so foreign to me. I wouldn't know where to begin.

"Gunnison Homes is the largest manufacturer," Dennis said. "I've been reading up on 'em. They've been around for a decade, and they've got several models to pick from—some with two bedrooms, three bedrooms. Some with garages or basements."

A cheer went up from the crowd nearby. A sailor had bent his girl over backward and was planting a kiss right on her lips while everyone watched. Other couples began following suit. Dennis and I grinned at each other. He bent me backward and kissed me for the longest time. I came up and arranged my hair, smiling.

"The houses are strong?" I asked. "I can't even begin to imagine what a kit looks like."

His dimples flared. "Just as strong as traditionally built homes. A kit is everything needed to assemble a house—delivered all at once by a truck. Thing is, once a dealership gets up and running, a prefab can be fit for a family to move in within less than a week."

My mouth dropped. "Less than a week?"

"Think about this," he said. "The construction industry in this country has taken a nosedive, right? While so many men have been gone and resources poured into the military. There's now a housing shortage." It was true. I'd seen the headlines. "It's only gonna get worse as more troops return."

37

I recalled that my grandfather had a friend named Peanut Jim who sold nuts to Reds fans at the ballpark. Opa had taught me that an entrepreneur finds a need and fills it, reports to no one. My husband had identified a need. His older brother was set to take over the farm one day anyway. Dennis would become an entrepreneur. After what had happened to my father and Opa in the brewing industry, I warmed to the notion that my husband might be less subject to losing a job.

"One of the best parts is this," Dennis said, sounding serious. "Gunnison dealers get to offer financing. Veterans under the GI Bill require no down payment to buy. So if I couldn't help the boys on the front line, my work could help them after they're back."

How I adored this man.

One day soon, though, we'd need to talk of my personal dreams. Of having children and my own job—of being useful both inside and outside our home.

"You and I will start a family, too." He winked, and I gave him another big smile. He already understood some of my needs. I was a lucky girl.

As church bells rang again in the city, I bent my neck to face the warm sky—a sky as blue as Mother Glenn's hydrangeas—while the odor of my own sweat lingered beneath my arms and confetti sprinkled my forehead like fat summer snowflakes.

Then I felt a familiar disappointing dampness coming on, one that meant I was spotting and hadn't conceived.

CHAPTER THREE

May 1946

Nine months after V-J Day, we still weren't holding an infant. Instead we stood on a concrete block foundation, overlooking a quarter acre of mud. It was Dennis's new baby, the start of Gunnison Homes by Glenn, his dealership for prefabricated homes. Leading to the street was a line of wood planks marred by our own dirty footprints. In two weeks, a truck would deliver Dennis's first model home in kit form: numbered joists, preassembled walls, shingles, furnace, and all. Even a white picket fence.

I was helping Dennis prepare for the grand opening. The model home's lot was on Egbert Avenue in an up-and-coming Cincinnati neighborhood north of Clifton—while we now lived like misers in a twenty-five by thirty-foot flat. We had waved goodbye to the farm life for good.

The weeks leading up to this day had been hectic for Dennis, what with finding and grading the lot, getting his first permits, hiring a crew that would erect the structure, and arranging for utility hookups. Dennis had asked for my help with budgeting and decor. So I'd postponed my job search. I worried about our financial risk, though. Dennis's folks had given their grown children each cuts of a recent land sale. They'd sold off some acreage to an aircraft engine factory moving into the county. What if the business my husband invested in failed?

Tori Whitaker

I spent my days at fabric shops, gathering up swatches of gingham and chintz, or catching sales at furniture stores. At night I studied the Gunnison manual and women's magazines to glean what young families wanted. I imagined myself at the model home, rubbing the chromium toothbrush holders to a gleam or polishing the kitchen's linoleum floor to a shine so perfect it'd reflect the new Frigidaire. It was all great fun. And useful. But it wasn't enough for me. I needed to do something more to assure the company a commission—and to provide myself some money.

The next morning, Dennis and I drank coffee in our kitchenette within view of our bed and a few feet from our couch. I said, "There's more I can do for the business than make things pretty. I've read the Gunnison dealer's manual twice."

"I'm all ears," he said. He'd finished his bowl of Cheerios and lit up a smoke.

"Advertising and mailings," I said, tightening the ties of my robe, nervous. "Things to get the word out. Gunnison's budget already allows for modest spending." Besides, I had seen at Kroger how well-timed newspaper ads and mailers sent droves of customers to the store. Could it work for our grand opening?

"I definitely don't have time for that stuff." Dennis stood up and kissed the top of my head. "I'm sold. If you can handle it that would be swell."

I took the streetcar over to a printer's office on Walnut Street. My arms trembled in the seat en route, the Gunnison manual like a security blanket in my lap. Surely I could follow directions as well as anyone.

Standing before the sign that read **BERGMAN AND SONS PRINTERS**, I straightened my shoulders. A bell tinkled as a businessman who was leaving held the door for me and tipped his hat. The shop smelled of paper and glue and ink and wax. Examples of the shop's work covered the walls: party invitations, posters, flyers in every color. I stood at the counter while the clerk served another patron. Both men. They glanced at me as if they were unaccustomed to seeing the fairer sex bring in projects, although I'd worn a skirt with pumps and a blazer—like a professional secretary in a Cary Grant movie.

"May I help you?" the short, balding clerk said as the other customer left.

"Yes." I willed my hands not to shake. I opened the manual to the page I'd marked. "I have a template. For producing a postcard."

A few hours after, I returned to inspect what the clerk had called a proof. "Wait," I said, pointing. "The name of the company is misspelled." I was appalled at the shoddy workmanship that would type Gunnison as *Gunnisom*. Did he think me dimwitted?

"Dear me," said the clerk. "My apologies. The apprentice missed it."

"Quite," I said, my lips firm, my confidence growing. "I trust you'll correct this for no extra charge. Now shall we discuss quantity?"

"The more you order, the lower the price per piece," he said, sliding a rate sheet in front of me. I scoured the costs to be sure I wasn't being bamboozled. I ordered a little more than I would need for the list of addresses I'd obtained.

When the final piece came off the presses, I couldn't stop staring at it. I taped the postcard to our refrigerator at home, so I could admire it each time I passed. I mailed one to my mother and one to Mother Glenn. I, Millicent Glenn, had produced a real publication. I was so proud.

The postcard featured a color rendering of the model house and the Gunnison manual's text:

> Picture your family in a house of tomorrow, today.
> Here is everything a woman dreams of: security and
> a place to call her own. Come learn what a Gunnison
> home would do for you every day in new comfort,
> luxury, economy, security, and family happiness. And
> you can own for less than paying rent.

I spent half a day licking and sticking purple one-cent stamps on the mailers until my tongue adhered to the roof of my mouth. I could barely taste the chicken and dumplings I fixed that night for supper. A feeling of accomplishment was my reward for working so hard, eating so little, sleeping so lightly, and having no leisure. We'd not gone to a matinee in weeks. But we did have one form of free entertainment.

"How am I supposed to eat this meal with you flitting around here looking so pretty?" Dennis had said the last time we got in the mood.

"You have to have your nourishment, to keep the pace you're working," I said, standing beside our Formica-topped table.

"So nourish me," he said. With one long, slow blink of his eyes that man could arouse me.

Dennis swept our plates and glasses aside with his arm. I pulled up my apron and lifted my polka-dot shift to my waist. I bent over our table before him. Then he unhooked my stockings and slid them down, slowly, one leg at a time, bringing fire to my skin with the tips of his fingers.

After each time we made love, a thought niggled in the back of my mind: Why wasn't I getting pregnant? My parents had been married years before I came along. Might something be wrong with me, the same thing that had been wrong with my mother? The thing she never spoke of . . . or something worse? Not that Dennis and I had hours in the day to raise a family yet anyway, I reasoned. We had lists upon lists of things to do.

Three days before our grand opening, a black Chevrolet parked in front of the model home site. Dennis and I were in the living room measuring the picture window for draperies.

"What are Nathan and Abbie doing here?" I asked.

"Nathan wanted to see the place before the crowds came. Didn't I tell you?"

Would I be wearing my dingiest denim pants and a scarf wrapped around my hair that's overdue for a wash if you'd told me I'd be seeing the perfect Abbie Glenn? I brushed sawdust from my blouse, which was splattered with the bedroom's green paint.

"You guys have about got it licked," Nathan said as they entered. "Proud of you, baby brother."

Abbie was neat as a pin, radiant in her starched red slacks and bright print blouse. She smelled of White Shoulders cologne. Little Margaret hugged my leg, and I caressed her soft cheek.

Abbie said, "Nathan, you need to pick Margaret up. There are metal screws lying all over."

As the boys and Margaret made for the kitchen, Abbie said, "Have you heard the news, Millie? I'm expecting again."

She had a smug cat smile that seemed to ask how I could stand doing men's work in a filthy hole like this. Why wasn't I doing a real woman's job, anyway—keeping the hearth fires burning somewhere clean and making babies every night? Was the work I did so different from her spreading manure in a garden on their acreage?

But how I wished I at least had on some lipstick.

$\smile$

Forty-two hours before Gunnison's grand opening, as we readied ourselves for bed, Perry Como sang "Prisoner of Love" on the radio. The telephone rang.

"What's wrong?" Dennis said into the receiver. I turned down the music and wiped the cold cream off my face over a washbasin.

"What does that mean exactly?" The corners of his bottom lip were tucked in. He was mad. Or upset. Was it his family? Was everything okay?

"I had understood the timing would work." Dennis lit up a Camel and took a deep drag.

It had to be the house. Our investment. Fright overtook my body. I didn't want to live in a one-room flat the rest of my life. I couldn't go back to the slums. Why hadn't I gotten a real job—one where the boss actually paid me a wage?

"But that delay will cause—"

My heart raced faster. Was it the electricity hookup? The plumbing connection? We couldn't put off the launch of the open house. The mailers had gone out the week before. In addition to my getting the postcards printed, I'd worked with the *Cincinnati Enquirer's* classifieds department to place three advertisements. The ads showed the dates and address for the house—and they'd already run.

"Look, I really want that shipment," Dennis said, firmly but not unkindly. "I'm afraid I need it by noon tomorrow." *Shipment?*

"Thank you. Whatever it costs."

Turned out Dennis was talking with the Gunnison factory in Indiana about shutters and flower boxes—accessories that weren't furnished with the basic home package, but which were items he'd ordered last minute. It wasn't the end of the world after all. But Dennis wanted the place to look like the brochure. He expected perfection.

"Come hell or high water. We only get one chance at a first impression," he said. The weight of the business was getting to him, too.

At midnight on the eve of the grand opening, by the light of a crescent moon, Dennis installed green shutters on the white house, while I planted pink and purple petunias in the window boxes—the first time I'd planted flowers all by myself. We'd cut it that close.

At noon on grand opening day, Dennis dangled the key on a cord and unlocked the door with a flourish. It was as if the Land of Oz awaited us. And though this house would never be ours to live in—it would be sold, and we'd use the money to reinvest—my handsome husband swooped me into his arms and lifted me across the threshold. He was so strong. So mine.

"Mrs. Glenn, with you at my side, we're gonna go places," he said, lowering my feet to the welcome mat inside. My heart warmed at his recognition of my role in his enterprise. In fact, it was beginning to feel to me more like *our* enterprise.

How different this moment was from the day Mama and I had stepped inside our new, shabby flat above a defunct saloon, while Opa lugged our cart up the steps. I had been in second grade and carried my drawstring bag filled with my most prized possession, my game of tiddlywinks. When Mama opened the door, a rat ran out and skimmed the toe of my shoe, and I screamed.

A man with greasy hair and bristly whiskers had leered from across the hall and said, "Well, look at you two sweet things. Don't worry about rats, they don't eat a lot. But I sure like to." He licked his lips and then whistled as Mama slammed and locked the door behind us.

My Dennis had little idea how far he and I had already come compared to where I'd been. And I'd make sure I didn't go back. In the next week we'd bring Mama and Opa for a tour.

"One hour till our future customers arrive," Dennis said.

We dashed about getting every last-minute detail marked off the list. I put the lid down on the toilet seat in the bath with its walls of pink tiles, because Dennis never remembered to. He set the doors ajar in the closets and switched music on a radio at a soft timbre. I touched droplets of vanilla extract on warm bulbs in the lamps, a trick to entice a wife into imagining herself baking in this very house. I fanned out pamphlets atop the sink's chip-resistant porcelain enamel drainboard. The kitchen had other features that young wives would love: a bright tone and sunny pictures; white enameled cabinets that easily wiped clean; a durable linoleum floor in blue with small geometrics in red and white; a drop-leaf table and red vinyl stools—and gingham curtains, a canister set, and a metal breadbox with a cherry motif.

The beautiful living room would greet potential customers. It was clutter-free, which was important; young couples needed space for their children. It had a summer rug and ample furniture: a streamlined blue sofa with striped throw pillows, a stand-in cabinet and table of blond wood, a flowery upholstered chair with an emphasis on red. Postwar families still valued patriotism, and new homes reflected the flag's colors.

Dennis and I had everything in place. Then we waited.

Beneath my cheery face, my jaw ached and my neck ached and my shoulders ached—all from clenching my teeth so tightly during what little sleep I got. What if my promotional campaign flopped? What if no customers came? What if Dennis didn't make a sale? He had to sell house kits for other lots in the neighborhood, or this dealership wouldn't last the summer. Had starting this business been a mistake? A waste of his parents' funds? Why hadn't I gotten a real job?

"Millie," Dennis said. "Look out the window." I peeked between the curtains, and goose pimples sprouted up and down my arms.

A steady stream of cars was creeping up the street, going both directions. Four-door Chryslers and Fords were parking in front of yards on both sides for as far as we could see. Families with fathers carrying toddlers and mothers carrying pocketbooks made their way by foot, casting huge bouncing shadows as they crossed our drive. One couple had already stridden past the petunias I'd planted in the window boxes.

Dennis shook the hand of the first husband to arrive. I smiled at the wife, whose mouth was open in awe as her gaze flitted about the room.

"Welcome to Gunnison Homes by Glenn," I said.

⌐

By the close of the fiscal year's second quarter it was November 1946, and we'd been married just under two years. Hundreds had toured the house in the first six months. Dealerships that promised the highest success closed three home-building deals in the first two months, the manual stated. Dennis and I had sold ten prefab houses in six months. Ten. We celebrated our good fortune at the Empress Chili parlor downtown.

My ongoing campaign had been a hit. I hadn't conceived a child yet, but I'd helped launch the business that would be the foundation of our future. It made me feel as if I could do anything—like Rosie the Riveter or Eleanor Roosevelt.

At Empress we ordered five-ways. This Cincinnati specialty had spicy meat chili simmered with cinnamon and allspice. Our small oval plates were mounded high with spaghetti and covered in chili, red kidney beans, chopped white onions, and heaps of finely grated cheddar cheese.

Dennis said, "I couldn't have done it without you, Mil, you know that, right?"

My cheeks warmed. I knew it.

"Your mother told me once," I said, "how when she was a bride she would labor in the cornfields if needed. She had once driven a team of horses when hay had to get to the barn." Mother Glenn and my mama had taught me that a wife does what she must.

"A farmer and his wife are partners," Dennis said. Indeed, this was the exact way I'd come to think of it, the way his mother had described it, too. I'd seen how farm wives gathered and cooked or sold the eggs. Husbands kept the coops in prime condition to protect the hens from thieves. "The farm isn't only my folks' home," Dennis said. "It's their business."

I liked the concept of our marriage being a business partnership, too. I could do meaningful work as I'd longed to do for some time. I would be fulfilled in being useful and actually contributing to our stable future—and contributing to our income. I could put money aside for a rainy day, the way Mother Glenn did, the way Mama had wanted to . . . the way I wanted to for myself.

I said, "Your mother was a business partner, and she raised the babies, too. She did both. Just as I hope to do." I hoped that more than anything.

Dennis sprinkled a handful of oyster crackers onto his five-way. I wasn't sure he'd heard me. Or was it that after being married so long, Dennis, too, quietly wondered if a baby would ever come?

~

The next day after Dennis left for work, I crawled into the dark corner of my side of our one tiny closet and slid out a wide-mouthed, blue clay jug the size of a cantaloupe. Mother Glenn had given it to me. It stowed the money I'd saved from being frugal with my housekeeping budget and the money I'd earned when we had a house sale. I didn't mind if Dennis knew about the stash so much as I needed the security the cash brought me. It belonged to me. I needed provisions in the event disaster struck—a landlord kicked us out without notice, or one of us got hurt and needed medical care, especially Dennis. I prayed my mother's history did not repeat itself with my husband. I poured all the cash into a heap on the rug. Down on the floor I meticulously counted every dollar and cent and recorded the totals on white, lined paper. I sorted the one-dollar bills from the five-dollar bills from the tens, making sure the presidents' heads were all facing up the way a bank preferred them. I separated the pennies from the nickels.

Soon I stood at Third and High Streets in Hamilton. My gaze followed up the eight stories of a limestone building that had an enormous sign atop: **1st**. That alone was enough for folks to know this was the First National Bank and Trust Company. Dennis's family had used this bank for years. I'd been here a few times with him or alone while handling matters on his behalf.

Today I was here on my own behalf.

I strode toward the row of tellers, who stood behind barred, marble cubbies—all the men in white shirts and wearing vests. I acted as if I knew what I was doing.

"I'm here to open an account," I said to the teller. He looked at me as if I'd just asked him to zip his fly. "A savings account." I wanted my money to be more secure and to grow by earning interest.

"And in whose name would the bank account be?" he inquired. He wasn't that much older than Dennis, but he had the manner of a high school principal.

"Millicent Glenn."

"That's you?" he asked.

"Correct." Was there a problem?

"Excuse me a moment," the teller said. He unlocked himself from his cubby and scurried to the back.

There I stood with other patrons glaring at me from the end of the line. I was the dreaded customer who had a special need, who was taking too long. My attention drifted to my left and to my right. A woman about my age was seated by a window across the way, presumably waiting on her husband. A child wiggled on her lap, a boy blowing spit bubbles. A pang of jealousy hit me. The baby was probably two years old and poked his index finger into his mother's mouth while she made sounds, pretending to chew his finger. Giggles from deep in his belly curtailed his bubble blowing. His other hand went for his mother's hair, and he coiled a lock around his finger. I wanted what that woman had. I wanted every bit of that.

The teller returned at last and asked that I follow him. I did so. I wanted to get this over and go home. I soon found myself sitting across the wide swath of wood that topped a businessman's desk.

"Mrs. Glenn, how are you?" I didn't know the man at the desk, but he apparently knew me.

"I'm wonderful," I said. "I'm here to open a savings account."

The man's desk nameplate said **MR. HATTER**, and he said, "We at First greatly appreciate the business your husband's home dealership brings to our bank. We have a longstanding relationship with all the Glenns."

"I know. I'm a Glenn. That's why I'm here, instead of at the bank down the street," I said jovially.

"You've come to the right place. I'd be happy to open a savings account for you. Right now, as a matter of fact. Can you show me your written letter of authorization?"

"What do you mean by 'letter of authorization'?"

Mr. Hatter cleared his throat. "You'll need your husband's permission to open an account in your own name."

"But I have my own money. Money I earned and saved." I had neatly arranged it in a drawstring bag in my purse.

"Perhaps Mr. Glenn is near a telephone?" Mr. Hatter said. He lifted the black receiver off his desk and poised a finger to dial. "Shall I place a call? Given our longstanding relationship, I'm happy to accommodate your request with his verbal consent."

"I'm sure Dennis would approve, though he's on a building site right now," I said, annoyed. "I can try down the street after all, I suppose." If this bank didn't think I was good enough, I'd find a bank that would.

"It's not just our bank's policy, Mrs. Glenn," the banker said. "It's everywhere."

"But the money's mine."

He picked up a pencil and tapped it on his desk. "Do you have something to hide from your husband, Mrs. Glenn?"

"Pardon me?" How dare he ask me such a question? How dare he insult my character? I couldn't get my mouth to close.

"Here's an authorization form," he said, "in case you decide to return with your husband's signature."

I snatched it out of Mr. Hatter's hand, and it was all I could do not to rip the page into pieces and toss them in his face.

Back at home I awaited my husband's return. Dennis would grant his permission with the bank. Wouldn't he? But why should he have to? Why did I have to lower myself to ask him? He wasn't my parent. We were partners. He was my husband. I'd worked hard for that money.

I poured myself a glassful of water and swallowed a big gulp. Without me, Dennis's business—our business—wouldn't be where it was. He'd said so himself.

2015

By the time Kelsey arrived at the gym, I'd already squirmed into my one-piece swimsuit. Several blogs had recommended water aerobics as one of the best forms of exercise for pregnant women, so Kelsey had asked if she could come to my class on her next day off. I was delighted. It would be just us two, a grandma-granddaughter moment like we'd had before her mother returned. Kelsey located me in the rear of the ladies' changing area and hugged me. I was resting on a low bench in the most remote U-shaped alcove of lockers, wrapped in my extralong towel like a pig in a blanket. A skinny pig.

"Am I in the right place?"

I turned. "Jane?"

"Finally found my bathing suit stuck at the bottom of a box of underwear yet to be unpacked. One of several boxes decorating my bedroom in the apartment."

"Yay," Kelsey said. "You came."

"Thank you for inviting me," Jane said, boring holes through me with her eyes, "*Kelsey.*"

I was ashamed to think my territorialism where Kelsey was concerned still lingered. A better mother would never feel this way. Kelsey smiled, and I knew what I had to do.

"Jane. I'm glad you came. And as for your boxes, you are both always welcome to store anything—boxes, furniture, what have you— in my basement. Plenty of room." I lightly clapped my hands. "Best hurry now, girls, as class starts in five minutes, and we've got to pull our plastic barbells out of the bin."

Kelsey pattered off to a restroom stall. "Did you bring water-safe shoes?" Jane said, but Kelsey didn't hear her. Indeed, the deck around the indoor pool puddled in spots, and I didn't want Kelsey slipping on the concrete in her condition either.

"We'll get her when she comes back," I said. "Best hurry up and change."

"Tsk, tsk," Jane said. "I'm one step ahead of you." She pulled her sweatshirt over her head, revealing her swimsuit underneath. "Voilà. I do hope that pool's heated."

"It's heated. But it's not bathwater," I said. "You'll have to buck up."

She rolled her eyes.

I locked my locker. I used number 103 every time, so I wouldn't have to try to remember where I'd stowed my clothes. When Kelsey strutted back out of the restroom, towel in hand, I said, "Good heavens, I see the baby poking out."

"I'm eighteen weeks along today," she said, and twirled around, her feet bare. The protrusion at her midriff didn't stick out that far, but it was nicely rounded. She glowed. Four and a half months? I still counted terms of pregnancy in months, like in the old days, not in weeks the way Kelsey did.

As if by instinct, Jane reached out her palm to touch her daughter's belly through the hot-pink one-piece suit. "I'm Nana," she said in a squeaky-grandma voice as she rubbed Kelsey's tummy with reverence. Then I had to have a turn. Kelsey's belly was warm and taut. To think, this was my great-grandchild growing inside. Would we have another girl?

"You two do know, of course," Kelsey said, "you're the only people in the world I'd let do that."

"Do what?" Jane said.

"Touch my body without permission. These days it's not cool to touch a pregnant woman's stomach without asking."

"Well, we're not just anyone," her mother said with a *hmph*.

"The swimming shoes?" I asked.

"I haven't forgotten, Mother," Jane said, and sighed. "Kels, put on my rubber shoes. I'll go without."

Now I hoped Jane wouldn't fall.

—

I grasped the metal rail and lowered a foot onto a step in the slightly cool water, careful not to slip. The first time I'd gone swimming, I was a child in Washington Park in my old neighborhood. The shallow wading pool had been in view of the old, grand music hall where rich people went to concerts. I'd worn rolled-up shorts, because my mother couldn't afford a bathing suit as some other girls wore. But to this day, I could feel Opa holding me up by my armpits so my face wouldn't go under the water.

"Good morning, ladies," the instructor said. "Let's warm up!"

We began with walking in the water, increased to a water jog, and then advanced to doing jumping jacks—those were hard on my shoulder joints, but I wouldn't relent. I wanted to prove to my girls I was fit.

Out of nowhere Jane said, "Marco!"

"Polo!" Kelsey called back. They giggled. The game was reminiscent of what they'd played in the apartment complex pool when Jane was in college as a nontraditional student.

She'd gotten financial aid when she returned from Arizona with the baby, unwilling to let Dennis and me help. She had a part-time job on campus, too, where they had a childcare center for employees.

I was proud of Jane's independence, though we always wanted to help, especially given that Kelsey had no father in the picture. Having the girls nearby had given me new purpose after Jane was away so long out west. Yet even when Jane went to work full time here, Kelsey didn't wear expensive Nike Airs or play Nintendo games. Jane got down on the ground, taught her about ant colonies and how all the ants had jobs—including the females. That made me smile. Jane took her camping in the Smoky Mountains, borrowing a pup tent from a friend. Although I had starched and ironed little Janie's shirts and shorts when she wasn't at the farm, Jane had always let Kelsey get dirty. If that child splattered Kool-Aid all down her top, "so what!" was Jane's response. They visited us most weeks during Kelsey's school years. And sometimes, like when Jane had finals to study for, we babysat for the weekend. Those days before Jane moved to Georgia—once Kelsey went off to Ohio State University—were simple days, because we all had Kelsey's best interest at heart. For the most part, Jane and I got along as if we were close, though something undefinable in our bond was missing. She spent more time in the garage with her dad and his tools than in the kitchen with me and the dishes. And if ever she thought my overprotectiveness horned in, like when I questioned her decision to let Kelsey ride a two-wheeler in the street, Jane let it be known who the mother was around there. So too with my hovering over Jane herself. Was the apartment kept too cool? Should Dennis install a humidifier? Did Jane have her annual pap smear yet?

One time when Kelsey was running a cross-country meet, I asked Jane as we sat in the bleachers: "Do I hear you're dating?"

Jane's lip had curled as she growled: "My private life is called private for a reason. It's my private life. Not yours." A typical reaction. Though whatever fling she'd had turned into nothing.

After aerobics class, Jane, Kelsey, and I dried off in the locker room where we'd begun. Thank goodness no one had slipped and fractured their tailbone. Or worse.

The remaining dripping-wet swimmers from class gravitated elsewhere. My granddaughter's cheeks were rosy from exertion, the way they were when Dennis had pushed her on the tire swing in our backyard during the summers. "Higher, Papaw, higher," Kelsey would yell. I hated that he hadn't lived long enough to play with the great-grandchild we were soon to have.

"Did you notice," Kelsey said as she pulled off her rubber swimming cap, "my breasts are swelling already too? Aaron sure has."

"TMI," I said, and Kelsey cracked up. I'd learned that acronym from her: *too much information.*

"Yeah, your boobs are getting bigger," Jane said, "while mine continue to shrink. Thanks, menopause." We all laughed. It was an unexpected moment of bonding, and I treasured it. Her wet swimsuit was unpadded and it clung to her torso, revealing every ripple and bulge of age and the cold perkiness of her nipples.

"Wait till you get my age," I said. I'd been a "sweater girl" back in the fifties—round, high, and firm, or pointy when wearing the right brand of bra. One would never know it now, to look at my deflated sacs of skin made flatter by the stretch of my suit.

"Well, actually," Jane said, "I might not have any boobs at all one day."

Kelsey frowned. "What's that supposed to mean?"

"She means she'll look like me when she's my age," I said.

"No. Not referring to you." Jane smiled tightly. "I don't know. I shouldn't have said anything."

Kelsey's eyes met mine as we stood in our wet suits and towels, the three of us in a circle between the low bench and the double-stacked rows of lockers. Pop music blared in the background. The fluorescent lights overhead revealed every line and crease in our faces, and the smell of chlorine hung in the air along with my nerves.

"Mom," Kelsey said. "You shouldn't have told us what?"

"I don't know. I had no intentions of saying anything. But all this talk of breasts, well." Jane waved her hand dismissively, but the note of sadness I'd seen on the day she returned from Georgia was back in her eyes. Dread crept into my limbs. She looked so much older in a bathing cap, too, without her shoulder-length hair to frame and soften her face. More like Opa. Directing her speech to her locker now, she said, "I guess I have a little complication."

"A complication?" I said, a rush of adrenaline paralyzing me.

"It's nothing, I'm sure," Jane said lightly. "But before I left Georgia, I discovered a lump."

My intake of breath might have been heard two locker rows away. This couldn't be happening. Not to my daughter. Could life be that unfair? No. It couldn't, it couldn't. She and I were just getting a chance to feel our way back together again. We were still trying to—

Kelsey stepped closer to Jane and put her hand on her mother's arm and was quick to say, "You're right, it's probably nothing. Lots of women get lumps, and most of them are benign."

"Exactly," Jane said. "I shouldn't have brought it up. The last thing we need is for you to be stressed. You're carrying my grandchild, after all."

If I had to describe my daughter's expression in that moment, I would say it was brave, defiant, reassuring. And troubled. And that's how Kelsey looked, too.

How dared I have thought for one millisecond that I'd rather Jane not have come today so I could have Kelsey to myself? What kind of mother was I? My body was numb. I pictured a poor lady at church whose son had recently died from cancer—her weeping over his coffin in the funeral home, and her tossing a fistful of dirt into his freshly dug grave. And Dennis. When Jane's father was about her age, he, too, had died of cancer.

"Where is it? The lump?" Kelsey said.

Jane pointed to the outside roundness of her left breast. Kelsey reached up to touch it, and Jane swatted her hand. Kelsey's lips were firm as she went in again. "Stop it, Mom," she said.

I stood immobile, shivering, as Kelsey pressed the length of her cupped fingers along the sagging curve of her mother's breast.

We heard voices coming nearer, women in for spin class. I stretched my towel out in the way a bat spreads its wings, shielding my girls. The pack of spinners turned back for a less crowded alcove.

"It's not cool to touch a woman's breast at the gym," Jane said sarcastically.

"I'm not just anyone," Kelsey said.

Kelsey moved her fingers up a little and then down, pressing in methodically. "Uh!" came from Kelsey's throat all of a sudden—and she yanked her hand away as if scalded. Her rosy face turned ashen. "It's the size of a grape. Mom, you've got to get this thing checked right away."

My skin went fire-red hot, and an urgent need to vomit was mounting in my gut. My daughter was to be a grandmother, oh yes, but her health was another reason she'd surprised me by moving back home.

I'd been right to worry after all. But how I wished I'd been wrong.

CHAPTER FOUR

April 1949

I waited in our car, alone, in front of a lot in a neighborhood that already had three of our Gunnison houses. Two white oaks had been spared at the rear of the lot, and it was good to see the leaves in full bloom. The house's slab foundation was already poured. I rolled down the car's window, and the air was fragrant with early honeysuckle from a neighbor's yard. With Dennis at Gunnison's Indiana factory learning about home warranties and customer repair claims, someone needed to accept delivery of a customer's three-bedroom kit. That was me. I thrived on handling the advertising, accounting, and some interior decor, but I pitched in wherever else I could. The customer's kit was scheduled to arrive by truck between ten a.m. and noon. On this particular day, the earlier the better.

At long last I was getting to plan a big surprise for Dennis. I had much to do before his return home. After more than four years of trying, I was going to have a baby.

I was going to be a mother.

It meant our family was starting, that I was not defective, that our hopes and dreams would be fulfilled. My husband and I would get to decide on a name. I had ideas on that, of course. I'd toyed with choices for years. It meant that Mother Glenn would assess whether *this* grandchild of hers resembled Dennis as an infant and pull out his baby pictures to prove it. I would get to dress the little baby in adorable outfits—blue or pink or white. It meant that I would have a little one to play with the Glenn family cousins at future Christmases. I—yes, I, Millicent Glenn—would get to enjoy all the things a mother enjoyed, things that I'd been missing. I could almost feel my baby Glenn growing inside of me; it was the physical definition of happiness. I already loved her or him. And I would create a wonderful nursery to welcome our baby home.

Dennis and I had a personal Gunnison house of our own now, in a lively nearby neighborhood filled with young families who rode bikes together and borrowed cups of sugar. A real home. It was the smallest model that Gunnison made, but it had two whole bedrooms and one private bath. We'd made friends as well. Pauline and Bob Irving lived next door in their prefab house the next size up. We'd met when they toured our third model. As soon as they'd walked into its light, bright kitchen, Pauline had asked, "What are you baking?" I had opened the oven to show there was nothing. She assured me the room smelled as if I had baked.

"Can you keep a secret?" I said.

"I'm the best gal at keeping secrets you'll ever meet," she said, crossing her heart with the tip of her finger.

I told her how, since our first open house, I'd used my trick of dropping vanilla onto hot lightbulbs. Drops would sizzle and send off an aroma.

"Why, Millicent," she said, having taken a cue on my name from the flyer, "if that's all it takes to make a house smell like a bakery, I can give up making Toll House cookies entirely."

I'd laughed. She and I might not have ever met under different circumstances, but we'd become fast friends—and she'd called me Millicent from that day forward. Pauline's family had sent her to college for a year to study home economics and to find a husband. She once referred to herself as "Pauline Loretta Irving née King." How implausible it was that "Millicent Marion Glenn née Kraus," once a tenement girl, now resided in a private dwelling surrounded by thick green grass, pristine sidewalks, well-kept homes, a milkman who delivered to her own metal box, and a shaggy-haired mutt named Raggsie.

It was getting stuffy in the car now. I strained to look down the block. No sign of the Gunnison truck. I checked my wristwatch. Half an hour had ticked by. I rested my head against the back of the car seat and closed my eyes.

I'd come to have my own home and almost everything else I could have wanted, almost everything my mother and Opa had dreamed of for me—though they hadn't lived to see it. I'd held Mama's hand as she died of pneumonia over a year back. When we buried her, Opa said, "I always thought I'd go before her. This isn't the right order of things, first losing a son in the Great War and now a daughter, too. Losing them both before me isn't right."

A few weeks later, he passed in his sleep when his heart gave way. Losing him felt as if the roof of my house had blown off, as if I were at risk, exposed to the dangerous elements outside. The feeling was irrational, given that I lay safe in the arms of my husband. In time, I would realize how my accepting the deaths of my loved ones was a sacrifice I had to make, so they could be together if only in heaven.

And finally I was going to continue their legacy.

I was delirious to tell Dennis that I'd skipped my second monthly cycle—at last—and Dr. Welch, the doctor all the Glenn women used, had confirmed the glorious news.

Pauline had a baby on the way as well, and she was the only one whom I'd told thus far. She'd lent me her manual by a Dr. Eastman, *Expectant Motherhood*. I wanted to understand the baby's development and start planning a layette. The night before, I'd rolled from one side onto my other, alone and wide awake, envisioning my infant's tiny fingers, dressing him or her in tiny sleepers, pushing my child in a carriage through the neighborhood while the morning birds sang.

I couldn't stop celebrating with my own self. I was going to be a mother.

I glanced out the window of the car and there it was: the long, forest-green truck pulling around the corner. Seeing one of the company's trucks and trailers—with GUNNISON HOMES painted down its side in big white script—tickled me every time. I was proud to be part of our dealership's success. I climbed out and waved at the two men who would unload. The driver backed the trailer into the dirt, positioning the rear doors adjacent to the concrete slab foundation.

No heels for me today. I wore slacks, flats, and a jacket. I put on my yellow hard hat and met the men by the trailer.

"Hello, Mrs. Glenn," the driver said, hopping out of the truck's high cab.

"You fellas made good time," I said. I'd only been waiting an hour, and I was glad of it. I felt a bit queasy.

Within another forty-five minutes, almost everything was unloaded. I methodically examined every item, checking it off on my chart: skids containing neatly stacked and secured doors, windows, walls, and gables.

But my head started swimming. I got dizzy. Nausea overwhelmed me.

"Excuse me," I said as the men lifted out the last crate.

On the walk back to the car, a great wind blew up, refreshing my face—exactly what I needed to let the morning sickness pass. I returned to the crates filled with packages wrapped in brown paper, their contents detailed with large, square labels—everything from standard thermostats to optional window screens.

"The shipment checks out, gentlemen," I said. "Be safe on the roads." I waved as the driver honked the horn and the men left.

Now I had the surprise to plan. I climbed back into the car. I was going to manage this all: job, home, husband, and family. A little morning sickness wouldn't stop me.

Sitting on my bed now, I counted out enough bills and coins from my blue clay jug for what I had in mind. Dennis had indeed signed for me to open a savings account, but I still kept some money hidden away at home. What if I needed cash fast, and banks were closed? One never knew. And with a baby in the house I would have to be particularly diligent. A baby had needs. Soap to wash his diapers. Vaseline to protect his bottom. Spoons and food and hairbrushes as he grew.

Mother Glenn had given me the jug for the purpose of saving, but I'd learned the importance of that from Mama. The hard way. I wouldn't go back to a day like when Opa tried restraining her flailing arms while neighbors watched—the day a landlord had thrown us out when I was six. Rent had been late. The landlord used his key when we were gone. Mama, Opa, and I had returned to the tenement to find everything we owned piled up in the street—right down to Mama's and my tattered undergarments strung on the legs of our upturned table and chairs like US flags on poles. Old Mr. Fletcher, a friend of my opa's, stood on the corner, gaping with his granddaughter, who was a girl in my class at school. My cheeks burned, and I stared down at my feet. My family had slept that night on the floor of another tenement family's flat, beside three people we didn't know, someone's second cousins twice removed.

I shook off the memory. My priority at present was to create a simple but special celebration for this most important day of my life: the announcement of my pregnancy. I was wrestling between staying in to cook chicken fricassee or planning an outing for Dennis's surprise. Perhaps we could return to the zoo.

When we were dating, we'd gone to see Susie, a four-hundred-pound gorilla who'd come as a baby from the Congo aboard a zeppelin. Susie had amazed visitors by eating real food with a fork and kissing her trainer on the lips. That day was the first time Dennis said he loved me. Or we could enjoy Eden Park—where Dennis had proposed on a snowy afternoon. It was warming up outside now, and we could spread a blanket across the lawn on the hill. That was it, yes, we'd have a picnic in the park.

The next day I made deviled ham salad sandwiches and wrapped them in cellophane. I filled a thermos with hot potato soup. I prepared a relish tray and a platter of cheeses and German sausage, and I cut slices of chocolate cake. I packed a basket with utensils and a blanket and plates—even a damp washcloth so we could clean up.

Scattered across our kitchen table were mementos of our life together. I'd bought a picture frame at Woolworth's with my jug money and covered the cardboard backing with a piece of white muslin. I arranged a collage with a Gunnison postcard, zoo ticket stubs, the Orbit gum wrapper from the prize Dennis had won me at Coney Island, and more. To drive home my surprise, I inserted a photo of a silver baby rattle that I'd cut from *McCall's* magazine. Before reassembling the frame, I wrote on the back in blue ink: "Made with love, in memory of our happiest day yet, a day that will only be surpassed by the glorious moment that our first baby is born."

With all my preparations complete, I went to the bedroom but felt sick all of a sudden. I leaned to the wall, dizzy. Had I overdone it? Earlier in the week I'd finished preparing the yearly taxes. I'd collected swatches of carpet for a customer. I'd had no intention of slowing down. But perhaps I'd been a mite too ambitious.

In my bathroom I found it was only morning sickness after all—or, as Pauline called it, all-day sickness. Nothing to worry about. I rinsed with mouthwash and changed into a slim tweed skirt. It had a matching sport coat that flared and oversize patch pockets that I thought would come in handy. I had only to do touch-ups to my makeup when the telephone rang.

I trotted into the kitchen to answer. It was Dennis. He was back in town, calling from his office, where he'd dropped off some boxes. How I hoped he wouldn't be late.

"Mil," he said. "I can't believe it. I'm so happy!"

Happy? About what?

"We're going to be parents!" he said.

My spirit deflated like a bubble pricked with a fork. I sagged against the wall, wearing my smart little slouch felt hat.

"Babe? You there?" he said, and I could tell from his breathing that he was puffing on a cigarette. "You all right?"

"How did you hear?" I fought not to faint.

"Why, my brother just phoned. Nathan's so happy for us. Abbie knows the nurse at Dr. Welch's and—oh, honey, I can't wait to get home. You haven't told Mother yet, have you?"

"I can't wait for you to get home either," I said, trying to sound chipper.

Abbie Glenn had beaten me to surprising my own husband? I slammed the receiver back in its cradle after Dennis hung up. I slumped onto a kitchen chair, my eyes welling with tears. My surprise was ruined. I was tempted to stuff all the picnic wares away—the food, the basket, the checkered napkins and plates. But I wouldn't. And I would not destroy the collage that I'd crafted by hand. I resolved myself not to show my disappointment to Dennis and to continue on with our celebration.

That night I wasn't nauseous anymore, yet I was utterly exhausted.

But I made love to my husband, freed from the tension of whether I could conceive. I fell easily to sleep, after ticking off in my head all the things to be done tomorrow: picking up another order of postcards, launching a new series of ads, and writing out checks for the bills so that Dennis could sign with his trademark large capital *D*. I dreamed of the infant I soon would be holding.

CHAPTER FIVE

August 1949

Four months later, on a hot August day, I was in the fabric shop, a popular chain that had begun upstate. Mrs. Reilly was a Gunnison customer whose house would soon be ready. She needed fabrics for her boys' bedroom, and I had homed in on the bolts I thought she'd like.

"Let's try this one," she said, fingering a blue-and-brown cotton blend plaid, her voice as light as her weight. Dennis might've said a strong wind would blow her away. "No, no, no. You're in no condition to carry this," she said. She made her way with the bolt to the huge cutting table. I was six months along and as active as most women who weren't expecting. But I was tired, so I relented.

Over the next ten minutes we considered several bolts, but I could see she needed guidance on how the room would come together. I pulled a notepad and pen from my purse.

"Here's the bedroom," I said, drawing a square. "I recommend corner beds." I sketched the narrow twins set with their lengths flush against each of two walls and a higher table in the corner connecting them. "This leaves the maximum floor space for playing. Games, Tinkertoys, fire trucks." She smiled and nodded. Next I added the two windows. "So you'll select two fabrics. One for the fitted top spreads—a solid, I would think—and a coordinating pattern for draperies, valances, and dust ruffles."

She laid the plaid bolt alongside a solid blue and unspooled a stretch of each fabric. "What do you think?"

"That combination looks very nice," I said. I handed her the diagram and rubbed my chest and throat.

"Are you feeling unwell, Mrs. Glenn?" she said.

"A touch of heartburn is all."

"I remember those days," she said. "Just wait until the baby wakes you up three times a night, hungry."

This kind of talk made me miss my mama more than ever. Had she had heartburn, as I did now? Mother Glenn had not. Had Mama felt a strain on her back? Her hips? What did Mama remember of the first time she felt me kick? If only I could've called her when my baby had quickened.

"I'm afraid I have to scoot," I said. "Another meeting."

"I'm all set," she said, and thanked me profusely.

I loved helping her. This customer would be a good referral source for us. Mrs. Reilly's boys were in first grade—she surely knew lots of young families.

I had to get downtown in a jiffy for a meeting with the ad agency.

⁓

I sat across from Mr. Drake in a chair much too hard for women in my condition. But I had sat on stacked cinder blocks and plywood crates. I traveled well.

Mr. Drake was new. I could barely hear him in the noisy open room with other men at other plain desks with typewriter carriages swinging. He kept ogling my belly. The only other woman I could see wore a slender black dress and breezed through the aisles delivering reams of papers and answering phones with a sharp yellow pencil tucked behind her ear.

"Mrs. Glenn," Mr. Drake said, handing me a file. "I've prepared the advertising agreement. I assume your husband will look it over and return it tomorrow?"

I smiled. It was a contract to run a month's worth of newspaper display ads—not simply classified notices as we'd done in the beginning. These ads would be three columns wide instead of one, have bolder headlines and pictures of the houses, too. And we now had two model homes to advertise, not one.

"That won't be necessary, Mr. Drake. I'll take a look right here."

His bushy eyebrows lifted. He set about typing something and picked up his phone when it rang. He paused with his hand over the receiver long enough to ask, "Can I help you with anything, Mrs. Glenn? Any of the language?" I had already read every line of the two-page agreement. Twice.

"No, Mr. Drake, I can assure you I understand the terms."

Some time ago I'd caught on readily to advertising jargon, such as the costs driven by column inches and the frequency of insertions—a fancy way of saying how many times the ad would run over a specified period—just as I had quickly grasped how to manage the government's rationing coupons when helping Kroger customers before I met Dennis.

"Everything appears to be in order," I said, feeling fatigued. It must have been because I'd worn pumps. My feet began to swell by late afternoon. "I'll watch for the first installment in Friday's edition."

Friday was just in time for families planning their weekends. They loved touring new homes on Saturdays. I loved showing them. I loved making decisions about interiors. Guiding customers. Crunching numbers. Saving the business money. Showing businessmen that I had a brain. And saving my own jug money for incidentals or emergency needs of my family. I didn't want to lose all this when I became a mother. Why should I have to?

I suddenly had an urgent need to empty my bladder. I recalled passing a men's room in the hall moments before. I walked briskly to the information desk in the building's main lobby.

"Can you direct me to the closest ladies' lounge, please?" I asked the man wearing an official coat and hat.

"There's a men's room on every floor, but only one in the building for women. Take the elevator to the basement. Then down the hall to your left."

That annoyed me. By the time I made it to the elevator, I had to go so badly I couldn't look at the man on it with me. Ding, ding, ding. The doors opened, and I ran out and to the left.

My six-month pregnant belly got in my way as I tried to close the stall door fast. I lowered my pants, which had an elastic panel in front, as quickly as I could. Then I sat there, gathering up the parachute of a top I wore so it wouldn't dip into the bowl. I tried to go. Nothing. The urge to go was fierce, but only the slightest dribble came.

Come to think of it, this wasn't the first time this had happened.

My medical visits had increased leading into my third trimester. The next day I headed to an appointment at Dr. Welch's office, not far from the farm. Dennis had ridden to work with Bob Irving so I could take our Buick.

Here I was, stuck on Ohio State Route 126 in a line of a dozen or more cars. Had someone run out of gas? Been rear-ended? I drummed my nails, which were painted the Cutex color Cute Tomata, on the steering wheel. I switched on the radio and twisted the knob around until I listened to Nat King Cole. Cars and trucks passed me going south. If only their lane had been the one stopped. I'd seen nothing in sight for a while. No gasoline station with its huge gold shell. No greasy-spoon diners. Nothing but the occasional house and lots of country land. I was past the stage of vomiting, and though I thought I could hold my bladder, I didn't want to be late for my appointment.

Two little boys with cowlicks and horizontally striped shirts waved to me from the rear window of the car ahead, a new two-tone Chevrolet. I waved back and watched them laugh. I couldn't wait to have rambunctious children in my own back seat.

Thank goodness the cars ahead started to creep forward.

By the time I turned off the state road I was fifteen minutes from the doctor's and had ten minutes until my appointment. Few cars were on this stretch of county road. I sped around a tractor going two miles an hour.

At last I arrived. I went to the door of the small redbrick building, which was in a row with a general store, the post office, and Roberta's Breakfast Grill. Feed stores and tractor sales were down the road.

Just as I placed my hand on the knob, the door opened and there stood Abbie Glenn on her way out.

"Millie," she said, as stunned as I was. A week after she'd told Nathan I was expecting, she'd called me as if nothing had happened. Abbie had already learned that she'd spoiled my surprise. When I brought up my disappointment, however, she'd said she'd assumed Dennis already knew. Two days later my postman delivered Abbie's trio of jars of home-made grape jelly, blackberry preserves, and apple butter with cloves.

"Are you all right?" she said now. "You look peaked."

"I'm fine," I said as we stood there with the door ajar, her blocking my way. "Just running late for a checkup appointment. A stall on the highway."

Abbie patted my belly, and I cringed. "That's going to be a big baby." It'd been a few weeks since she'd seen me. "Nothing is more important than your health," she said. "I've got to run. Cooking a crown roast of pork for dinner."

"Bye-bye." I was thankful she hadn't listed her whole menu.

In Dr. Welch's office for his general family practice after my exam, I stared at a chart hung on one wall with its huge letters of the alphabet: *A*'s and *E*'s at top, and progressively smaller rows of *K*'s, *B*'s, and *Q*'s. Clear glass canisters with silver metal lids lined an old counter, each filled with tablets, cotton balls, or long cotton swabs. Dr. Welch perched on his swivel stool, looking at me from over the rim of his black-framed glasses.

"You've developed a complication," he said without preamble.

A complication? I pressed my hands to my bulging abdomen.

"What is it?" I said.

"You have pyelitis," he said matter-of-factly. "It's not that uncommon, but you'll need to avoid infection."

"Say it again?" Had I ever read the term before? *Pyelitis?* I couldn't think. "Is it serious?"

The doctor had a kindly face, but I detected superiority there, too. In an earlier visit when Dennis had come, the old coot had spoken directly to my husband about my health as if I weren't the one carrying this child—as if I weren't in the room. But I had dared not show my annoyance. He had delivered all the Glenn grandchildren. And besides, a doctor was the expert. He was in charge.

"By the time an expectant mother reaches six or seven months," he said now, "her enlarged uterus can put pressure on her bladder, and if inflammation occurs this can make urination more difficult, a symptom you've experienced." That was true. He patted my knee and took on the tone of a kindergarten teacher. "You've registered a slight fever, and given the discomfort you've reported on your right side in the back, and your hip area as well, the diagnosis is clear."

"But is it serious?" I asked again. "Will this complication hurt my baby?"

"It's rarely serious, providing you follow my instructions to a T."

I fumbled for a pen in my purse. On the back of a Gunnison post-card I wrote the doctor's advice.

"Consume forced fluids, that is, drink fifteen full ten-ounce glasses of water a day—to keep your kidneys flushed out. Lie down periodically, too, flat on your back with a low pillow and your legs elevated."

That didn't sound as if the baby and I were in danger. Did it? But what about work? Running out to the newspaper and fabric shop?

"And another thing," the doctor said. "Slow down. Take it easy. Don't try to do as much as usual."

I could barely hold back tears as I drove home, worrying about my baby the whole long way. I wished for Dennis, Mother Glenn, Pauline—or Mama—to be with me. I felt as alone and afraid as a child lost in a department store when the lights went out for the night.

Had my mother suffered this medical complication? *Not all women have babies the way alley cats squirt out kittens.*

I felt my baby flutter. It was the most wonderful sensation in all the world.

Had Mama ever lost a baby midterm? Or, heaven forbid, delivered a stillborn?

2015

Jane crumbled saltines into a hot bowl of vegetable soup. Kelsey and I had convinced her to stop back at my place for lunch after water aerobics. How could Jane decline when I'd made vegetarian vegetable soup, without the beef, just for her? I'd stirred up the batch the night before just in case we all got together. Mother Glenn had taught me that second-day soups always tasted better.

"You guys," Kelsey said, her hand on her stomach. "I feel flutters."

It was still too early for Jane or me to see or feel the movements by touching. But it was wonderful to know this grandchild was alive and kicking.

"The baby likes your soup, too," Jane said to me. Sweetness. We both had a baby to look forward to—providing nothing drastic happened to Jane.

"Mom," Kelsey said to Jane, trying to keep the tone upbeat. "I believe you're going to be fine. I really do. But you need to get a mammogram. Fast."

"Honey, you just focus on your own well-being. You already have one other person to care for. I'm capable of handling myself."

"You just moved here," I said. "Do you even know where to go?"

Jane glared. I flinched. I couldn't take confrontation right now. I couldn't.

Kelsey got her cell phone out and started tapping with two thumbs. "There's an imaging center in the women's health complex where I get my annual pap."

"I told you," Jane said. "I'll take care of it."

"Mom, seriously? Let's just give these people a call. I'm not leaving until you have an appointment."

Jane put her spoon in the bowl with a clang. "Wasn't it you the other day who said you didn't want to go anywhere near a hospital? Nor machines? Now you're cramming doctors down my throat?"

"Jane, she's just—"

"I know what she's doing, Mom."

Jane took her bowl to the sink, leaving half of her soup untouched. My own appetite fizzled.

Kelsey keyed more numbers into her phone. "Hello, I'd like to make an appointment," she said. Jane folded her arms across her chest. "For my mother."

Jane returned to the table, stiff, once Kelsey had hung up. Jane said, "Aren't I the one who's supposed to be helping the aging mother? Not the other way around, with my own daughter helping me?"

I bristled at the word *aging*. But I agreed. Jane shouldn't be the one we were all worrying about. "So what'd they say?" I asked Kelsey.

"They won't give her a screening mammogram, not since she's already found a lump. She needs a diagnostic mammogram, and that takes a doctor's order first. I'll make an appointment for her with my doctor."

"Hello, I'm right here! You two are talking about me in the third person?"

Her protest resonated; I'd never liked when someone did that to me.

Jane pushed away from the table again and stormed to the front door. "How did I manage to take care of myself for twenty years in

Georgia without you two hovering around? Next thing you know, you'll be whipping out the Vicks VapoRub or hot mugs of Ovaltine." The door slammed.

My eyes locked with Kelsey's. "She won't be gone long," Kelsey said. "She didn't take her purse or her keys."

"Or her coat," I said. "She's going to need her coat or she'll catch her death of cold."

Jane was sitting on the stoop by my mums when I found her. Pitiful thing. It's hard to see your child look so alone. Downcast. It's worse knowing you pretty much put her there. She slipped on her coat.

"What do you say you and I go for a walk?" I said.

"You're kidding, right?"

"Would I kid about that?"

She reluctantly agreed. Jane and I hadn't strolled this neighborhood together in many years. It had been 1955 when Dennis built the ranch house in which I still lived. There were Gunnison prefabs that he had built on our street, but our house was the first custom home we'd designed. Janie had been five. Dennis had later transitioned the business from all prefabs to Custom Homes by Glenn. He would have loved to have built other houses for us, too, but I'd resisted it. I wouldn't shuffle Janie around as I'd been shuffled as a child. And I hadn't needed anything bigger or fancier in a home. I had needed stability.

I still did. Jane and I walked in silence, but we were together.

We passed Pauline's old house next door, and I got a pang. The Irvings had relocated here, too. A young family had moved in after my friend died. Farther up was an early Gunnison house, now painted yellow, and the owners had added on a sunporch a couple of years back. It favored their huge rear yard with old trees. Dennis would be pleased. Up a little ways more was another house I remembered him building as if it were yesterday—it had what Gunnison called the wind-o-wing that extended the space in the bedroom. One thing I loved about my neighborhood of Terrace Park was the variety of homes families here shared. Homes from before the 1920s. Homes that were updated or modern. As Jane and I walked slowly without speaking, I imagined I heard the trumpeting of elephants in the way she and I had pretended to do years ago.

"Do you still hear the elephants out here?" Jane said, breaking our silence. I laughed out loud.

"I do. Just now, as a matter of fact." In the late 1800s a traveling circus had wintered here. The Terrace Park Historical Society had black-and-white photos of elephants roaming the fields before the neighborhood grew up.

"I thought so. I heard them too," Jane said. I caught a glimpse of her smile. We'd connected, and I breathed that feeling in. "Looks like it might rain," she said.

"Remember those black-and-red rubber boots you used to have?" I said.

"Ha. The ones I left on the school bus because no other kids' moms made them wear galoshes?"

"You've always hated having to bundle up in the rain and cold."

"Or maybe we've just had issues over boots. You weren't wild about my Nancy Sinatra go-go boots in high school either."

"No, I wasn't. Nor the miniskirts you wore with them." And my, that girl had had the legs.

In the midst of this shared glimpse of lightness between us, it scared me more than I could measure to think that, in months ahead, all I might have left of her were my memories. And my regrets.

We walked to the end of the block and turned back around. Quiet. Jane had been glib when she'd told us about her breast. But underneath she was frightened. Who wouldn't be?

"Janie—I mean, Jane. Sorry. You are going to be fine." She needed to hear a positive outlook. I could do that for her.

"I know. I know." Her voice sounded hoarse. I hooked an arm through hers and was relieved that she let me.

"Breast cancer doesn't run in our family," I said. "On either side." I think I said it as much to reassure myself as to reassure her.

"I've done a little research on my own," Jane said. "Heredity isn't a requirement. But, as Kelsey said, most lumps are, in fact, benign."

A car passed. The neighbors waved. For a split second I was deceived into everything feeling normal.

"But in women over sixty years old," Jane said, and I felt her arm tense up, "the chance of a lump being cancerous is higher."

I felt sick, the way I had one day long ago: I had heard bad news outdoors that day—in Eden Park, not here in my neighborhood—but I had lost control and vomited over and over right there in the grass.

I held myself together now. I did it for Jane.

"Mom, you know what bothers me even more than the fact that Daddy didn't survive his cancer, and I—"

"That was years ago," I said, cutting her off. "They've come so far with treatments since then, especially with breast cancer." I tried to keep my optimistic front, but inwardly I was scared to death.

"I don't want to waste away to nothing the way Daddy did," Jane said, a hint of her Southern twang coming out. "That's for sure. But that's not what I'm really afraid of. And it's not so much that I'm scared to lose my breasts." She stopped and turned to me, a sudden wind making her thickly lashed eyelids flutter.

"What if I don't live to see my grandchild grow up? What if I die before Kelsey's baby is even born?"

I shook my head no, no. "That can't possibly happen," I said decisively, as if it were scientific fact. But I was frightened for her. Bad things happened all the time.

CHAPTER SIX

August 1949

I was ready to tell Dennis of my complication. I'd read up on pyelitis in a maternity manual and accepted its treatment. I knew it might mean hauling myself out of bed to urinate three times a night. The part about slowing down was another thing. I wouldn't broach that topic.

Dennis took the news without much alarm, based in part, I'd believed, on how smoothly I'd delivered it.

Or so I'd thought.

"Honey," he said as he'd crumbled a thick leftover square of corn bread into a glass of cold milk. "I've been thinking." He dunked his spoon into the milk mixture, gave it a stir, and stuck a sloshy spoonful into his mouth. Corn bread and milk was a favorite among all the Glenns. They ate it like late dessert. I didn't care for soggy food.

"Thinking about what?" I said, scraping the remnants of macaroni and cheese off his dirty plate onto mine, preparing to clear the table.

"Maybe you should cut back," he said. "Let me take over the paperwork duties for Gunnison. You can rest more. Reserve your energy these last three months before the baby comes."

I felt my blood pressure hike. I was unprepared for the suggestion, no matter how reasonable my cutting back on work might sound. There were plenty of duties I could handle from home anyway. There were calls to make. Ledgers to manage. Bills to pay. I accidentally let the fork I'd been scraping with clang to the plate. He startled.

"Sweetheart, I'm fine. Dr. Welch did suggest I slow down a bit," I admitted, "but he doesn't really know what I'm capable of. You do. Yes, I've had a little heartburn and whatnot, and now this new hiccup. I've done some research. It's not as if we learned our baby is breech."

"Just think about it," Dennis said. He looked thoughtful. "Especially given that the doctor recommended it. I can let the girl answering the phones help more with something. You could show her a few of your tricks."

I wasn't sure whether I was more angry or hurt. I felt as if the king had just told the queen that her lady's maid might suit better, and he'd next be announcing to his kingdom—about his queen—"Off with her head." I stared him down. Taking care of the Gunnison Homes by Glenn accounts was my work.

"Dennis, I'm fine. I'll stay fine. I'm pregnant, that's all," I said. "Your mother worked through every pregnancy. Remember? Have you seen any slips in my output?"

"Of course not. I was only trying to help, honestly." He leaned to kiss me. "Please don't be sore."

We never spoke of the complication or my work again. Until we had to—after my hospital stay.

~

Among other manuals for mothers, Pauline and I had read British Dr. Grantly Dick-Read's groundbreaking book about "natural child-birth"—about how women shouldn't fear labor, for it was never intended to be painful. Partly rooted in Darwinian theories and partly on primitive societies, the doctor advocated relaxation methods and controlling one's emotions to improve the birthing experience.

But in the end, there was nothing "natural" about either Pauline's or my first deliveries.

She had gone the "I don't want to feel a thing" route—Demerol, scopolamine, forceps, and all.

Less than three months later, it was my turn.

～

When I arrived at the hospital that November of 1949, a nurse asked me to sit in a wheelchair. Dennis kissed me goodbye and rubbed his hand over my hair, his face nervously hopeful. He would get me admitted and go from there to the lounge where fathers gathered to wait. My contractions were six minutes apart. I had five or six minutes left until the next one. As I rode up that elevator with the quiet, middle-aged nurse—one floor, two floors, three floors with the elevator's screeching of cables—I thought: *This is it. No turning back. The time has come, and one way or another, this baby is on its way out.*

A bell rang, and the doors rattled open. I smelled cleanser and the wax on the spotless, shiny floor, and I heard an infant cry. Directly across was a sign with big, black, bold letters: **MATERNITY WARD**. There were no pictures of bunnies or duckies or teddies. The tiled hall was like a hall in high school, only with nurses in their starched white dresses and white stockings passing by, instead of teachers in suits and ties.

"How are you doing?" the nurse asked.

"I'm great," I said, for as scared as I was—and I was scared—the only way I could answer was great, because the next time I would be in this chair, I knew I'd be heading back to the elevator, my arms cradling an infant boy or girl.

The nurse rolled me to a single laboring room, but she said, "You'll be in this room long enough to get prepped. That's it."

My next contraction came, and it was a doozy. My head went back, my jaw tightened, my legs locked, my hands clutched the wooden arms of the chair, and my whole abdomen and buttocks and lower back tensed, tensed, tensed. I came out of it huffing.

The nurse told me that before my next contraction I should have time to remove all my clothes, put on the nursing gown, use the toilet, and climb into the bed and lie on my back. Then she left the room.

I followed her instructions with no time to spare.

The pillow was cold, the top sheet crisp, the mattress hard. There was no blanket; I wouldn't be here long enough for that, I supposed. I snuggled under the sheet. The walls were beige. The light dim. A ladder-back chair stood beside the bed, and I wished that Dennis, or Mama, was in it.

The nurse returned and flipped on the bright ceiling lights. For what she planned to do to me next, she'd need better light to see.

Pauline had warned me about the full shave. This hospital was a different one than hers, mine being outside of the city. I'd like to say that the shave wasn't as bad as she said it would be. But it was. The nurse slid the sheet down to my knees. She slipped my airy cotton gown up over my hump, letting it puddle on my tender, swollen nipples and exposing parts of me below that no one but Mama and Dennis and Dr. Welch had ever seen. Goose bumps formed on my thighs with the chill. The tight skin of my belly felt warm to my hands, though, as I cradled my baby inside me.

"Spread your legs apart, Mrs. Glenn," the nurse said, "until I tell you to stop." She wore white rubber gloves—which somehow made it easier on me than her touching me skin to skin—and she guided my legs by holding on to my knees.

Another contraction came. "We'll wait," she said, and slipped the sheet back up to cover me. My gown stayed pooled on my breasts. And though she had covered me back up, I felt humiliated to shudder and rock with the pain with her beady eyes watching me. Afterward she pushed the flimsy sheet down again.

"This is going to be a bit cold. Hold still," she said. She applied lather while I stared straight up to the ceiling. "Now it's important that you don't move, Mrs. Glenn. I know it's not comfortable, but no different than when you shave your legs." I glanced at her then, and all I saw was the glint of the light on the blade that was four inches long and half an inch wide. That's not something I'd ever take to my calves, I thought. I closed my eyes again and heard the swipes as much as I felt them—one swipe, two swipes, three swipes, and so forth. She removed the razor and dabbed me with a cool, wet cloth.

"After your next contraction, it's time for the enema," she said. I gritted my teeth through my next wave, while hearing her stir up the soap suds.

When the prep was finally over, I was put in a rolling bed and pushed through the halls with merely a sheet covering me. Another bed passed coming from the opposite direction, the woman in it drenched in sweat and her hair a big tangle. At least a blanket covered her. I heard the labor room before I saw it—with its low murmur like that of the crowd when Dennis and I had approached the V-J Day celebration from blocks away. The nurse swung open the door, and I raised my head up to behold a large room, a ward in itself, with lights dipping from the ceiling at equal intervals—a room that, as I was soon to learn, held twenty laboring women.

"Why is this room so crowded?" I asked.

"It's been like this since the war," the nurse said. "So many babies, we can scarcely keep up."

There were two rows of narrow beds that faced each other end to end, but with an aisle running up the middle. Two men awkwardly slid my bed into a slot at the center of one row. One dropped a folded blanket on my feet. All the women's heads backed to the walls. My metal-framed bed was less than four feet from the women on either side, where one of them wrenched in anguish, squealing as a contraction gripped her. I had no sooner shuffled under the welcome navy felt blanket than my own contraction took over.

A different nurse came to my side. "I need to examine how far you've dilated," she said in the manner of a gasoline attendant filling a tank. Then she proceeded to slip her gloved fingers under the covers, between my legs, and deep into my most private place.

Over the course of ensuing hours, doctors went up and down both rows giving shots to the women. Nurses told us over and over to keep quiet. But there was a steady stream of moans and cries. I tried to follow the rules. But it hurt. We watched as every so often they wheeled an expectant mother away to a sterile delivery room. And a fresh patient was brought in. The maternity ward was an assembly line for newborns—the laboring women rolled along from station to station to station while doctors and nurses mechanically took their turns with the women to get the product out. A baby factory. Had Henry Ford still been alive, he would have patted himself on the back.

The woman lying in the bed next to me screamed. She was a girl, really, maybe seventeen. A burly nurse leaned in close to her. The girl quieted long enough for me to hear the nurse say, "Shut up your crying at me. I didn't make you pregnant. Suffering is what comes of all the fun you had." The girl went mute. Why would a nurse condemn this girl so? Hadn't a man shouldered 50 percent of the responsibility for the "fun"?

When the nurse left, I smiled at the girl, but she turned her head the other way.

After contractions had ripped through my body for hours, I was finally in a delivery room with my feet in stirrups and knees high. I was groggy and in some moments disoriented between pushes. Dr. Welch, the country doctor who'd delivered all the Glenn grandchildren, came to my ear.

"Mrs. Glenn, I must perform an emergency surgery. Your baby can't come without it."

My baby? Emergency surgery? No one else in the ward had been told that.

"The baby can't fit through your birth canal," the doctor said anxiously, sweat beading on his forehead. "You need a cesarean section."

I'd scarcely even heard of it. Certainly no one I knew had had that done.

"Does this mean my baby may die?" I imagined all the women's heads rising across the labor room down the hall, hearing the terror in my voice. "Might I die too?"

—

I'd been sliced up the middle, from the line where my pubic hair used to be to just beneath my navel. Like an autumn pig at slaughter. The hospital kept me and baby Janie for almost three weeks—though we were mostly separated as a precaution against her getting an infection. The last words I recalled Dr. Welch saying as he discharged me were: "Once a cesarean, always a cesarean. And no more than two babies, Mrs. Glenn." But I paid him no mind. Who was he to tell me how many children I could have?

The first night I was home, when Dennis and I watched our baby sleep with the door cracked to the hall light, he kissed my temple and said, "Janie is an angel." She was. She had a feathering of dark hair. Smooth skin without blemish. Tiny perfect fingernails. Ears that laid to her head as if she were a doll. I lifted Janie out of her cradle, and she stayed fast asleep. I brought her to my cheek and my lips—what a wondrous miracle she was. Her smell, her lashes as long as mine, her tiny doll-face nose. I kissed it. I knew in that moment that all the pain I had suffered did not matter.

I would go through it all again for more babies like this. Enough babies to fill a birthday party . . . the kind of party boisterous with romping children that I'd never had myself.

—

The surgery wasn't the worst of my pain.

Dennis was on a construction site a week after I was home, the day my sister-in-law called me. "Just thought I'd check up on you. How are you doing?"

Abbie had visited in the hospital with Nathan, of course. She'd even gone so far as to say Janie was a beautiful newborn.

"Janie and I are doing splendidly," I said. "Home a week and already I'm cooking dinner every night." I thought Abbie would be impressed.

"Very good," she said. "You don't miss the business?" Her voice was flat.

"It's only been a month since Janie was born. I'll be ramping up soon." I'd had all the ads and accounts up to date before I was admitted to the hospital. "I am itching to start back, though."

"But what about the support person Dennis put in place?" she said.

"Support person?"

"You know," she said, "the one taking your place. Maybe it's just temporary."

I hadn't known. Had I assumed Dennis would wait? Of course I had. Or else I'd have asked.

"This is a wonderful time in a woman's life," Abbie went on. "Shouldn't the children and homemaking be your only priorities anyway?"

I bristled when Abbie Glenn, Housewife of the Year, needled me. But apparently, as I came to learn, my husband agreed with her.

It turned out Dennis had shifted some accounts payable work to an assistant when I was confined in the hospital. He hadn't wanted to disturb me while I recovered. But he'd had someone step in on ads with the creative agency as well. He'd sent one customer to someone else who could help pick out decor colors, too—sent her to a seamstress. I thought my skills exceeded sewing.

Perhaps I shouldn't blame him. Money had to come in the door each week. But I did blame him. Didn't partners tell each other what was going on in the business?

That night, as Dennis opened the newspaper to the sports section, I said all bright and perky, "Dennis, I'm back up and at 'em, I can handle the accounts from home while Janie naps. I can make calls. I can get out once a week to the newspapers, too, toting her along. You know, do the occasional decorating consultation."

"Mil, you don't need the pressure."

"Honey, just because a seamstress knows how to design and sew curtains doesn't mean she can walk a Gunnison customer—a future referral source, dare I say—through the thought process of laying out a whole room."

"Like I said, you don't need to concern yourself." He smiled.

A seamstress wouldn't contemplate the scale of a space, wouldn't take resale worth into consideration. She'd sew. Why was Dennis diminishing my value in our business? It wasn't fair. He was muffling my voice, and I didn't like it.

"Dennis, you have to—"

"You're such a good mommy," he said.

Yes, I was. That wasn't up for debate. But I could be both.

He folded the newspaper, tucked it under his arm, and stood. "Just take care of yourself and Janie. I've got the work bases covered."

I wilted.

If Mama were still alive, she would urge me not to give in—she would support my wanting it all: raising my children, managing our home, earning some money. Feeling fulfilled.

But surely Dennis had my best interests at heart. He was my husband. He cherished me above all others. Were he and Abbie right, then? Should I accept my woman's lot and move on? Was I wrong to want both a family and a job? Would a better mother than I be satisfied and not seek the thrill of a deal or sale?

What if I couldn't slow down?

CHAPTER SEVEN

August 1950

I wiped the countertops and ran my cloth-covered thumb along the stainless-steel edging that overlapped the red surface. It was Sunday night, and that meant our neighbors would soon pop over to watch *The Gene Autry Show*. The Irvings rotated each week with Dennis and me, gathering in front of the singing cowboy on either their television set or ours. Janie was nine months old and amusing herself with an orange Jell-O mold in her high chair. Pauline had telephoned to assure me her husband, Bob, would keep his repeating cap pistols—yes, his toys, not their eleven-month-old Tommy's—at home next door in their holsters this week. We'd laughed. Our phones didn't have party lines anymore—no one could overhear our conversations—but I'd given Pauline no hint of my new dilemma. Tonight I would let her in on the news that was at once thrilling me and terrifying me.

Dennis wandered into our kitchen while I was assembling my glass chip-and-dip set. It had a smaller bowl that perched on the rim of a larger one with the aid of a tiny metal rack. "Have I told you lately you're the prettiest girl a guy ever got?" Dennis said. "Not to mention the smartest."

"Only about a thousand times." I smiled at him, suggesting he could tell me a thousand times more. I pressed my index finger into one of his dimples. "And you're the most charming guy a girl ever snagged."

He kissed me and patted my behind. This could be the perfect moment to tell him my news. So spontaneous. But no, Pauline would be first to hear I was pregnant again—and help me form a plan to tell Dennis. I couldn't wait too long, for who knew if Abbie would find out and blab it again?

My larger concern was that my husband and I still didn't see eye to eye on my workload.

Papa Glenn might've said I was damned if I did and damned if I didn't: I was beyond excited to be pregnant again . . . I could hear the chorus of children's voices singing happy birthday in my home, the way I'd longed to hear as a girl. Lots of children, my children, running about in play. Yet I yearned to contribute to the business, too. I wanted to earn my jug money, and build my savings account, and I craved the feeling of accomplishment in making our business succeed.

Back when Janie was a few months old, I'd convinced Dennis to let me resume doing promotional mailings two afternoons a week from home: "Your mother didn't stop picking cabbages when she had four kids underfoot," I'd said. Mother Glenn had told me so herself. What I didn't relay to Dennis was how his mother had said I could cut back on the number crunching for a while, and Dennis would see that he needed me again soon enough. *Soon enough for whom?* I'd thought. I told Dennis, "Can you imagine the farm without your mother directing the annual cider squeeze? Do you want a stranger handling our finances?" So Dennis had seen how I managed our home and Janie so well, and he'd agreed to a few discrete duties. "Not too much to overwhelm you," he'd said, fearful that my surgery's scar might split open or something. But besides the mailings, I was soon reconciling the bank accounts each month from the couch at home, too. My family and my work made me happy.

I was afraid that with another baby coming, though, Dennis would shift these tasks to his new "guy Friday," and I'd never work again. As a matter of fact, most of the time I felt I could take on more work.

As it was, I'd thrown myself into sewing for Janie to help fill my days. Dennis had bought me a Singer sewing machine. Its owner's manual advised me to prepare mentally for sewing: to never begin a project with a sink full of dishes. Seamstresses should wear a neat dress, freshly clean, and lipstick as well. One's sewing mustn't create undue stress if a visitor should stop by. Be ready. For me, though I followed the guidance to the nth degree, the feel of the cloth on my palms, the pull of the thread, and the spinning bobbins somehow, surprisingly, brought me closer to Mama.

And with everything I did I felt productive. Useful.

I was frazzled some nights, I confess—the chores, caring for Janie, my business work, getting dinner on the table in time—all while looking magazine-mother pretty. No one ever said that doing some of everything would be easy. Mother Glenn's wide array of duties had never been easy on her either. Partnerships were hard work. But these were all things I loved doing. In the beginning of our marriage, I was driven more by my need to not depend solely on a man. I still had that need. But as time had evolved, I sought to make a difference with the business, too.

Now that our family was set to grow, I at least wanted a chance to prove what I could do.

I went to our daughter after Dennis patted my bottom, and I said, "You didn't catch that frisky move your father just made, did you?" I nuzzled her silky, scrunched neck. Janie squealed and pulled her bib up to her face, trying to lick off the last of her Jell-O. Raggsie scampered to the door, barking.

"They're here, Mil," Dennis said. The Irvings never used our front door; they crossed through the gate at the yard in the rear and came through the arcade between our house and the garage.

Our living room was comfortable enough for two couples to mingle, though the playpen cramped our path to the kitchen. Dennis claimed his favorite seat, of course, the womb chair. Buying that had been a splurge. It was a roundish, padded designer piece all covered in red wool. I thought it, like so many modern designs, looked born of a spaceship. Dennis admired its wide molded arms and skinny pole legs. Pauline had called the womb chair "deliciously avant-garde."

As parents, we couples had no trouble hearing the television program over the children's blabbering. We were used to a ruckus. In no time the show's intermission came. I got a twinge of butterflies in anticipation of Pauline's reaction to my news.

Bob, who was an up-and-comer at Procter & Gamble, was spouting off about how the Reds would lose the pennant again. Dennis rose and reached into the playpen to stack blocks with the babies. "How's it going, kiddos?" Such a good daddy.

Pauline trailed me into the kitchen for refills, wearing an outfit that might have come out of a photo spread in *Life* magazine. Tonight, while I wore a belted A-line dress and pumps for casual entertaining, Pauline had said her costume was designed expressly for women to watch the television. Her mother had picked it up during a seasonal spree to New York. It paired a snappy red, short-sleeved top with some sort of gold-striped slacks. The cut of the legs was so full, it was hard to tell if the gear was a spinoff of a sailor suit's belled bottoms, or a floor-length, billowy wrap-around skirt one might wear someplace like Morocco. The outfit, I had to admit, was ideal for stretching out on the floor in front of the set or lounging on one end of the sofa with a cocktail dangling in one hand—or sitting spread-eagle on our ottoman while lighting a cigarette and laughing gaily as she did.

"No more gin gimlets for you?" Pauline said as I arranged another round for everyone else with my glassware and pitcher.

"Water's fine for me," I said. *Expectant Motherhood*, our popular pregnancy manual, advised that a single cocktail was harmless, and ten or fewer cigarettes a day were fine, too. But regardless of how movie stars smoked on the silver screen practically as a means of foreplay, I'd never picked up the habit like Dennis had. Mama had always said that people who smoked had money to burn.

Pauline checked to make sure the guys had stayed put. Then she looked me square in the eye and said, "All right, Millicent. Spill the beans."

Pauline and I'd been neighbors for three years. She knew I roasted chicken on Tuesdays, dusted on Wednesdays, washed laundry on Thursdays, and went to the beauty parlor on Fridays. She knew my preferred brand of lotion was Jergens. She knew that Abbie wasn't my favorite Glenn relative. She knew I loved the songs by our hometown girl Doris Day, and I was so-so about Dinah Shore. Pauline sensed something was up, and she was right.

"I'm late. For the second month." I grinned, but her eyebrows spiked.

She slipped the ice cube tray out of the freezer compartment and whispered with a sideways stare, "Good Lord, Janie's not even a year old." She pulled up on the tray's metal handle to crack the ice and unstuck her fingers from the frost, and then she plopped four cubes into the metal shaker.

"True. It'll be a circus. But I'm happy, you know?"

"I recall the first time we met," Pauline said, "you were touring me through the model house and said you'd always wanted enough children to fill a birthday party. I'm happy for you. I take it you haven't told Dennis?"

"Not yet."

"Why not?"

I leaned in and whispered. "Will Dennis let me work at all once I have two children to raise? How will I react if he doesn't?" Pauline appeared to ponder this predicament.

I scooped more chip dip into the serving bowl. I'd sautéed sweet onions in butter, stirred them into sour cream and Hellmann's, and added three drops of Worcestershire sauce. I reached for the big red tin of chips and pried off the lid, distracted.

Dennis called Pauline and me from the living room. "Girlies, Gene Autry's back, and he's getting ready to sing."

"Coming," I said. "Wish me luck for when I decide to tell him."

"There are two ways to a man's heart—I mean, two ways to a man's head," Pauline said, giggling. "Either through his bed or through his belly. I recommend you first serve his favorite dinner, and then . . ."

"I'll take that under advisement."

"You'll have to buy a bigger house, you know," Pauline said as she spooned Jell-O into cups for the kids.

"We're not ready to move up." I lifted the serving tray of drinks and chips and nodded for Pauline to follow. To her, their place was a first home. To me, after the way I'd been raised, our place was a palace.

"If having another baby will move us up to a newer model," Pauline said, "I'll wear Bob's favorite peignoir set tonight." She winked, and I rolled my eyes.

The next day, I had to get past the hurdle of telling Dennis I was pregnant—and hope he didn't cut back on my business duties. When would I get to squeeze the conversation in? He had hurried off to a job site that morning, and we had a neighborhood party to attend that night.

I sprawled on the sofa and rubbed my hand across my flat tummy, feeling a tad nauseous. It wouldn't be long until I was big and round again. Maybe our next one would be a boy. The children might almost be like twins, live-in playmates at a mere sixteen months apart. The idea of doing double-duty with diapers didn't faze me. Well, perhaps it did a tiny bit. But I had every modern convenience, including a Maytag AMP automatic clothes washer and a built-in wall oven. I didn't have to bend over. I had a Hoover electric vacuum for cleaning our wall-to-wall carpeting and owned one of the first dishwashers among our set. But still, I'd have to manage my time well to do the construction company's paperwork and call in some ads along with everything else. Getting the children down to nap—both babies at the same time—would be key for tackling the messier chores such as cleaning the bathroom and the tasks requiring more concentration, like handling the checking account. There were nights that Dennis worked late, too, especially during long summer days like this when daylight lasted longer. So I'd have that time as well.

Was Janie stirring in her room?

Raggsie scampered in and propped his paws on my legs, wiggling his shaggy tail. That confirmed it. Naptime was over. I rose, my stomach settled for now.

I cracked open the door to Janie's room and smelled Johnson's Baby Powder and a hint of wet diaper. She sprang up and down on her crib mattress to greet me. Her cheeks flushed, and she had a full smile—a smile with four teeth, two on top and two on the bottom, and dribble stringing from her lip to her chin. I kissed the tiny wrinkle marks the sheets had left at her temples, that salty-sweet sugarplum skin where her curls were matted from deep-sleep sweat. Preciousness. I lifted her warm body, and she nestled her head into the well between my shoulder and neck. I caressed her plump, padded bottom, clothed in Minnie Mouse pants that fastened down the inside of each leg. Her cloth diaper hadn't leaked outside of her rubber panties.

I closed my eyes, imagining a baby in each arm. It would be hard. But I was strong.

～

By the time the mailman dropped our letters into the black metal box on the porch, Janie was in her bouncy seat, and I had time to scan the latest Gunnison Homes catalog that just arrived, produced by the manufacturer for dealers like us to use. Its headline got my attention, with its big, bold print: **Man's Greatest Gift to Woman.**

I wasn't sure I liked it.

I skimmed through the catalog while Janie played her toy xylophone with its metal keys in primary colors. The catalog was a slick full-color piece with pictures of all the home models, interior floor plans, and new optional features like fireplaces and porches. When I came to building specifications and engineering data, the section was titled "For Men to Read." It explicitly targeted potential home buyers—husbands. There was also a dedicated section called "For Women to Read." It dealt more with a floor plan's convenience and decor and addressed the needs of the wife:

> **Nothing is more conducive to happy family life than a cozy, comfortable home. It is a woman's contribution to the marriage union.**

I grimaced. So women couldn't make contributions to the marriage besides cooking and cleaning? My sister-in-law Abbie Glenn could have written that copy herself.

My occupation was housewife. Did that mean I was married to a house?

While I enjoyed sewing, I didn't want to be a paid seamstress as Mama had been. I didn't want to be a nurse or to teach second grade either, though these were all considered appropriate feminine pursuits. During the war, I had worked at Kroger and assisted customers with their ration books. Other women had driven ambulances on battlefields or built planes in factories. Women had helped win the war. Since the men had returned from serving our country, many of these same women had lost their manufacturing posts. The production lines turned back over to the male breadwinners. The women could go back home to bake bread.

⁓

Thank goodness the birthday party that night for one of the husbands in the neighborhood was casual and held indoors. It was muggy outside. I wore slim red slacks and a sleeveless checkered top and sipped on a Coke through a straw while the wives rambled on about meatloaf or steak. The topic of hobbies arose—knitting, embroidering, and flower arranging.

"What about you, Millie?" the hostess, Deloris, asked from her living room filled with vases of thornless red roses.

"I love to cook and am learning to sew for Janie," I said, "but as for true hobbies, I don't have time. I help with the business from home—handling ledgers, getting out mailers, developing newspaper ads. That's what I like to do."

Deloris's mouth opened into a wide O. The men in a circle nearby looked over and laughed. Her husband, Ray, the birthday boy, slapped Dennis on the back, saying, "Good God, man, you don't work the little lady's fingers to the bone, do you?"

I suspected I'd gone too far. This crowd of suburbanites wasn't ready for the likes of me.

"Get her a girl to do the floors," another husband said before plopping a plump green olive into his mouth.

Still another guy said skeptically, "So Mrs. Glenn's taking a job away from a man?"

Taking a job away from a man? I bit my tongue. Were men so much more important then? I wanted to jump back into the conversation, but although I'd already created a fiasco, I wouldn't make a scene.

Another husband put in, "My wife's always saying that keeping house is job enough in itself." He snickered.

"I'll say," Deloris said, bringing attention back to herself. "I scarcely have time to file my nails."

All the wives tittered. Except for Pauline and me. My jaw was too clenched to even fake tittering. While my best friend wasn't driven to be the absolutely perfect housewife, she didn't long to be something else. But she knew me. She sipped her martini and shot me a compassionate look over the rim of her long-stemmed glass.

I turned back around to find Dennis, hoping he'd jump in and support me. But he was stabbing a cheese cube with a toothpick, pretending he hadn't heard.

~

After last night's embarrassment at the party, I felt more guarded about approaching Dennis than ever. I had to get this right. There was too much at stake: my job, my fulfillment. Pauline had suggested I butter him up with a lovely meal before telling him my news of another baby. And before telling him my . . . demands? No, my *requests*? My *opinions*. Yes, I'd tell him my opinions about work. I'd allow myself the best odds and follow my friend's advice. Swiss steak with tomato gravy was one of my husband's favorites.

I flipped the raw pieces of round steak over on my cutting board, sprinkled them with salt and pepper and flour, and picked up my aluminum meat tenderizer. *Pound, pound, pound.*

The neighbors' comments still annoyed me—I wasn't being worked to death, and I certainly did find time to file my nails. *Pound, pound, pound.*

The Gunnison catalog still irritated me every time I thought about it, too. I was feeling nauseous. *Pound, pound, pound.*

Then an image of old Mr. Hatter at the bank, from a day back before Janie was born, squirmed into my head. I needed my husband's permission for a savings account? Phooey. *Pound, pound, pound.*

I dropped the metal meat mallet into the porcelain sink with unexpected force. Janie shrieked from her high chair. The mallet crashed and splintered a dirty water goblet. Damn it.

Now I had a bigger mess to clean up before I prettied myself for my husband.

2015

My granddaughter and I busied ourselves by making a mess in Kelsey's kitchen while Jane was at the doctor's. Jane would return to pick me up later, and she'd be in possession of her written order for a diagnostic mammogram. As a treat, we'd have monkey bread warm from the oven awaiting her. Kelsey had taken the day off, and the bread had been her idea. She was smart, because baking had also allowed us a reprieve, however briefly, from our worries over Jane.

Kelsey had a gorgeous kitchen. She and Aaron had bought this condo within the last year. I'd been astonished when we'd pulled up in their car out front the first time. The condo was on Republic Street in Over-the-Rhine—in a refurbished nineteenth-century tenement on a block where I'd lived as a child. Before I was born, the street had been named Bremen. But anti-German hysteria during the Great War had changed all that. Even President Wilson had referred to German-Americans as "hyphenated" Americans. On the day Kelsey moved into her condo, I would have been no more taken aback by where they lived had it been Neuschwanstein Castle in the Bavarian Alps.

Republic Street was one street over from Washington Park, where I'd first waded in a pool with Opa. This urban Cincinnati neighborhood was now called the OTR, and it had climbed out of a shambles and was hip and chic, as Kelsey would say. Craft breweries, cocktail bars, restaurants, and boutiques lined the streets. Mama had always made sure the inside of our home was safe and clean—furniture dusted, floors mopped, dishes done, and cobwebs cleared. But for a time in this neighborhood I had played outside with older kids who hit balls with sticks in the streets, dodging cars that zoomed past. I played with kids who dared each other to climb wooden fences that were falling down from disrepair. A boy in knickers once shoved me to the cobbled street for fun—and I had run home crying with my knees and palms scraped, my wounds bloody and filled with tiny gravel.

The first time I had come to Kelsey's place, I'd said, "Can you imagine what Mama would think of all this?" It was beautiful. A dream.

Kelsey's two-bedroom condo on an upper floor cost more than three hundred grand. Mama and Opa had barely been able to scrape up the rent. In 1930, that'd been about twelve dollars a month. Maybe less.

Kelsey's kitchen was open to the living area. She had two walls of exposed brick and engineered floors of red oak. Large, silver ductwork ran across the white ceilings for function and to make a fashion statement. There was a small faux fireplace painted matte gray, and a dark-gray sectional unit with throw pillows of red velvet and fluffy white fur. The furry ones played off the thick shag rug—and both brought to mind my burying my fingers in old Raggsie's fur years before. The kitchen picked up the color scheme, too, with glossy red cabinets, a white quartz island, and barstools with gray seats and sleek legs. We stood at the island beneath its hanging light that was designed like something from Mars. It had sixteen prongs—I'd counted each one—tipped with bright, warm bulbs.

My granddaughter peeled the outer wrapper from a tube of store-bought biscuits. Then she gave the tube's seam a whack on the corner of the counter, and the fresh dough popped out. Mother Glenn would've had our tails. Her farm table saw only biscuits from scratch—with flour and buttermilk, lard and leavening. She'd taught me to smear the biscuit tops with grease from fried sausage, using the back of a spoon. Pauline was the one who'd introduced me to monkey bread. That was back in the 1980s. While canned biscuits couldn't hold a candle to Mother Glenn's, they could be finagled into a coffee cake pretty darn quick.

Kelsey quartered the unbaked biscuits with a paring knife. Despite how my knuckles ached, I coated the chunks with melted butter, cinnamon, and brown sugar. And we both artfully plopped them into a greased Bundt pan to bake. I savored my girl time with Kelsey, but I was grateful Jane had moved back—and grateful that Kelsey and I could care for her.

"Think your mother will be in good spirits?" I said while we washed up.

"I think Mom's still adjusting. To a lot. We need to get this diagnosis out of the way," Kelsey said. "But she misses her work."

Kelsey was coping by being pragmatic. Yes, Jane had dedicated years of her life to a mission—between her volunteering and then working with the Cincinnati chapter, and then moving south to join Habitat's management. She missed her career. And while I totally agreed with Kelsey, this failed to mask my underlying fear. What would Jane's health hold in coming months?

"You're right," I said. "Of course she misses her work."

Maybe Jane could return to volunteering with the local chapter of Habitat. Maybe she would dodge this health bullet. Her lump could be benign. And then she could revel in being a grandma. But the sinking feeling in my stomach would not wane until this period of limbo ended.

I returned my gaze to my granddaughter. Her blue irises had gone glossy. She was as worried as I was, and that made me worry more. Kelsey might be feeling more pain than any of us realized. She'd never had a father. She didn't want to lose her only parent.

"Let's move out to the cushy gray seats," she said, shaking it off. "I'm trying to decide what I'm going to do regarding work myself. I mean, I really love my job."

More pragmatism. Her approach was to not delve too deeply into her mother's state, or her own fear.

"The History Library values your work," I said. "You've got a great boss." Kelsey had gone to school for seven years to get where she was. She had met Aaron at Ohio State, hence the red-and-gray colors in their home. I'd gotten to meet Aaron long before Jane had. Jane had moved to Georgia to pursue her own dream career once Kelsey started college. When OSU won the national championship during Kelsey's last year of grad school, which was also Aaron's last year of law school, I'd fixed them a dinner the following weekend to celebrate. I served homemade chocolate-peanut-butter Ohio Buckeye candies for dessert. I treasured those times, being less than two hours away—Kelsey's closest family connection while she was at school. And then I got to send her off on her first day at the museum, in Jane's absence. Kelsey's first career job. When Jane later visited, she demanded Kelsey time alone. I understood. When the three of us gathered, Jane was perpetually behind on things Kelsey and I took for granted. Kelsey had wanted a dog, but she and Aaron had decided to wait; Jane was the one who barked—about how no one had told her. Kelsey had tried a new diet, something called Paleo; Jane picked at her plate, having lost her appetite from being left in the dark. Kelsey and I had gone to see *Harry Potter and the Prisoner of Azkaban* on opening night; Jane had exclaimed that that was going too far. "That's cruel and unusual punishment," she'd said. We hadn't left Jane out on purpose. But my having Kelsey to myself in some ways replaced the time I'd lost with my own daughter during her commune years.

I closed my eyes for a moment. If God saw way to make Jane okay, I'd never again resent not having Kelsey all to myself.

"You're good at your work," I said to Kelsey now.

She sat with her hands cradling her stomach. "It's cool to know that my hours with the manuscripts will help historians in the next century." Kelsey's ancestors' lives in the beer-making industry had inspired her

Tori Whitaker

life's work. In her position at the museum, she documented everything from the defunct old breweries to lager beer caves hidden beneath the streets of OTR. "And I love having my own purpose in addition to my role in my marriage," she said, "if that makes sense."

I got what she meant all too well.

"What are your options?" I asked.

"I can return when my maternity leave is over. Or I can stay home and raise the baby. There may be opportunities to work from home or even go part time. Mom's offered to keep the baby a day or two a week."

Oh, the choices women had now, compared to my day. The paradox was that Jane could care for the baby now that she'd returned to Ohio—but we had to ask how realistic it was to plan for that with her health issue. Was that really an option at all? The question lingered unspoken between Kelsey and me.

I didn't know whether I should ask this different question, but I did it anyway: "And Aaron's opinion about your working?"

"He's up for whatever I want. We're lucky. If we cut back, we can afford for me not to work. If I stay on the job, we can afford good childcare if need be. And with his law practice, he's got some flexibility to pitch in on snow days and whatnot once our child's in school."

I gloried in how Aaron supported his wife, not in the financial sense, but rather the marital-partnership sense. There was a time when it had been very unlike that for Dennis and me. No matter how old I became, I never forgot my warring feelings during that period—the angst between my love for my husband and the loss of my identity by his having marginalized my work.

Kelsey pulled the monkey bread from the oven. "But I'm freaking out. I should let my employer know my choice two months before I'm due. I think I would miss being part of the action. But part of me doesn't want to miss the small things as a mother either, you know? I'm only going to do this once—an 'only child' in our family again. As you were, and I am. And Mom is."

My skin heated. I'd let that observation pass.

"I'll get the whole job thing figured out," Kelsey said with a smile. "Let me show you my plans for the nursery." She logged on to her laptop as we scooted together on the couch. She googled knitting patterns for booties on something called Etsy. Kelsey then dragged out her motherhood manuals. Should she lay her infant on its tummy or on its back to sleep? One way, the child might get a flat head—but the other way he might risk choking on his own spit-up. Didn't the experts' opinions flip-flop every couple of decades? And how was I to know that nowadays the practice was no sheets, no bumper pads, and no blankets in a crib? Too much chance of suffocation.

Echoes of past conflicting advice circled in my brain. Breastfeed your baby. No, bottle-feed your baby. Let your baby cry. No, pick your baby up. When it came to guidance for caring for infants, one thing hadn't changed: it seemed there were many ways in which a loving mother might inadvertently harm her child.

⁓

"Well, that was a big nothing," Jane said after returning. She slid her mammogram order across Kelsey's counter.

Relief rolled over me. Jane was practically her usual irreverent self.

"What's next?" I said more casually than I could have expected, given the tension in my neck minutes before. I pinched a chunk of sticky monkey bread off the loaf and stuffed it into my mouth. These days they called this comfort food.

"Damn," Jane said, doing the same. "I almost forgot how gooey, melt-in-your-mouth good this stuff is." Buttery brown sugar syrup dribbled on her lip. She licked it clean. Kelsey's idea had been a hit.

"Daughter dear," Jane continued, "you'll be happy to know I've already scheduled my appointment for the diagnostic mammogram, too. One week from tomorrow."

Kelsey looked crestfallen. "Ugh. I wish I could go with you, but I've got a big meeting at work about the upcoming renovations at the Terminal."

"That's fine, I don't need—"

"I'm going, anyway," I said, interrupting Jane. "We don't all have to be there."

"You're kidding, right?" Jane said. "I don't need an escort. I've had plenty of mammograms in my day."

"Only screenings," Kelsey said. "Not diagnostic."

"I'll be fine."

"I told you, I'm going." I held my ground. "I need to be there, even if you don't need me to be."

"OMG," Kelsey said. "A week from tomorrow is October 6—your birthday, Grandma! I can't even believe it—with everything going on, the date crept up on me. What do you want to do?"

I looked at both of them. "We're not celebrating my birthday or anything else until all of this is settled." I waved the page with the medical order.

"Don't be crazy." That was Jane. "We'll go to dinner. We'll have some wine. Or at least, two of us will. We'll have cake with ice cream and candles."

"I want to go to a fancy place, but I want to go at a time when no concerns are hanging over our heads."

Jane put her hands up. "Have it your way. We'll wait."

Kelsey shrugged.

"But I am going with you for the test," I said.

"I'm not your baby anymore," Jane said, impatient.

"Yes, you are," I said jokingly, trying to loosen us back up.

"I'm. A. Big. Girl. Now. Mother."

Be a big girl, Abbie Glenn had once said to me. Memories clogged my mind. More every day. So many memories rushing, rushing.

I felt light-headed. I felt—

"Grandma, are you okay? Grandma."

"Let's get her to the couch," Jane said.

My head lolled back onto the cushioned sofa. Memories were spinning faster than I could sort through—Kelsey in college, Jane as a girl, my baby kicking, doctors and tests and results.

The woman with the beauty mark.

Kelsey forced me to sip some water. I opened my eyes.

"Grandma, say something."

"Mom," Jane whispered, squeezing my hand gently. "I didn't mean to upset you."

"I'm okay," I said. I sat erect to try to prove it. I set the tumbler of water on the end table, not too shaky.

"You had me worried." Sweet Kelsey.

"Too much monkey bread?" Jane said. We chuckled.

I said, "Please let me be with you at the mammogram."

"Fine. I don't get why you've always been so protective. But you can take me for the test, if it will make you feel better."

I exhaled, relieved. I'd ensure no one hurt my daughter.

But after today there was no question left in my mind. The time was coming. I would tell the girls my story. I had to get it out.

Jane and I must fully reconcile before it was too late for either of us.

CHAPTER EIGHT

August 1950

"That was delicious," Dennis said from his seat at the head of the table. After Swiss steak, I'd served him baked Alaska for dessert. It was a layer of vanilla cake beneath strawberry ice cream and toasted meringue, which I'd scrolled into peaks and curlicues—simple though extravagant-looking, just like in the magazine. I had set the table with my Fiestaware plates in their hallmark color of old ivory. Black-eyed Susans graced the coordinating yellow vase. And two lit tapers flickered in the candleholders of classic Fiesta green.

"You make a man feel like a king," Dennis said. "No one makes Swiss steak as good as you. And with this dessert, it's a whole meal fit for royalty."

I was genuinely glad he thought so, and not merely because it played into my plans. I liked to cook. And I liked making him happy.

As I poured him coffee after clearing his plate, my hands shook. It was do or die, as they say. Either my plan—well, Pauline's plan for me—would work or it wouldn't. By evening's end I'd know my future fate when it came to the business.

"Honey, I have news," I said, standing beside him and stroking the cloth of my apron. No matter how this all turned out, I was sure to have one thing I wanted: another baby, another step closer to the big family of my dreams. "Janie's going to have a little brother or sister."

"Mil, that's wonderful news. Hot diggity-dog." He scooted back his chair and stood, almost knocking it down in his excitement.

Half an hour later, breathless and sated, I looked up to Dennis, who was atop me in a tangle of damp bedsheets. "I'm feeling better at this stage than I did last time, far better," I said. "Fewer signs of morning sickness. This pregnancy is going to go smoothly. You'll see."

"More wonderful news," he said, and kissed the tip of my nose. "Maybe that means it's a boy?"

I purred. "So there's no need for my business duties to lessen this time."

Dennis rolled off me and flopped onto his back in the bed.

"I mean, I can continue as I do now," I went on. "With some work for the business from home."

"With all the mailings and accounting? I don't think so, Mil."

I felt myself sink into the mattress. Managing to summon the voice of an angel, though, I said, "I *do* think so."

He still faced the ceiling. "Janie hasn't even started to walk, and you'll soon have two little critters darting around." He turned on the pillow to get a direct look at me. "I won't put that kind of pressure on you. You can leave all the business worries to me."

It was as if the metal coil springs of the bed had sprung and dug into my back. My legs stiffened beneath the damp cotton sheet. "Worries? Phooey. I—"

"All our friends' wives care for their homes and children; they don't have jobs. They don't even want them. And they certainly don't need them. You don't either. Things are different than when I was just starting out and couldn't afford any help. And we didn't have kids then."

"But I—"

"But nothing. Come on, I'm proud to support my family."

My face burned. I couldn't even speak anymore, as my teeth had locked together. The Gunnison home catalog echoed in my head: *Man's Greatest Gift to Woman*.

Dennis brushed a strand of hair from my sticky forehead. "Running this home is job enough." He propped up on one elbow and swept his other arm about the room. "You're in charge of this whole domain."

Whole domain? I wanted to oversee all these things in my domain. I loved them. I didn't mind the dishes or running the vacuum. But I wanted my homemaking and mothering missions both—and the business, too. The business contented me in ways Dennis didn't understand. Seemed he'd forgotten that I'd been there since the beginning—we had begun as business partners, much as his parents were on the farm. Without me Dennis wouldn't be where he was. He had long called me the prettiest girl a guy ever got, not to mention the smartest; so why wasn't he letting me use all my smarts?

Then my wedding vows rang in my head like tinkling little nuptial bells: I had promised to love, to cherish, and to *obey*.

The bells resounded in my head louder and louder. How literally was the vow "to obey" to be interpreted? And if Dennis cherished me, as the words of his vows had proclaimed, would he not in these matters consider my true heart's content?

"Mil, you don't need to mope," my husband said, climbing out of the bed. "This case is closed."

⌒

Pauline and I pushed Janie and Tommy through the Cincinnati Zoo in the kids' matching blue strollers we'd bought at Shillito's department store. The weather was less humid, and the zoo—the second oldest in the country after Philadelphia's—boasted lush gardens and canopies of trees for shade. It had opened the year after Opa was born, and he'd told me of his grandfather bringing him here back when the guidebooks were printed in German. Our metal strollers were a godsend, steering easily around the path's bends with three wheels. And they had built-in snack trays and attached colored beads that kept small, idle hands busy.

In the last two weeks my second pregnancy had continued along splendidly, yet Dennis had reduced my duties just as he'd said he would. I had only one mailing to send out per week now. And even my balancing the checkbook was in question.

"Don't overtax yourself," Dennis had said. "Wouldn't want anything to lead to another medical complication. Like the first time you were pregnant."

It was clear there was no hope for expanding my duties once my baby was born. No decorating consultations. No waiting at lots for kits to be delivered.

That morning, before leaving for the zoo, I had fried Dennis's over-easy eggs a tad over-hard and left his starched white shirts with wrinkles.

The kiddies jiggled in their seats as we passed the giraffes eating leaves off treetops. We all enjoyed other African animals, too. "Janie, see the mommy elephant and the baby elephant?" I said, pointing. "See how their long trunks help them drink water?" Janie was only nine months old and Tommy nearly a year. They wouldn't remember this day. But our excursion was as much to get Pauline and me out of the house as it was them. I only had a finite amount of clothes to fold while Janie napped. And it wasn't productive for me to sew more clothes than she could possibly wear. I was beginning to be bored out of my head.

I needed to earn. I needed to feel useful. Were I a painter, I'd need to paint with my full palette of colors.

"Tommy," Pauline said. "Honey, sit. You mustn't climb out of the seat."

We stopped at a food stand, and I bought a big soft pretzel. I brushed most of the coarse salt off it, tore it into many tiny bites, and dropped them onto the children's snack trays a few at a time. Pauline and I shared a whole one ourselves.

We soon came to the apes, chimpanzees, and monkeys. Given the season, some gorillas were exhibited in outdoor cages, instead of indoors behind glass. As I took in the sight of a female gorilla lazily lying in a hammock in her cage strewn with straw, a feeling overcame me as if I would be sick—but it had nothing to do with my pregnancy.

"Did you ever see Susie while growing up?" I asked Pauline while noisy monkeys entertained the kids.

"*The* Susie the Gorilla? Yes," she said. "The one who ate table food."

"That's the one." While on a date years before, Dennis and I had seen Susie, the gorilla who'd come over in a zeppelin as a baby—but who had matured into the famous "World's Only Trained Gorilla." I had been enthralled with her. While I was growing up, the zoo invited children to her birthday party each year, and the newspaper showed pictures of kids getting to eat cake and ice cream, with Susie eating it, too. My family couldn't afford to take me. But Dennis had later found a way to let me see Susie, even if it wasn't her birthday. We'd been amazed at how Susie sat on a stool at a small dining table beside her trainer, inside the cage. So polite. She drank malted milk and fed herself with a fork . . . strawberries, pineapples, and rice. When the trainer asked her to kiss him, she puckered up her full, fat lips and smacked him right on his chops. We had applauded with all of the crowd.

Now as I stood before another adult female gorilla, the only images floating through my head were of Susie surrounded by metal bars, eating with a fork, and kissing her trainer. Silverware, kisses, a trainer. And a cage.

Was I any better off than Susie?

"Millicent?" Pauline said. "Time to get off your feet for a bit?"

"I'm fine," I said. "Let's move on."

Pauline was first to speak after a long time strolling. "I've found a new doctor. A new OB. You may like him, too."

"Oh, really? So tell me about him."

When Thanksgiving rolled around a few months later, the entire family gathered at the farm. The men huddled around the radio in the living room to listen to the football game. Our gaggle of nieces and nephews sprawled on the rug playing a game of Chutes and Ladders. Seven-year-old Margaret grinned up at me with her front teeth missing and said, "Auntie Millie, Mommy's belly is bigger than yours."

"Sweetie," I said with a chuckle, "your mommy will have your baby brother or sister before my baby comes." Abbie's baby would be born in January. Mine was due in late March.

Mother Glenn's kitchen was abuzz with the women preparing the feast. She, of course, had first baked pies with all her grandkids—letting each in their turn spoon out the pumpkin or pinch the doughy rims of the crusts. I set to chopping apples and walnuts with Abbie for the Waldorf salad. Dennis's oldest sister basted the gobbler, a fat twenty-three pounder, and said, "This electric roaster is the most wonderful contraption Westinghouse ever invented."

"Your Margaret is so good with Janie," I said to Abbie in the spirit of what the day meant. Janie had loved Abbie's daughter to play peekaboo with her months ago, and Margaret still made her laugh. "Margaret is excited about becoming a big sister."

"She'll be a huge help," Abbie said. "I don't know what she'll think if it's another brother, though. She's got her heart set on a sister."

"She'll love the baby either way, I imagine," I said.

"How about you? The way you're carrying so low, everyone thinks you'll have a boy," she said. "What does Dr. Welch predict?"

"Actually, I'm thinking about moving to a different doctor."

Abbie stopped chopping. "Why would you want to do that?"

"For one thing, he's closer in. Mount Auburn. And he's a specialist." After more visits with Dr. Welch in the country, I had come to conclude that he was too old-fashioned. He still referred to me in the third person, and he hadn't veered from, "Once a cesarean, always a cesarean. And no more than two babies." Besides, I still held a grudge that his nurse couldn't keep my private medical records to herself the last time around. She'd had no business telling Abbie my news.

Abbie resumed her chopping, her eyebrows arched. "Well, Dr. Welch is no young specialist, but he's quite experienced," she said so loud the others couldn't miss it, and I caught our mother-in-law eyeing us. Did Mother Glenn side with Abbie? Or think Abbie was butting in?

Then for my ears only, Abbie muttered, "He's talented, despite his being way out here in the sticks."

"I just want to see what the other OB says," I said innocuously.

Then I stood there wondering why I'd opened my mouth to her to start with—and also wondering why her opinion should matter to me. I wasn't set on the new doctor yet, but if it meant Abbie Glenn wouldn't have access to my medical records, perhaps that'd be the main reason to go. And I could show her that I had a mind of my own to make my own decisions.

"Well, if you insist, then—" Abbie said, dogged to have the last word.

"Papa Glenn, time to carve the bird," Mother Glenn called out while looking warmly at me. It was as if I'd just been saved by the bell. I couldn't help but smile at her.

CHAPTER NINE

December 1950

Dennis rolled up the blueprints for work, his gaze not meeting mine. We'd had a wonderful weekend sawing down our Douglas fir at the farm after hunting for just the right one, and stringing on electric lights with bulbs the size of my thumbs. Dennis had climbed up four rungs of the ladder to top the tree with a gold metal angel, and we'd hung glittered glass ornaments all about. Janie had squealed with delight and pointed her chubby fingers at the glow of red, green, yellow, and blue in the window of our living room. Now Dennis packed the last of his files in his briefcase.

"I'm meeting the new doctor, Dr. Collins, tomorrow," I said in case he hadn't heard me the first time. "Pauline will drive me if you can't get away."

Dennis hoped to finish one more house before the first snow, so he'd had his mind on his jobs. But he frowned as he took a rubber band and wound it around the last set of rolled-up blueprints.

"I thought we'd decided after Thanksgiving that you'd stick with Dr. Welch again."

The conversation to which he referred had been mostly one-sided. I'd said I was going to look into a new OB. Dennis had said, "Why not stick with who the family uses? Even though he's a little farther out." I'd said, "It's more than a 'little farther' out, but that's beside the point." And he'd said, "Can't beat Dr. Welch," and he'd left the room with my mouth poised to speak.

Now when I didn't reply, Dennis looked up. "You've changed your mind?" He picked up his hard hat and went for his coat.

Nothing had changed. I had decided all by myself. I would try the OB Pauline recommended.

"I'm going to Dr. Collins. See what he says." I smiled. "Building houses is your business," I said. "Running our home, caring for the family, and caring for myself is mine. Choosing a doctor is in my domain, then, right?" I resisted the impulse to stress the word *domain*, what Dennis had called my kingdom.

"I'll be late," he said, ignoring me. "I've got an appointment tonight to review plans for a couple on the hill."

What couple? A new house on the hill? I felt more and more left out.

"Of course. I'll keep some tuna-noodle casserole warm. And Pauline can take me to the doctor tomorrow." Until Pauline got her own transportation, we'd traded off. One day each week Bob left his wife his car, and on one day each week Dennis did the same with me. The Irvings were a two-car family now. Pauline had her own Chevrolet in vista gray metallic—quite the neighborhood sensation.

"I'll squeeze it in," Dennis said. "If you want to meet this guy, Mil, so do I."

I felt proud of my assertiveness. I reached to hug him, but he put on his yellow hard hat and was off. He'd left me feeling chilled.

I had my daughter to focus on, though. It was the holidays, and for the first time she had picked up on some of the season's magic. I looked forward to the years to come. Lots of children. Milk and cookies for Santa. Carrots and celery for Rudolph. And dollies and tricycles and stuffed bears beneath the tree. I rubbed my belly, and my baby kicked. Janie's baby sister? Brother?

Janie toddled from the ottoman to the red wool womb chair, jab-bering, "Mommy, Mommy." Her little white lace-up leather baby shoes crossed the carpeting as quick as they could go. I already planned to have those ankle-high shoes bronzed and mounted and put on display when she grew out of them.

I sat her in her high chair with a lidded cup filled with juice. Janie had four sprouts of teeth, two up and two down. I took out a piece of dense melba toast she could chew until it softened enough to swallow, which seemed to feel good on her sore gums. I put a record album of holiday carols on Dennis's new hi-fi set and sang along to "Frosty the Snowman" with Jimmy Durante.

I wrapped gifts and washed Janie's sticky hands with a damp cloth, attending to each tiny finger in its turn. I took my precious girl in my arms and went to change her green-knitted top and diaper. Then I car-ried her to the big, red womb chair.

"Janie want a Christmas story?" I sat her on my lap, though I had a lot less lap than before.

"The year was 1932," I began. I had a mind that my personal Christmas story would be one that I'd tell her year after year.

~

Cincinnati was still in the drought of Prohibition and early in the Depression both at once. I was eight years old and sat on the floor beside the burlap-covered chair Mama used for sewing, though she had run to the market. Opa snored on the couch. I was thumbing through a week-old newspaper, looking at pictures of movie stars.

My family had no tree, no blinking lights. We had Opa's holey old socks for our stockings, but they would remain empty. It was several days before Christmas when a knock came at the door. A timid knock, not the Big Bad Wolf knock of the landlord. Opa continued his nap.

I opened the door a crack. There was a lady—a real lady like the newspaper's movie stars, who wore mink stoles with tiny feet and claws and heads on them. She even had one on. Some kind of fur anyway, even if it didn't have feet. She held a package big enough to take up both her arms. It was covered in cloth the color of Santa's suit.

"Are you someone to get sewing done by Mama?"

"I'm Lillian Partridge," she said, "from the Ladies' Aid Society."

The name Lillian Partridge sounded musical, like the "partridge in a pear tree" song I'd learned in first grade.

"Merry Christmas," Miss Partridge said with a kind, beautiful smile, and she held out the basket, removed the cover, and revealed a bounty of juicy, ripe oranges. "For you and your family, little one."

"Thank you." Oranges came all the way on trucks from down south, Opa once said. No one we knew could afford them at the store.

Lillian Partridge wished me a merry Christmas and waved goodbye, and I thought I heard jingle bells as she disappeared down the dark, rickety stairwell. "Merry Christmas," I called out.

After Opa awoke, I got to pick the first orange. I inhaled its sweet citrus scent that came from growing in so much sunshine. Opa used his pocketknife to bore a hole in the stem-end, a hole the size of a blueberry. Then I pushed the orange's opening to my mouth and squeezed with all my might. With every compression of my palms on the dimply peeling of the fruit, I sucked out the juice. I tore the orange open and gnawed every bit of pulp from its peel. I was still chewing, juice dribbling down my chin, when Mama came home. She had a day-old loaf of pumpernickel, a surprise, and a grin on her wind-reddened face.

Then her grin vanished. "What's this?" she asked.

After she heard my story, she shouted, "Who said you could take fruit from a stranger?"

"Opa was here. I didn't eat it until I had permission."

Mama stomped to the window and stared out. A minute later she took hold of the sill and forced it open. A freezing gust blew in. Then

114

she grabbed the basket and threw the oranges out. One. Two. Three. "We don't take no charity from fancy-dressed, filthy-rich, movie-star women in their high heels on their high horses. Not in my home."

But Opa had said I could have an orange, so I didn't understand Mama's anger. We needed food every day; she was always griping about that. So why would we not accept the fruit? It was a gift.

Two days later it was Mama's laundry day. Mama and five wives who lived in our tenement building took turns doing their family's washing in the attic. I hated that attic. It had a splintery wood floor and stark gray walls with dark shadows. It was freezing cold. The walls and ceiling showed cracks you could see light through. The walls held pegs up high, too, and eight ropes hung from one wall to another. Mama and I hung our wet clothes there after carrying the water up from the spigot in the hall outside our flat. Laundry day was the one time Mama was glad we lived on the third floor, not on the first floor. I sat on a short-legged stool, scrubbing Opa's overalls on a rubbing board in the zinc metal tub. The soap flakes helped hide the attic's stink of something rotten. I did one rinse in a second tub, and Mama did the second rinse in a third. She said we must always have clean clothes. We must take care for nothing to be spilled down the front. We might be poor, but we weren't ragamuffins. And never was I to have a dirty face. If Mrs. Shultz had apricot jam to spare, I mustn't let my cheeks get smeared when I ate it on a crust of bread.

Mama was pulling shirts through the wringer one at a time, her hair high off her face for fear it'd get caught in the rolling tubes, when she said without looking at me, "I shouldn't have thrown those oranges away. I'm sorry."

I stopped scrubbing. I didn't think Mama had ever apologized before. At least not to me.

"When I heard that charity lady had come, my pride got the better of me. Sometimes a woman cuts off her nose to spite her face." She started rolling another shirt through the wringer.

I was confused. Had Mama's nose been cut? I didn't see a scab. Or was it somehow that the charity lady made Mama feel less useful? After all, Mama had brought the pumpernickel home. While I loved pumpernickel, it didn't compare to a sunny, plump orange.

Then before I could ask for clarification she said, "We have to move again. Somewhere cheaper."

"I don't want to move away," I said, pouting and letting soapy water splash outside the tub. Even at my tender age I remembered the two flats before and friends I'd had to leave. If I had a sister, it might not have been so bad. A mouse with a long, skinny tail skittered across the floor behind Mama's feet, and I squealed.

"Shush," she said, her wide blue eyes boring into mine. "Listen. When you grow up, you must have a trade—be better at sewing than me, or teach. You're a clever girl, you'd like that, wouldn't you? Wouldn't it be grand to do something you liked?"

I didn't know. I'd never thought about it before. Mama let her chapped hands dangle, dripping, and she huffed. "You can't depend on a man all your life, you know."

She'd confused me again. "But we have Opa to get coal for the stove. We have him to haul garbage to the alley in the snow."

She worked her yellowed white blouse through the wringer without speaking. I could not tell from her face if she was angry or sad. Why hadn't she responded?

"I used to wear fine dresses when I was your age," she said. She had? "My favorite one," Mama continued, "was dainty, made of dotted Swiss muslin in a color of pale cream. Had the prettiest green sash along here." Mama swiped her wet hand in front of her chest from one shoulder to the other. "And when your papa and I were young marrieds, he bought me pretty dresses, too. He and Opa earned a good wage brewing lager in those days. Papa oversaw the crew that stored the kegs in the vaults beneath the streets, where the beer stayed cool." Mama sighed heavily as if this story pained her to tell.

"That was before Prohibition," she said. "Then Opa and your papa lost their jobs. Opa's own grandfather had learned to brew before moving to this country. So the men in our family had lost their heritage, too, not just their work. We all did.

"The beer gardens with their oompah bands where our family gathered for fun were never the same. We lost our home, too. I had to start sewing for other people. For your father, making root beer in the old factories, or potato chips, didn't pay the wage we needed—that's if he could get the work at all, which often he and Opa could not." Her bottom lip poked out. "Gone were the days of my having nice dresses."

"But the brown dress you sewed last summer is pretty," I said. I truly thought it was. She smiled but shook her head no.

"Things got worse when your papa died of fever," she said, and I thought of the photograph of her with him—the only one we had, dating to 1918. They were seventeen years old and married. He'd been too young to fight in the Great War, but their picture was taken before Prohibition. They posed—their smiles evident in their eyes more than by their lips—in front of a drapery and a wall painted with a stained-glass window at Rensler's photographic studio. Papa was taller than Mama by a whole head and so handsome.

I watched as two tears trailed down Mama's chapped cheek.

"Then it was only Opa and me," she said, "to scrape up a dollar. Opa had his limp, so he was slow. And I didn't have my brother, who'd been shot in France."

Mama's story made me feel sad.

"So you see," she said, "men get jobs. Men lose jobs. And sometimes men die."

She reached out and gripped my chin in her wet, calloused fingers and yanked it up to be sure I was paying attention. She said: "Don't trust the wedding vows that say, 'And with all my worldly goods, I thee endow.' You have to have a means of earning. Do you hear me? Lest you find yourself without a bed or a soupbone to your name."

She let go of my chin. I gulped. I'd remember. I'd remember many lessons from that day: I must earn my own keep. Sometimes mamas make mistakes. Pride can get in the way. We can grow up and do things we like to do.

And a single orange can be the best present a girl ever got.

⌐

The next morning Pauline kept Janie, and Dennis and I sat in the waiting room at the medical office one block away from the hospital. He'd come with me, as he said he would the day before. The walls were painted pea green, like peas from a can. The floor was commercial linoleum square tiles with enough multicolored specks and spots that scraps left by the youngsters with their pregnant mommies would barely show at all. I liked practicality. This doctor and I would get along well. Dennis tapped his foot and kept looking to the window. It was placed too high to see out, but it let in light while he must have obsessed about concrete sidewalks that needed to be poured or roof installations.

According to the article Pauline had, Dr. Collins had gotten his medical degree from Johns Hopkins, a university in Baltimore. He had contributed to a journal while in medical school. The Cincinnati hospital at which he now worked had all the latest equipment.

"I have to admit," Dennis murmured, "one day when we move not far from here, it will be convenient when we have Glenns number three and four."

A lopsided smile appeared on his face. Maybe he'd warmed up after all.

Following my examination, this new Dr. Collins allowed, "Unlike what some old-school doctors think, I've found a few women can deliver vaginally after undergoing cesarean. It depends on the situation." I looked at Dennis with a glimmer of hope. "I've reviewed the charts from your last surgery," Dr. Collins said, "as well as from my own

X-ray exam, and I see you have an unusually small pelvis. I must advise against a vaginal birth in your case."

I was crestfallen. Dr. Collins, with all his silver-spoon-fed education and framed certificates on the wall, had advised us the same as Dr. Welch had out near the cornfields. *Once a cesarean, always a cesarean.*

Mama's face flashed in my mind. I'd inherited a problem with birthing children.

At least this doctor had directed his concerns to both Dennis and me, and not acted as though I were a child from the last century—better seen and not heard. Regardless of the bad news, that alone was enough to win my patronage. Dr. Collins handed over the forms for us to review, and he'd actually passed them to me. I appreciated that.

But then Dr. Collins said something else the same as Dr. Welch had: "It's not recommended for mothers to have more than two cesarean babies. After the birth, I recommend you have a tubal ligation."

Dennis stared at me as if wondering whose turn it was to speak. I was incapable of speech.

"Dr. Collins, can you explain more of what that procedure is?" Dennis said.

"Of course. The main concern is that after a surgery, the scar tissue in the uterus creates a weakness in subsequent pregnancies. After two births there's a very real risk of the uterus rupturing during labor, which is deadly. So getting one's tubes tied, as it's sometimes called, prevents more pregnancies."

Dennis started fidgeting.

"Dr. Collins," I said, "have you ever known of any cases anywhere— one of your patients or not—where the mother survived a third cesarean and bore a healthy child?"

"The risks of something going wrong with a third are great in my estimation."

"Humor me, please. Have you knowledge of such cases?" I said, and I felt heat emanating from my husband.

"It's been known to happen." Dr. Collins shuffled my papers back into his folder. "But you've had one surgery already. Even now, no matter what, you must deliver early in labor, or your uterus can rupture."

⌒

"Millie. Babe, listen," Dennis said once we were home. "I went there with my mind about as open as a guy's could be—"

"I won't do it, Dennis. I won't consent to the other procedure."

"You wanted to see this crackerjack expert. He agrees with Dr. Welch," Dennis said. "It's too risky to have more children after two cesareans."

"I can't submit to having my tubes tied. Please understand—"

"I do understand. Your life is at stake. What would I do if something went wrong? I love you too much."

I'd wanted many children since before we married. I'd envisioned all my little ones gathered around Mother Glenn's country table, helping her pinch the doughy rims of pie crusts. I wanted a large family like I'd never had while growing up, one that turned heads in the park on spring days and made people smile and wave. I had imagined a whole clan on Easter Sundays, hunting for eggs, each little tyke dressed in frilly go-to-church dresses and suits in pastel colors. Society expected families to be big. I wanted to fit in. Be the perfect mother.

This dream I would capture on my own. Neither Dennis nor the doctor would stop me.

"Do you think this all doesn't hurt me?" Dennis said. "I want to throw big birthday parties. Pin the tail on the donkey and all that jazz." His eyes drilled into mine. "But we have one precious angel and another on the way. Two babies are plenty. A blessing."

I folded back into his embrace. Yet my mind would not be content.

Having my tubes tied was nothing but sterilization. Hadn't the evil Germans, those of whom my family had been so ashamed, forced sterilization on Jewish women not so long ago? The practice was repulsive to me. Like slavery or incest. I'd read that over in Indiana even now, for Pete's sake, eugenics laws allowed for "imbeciles" to be neutered like cats. And, pray tell, what criteria determined an imbecile? Was I an imbecile? Was I flawed?

"Look," Dennis said. "I'll strap on the raincoats in bed—we aren't going to go cold turkey. But what if you conceive anyway? Can we take that chance?"

I didn't know how to respond.

That night, lying awake in bed beside the soft rhythm of my husband's dream-filled sleep, I pictured Opa telling me how Oma passed away before I was born. It was in the epidemic of 1918. The Spanish flu's dark spots had clouded her cheeks before her skin turned blue. "I lost the love of my life," he'd said.

If Dennis and I didn't consent to the tubal ligation and something happened to me, he would never forgive himself.

But Dr. Collins knew of mothers who'd had multiple surgeries without problem. I didn't have to make this decision now. I could always go back and get the procedure done later if I changed my mind. I couldn't think about becoming barren right now. I just couldn't. I didn't want to be forced to choose so quickly—to sign papers this minute.

And it was my body, wasn't it?

"We're not signing the papers," I said the next day. "It's my body. It's my domain."

2015

It was my ninety-first birthday, and Jane and I were at the imaging center for her diagnostic mammogram.

We found two chairs together in the waiting room. She'd already signed in, shown her new driver's license, and provided insurance information.

The whole waiting room paid homage to pink. Nubby brown carpet and crisscrossed pink stripes. Wallpaper with muted-pink shades. All but a few chairs covered in muted pink vinyl had a woman wedged into them. Patients thumbed through magazines, turning pages too quickly to be reading. Near the ceiling in one corner was a small TV. Two guys were rehabbing a bungalow for some newlyweds. Dennis would've loved today's craze for home-and-garden television on cable networks. I smiled. He might have hosted his own show: *Prefab or Rehab with Dennis Glenn*. I bowed my head. How dare my brain think up such folly at a time like this?

My worries returned. Jane. My secret that I would soon tell her in hopes of drawing us closer. For now I felt cold as stone.

"I still don't get why you insisted on coming," Jane said. She let out a ragged breath. "You could find better things to do on your birthday.

You could be home watching the Pioneer Woman cook breakfast burritos."

"I'm here because your daughter wanted to be here but couldn't," I said, undeterred. Jane's eyes widened despite herself. "And because you, yes you," I went on, "can't anticipate everything you may need. You might need a cheerleader while you're here."

"Rah rah," she said without any cheer. "I've got to fill out the history of my life," she said, holding up a stack of forms. "And everybody else's medical history in the family, too."

Adrenaline hit me down low. *My* medical history, too? Why?

"What do they need to know?" I asked.

"Hold on," she said, scribbling on one of the sheets. She shuffled to the next page. "I'm putting checkmarks by everyone who had cancer in our family. I have no clue about my grandparents' high blood pressure or heart disease. Help?"

I helped her complete the forms, thankful that my "sensitive history" had not been probed.

"Ms. Glenn."

Of habit I turned to the voice at the door and saw a nurse holding a chart. But it wasn't me she called; it was Jane. Jane sucked in a big breath and let it out through her nose as she stood. She followed the nurse wearing baggy blue scrubs, and I followed Jane.

"Next door on the right, ladies."

We entered another space in the rear, where in an adjacent, enclosed cubicle Jane was to cleanse any deodorant from her armpits and put on a hospital gown, open in the front. Then we waited to be called to the exam room. My skin felt as numb as if a dentist had shot me all over with Novocain. A bodily defense? My body preparing for the assault, that is, perhaps bad news that might soon come? I wondered if Jane's felt numb, too.

We waited. The digital clock on the opposite wall flipped its minutes instead of ticking.

I remembered rocking and humming and nursing my Janie when she was an infant. Her waking from a nap all warm and cuddly. My changing her diaper and nursing her again. How odd to think I'd nourished this woman with the bounty of my body, and today her own breasts were at risk. If only what she was facing in the present had happened to me instead.

"Hi, Ms. Glenn." This time I looked to Jane before I looked at the nurse in the doorway, and we got up and followed her.

The exam room was dim, with indirect lighting glowing from under the top cabinets. I took the one chair with metal legs, while the technician named Tammy taped sticky markers to the tips of Jane's nipples. I don't know how many X-rays Tammy took while Jane stood tied to the machine—her breasts sandwiched between flat plates that compressed tighter and tighter, like materials squeezed in the iron vise on Dennis's workbench.

"Time to hurry up and wait some more," Jane said as we were led back across the hall. She was trying to be strong by using her humor. She still had that.

My old heart caved at the thought of watching her ill, draped on a bed, seeing her color fade, the light of her eyes extinguish, her becoming disoriented from bodily toxins and having to be fed and changed like a baby again—like I had done for Dennis. I knew the utter lack of dignity he'd felt in his lucid moments. Jane didn't want to undergo that. This much I knew. Yet what could I do to stop the train if that was the route it would take?

I was helpless.

"The radiologist will see you shortly," said the nurse. "You'll have your results soon."

Jane's eyes darkened in a human fight-or-flight mode. "I'll learn today?" she said. "I don't have to wait a week for a letter as with my past mammograms?"

I'd known this was a possibility. But was it a good sign or bad? I was as impatient as she.

I'd been holding Dennis's hand when an oncologist relayed that he had a tumor in his lung: the death sentence that led to the rest. I'd never get over the fright in my strong husband's eyes. I couldn't bear to see that again. Not in my daughter's eyes.

Jane was sniffing and smacking her lips. Nervous.

"You okay?" I asked, praying for God to help me accept Jane's answer, whatever it was.

"Better with you here."

An audible release of air escaped my lungs. Goose pimples raised the hair on my arms, and my eyes stung. She'd been glad I came after all. I was useful. I had a new purpose, to be there for Jane.

I took her hand and was astonished at how tight her grasp was. So tight it hurt.

"Ms. Glenn, please follow me."

We landed in an exam room even smaller than the last, though now Jane and I each had a chair. The space was dimmer than the last, too. It smelled of antibacterial cleanser or something clinical. It was quiet. We waited.

"I'm thinking about getting a puppy," Jane said. "Do you think that's senseless?"

Jane, and her daughter after her, had long been ones to throw questions at me out of nowhere. "Mommy," Janie had said in third grade as we drove down a road, "when you look out the window, how do you know the trees are real?" And then there'd been Kelsey when she was in grad school: "Grandma, do you think Aaron and I should live together before we marry?" My girls' questions required thoughtful answers that I wasn't always ready to give.

Jane's question today was no exception. But I figured she had duly considered it before asking. Pragmatic, like her daughter. If Jane were to require chemo treatment or radiation, would she be physically able to care for a pup? And if she weren't to survive, would it be fair to a pet to leave it an orphan? Jane was missing her friends in Georgia, her career, and now she had uncertainty looming about her health. She had Kelsey and me. But she was still lonely.

I said, "Do it. If that's what your heart is set on. We can go to the pet shop today—or to the Humane Society. Kelsey and I will support you and the puppy in any way we can."

Her shoulders relaxed. "Thank you. I think I'll wait till this is all over. But I just wanted to know in case I get spontaneous." She smiled.

How I loved it when she smiled. I remembered her first smile, an adorable toothless grin when she was a few weeks old. Mother Glenn had said it was gas. But that smile was cute to me all the same. I'd missed her smiling at me during all her years away.

"What breed of dog would you—"

There was a knock, and the door opened. "Hello, Ms. Glenn. I'm Dr. Patel, your radiologist." She spoke so quickly I was glad we had two sets of ears to take everything in. "We don't have a clear answer for you based on the X-rays. As long as you're here, we want to do everything we can."

I looked at my daughter out of the corner of my eye, and she was composed. Only one finger, slowly stroking the small scar at her brow, gave a hint as to what was going on inside. And a flash of a long-ago day rose up in my mind: my holding her while her face bled, my trying to stop her suffering.

"I'm having another technician come in and perform an ultrasound," the radiologist said. "It's painless and won't take terribly long. It'll give us a fuller picture of the lump you felt. Sound good?"

"Makes sense to me," Jane said, and I was glad of it.

I adjusted in my chair. Stiff as I was, I wasn't going anywhere. I'd be here with her to the bitter—or sweet—end.

CHAPTER TEN

March 1951

For my shower, Pauline served petite sandwiches garnished with sliced sweet pickles, and she'd mashed sherbet into a bowl of punch. It was a lovely spread on her new chrome dinette table amid yellow and white decorations in a baby carriage theme. I was due in a couple of weeks. We women sat in Pauline's sleek living room, its white and cool-green decor bringing to mind a luscious mint frappé. One of Dennis's sisters jotted down all the gifts for my soon-to-be second child. I received hand-knitted sacques that opened down the front to free a baby's bare legs. Pads and sheets and a bathinette—unlike Janie's tiny tub, this one was the folding type with pockets and a canvas top. From Pauline I got two dozen cloth diapers, complete with a coupon for a laundering service while I recovered.

"Are you going to chug castor oil?" one of the neighbors asked as the gifts I'd opened passed around our circle. "That'll get the labor in gear." Everyone enthusiastically agreed.

I said, "I took my teaspoonful of cod-liver oil all winter long, never missing a day, you'll be pleased to hear. But, ladies, I think I'll pass on the castor oil." They all chuckled.

"Come on," Abbie Glenn said, rolling her eyes with exaggerated amusement. She was in the folding chair beside me. "Be a big girl." Everyone laughed. Except Pauline and me. This was my baby shower. I didn't care to be teased.

I'd once asked Dennis why Abbie didn't like me. Was it because I was German? It could be. Her mother's house had a gold star hanging in the window, meaning that a son—Abbie's older brother—had died in the war. Or was it because I'd grown up poor? I had even speculated that Abbie didn't care for me because when she'd been a girl, she'd had a crush on Dennis. He'd laughed and said, "Don't worry about Abbie. She rubs people the wrong way sometimes."

Mother Glenn concurred when I asked her. She went so far as to suggest Abbie felt threatened; she craved having center stage. So Abbie wanted to be the favorite Glenn daughter-in-law—and Housewife of the Year to boot. "But Abbie doesn't realize we don't play favorites in our family," Mother Glenn had said. "And we love you, Millie dear, like you're one of our own."

Abbie was my sister-in-law. I'd try to be less judgmental. But it was hard.

Abbie had gotten pregnant with her third baby a couple of months before me and had already given birth. Now she entertained everyone with how she'd spurred on her labor. She'd coated a glass with a quarter cup of orange juice, poured in the castor oil, and then added more juice. "I held a cube of ice as round as a walnut in my mouth, trying to freeze my taste buds," she said, "then I washed the icky potion down, keeping it as far to the back of my tongue as possible. I went into labor that night, ladies. Linda Jo was born eight hours later."

"But remember, Abbie, our mother-to-be gets to set a date for her delivery," Pauline said. "Gets to skip most of her labor this time."

"Getting to set a date for surgery may be better than having to go through all the old wives' remedies," said Deloris, my neighbor—the one who'd once hosted a party for her husband's birthday and been baffled to learn I'd rather work on ledgers than have a hobby. Sadly, though, Dennis still had my role reduced to one mailing a week and the occasional ad since becoming pregnant the second time. I wouldn't "overtax" myself or create a complication. I remained pleasant, though, because Janie was at a delightful age, and I was holding out hope that once Dennis saw how capable I was of running our beautiful family of four, I'd get back involved in the business. It wasn't a matter of if but when.

"And a date for surgery is better than going through hours of contractions and pushing," said another friend. Most everyone agreed.

That was fine but for the fact that I might lose my water before that scheduled date arrived. And there was no accounting for my recovering from all the stitches later.

"Ladies, shall we have refreshments?" Pauline said, ushering us to her table, where we would fill dainty china plates and carry them back to eat in our laps.

"My goodness, this cake is to die for," said a neighbor. Abbie had insisted she bring a coconut cake.

"Why thank you," Abbie said. "It's one of my husband's favorites. He likes extra coconut on top."

"You've outdone yourself, Abbie. So moist." That was Deloris. "And the buttercream. Scrumptious."

The room filled with the sound of women conversing about the *Ozzie and Harriet* radio program. But rather than join in, Abbie scrutinized my plate.

"No cake for the guest of honor?"

"I, uh—"

"I'm so sorry," she said, pressing her fingertips to her mouth. "I completely forgot. You don't like coconut."

"Don't worry about it," I said. Mother Glenn looked on sympathetically at me. "Pauline baked my favorite cookies." I smiled and bit into my second snickerdoodle sprinkled with cinnamon.

But Abbie being Abbie, she couldn't let it go. "Again, my apologies. I should have left a corner of the cake's frosting plain. Just for you."

That woman grated on my nerves. Then Mother Glenn winked at me, and that made me smile.

I heard my name and shifted left. Deloris was trying to get my attention.

"Millie, did you know Sally here just found out she's expecting?" Our new neighbor, Sally, was sitting right there, bright as the torch lamp lit up behind her.

"How wonderful," I said. "Congratulations."

Deloris went on, "What OB do you use, Millie?"

I could sense Abbie's ears had gone on alert. "I'm a patient of Dr. Collins," I said. "Pauline recommended him." I hoped the inquiry would end there.

"As men with stethoscopes go, he's a jewel," Pauline said.

"Millie didn't use him the first time, though," said Abbie. "Dr. Welch, the OB who delivered all the other Glenn grandchildren, delivered her Janie." Abbie looked to the Glenn sisters for affirmation. They nodded politely but not overly politely.

"Why did you switch OBs?" Deloris asked.

Because I didn't want to use a doctor Abbie used, I thought. "Because he's closer in, more convenient," I said.

"Oh good," Deloris said, and lit a cigarette.

"Millie didn't think our doctor was good enough for her anymore," Abbie said, laughing.

It wasn't funny. Mother Glenn frowned at her. Perhaps that'd shut her up.

"Well, honestly," I said, wishing I were in the half of the room that followed a different conversation, "I owed it to myself to check around, given my circumstances. The surgery and all." I glanced to my right, and Abbie was looking at me as though she were mystified—and that made me mad. "And for another reason," I continued, "I like a doctor who speaks directly to me better than one who talks about me in the third person when I'm sitting right there."

Dennis's sisters' eyes were wide, and I felt myself burning red.

I laughed and said, "Just teasing."

Then they broke into a hearty laughter.

Deloris said, "I guess that's particularly important to you, Millie, given you work with ad men and Lord knows who else."

"My sister-in-law thrives on juggling a job and caring for the baby and the house," Abbie said. "I'm afraid she spreads herself too thin."

Please, Abbie, just shut up.

Mother Glenn didn't think I spread myself too thin. And that was good enough for me. "A wife's gotta do what a wife's gotta do," she was often known to say.

Fortunately, Deloris rose to refill her punch. Some women were gabbing about Camay beauty bars. Others needed to get home and get supper started. I thanked each guest as they shuffled out the door, and they hugged me and said they couldn't wait to see the new baby. Abbie still lingered.

My back was sore, my ankles were swollen, and I was ready to lie down and rest. Good thing I lived right next door. Pauline and Abbie insisted I not stay and clean up. The husbands could cart all the gifts home later. I waddled to Pauline's room, and I'd no sooner fetched my trench coat off the bed than Abbie breezed in. She was always pretty at first glance, but sitting beside her today I had realized that in profile, her face was quite ordinary. No bone structure, nor depth or dimension.

"I hope you aren't mad," she said, wringing her meticulously manicured hands. "About the coconut."

"Nope," I said as I slipped one arm through a sleeve.

"Swell," she said, picking up her coat. "So it won't be long now. I'll be an aunt again."

Even the birth of my child was more about her than it was about me.

"Millie," Abbie said. "I'd like to talk to you, friend-to-friend."

"About what?" I asked, pulling on my coat the rest of the way.

"Why do you spend so much time making up newspaper ads or bookkeeping or whatever you do anyway? Isn't being a mother and keeping a nice home more important?"

I stood there, dumbfounded. "Listen," I said. "My floors may not be as squeaky-clean as yours. Though I doubt it. My clothes hampers may pile up a little higher than yours. Though I doubt it. And you can bet I'm a good wife. Don't you doubt it. And I'm a damn good mother, too."

"Well, well, yes, Janie's a wonderful child," she said. "But—"

"But? I'm standing here eight and a half months pregnant, and believe it or not, I'm tired. I want to go home, Abbie. Alone."

"Of course," she said, picking up her purse, her cheeks pink. She looked remorseful. "Good wives never let a house fall apart. I'm sure you never do that. And I'm sure your new doctor will be fine, too," she said, buttoning up her coat.

"Millicent?" Pauline called from the hall.

"Coming."

I soon walked through the grass between our houses, carrying a half dozen snickerdoodles wrapped in tin foil. Abbie had needled me until I felt like a pincushion. But why? She had a wonderful family. She was Betty Crocker extraordinaire. Some of the things I chose to do weren't as fancy. I enjoyed working with numbers. Could she not accept that?

If only my opa were here. He'd know how I should handle her.

He had taught me that there were three kinds of people in the world: Some were just plain evil—like Adolf Hitler. And then there were good people who occasionally did bad things; they made a wrong decision. And then there was the bad person who had a nice streak every now and again. Opa never told me what category the men who'd beaten him up fell into—the rowdy ones who'd busted out his eyetooth in an alley and had twisted his leg until it snapped. That had been about anti-German hysteria in this country during the Great War. Opa had shared his story when I was eight, when he'd taken me to Union Terminal for the whispering fountains. That day, a fancy lady had pointed and called me a German urchin. I hadn't known what that was, but it had almost made me cry.

I wanted to think Abbie was the good person who sometimes made mistakes. Like me. But she was constantly hurting my feelings or embarrassing me or trying to make me feel inferior or casting doubt on my decisions. It was insulting. I shouldn't have had to put up with it. She and I would have many years ahead of being the rival Glenn sisters-in-law. Couldn't we just get along?

I took from my shelf a small cherrywood box that Dennis had made. It preserved a memento from my grandfather: it was Opa's last surviving boyhood marble and my only keepsake of his. I could manage Abbie. I could. On that day in Union Terminal with the drinking fountains when I was a child, Opa had ended his lesson by saying, "Your name means strength in German. You're Millicent the Strong. Don't you ever forget it."

~

The day after the baby shower I spent admiring the dressing table that fit snugly between the chest of drawers and the closet in the bedroom Dennis and I shared. I placed a dainty hobnail milk glass lamp on it, so its dim little glow for midnight feedings wouldn't disturb Dennis. I had put sturdy baskets beneath the dressing table, and Dennis had installed three shelves above it. I'd laundered everything. I folded the miniature terrycloth washcloths, the pink-and-blue striped receiving blankets, the tiny flannelette kimonos. I'd lined up covered jars for diaper safety pins and absorbent cotton, and I picked a place just for booties. Mother Glenn had gone overboard crocheting them in yellow, pink, blue, and white yarns, some with tiny pom-pom ties.

We were getting closer to being ready, and this bonded Dennis and me together despite my frustrations. There was time enough to fix those. We were married. And our marriage was more than a series of business decisions. Dennis and I had our baby's names picked out. If Janie got a brother, his name would be Dennis Junior—Denny—and if she got a sister, her name would be Kathleen, and we'd call her Kathy. I imagined it would come out Kitty when little Janie tried to say her sister's name. Dennis and I were head over heels excited for our expanding family.

I peeked in on Janie in her crib. After cooing and playing with her toes for some time—a by-product of "This little piggy went to market; this little piggy stayed home"—she had at last turned on her side and dozed off.

Tea was steeping in my kettle, and I poured myself a cup to soothe my nerves from the day before. I turned the radio on with the volume down low to listen to *The Guiding Light*. I tuned in just in time for the opening message from the sponsor: "Duz, for bright-white washes, without red hands." During every episode, I mused about how every time a housewife bought that detergent, it put cash in Bob and Pauline Irving's pockets. What was good for Procter & Gamble was good for our city—and good for my best friends.

With some effort, I lowered my walrus-like body into our red wool womb chair and heaved my swollen feet onto its matching red ottoman. Fifteen days left to go.

On the side table I'd laid the baby album I'd received at my shower. Its dimensions were smaller than a sheet of typing paper, and it was an inch thick. I removed it from its box, and it smelled of bindery glue. The cover was padded in pink satin with embossing in baby-boy blue. *The Story of Our Baby.*

I enjoyed wandering its pages, eager for the day to come when I'd fill them in with ink beginning on page one: "Baby's Arrival." There were decorative spaces for the name, the date of birth, the baby's weight, the length, and more. There were cartoons of sweet cherubs with long, colored ribbons, pictures of lambs and puppy dogs, too.

Yes, I was ready to have this child. I was constipated. My back had had enough. My wedding band was so snug I'd have to use Ivory soap to get it off so my finger would quit hurting. My suitcase was packed for the hospital.

Dennis was ready as well. He kept the Chevy's gas tank full. He stayed within earshot of a telephone as much as he could. And he'd bought a box of cigars to pass out to the guys.

Baby Glenn kicked. I lifted my top and watched him or her lean far to my right. Then Baby Glenn leaned back, getting comfortable. How I loved these moments. I caressed the stretched skin of my tummy so the baby would feel my energy. I hummed a lullaby, as I did every day, so he or she would know my voice. I cradled my baby inside my womb, so it would know I already loved it.

My date for admission was two weeks and one day away, unless this baby wanted to be introduced to the world ahead of schedule.

CHAPTER ELEVEN

March 1951

Baby Glenn was determined to be the early bird. It was past noon on March 23, and contractions were twenty-five minutes apart. I wasn't scheduled for surgery for another three days. I had yet to track down Dennis. Pauline was getting her hair cut. Mother Glenn had hopped in the truck as soon as I phoned and was on her way to take care of Janie. Per Dr. Collins's instructions in this case, I was to call his office at my first sign of labor.

"Dr. Collins is at the hospital," the nurse on the telephone said. "Several other patients are in labor there already, and we're short-staffed."

"What should I do?" I said.

"I'll alert the hospital so a bed can be reserved for your surgery. Prepare to go immediately, but await my return call."

But Dr. Collins had drummed into me that if I didn't have the operation early in my labor, my uterus could rupture. Was it my imagination, or had my last contraction felt stronger?

"I'm worried," I told her.

"As I said, I'll reach the doctor," the nurse said, "and phone you back within fifteen minutes to confirm all is ready."

I tried Dennis's office again. My finger trembled as I cranked the rotary dial. Six, four, one, six.

Ring, ring, ring. *Answer, please answer*. But nothing.

"Tot, Ma, tot," Janie said, and latched on to my leg. She wanted me to play "Trot, trot to Boston," something Dennis usually did, bouncing her up and down on his crossed leg, while he sang a silly ditty. I hadn't had the strength to play that game in a month.

I pried her arms off my calf and padded across the kitchen. "Here, baby. Want a treat?"

She worked her fingers as if making number fives over and over. "Pig noo, pig noo." She confused the word *fig* with the pigs at the farm. I gave her a Fig Newton torn in two, one half for each hand. Let the crumbs fall where they may.

Janie was an advanced talker. I'd sit her on my lap and say, "Baby, baby," and point to my belly, letting her know she'd soon be a big sister. She was too young to get all that, but she wandered the house saying, "Bah, bah, bah," like a sweet little lamb.

The phone rang. I reached over the counter and grabbed it on the second ring. "Hello?"

"Hi, Millie." It was Abbie. Oh my gosh, no. "Just checking on you. Heard Mother Glenn is on her way."

"Abbie, I'm going to hang up now so Dennis can call me." Click.

The phone instantly rang again. I prayed it wasn't her calling back.

"I'm home." It was Pauline. "Right next door if you need me."

I inhaled deeply and let it all out. Relief. And then a contraction kicked in. Mild. "Guess what," I said.

"What? No, no, Tommy, honey. Don't play in the plant dirt."

"This baby is coming."

"Oh my gosh. Millicent, you need to get to the hospital."

What I needed to do was get off the telephone, in case the nurse or Dennis was trying to call me back. So I did.

I checked the teapot-shaped clock above the refrigerator. Pauline could watch Janie or rush me to the hospital if need be. But I expected Mother Glenn in twenty minutes. I thought about arriving at the hospital, climbing into a wheelchair, being rolled by a nurse onto an elevator, and riding up to the floor with the big black letters: **MATERNITY WARD**. But I'd be in surgery instead of a single room with twenty women laboring at once. There would be the metal table on rollers, lined with a crisp, white sheet and sterile implements arranged neatly in a row: clamps and forceps, scissors and scalpels.

But it would all be worth it. I would come home with another beautiful baby. For that I'd go through it all again. And again. And again.

"You're a star patient," Dr. Collins had said just this week at my checkup. *A star patient.*

The telephone rang again. I didn't know who I wanted it to be more—the nurse or my husband.

Dennis. I was so relieved. He'd just returned from meeting with a customer.

"I'm out the door," he said in a rush. "Hang tight. Love you."

And I loved him. We were on the cusp of being parents for the second time. I slipped the receiver back into its cradle and prayed for it to ring again. I was afraid to go to the bathroom for fear I'd miss the nurse's directive.

Strangely, I remembered in that moment the carefree days of dating Dennis. When I lived with Mama and Opa, Dennis had had to call the Fischers upstairs—the only family in our building with a telephone—and little Adeline Fischer would come running down two tiers of stairs to get me, and I'd go running back up. Because of the party line, we never knew who else in the city was listening. Our calls were short and clipped.

How I needed a short, clipped call right now—public or private, I didn't care—just a call from the nurse.

By twenty minutes to four, Dennis was helping me from the car under the hospital overhang. Mother Glenn had Janie at home, so I need not worry about that. I tottered inside the building with Dennis at my arm. He would park later. An orderly greeted us and apologized—they'd been so busy, no wheelchairs were available. We'd have to wait.

Soon I reclined on a rolling bed with metal tubing at head and foot alongside a wall in the wide, brightly lit beige hall of the ward. My bed was one in a row of beds positioned end to end, each filled with a woman whose stomach rose up out of the sheets like a whale.

Over an intercom a woman with an official voice called for doctors: "Code Blue in room fifteen." Nurses in white dresses and hosiery, some with navy sweaters, whizzed by. I wondered how they kept their caps from slipping off, perched on the backs of their heads rather than on top.

I suddenly wanted to go back home. No, I wanted to be in the rose-floral bedroom at the farm. Safe in the Glenns' old sleigh bed with piles of handmade quilts.

"My sister told me," said a red-haired woman with a gravelly voice in the bed at the foot of mine, "that her hospital in Texas was equipped to deliver sixteen hundred babies last year, but their births topped six thousand."

"Those poor mothers," I said, with a mental image of women giving birth in the halls.

"You have to wonder," said the redhead, "how many of those Texan babies might have gone home with the wrong mothers."

We both laughed. But it wasn't funny.

There was a hubbub in a room near where I'd been parked. Snippets of women's voices floated from the delivery room to my ears:

"Lie still."

"That pinches."

139

"Calm down."

"Please, you're—"

"Control your hysterics now, Mrs. Lutz. Or do you want to give birth to a misfit?"

Silence.

That poor woman.

Click, click. Click, click.

A man's dress shoes were coming my way from behind. Not the quiet, rubber-bottomed, white-polished shoes of a nurse.

The doctor wore a spiffy white coat, his name embroidered beneath the left front lapel in official blue letters. He was clean-shaven and deep-voiced.

"Nurse, what is this patient doing planted here?" He was talking to her while pointing to me.

"I'll move her. Right away, Doctor."

"And slow this patient down. Speed that one up. We can deliver only so many at a time."

I didn't appreciate the way this doctor ordered people around. But I was equally concerned that my own doctor, Dr. Collins, was nowhere in sight.

2015

Jane and I still waited in the doctor's dimly lit office. She had welcomed the chance to get the ultrasound behind her on the same day. So had I.

"The weird thing about waiting," Jane said matter-of-factly, "is how every minute you think: this could be it. This could be the day, the hour, the very minute I learn I'm going to die."

Her words stabbed me. I felt the weight of every ticking minute, too, and I ached for her. I wanted to reach out and heal her with the palms of my hands and calm her innocent pinked face. This was the most revealing she'd been since we'd arrived. She trusted me to hear it, and the irony was that it made me feel closer than we'd been in years.

Yet what was I to say? Helpless with a capital *H*: that's what I was. When Dennis was ill, I felt as if I were losing half of my own being. With Jane it felt as if I were losing *all* of myself. But I could not tell her that.

"My dear Jane, darling girl," I said instead. "I love you so much."

"I know you do," she said quickly, warmly. And that meant more to me than had she said she loved me back. She turned to me then and added, "I know you do in your own way."

My heart dropped. *In my own way?* Did that mean my love for her was lacking in someone else's way? In hers?

I'd gone wrong somewhere with her. If I knew where, I'd have fixed us years ago.

Did our deeply rooted rift begin when she was a young girl? She'd lived through the worst part of my life without even knowing it. Yet my memories were filled with my being a good mother to her. Rare were the times I'd failed her, or so I thought, but given our unstable history it seemed that her bad memories held the most weight. Had the downfall between my daughter and me occurred when she was a teen? Or during her twenties, when she lived in the commune, before she brought Kelsey home? No, it was earlier than that. Had to be. In her midteen years our relationship became rocky, but Pauline had assured me it was common for mothers and daughters to squabble. But was it?

At age seventeen Jane ran away with a flock of flower children. She was in San Francisco in 1967 during the infamous Summer of Love. Dennis and I, beside ourselves with worry, had flown out to hunt her down. Save her. After two frantic weeks we'd spotted her while we rode the Gray Line bus—on the sightseeing company's special hippieland tour. She was braless in a white blouse with long, flared sleeves, beads strung from her neck to her navel, and wide, bell-bottomed jeans with the hems ripped out, frayed and dragging the ground with filthy, shoeless feet. A long-haired guy nearby wore a tie-dyed shirt and held a protest sign that read, MAKE LOVE, NOT WAR. With a crown of daisies in her own hair, our daughter had proclaimed on that day that she was no longer Janie like a baby. She was to be called Joan, "like Joan Baez or Joan of Arc." But I had laid down the law: "You're seventeen. You'll return with us, and you'll return to school until I say otherwise, which is at least until your next birthday." She'd looked to her father's nod of concurrence and fumed. But Dennis's soft touch had eventually convinced her to shorten her name to Jane, not change it altogether.

In the end something had changed. She had changed. And something had changed between us.

All I knew now was that we had to get Jane well. And she had to know my secret. I was more convinced than ever. She would never comprehend the fierceness of my love nor the depth of my devotion until she'd heard it.

Time. We needed time. Would the moon and the stars and the sky contrive to provide it?

I dipped into my handbag for a pack of mints and asked Jane to unwrap one for each of us. I'd woken up with my arthritic knuckles sore. With the nerves I had vibrating now, I couldn't have opened the pack on my best day.

The new medical technician entered, and I watched her prepare the equipment. "Now, honey," she said to my daughter, sounding as if she'd grown up in the South, where Jane had lived for a time. "This is going to feel a little bit cold at first." Her "cold" had two round syllables. She applied gel to my daughter's goose-pimpled skin so that the transducer could glide over easily. "Just relax. We're only gonna do your left side. You can watch everything right up there." She pointed to a computer screen on the wall.

The tech rolled her slick instrument from one place on Jane's breast to another slowly, letting it rest in a few spots for longer periods, and I pondered what each pause meant. Had she come upon something? A spot? A mass? She studiously monitored a smaller screen beside Jane's shoulder as she went back and forth as if stirring a pudding.

I honestly couldn't interpret a thing.

Soon Jane got wiped up, and again we waited. Jane had been right. Every minute of every hour we waited for the ax to fall. But surely there was equal chance that the lump could be benign. *Dear Lord God, help us focus on the positive.*

The loud tinkling of a text on Jane's phone startled us. It was Kelsey checking in. Jane texted back that she was still waiting.

There was a faint knock at the door. It was Dr. Patel. I could feel Jane and me both tensing up, our bodies shrinking as if we were lilies in snow. Was this to be *the* minute?

"That wasn't bad, was it?" the radiologist said. "I have a couple of conclusions for you. First, we've confirmed the lump you felt is an ordinary cyst. Lots of women have them. They're noncancerous. So is yours. This is a good thing."

"Hooray!" I blurted. I dug my fingers into Jane's thigh as she wiped her hand across her mouth roughly from cheek to cheek. Then she thrust her head between her knees. When she raised it, her face was flushed and puffy—but relief radiated from her glistening eyes in the dim light of the room. She took my hand and smiled at me.

My eyes shifted back to the doctor. Time stopped. I wanted Dr. Patel to smile more broadly.

"I recommend we aspirate the cyst," the radiologist went on. "It's a matter of inserting a needle to withdraw the fluid. You'll be numbed and hardly feel a thing, much like having your blood drawn. We can take care of that now, or you can come back when it's more convenient."

"It's a no-brainer," Jane said. "Let's get it over with."

"No problem," the doctor said. Then she looked contemplative as if she was thinking, *hmm*.

"Dr. Patel," I said hesitantly, "you mentioned 'a couple' conclusions. Is there more?"

Jane's hand squeezed mine. Or was it mine squeezing hers?

"Yes. While the lump that brought you both here turns out to be nonproblematic, the tests reveal another abnormality. It's called calcifications. Now, again, these are very common, and you could go the rest of your life never knowing they're there. You won't detect them in a monthly self-exam."

"Then why are we talking about them?" That was Jane.

"We still cannot determine the result of your condition, so we require further workup. I'm going to order a biopsy for you. A nonsurgical biopsy."

My heart sank all over again for Jane. I hadn't wanted to hear that word: *biopsy*. I was sure she hadn't either.

"These calcifications could be cancerous?" my daughter asked.

"Could be. But could very well not be." The doctor's eyes and tone were kind. "We don't want to make assumptions or take any chances."

I realized my body was trembling, not for the first time since we'd arrived.

"Will you do the biopsy while we're here today too?" Jane asked. Good question.

"I'm afraid not," the doctor said. "I'll have to send you over to the breast center for that. It's state-of-the-art. You'll meet with a breast doctor, and he'll perform the further evaluation. My staff can arrange the appointment over there within a week. You won't be left hanging for long."

A week was a long time to me. Jane's hand had gone clammy in mine. My eyes were fully adjusted to the shadows and light of the room, so much so that I could see her face had blanched white.

⌇

Jane called Kelsey's cell phone the minute we climbed into the car. Everything had taken longer than expected, she'd said. "Now I wait another six days, then go get the biopsy. But Dr. Patel emphasized that this too could be nothing."

Kelsey wanted to see her mom after work. Aaron was out of town on business. And I really didn't want to be alone. It had nothing to do with it being my birthday. Jane and I had experienced moments of closeness today, and I wasn't ready to let go of those. I wanted to remember these more than what she'd said about my love for her. *In your own way.*

Perhaps she needed togetherness, too, but would never ask. I invited the girls to spend the night. We could have hot cocoa and tuck in early.

It was after six when Kelsey arrived with two sacks of Chinese carryout. Shrimp spring rolls for herself, General Tso chicken for me, and vegetable fried rice for Jane.

"It's not the swankiest dinner," Kelsey said. "But it is your birthday. Besides, I've got a craving."

"Thanks for getting the food," Jane said.

"I want to hear every tedious detail of your appointment," Kelsey said, refusing to let her tone be a downer. She tore open a tiny pouch of hot Chinese mustard with her teeth.

"Fine," Jane said. "But once we get through that, we're done. I'm not going to sit around all evening moping. There's not a damn thing I can do but wait."

We ate with chopsticks, and Jane told Kelsey everything. "And the last thing the doctor said was that, no matter what, I'd caught it early."

"Mom," Kelsey said, "I have to think it's all going to work out in the end. Just like with the cyst."

"I agree," I said.

Kelsey jumped out of her chair and bowed to me. "In lieu of birthday cake—which we will have at a fancy restaurant of your choice whenever you're ready for a real celebratory dinner—we have three fortune cookies." She held up three fingers. "Birthday girl, you pick first."

I scrambled the cellophane-wrapped cookies around and picked one. Jane unwrapped it for me and removed its tiny white slip of paper without peeking at the fortune. When Kelsey had been in college, her friends had insisted that everyone read their fortunes aloud—and that they add the statement *in bed* at the end. Kelsey had prodded her mother and me into playing the same game some years later. Somehow it stuck.

I adjusted my eyeglasses, previewed my message, and then read, "You will soon reveal your soul to someone close, in bed."

When the girls picked themselves up off the floor from laughing, Kelsey said, "My turn."

She cleared her throat. "A surprise awaits you within the year, in bed."

Jane's hearty Midwestern laugh filled the room, and it was the most melodious sound I'd heard in days.

"So what this really means," Kelsey said, "is I'll deliver my baby at home and be surprised by its gender." She preened.

"My turn." Jane ripped the wrapper off the last cookie. "Those who swim the farthest hold the highest hope, in bed." She grinned.

Her fortune boosted me. She could swim far.

"I swear this silly game never gets old," she said.

Kelsey applauded.

~

As dusk turned to night, we drank chamomile tea instead of hot cocoa and burned essential oils that Kelsey had brought. The scent of eucalyptus gave the illusion that we were relaxing at a four-star spa. We wore crushed-velour robes from my closet with thick, fuzzy socks and snuggled up in the den before a flaming gas log.

"This is so fun," Kelsey said. "We haven't done this since, I don't know, since I was a sophomore in college and Mom was home for a visit?"

"Sounds about right," I said. Kelsey had slept over numerous times while Jane lived in Georgia, but we wouldn't mention that. Besides, I had come to appreciate how it truly was better with the three of us.

"What names do you have picked out?" Jane asked.

"That's a big question," Kelsey said. "All we know for sure is, if it's a boy, he won't be Aaron Junior."

"I almost named you Summer Star," Jane said, making a funny face. A spur of old resentment poked at me. I'd been left out of Jane's life at that time.

"Thank you for coming to your senses," Kelsey said dryly. "You guys. How did it feel to push a baby out? Isn't it, like, the most incredible human experience ever?"

My experience had not been the most incredible human experience ever. I had been put under. The whole thing was beyond my control. Then there was the awakening—

"It was," Jane said. "I can still feel it when I think back. And that instant majestic love I was filled with."

Kelsey blew her mother kisses. "Grandma? Do you remember delivering, or were you under the legendary twilight sleep?"

"I actually had a cesarean."

"No way." That was Kelsey. "You had a C-section?"

"Yes way," I said, adjusting my hearing aid. "Janie couldn't fit through my birth canal."

"I can't believe I never knew that," Jane said.

I hesitated. "You and I didn't have all those mother-daughter talks about pregnancy and heartburn and babies kicking." Looking back, that was a true shame. Jane had deprived me of that. But she'd missed out, too.

Jane said, "I should've told you and Daddy I was pregnant with Kelsey the minute I found out. I thought I had my reasons for withholding that news at the time." Her eyes shifted low, not meeting mine. "I'm sorry."

I had waited more than thirty years to hear those words, and they were sweeter to my ears than I could've imagined.

"Thank you," I said. "I remember you walking up to our front door, carrying that rosy-cheeked Kelsey, who was three months old with the most chubby, squeezable little legs. I remember it as if it were yesterday."

I had never understood Jane's reasons for withholding Kelsey. I would ask her again one day. But I was waiting to tell her things, too. Personal things that weighed heavily on my heart. So in this moment it didn't matter that Jane had rebelled and tried to punish us back then—or perhaps to be more precise, had tried to punish me. While it had crushed Dennis and me both, I wouldn't throw all that in her face. Not now. Not ever. Jane and I were together. That's all that mattered.

Then she looked back at me and said, "I'm sorry I denied you the shower, the announcement, the pictures, the gifts." Only now did my daughter understand part of the impact of what she'd done to me. She was soon to be a grandma herself. Jane continued, "And I'm sorry for taking away your chance to hold Kelsey right after she was born."

Her words touched me. "Not holding Kelsey was the hardest part. But it means the world that you're seeing it clearly now. The good news is," I said with a warm smile, "we're all together."

"Pure love, here, ladies," said Kelsey, her voice high like a child's. "Pure love."

I hoped so. I hoped Jane was beginning to see my love was pure.

"And remember, Kels, my birth canal was obviously fine," Jane said. I was glad she said that. I didn't want Kelsey to worry about herself or her delivery. I'd do that enough for both of us.

"I'm really glad my legs aren't chubby and squeezable anymore, too," Kelsey said, and we chuckled. "But, Grandma, I'm still shocked that you had a cesarean. That was pretty rare in those days."

"True. I was the one in fifty. Yippee for me." I didn't care to continue this part of the conversation. I couldn't control what might be asked next.

Kelsey fell silent again.

Jane said, "Kels? What's up?"

"Nothing, really. I just want to deliver vaginally, that's all."

"You probably will," Jane said. "No need to worry about it, at least not at this point."

Kelsey scoffed. "You guys, it's not the seventies or eighties anymore, the age of natural childbirth. One in three hospital births is a C-section now. What do you think of that?"

One in three? That sounded high.

Jane sat up straighter. She said, "You're telling me that out of every three women who walk in a hospital in labor, one of them walks out having needed surgery?"

"Needed? I don't think so," Kelsey said. "Don't get me wrong. The operation can save mothers' and babies' lives. Grandma's experience is living proof. But that many cesareans? That. Is. Craziness." She swirled her tea with her spoon. "Giving birth is the most natural thing in the world, isn't it? Some experts say surgery makes it easy on the doctors. OBs go home sooner to little wifey or little hubby and eat din-din with the kiddies."

My mantel clock chimed nine. I had grown weary. How long would this talk of surgery go on?

"Hospitals have their way with women these days," Kelsey said, and my weary eyes snapped open. "Despite the baby boom being over, some things haven't changed."

A sudden feeling overcame me—maybe I should interrupt Kelsey. Now was the perfect time to let them know my story of a long-ago day. If I had but one year left with my daughter—say, if she were to face the worst with her health, or if I were to not be long for this earth—I was determined to be the best mother a woman could be. I would be there for her. I would be there for Kelsey, too. And for my great-grandchild.

To be the best mother surely started with the truth. Now was the time. I moved my mouth to form words, but I couldn't get my vocal cords to work. I swallowed, licked my lips, cleared my throat. But nothing came out.

Why was I still afraid?

I'd always been afraid. When Janie was a young girl, I feared she was too immature, too impressionable to handle the truth. She might have nightmares. When she became a teenager, I feared that if we opened up about our second baby, the Glenns—Abbie in particular—would suggest to Jane that everything was *my* fault. I shouldn't have "spread myself so thin." I was concerned that Jane would resent me. Years later I did try to tell her, several times. But circumstance prevented me—or so I convinced myself. I was afraid. I feared Jane would reject me for having kept the secret for so long. I was afraid I'd wind up alone: I had no father, no mother, no grandfather, no siblings, no husband. I was afraid there'd be no Jane. And if I had no Jane, I'd have no Kelsey.

Yes, I was afraid of being alone.

No, that was the kind of thinking that Papa Glenn would call bullshit.

There was something else that scared me, something worse than being alone.

I was afraid that if the truth of my tragedy came out, the world would know I wasn't the perfect mother. They'd have to know of the guilt I'd dragged around my entire life—guilt sunken inside of me, an anchor overgrown with seaweed. Hidden, but there. Tangled and lurking. But that guilt had less to do with Janie than with . . .

I had to trust that these two women, both strong women—Jane and me feeling the closest we had in years—would accept my truth. Would accept me, too. I had to tell them while there was still time for us to heal.

I swallowed hard. This time I'd get the words out.

"Girls," I began softly. "I—"

"They were inducing women and holding them back in your day," Kelsey said. She was still on her roll. "Grandma, you know it. I've seen YouTube videos and have read the books. I will not be induced. The Pit is prohibited in my birthing plan. That is, I mean, Pitocin. And, you guys, if I happen to land in a hospital where a caregiver says I have 'failure to progress,' just know that's code for sending a woman to get sectioned off. To keep on their own schedules, not my baby's. I won't consent to surgical intervention—not without a warranted medical emergency."

"Whoa, down, girl." That was Jane. "I'm beginning to see why you want a home birth."

I blew air out of my mouth, my thin cheeks ballooning. Kelsey knew her stuff. Yet could any of us ever be prepared for everything?

"Girls," I tried again, louder this time.

"Mom, I'm sorry to say I'm zapped," Jane said. Of course she was. It had been a difficult day. "I have to call it a night."

Kelsey yawned. Then Jane actually gave me a hug and a kiss and said, "Night-night, Mommy. Love you." That tickled me. I was buoyed beyond measure.

The girls were returning in a few days so they could store some boxes downstairs. I'd tell them everything then.

No going back.

CHAPTER TWELVE

March 1951

I still hadn't seen Dr. Collins. Hadn't his nurse on the phone said he'd check in with me when I arrived?

An hour or forty-five minutes from the time I got off the hospital elevator—I didn't know how long, for they'd removed my watch and rings—I was settled into a stark white surgical room with a large, round metal light hanging above my bed. Presumably Dennis had completed the admissions forms and was hovering in the waiting room with green vinyl chairs, smoking Lucky Strikes with the rest of the dads. *Ohhh*, another contraction came.

"Mrs. Glenn, I'm Nurse Tibbers."

The nurse's entrance startled me. No "hello," no "how are you doing" after all my waiting.

"What's taking so long for Dr. Collins to see me?" I asked.

She looked at me blank-faced. "It's best that you keep quiet."

Was this the nurse who'd referred to new mothers' precious infants as misfits? Her back was now turned. She wasn't fixing a needle for me, was she? Maybe I would stay quiet. I wrapped my arms around my baby who'd yet to be born.

"Dr. Collins," Nurse Tibbers said in a submissive voice when my physician stepped in. "Meet Mrs. Glenn."

Thank goodness he was here.

"Of course, Mrs. Glenn and I know each other well," he said. I longed in that moment to be back in his practical office with the pea-green walls and speckled floor tiles. And with Dennis beside me.

Dr. Collins glanced at his watch and turned to my medical chart. Tension squeezed my groin and reverberated through the trunk of my body and killed my back halfway up my spine. The brunt of the pressure was at my tailbone: the baby's weight was crushing it.

"What about a rupture?" I asked between my gritted teeth. "Am I in danger?" I breathed, I breathed.

"You're a star patient, Mrs. Glenn. You won't have long to wait," the doctor said. "You're scheduled for your operation at 6:15 p.m. Today is your little one's birthday."

Today, March 23, two days after the first day of spring. It sounded lovely. And he'd again called me a star.

So why was Dr. Collins checking his watch again? Was there a problem?

"I've already spoken to Mr. Glenn—"

"What about?" I asked, pressing my lips together. Dennis first? Not me?

"The paperwork," the doctor said. "The maternity ward is over-crowded. I've called in my colleague, Dr. Reynolds, who will perform your operation."

My eyes were wide with surprise, and my limbs began to tremble. "Why a different doctor?"

"I'm caring for eighteen other mothers who came in before you. Don't worry. Dr. Reynolds delivered my own son. He's performed as many cesareans as I, maybe more."

Who could ask for a better referral than that? I turned my head on the cool, crisp case of the pillow.

"Mrs. Glenn?" A woman's voice.

My eyes fluttered open, just a crack, for looking into the overhead light was like glaring into an eclipse of the sun. I was groggy, but the noxious scent of antiseptic or medicine assaulted my nostrils. There was a faint smell of something soft, too. Sterilized cotton? Somewhere close by, metal clanged as if servers at a restaurant were clearing away cutlery. I rotated my head from one side to the other on the pillow and back. Where was I? But I couldn't speak.

"Mrs. Glenn, you're still in the maternity surgical suite."

I lifted my right hand, but it stalled. I didn't have the strength. No, it wasn't that. My wrists were bound. I lifted my head up from the neck, my eyes adjusting to the glare, my chin almost tapping my chest, and I saw that my baby was gone.

Good, my child had been born while I slept. Boy or girl? How long had it been?

"Mrs. Glenn," the woman said again with compassion. "I'm Nurse Breck." Not Nurse Tibbers. I could tell that much from her tone.

I tilted my head toward her face. She was young. Pretty. A caring warmth exuded from her smile, the first genuine smile I'd seen since my arrival. Above one end of her top lip was a dark, round beauty mark.

Her moist hand rested on one of mine contained by its strap. Her touch was gentle.

"When can I see my baby?"

"Mrs. Glenn . . ."

Fear surged in my empty womb.

"Mrs. Glenn, lie still," she said kindly. "The doctor will—"

"Where is my baby? Please, tell me." My voice rose, since my body could not. "Where's my baby?"

My eyes caught a shift in the light by the door behind her. Was it the doctor? Then the door opened wide and a shadowy figure came into view. It was Dennis.

PART TWO

CHAPTER THIRTEEN

April 1951

Dennis and his mother looked from me to each other and then to Janie and then back at me. We all stood in the entry of the house that my husband had pushed everything else to the side for, the second new Gunnison home he'd built just for us. He'd constructed it while I'd been hospitalized for three and a half weeks in recovery. Today was my homecoming. The house smelled of fresh plywood, carpeting, and varnish. There'd been no carrying me across the threshold this time—the incision that ran up six inches of my stomach was far too tender for that. Mother Glenn and Dennis didn't utter a peep, didn't know what to say. So I repeated myself.

"It's got to go. I can't take a womb chair under my roof anymore." The sound of the word *womb* made me want to retch. That chair was a big red reminder of our loss, of my failure to birth a healthy baby. The operation had been timely; there had been no problems per se, no rupture; and my lengthy physical recovery, though difficult, had progressed normally.

But our daughter had not survived her first day.

"Haul the chair to the yard, to the garage, or out to the garbage pickup, I don't care. But now. Please."

Mother Glenn nudged her head toward her son, a sympathetic crease across her brow.

In the car on the way home from the hospital, Dennis and Mother Glenn had chattered about our very first fireplace and the shaded backyard with a swing set and slide. The shiny appliances, the larger space with light from abundant windows. Mother Glenn had set up the whole kitchen—unpacked every skillet and pan herself, washed every bowl, and stored all the dishes in convenient spots.

"We considered yellow for Janie's room," Dennis had said, "because you love yellow. But we haven't hung a picture or bought new linens. The room needs your special flair for decor."

Dennis had forced a smile in the driver's seat beside me. I had not smiled back. I didn't care about decorating.

"And you have a third bedroom for all your sewing," Mother Glenn said from the back seat, as Janie squirmed on her lap. Dennis's face froze as he drove. He knew what I was thinking. That spare room in a new house should have been our second daughter's. No one had spoken the rest of the ride home.

Standing in the entry now, I turned my head, and Mother Glenn's eyes locked with mine. Her face swirled with emotions. Her smile-be-pleasant expression fought with her horror of seeing her son and daughter-in-law so beaten. Dennis had lost his child. And Mother Glenn had lost her grandchild. Was there anything on earth she cherished more than her grandbabies?

But poor Dennis.

When I looked at him, his eyes, unlike his mother's, did not lock with mine. He looked at Janie or out the window or at his shoes. Anywhere but at me. With this house he'd bestowed on me a gift I didn't want. All he'd hoped for, all he'd wished to see, was a tiny hint of a smile when I walked through the front door. He'd needed a sign that we'd be okay.

I hadn't meant not to give it to him. It just hadn't come.

Dennis was downcast, his shoulders slack as he lumbered across the room and manhandled the womb chair out the back door. Mother Glenn busied herself, rearranging Janie's bangs with her fingertips, which she'd licked.

I had supported moving from our old Gunnison model to this new one. No matter what, I was never going back to the house on Grace Street. I couldn't sleep in the bedroom where I'd organized the layette on the perfect dressing table tucked between the chest of drawers and the closet, the diapers and booties and blankets I had aligned just so.

Mrs. Glenn, I'm afraid I have bad news.

In months to come Dennis and I would try again. And I still had my precious first daughter. If anything at all promised to get me through this loss, it was Janie—and my having a third child. I wouldn't fail the next time. Kathleen, my departed baby girl, was my responsibility. I'd failed her. I had let Dennis down, too. And now Janie had no sister.

Where had I gone wrong?

I sat on the sofa now with Janie snuggled beside me, my arms around her waist. I kissed her clean-scented hair. She'd grown so much in the weeks I was gone. Her hair was longer, her teeth slightly larger, her vocabulary broader. "Mine," she said when I held her stuffed puppy and tried to play. She wriggled to get up. Our reunion didn't mean as much to her as it did to me. She scooted off the couch saying, "Bah, bah, bah," and though she wouldn't understand, it pierced my heart right in the center. We should have had a baby to bring home for her.

Then Janie took off at a pace I'd never seen before, a toddler's all-out sprint across the green carpeting like a new, wide-open field to her, her little arms flapping, her voice babbling with glee.

"Slow down, Janie. Slow down." My shout startled her, and she collided with the middle of the floor almost face-first.

"Oh no," I cried. I could not run, was not supposed to make sudden movements at all, but my child was hurt. I pushed myself up. I had to protect her.

"She's fine," said Mother Glenn as Janie looked back at us all, poised on her rump, her expression one of indecision as to whether she'd laugh at her blunder or cry for effect.

"See, she's okay," Dennis said, looking at me now. My heart pounded, and I felt my face grow hot.

She was fine. She was fine. Janie was fine.

"She's gonna be an athlete," Dennis said lightly. I didn't laugh. He worked his fingers into a crumpled cigarette pack and pulled out a smoke. Janie was already off to the toy basket, jabbering all the way.

The doorbell rang. We had a doorbell now? "Who is it?" I asked. I didn't want to see anyone. I didn't want anyone seeing me.

Mother Glenn answered the door. I heard voices.

"We're here. How's Millie doing?"

Abbie? I thought. *And Nathan?* Oh no.

My brother-in-law and sister-in-law tiptoed into the room. Nathan hugged me—gently, as though I might crack. He said, "I'm so sorry for what you've been through. It's terrible."

Yes, that's what it is, I thought. *Terrible.*

"I'm sorry for your loss, too." That was Abbie.

"Thank you."

"I've brought some gifts," she said. "I'll put this stuff away in the kitchen for you."

Mother Glenn and all the sisters-in-law had sent meals for us. Casseroles in the freezer. Sliced ham in the fridge. There were soups and eggs and vinaigrette dressings. They'd already stocked the cupboards with peanut butter cookies and banana-nut bread.

Mother Glenn went to change Janie's diaper. Dennis toured Nathan through the house.

With her hands fidgeting in her lap, Abbie said, "How do you feel?"

"I'm on medicine, so the incision isn't that bad." That part was easiest to explain. As for how I felt in my heart, that was harder to answer.

"The children wanted to come, especially Margaret," Abbie said. "She adores you, you know."

I was mute. I supposed Abbie meant well, but how could I possibly enjoy a visit from her bubbly brood of healthy children?

Abbie fiddled with the hem of her dress. Her vision swept about the room, a frown forming on her face. Was she looking for cobwebs? For dust? Must I get out a white glove for her to test my housekeeping on my first day in this house?

"Something's missing in this new room." Abbie pondered. "Oh yes. Where's the big red chair, the modern one with the matching ottoman? In the bedroom? I like that set," she said, and smiled. The womb chair.

"Abbie, I don't mean to be rude," I said. "I'm feeling rather taxed and need to go rest." I rose and retired without saying goodbye.

~

After Dennis's brother and his wife left, my mother-in-law served Dennis and me a dinner of pot roast with potatoes and carrots. She cleaned up the kitchen and bathed Janie. She'd be back in a couple of days for more help.

Standing at the front door now, I embraced her. I rested my head on her strong, soft shoulder. I didn't let go for the longest time as I pressed my face into her thick felt coat.

She said, "I know you're devastated, honey. I hate it for you. You'll live through this, somehow—though you'll always carry its scars. I'd bear them all for you, if I could."

I respected her for not pretending that time would heal all. She knew it wouldn't.

"I never got to hold my baby," I said. "Never even got to see her. I know it sounds crazy, but I can't stop thinking about who will rock her to sleep. Who will feed her? Who will change her diaper? She needs me."

Mother Glenn's round cheeks were wet against mine. She said softly, "There are angels in heaven whose sole job it is to rock the little ones and give them comfort." I pictured that heavenly sight. Then Mother Glenn added, "I bet your mama got that job."

Dennis's mother had said just the right thing. And she held me as I wept.

CHAPTER FOURTEEN

April 1951

Two weeks later, Dennis and I received a letter from the hospital.

"It's signed by Dr. Collins," I said frantically.

The mail had come, and I'd caught Dennis in the garage just in time. I was still getting used to our new garage, to our new house—to our new place in life. Every time I changed Janie's diaper, I'd think: *I should be changing two babies' diapers.* Every time I heard her cry, I'd think: *Which baby is it?* And then I'd remember I had only one. How often had I said to Dennis, "I can't believe this happened to us." He'd shake his head. He couldn't believe it either. Now with this letter, thank goodness I'd stopped him after he filled the car's oil tank. The burnished smell of the empty oil cans mingled with the scent of his aftershave. Two minutes longer and he'd have been off to check a house for new storm doors.

"I can't read this," I said, turning my head away and handing the letter to him.

My husband stood between his open car door and the car's interior. His engine was humming, and the garage was open to the breeze.

The hospital administrator had also signed the letter. Dennis summarized for me that an investigation of my operation and delivery had been concluded; investigations were routine when a child expired. The letter had used that word: *expired*. Was that more formal than writing the word *died*? More medical than saying *passed away*? Was the word intended to be softer for a mother like me to hear? If so, its author was gravely mistaken.

Then Dennis read aloud, struggling to pronounce an even worse medical term, "The baby expired of encephalomalacia due to undetermined cause." He looked up, his mouth twisted and his forehead scrunched. "What the hell is encephalomalacia?"

I grabbed the letter back and scanned it. "No explanation? They spit out some two-dollar word without telling us what it means?" The letter went on to express the administration's sincerest sympathies, because "there was nothing the maternity staff could have done."

"You'll have to drive me to the library," I said, already heading into the house to pack up Janie, who was asleep. "I've got to look this word up."

"First, I've gotta take care of—"

"Storm doors can wait. This can't."

Dennis didn't speak while we loaded up to go. As with the womb chair, he honored my wishes without more debate. He'd ceded to me a lot lately. He'd held me in his arms even more.

Janie squirmed and fussed in her canvas car seat attached to the back of the front seat with metal hangers. It was positioned between Dennis and me so Janie could see out; the seat even had a plastic steering wheel—but it didn't help her temperament today. I had woken her from a nap, so she was fussy. Dennis was sullen, and my soothing-mommy voice wasn't working. My mind was in chaos. What was encephalomalacia? Had my second child been born as a misfit, the word the cruel nurse on the ward had used? I loved my lost little girl with my whole being, whatever way she was, sight unseen.

While I had still been sedated in the hospital, Dennis had gotten to peep at her through the nursery observatory window during the posted viewing hour. Tiny Kathleen had been swaddled among a score of newborns, each in their glass bassinettes. She'd had pretty little lips like Janie's, he'd said. She'd also had an inflamed, swollen spot on her head, but other fathers remarked on their infants' soft heads being misshapen, too—or having unsightly red marks left from forceps. One father assured the rest that this was his third child, and he could attest that such marks and the uneven pointiness of their heads eventually faded away.

If only we could have been so lucky.

I didn't know what encephalomalacia was, but I did know one thing: I'd done something wrong in carrying Kathy to term. I had to have. My temples pounded as echoes of Abbie's warnings crowded in: *Why do you spend so much time making up newspaper ads or bookkeeping or whatever you do anyway? Isn't being a mother and keeping a nice home more important?*

Dennis pulled the car up in front of the library. "I'll swing back around in thirty minutes," he said, surprisingly gently.

"Thank you," I said, and our sad eyes met. "I'll hurry." Janie was crying as I closed the passenger door.

I stepped inside the library's main hall. For an instant I imagined I was here for a fun task, not an emergency one. The scent of books and old mustiness filled me with memories of Opa. This library had been built before my grandfather was born, and he had walked me here a lot when I was a girl.

"No matter how much money we have or don't have," Opa had once said, "you can always read books for free."

I made my way across the floor with its familiar pattern of large, diagonal marble tiles. Cast-iron cases housed stacks and stacks of books around the hall's perimeter. They reached several lengths up to the coffered ceiling fitted out with skylights.

I had no idea where to begin a search in the card catalog for a medical condition so foreign to me. I headed to the circulation desk for direction. I realized how I'd been slogging from day to day without helping our business. I hadn't missed that work, not yet. But I would. I would heal, and I would return. I was on a different mission now. I had a purpose. I got what I needed at circulation and headed back to the card catalog.

By the time I returned to the desk with a slip of paper noting the book I required, twelve minutes of my thirty-minute limit had ticked by. I handed the paper to a college-aged page boy, and he glanced at the Dewey decimal number I'd written down. He ran off as if he knew exactly which metal spiral staircase would lead him to it. He came back within six minutes, carrying a reference book that I was not allowed to check out.

"Thank you for your haste," I said. He gave a little bow.

I lugged the weighty leather-bound volume to a weathered table, trying not to put pressure on my tummy. I had to share the table with a businessman. He didn't bother looking up. All the seating areas in the hall had quiet patrons stationed at them, mostly men with their fedora hats and periodicals spread across the tabletops.

My hand shook as I opened the medical tome's back cover and thumbed through the index of human diseases and conditions. There it was: *E. Encephalomalacia*. I flipped to its chapter and quickly traced my finger along the technical text:

> Several things can cause encephalomalacia, such as a cerebral infarction—most commonly known as a stroke. This occurs when oxygen flow to brain tissue is blocked by a blood clot or hemorrhage of one of the brain's blood vessels. Cerebral softening may occur as a result. A traumatic brain injury, such as one sustained in an automobile accident, can also deliver a violent blow to the brain, and the body will interrupt normal brain function. A number of infections

may also lead to inflammation and cerebral softening. Encephalomalacia is a serious form of brain damage. The softening of brain tissue can occur in one part of the brain and then spread to contiguous regions. The condition may occur at any age, though in infants diagnosed with the disorder, it is often fatal.

Fatal.

My daughter counted among the fatalities.

It was easy to rule out what hadn't happened. We'd certainly not been in a wreck. So it had to be me. I'd carried her. I'd done something wrong. Did something I ate cause an infection in my womb? Had my rigorous activities—my workload—caused a deadly blood clot or hemorrhage to develop in my body?

I scribbled notes of the text on a card. I slammed the thick book shut and left it there. The stranger at the table scowled at me.

When I climbed back into the car, Dennis said, "You okay?"

"Not really."

He nodded. As if by intuition we knew my findings would wait until we were safely off the roads.

Once we were home I let him review the description intact. I braced the whole time he read it. Then he said, "I don't know about this mumbo jumbo. I know what I learned about life on the farm. I suppose babies aren't that far off from foals. Not all newborns survive. It's Mother Nature's way."

I could not have predicted what that man would say. He spoke with such finality, though, such reason, it signaled to me the matter was closed. I needed to dissect the findings or wallow in the pain of them or hear him speak his wisdom some more. But once would have to be enough. He didn't blame me. That much was good.

I could do all the blaming myself.

~

Business always flourished in the spring—and that was a blessing, because I needed something to flourish. I needed something to talk about over late dinners or early breakfasts—chitchat to fill that space where my chest was hollowed out like a tooth with a monstrous cavity.

Dennis was working more Saturdays, staying out later every night during the week. Was he throwing himself into his job to cope with his grief? Did he seek refuge from our house, where his wife's eyes held telltale signs of tears most days—such a contrast to Janie and Raggsie, who thrilled when he arrived home? He never asked if I was ready to return to more business duties. I wasn't.

But it might've helped me if he'd asked.

It was now Sunday afternoon, a rare day home for him. Dennis said, "Honey, I'll run a load of wash for my work clothes this week. You rest."

What? Had I missed laundry day on Thursday? No one—I do mean no one—in our circle of friends or in Dennis's family had ever heard of a man doing laundry. It pained me to think what Mother Glenn would say if she heard.

My eyelids shut, sickly. And there was Abbie to consider: she would never let me live this down.

"No, no, I'll do a load," I said from where I lay on the couch. "In a few minutes."

Moments before, Dennis had given me another pill in hopes of lifting my mood. At the doctor's suggestion Dennis had already purchased more medication since I was discharged from the hospital. The pills helped me to sleep. They helped me cope.

I would never get over losing my baby. But this part that went on all day—freed only if I managed an hour's sleep—wouldn't last forever. I wouldn't feel this blue forever. Would I?

Dennis carried an armful of work pants and shirts out of the bedroom. The washing machine was behind louvered doors in the kitchen.

"I told you I'd do that," I said groggily, angrily, as he passed through the living room.

"I don't mind. Really," he said. "It's not as if I can't figure out how to push a button on a machine."

His words felt like a smack—as though the menial work I'd done at home for years was nothing. A silly, mindless push of a button.

I was sitting up on the couch now, but I hadn't moved to stand. "I don't know why you couldn't have waited a few minutes. I said I'd do it." I sneered.

"Janie needs her diaper changed and to be tucked in," he said. He'd already carried her from the playpen to the crib. "Can you do that?"

I rose. Then I came within an inch of Dennis's nose in our living room and shouted in his face: "Can you let me know you feel this agony I'm feeling? How can you keep it locked up so tight?"

He jumped back, confounded. Speechless.

Janie whined. My little girl needed me. I padded to her room and changed her diaper in her bed. She smiled and grasped hold of her bare feet, and for a flash of an instant, I thought my life was normal. Happy. I lifted her up, using my arms and my shoulders as the nurses had shown me, not my core or my back. Janie smelled of sweet innocence. I kissed her night-night and laid her back down for her nap.

I found Dennis in the rake-back wooden armchair that he'd gotten to replace the womb chair. This one, too, had red upholstery on its cushion. He had one leg crossed on his opposite knee, presumably reading the magazine splayed open in his lap. Without acknowledging my presence, he lifted a glass of milk from the side table and sipped. He laid the magazine down. It was only when his gaze met mine that I saw the misery in his eyes after all—and I knew that pain. It mirrored my own.

I wanted to reach out. For us to come together. Hadn't I declared that I needed to know he suffered, too? But in that moment it was hard enough for me to survive my own loss, let alone to bear the weight of his, too. I couldn't look at him any longer. I retreated to our room and buried myself beneath three layers of covers.

⁓

Monday had come, and Dennis was out providing for his family as the world said good husbands should. Janie slept while I let the house fall apart—in the way Abbie Glenn had said good wives shouldn't. I didn't frost cupcakes or organize next week's calendar. The sink full of pots and pans lasted longer than before. I forgot the baseboards needed cleaning. The bed went unmade, and the sheets went unwashed. And I let the telephone ring off the hook. I dragged every morning, lay down every afternoon. Dennis rarely commented. "Unmade beds aren't the end of the world," he once said. And he knew that if anything got done besides simple dinner prep, it was my caring for Janie—she was clean and fed and cuddled—and my licking stamps for mailers. No way was I letting these go.

I retrieved the pink-and-blue baby album, the one I had gotten for my shower, and sank onto my bed. I flipped to the page for Baby's Arrival.

I tried to write in my meticulous penmanship, but the ink ended up wobbly on the page. I completed what few facts we had of our daughter's short life. Her birthdate, her name, her weight: seven pounds, two ounces. I ran my fingertips along the hospital's inked imprints of her feet—two perfect, tiny feet. I mused about how her soles had the deep curves of my own arches. Had she also been born with Dennis's dimples? I completed Kathy's family tree, where little birds fluttered their angel-fairy wings in its branches. And I wrote on the designated line her doctor's name—Dr. Reynolds, who'd delivered her. Forever to remain blank were the festive pages for her Visitors Who Came, her Favorite Playthings, her First Birthday.

2015

The day had arrived. The girls would store some belongings in the basement. And I would finally let go of my story and bring us even closer together.

Aaron's SUV pulled up out front, followed by Kelsey and Jane in Jane's car. Kelsey's husband had to write up a contract for a corporate client that Saturday, but first he'd loaded up their SUV and Jane's midsize car with stuff to store at my house. Jane had extra boxes that cramped her temporary apartment. Kelsey was itching to decorate her nursery and needed their spare room emptied. We'd hired my capable neighborhood lawn boys, who never turned down a buck. The two teens, freshman football players, would arrive within a few minutes. I only hoped they'd get everything out of the girls' cars before the skies opened up and it started to pour.

Aaron made his way up my sidewalk with his first load in his arms. He had a stocky build, was no taller than Kelsey when she wore pumps, and had the curliest crop of black ringlets. Aaron's father was an attorney, too, and his mother a judge. Aaron had made partner and opened up the OTR outpost of Goldberg LLC and was doing quite well, albeit working weekends. The first time I'd met him, Kelsey brought him down from the university when they were seniors. She'd been animated and glowing and said, "Aaron, this is my beloved grandma, Millie." And he'd smiled wide and said, "Hello, Grandma Millie." He'd ignored my extended hand and given me a friendly hug instead. I'd loved that boy from the get-go.

"Hey, Grandma Millie," he said now, and winked.

"Hi, sweetie-pie Aaron," I said. "You can put that box right over there." I pointed. "My plan is for you and the guys to haul everything into the house, then you can go on your merry way. They'll lug everything to the basement for us."

"You're a jewel," he said. He set the box down and then touched Kelsey's shoulder with utmost tenderness, reverence.

My heart smiled. How fortunate it was that she had this bountiful love. I'd not gotten to see it with Jane.

"Kels and I appreciate you letting us store our junk," Aaron said. "Someday we'll have three bedrooms."

"Happy to do it. I just can't wait for your little baby to arrive."

As for my pending confession to the girls, I hadn't changed my mind for a minute. I'd tell them about Kathleen. Jane and I had talked by phone or texted twice a day since she'd been here for Chinese food and the sleepover. I could hardly believe how close we seemed to be becoming. But for Jane's medical testing hanging in the balance, it was a dream come true. I'd already figured out how I would begin my story once the movers left: I'd prepare the girls with memories of my overcrowded, baby-boom maternity ward. Then I'd simply tell them about the worst time in my life, in Dennis's life, and how Janie had been too young to remember. I would let them hear of my deep remorse for withholding this story for all these years, but how now, my deepest hope that was the biggest truth would forge in us an unbreakable bond.

I would go through with the telling, no matter how afraid I was of them knowing my guilt, my failing as a mother. Opa's words echoed: *You're Millicent the Strong. Don't you ever forget it.*

Aaron went for another load, and my girls insisted on getting the lay of the land in my basement as the boys arrived. Jane went down the steps first, ducking when reaching the bottom step and avoiding the low overhead beam. I descended slowly, gripping the handrail while Kelsey steadied me with my other arm. We inhaled the musty smells born of the sixty-year-old cinder-block foundation in this house my husband had built. No sump pump glitch, no flood or mildew could ruin containers stored here—Dennis Glenn had seen to that. I batted away a cobweb and grasped the yellowed string dangling from the low ceiling. I yanked, and the bare bulb cast shadows across Dennis's old workbench and containers stacked along walls. My girls scanned the rows of crates and trunks. There would be much for them to clear out once I was gone. So many memories to unpack, like fragile little heirlooms, memories to grieve over or laugh over and settle into new homes—or to dispose of and to forget.

"There," I said, pointing. "In addition to the floor, there's some open space high on those shelves." Along the lower shelves were ornaments, wreaths, and canning jars once filled with bread-and-butter pickles.

"If I store something on the highest shelf, what can I stand on?" Jane asked, rubbing her forearms. It wasn't as warm down here as in my cozy den.

"I used to have a small stepladder." I poked around. "It's probably in the garage. We'll get it when we go back up."

"That couch has seen better days," Jane said, indicating the gold one I'd had upstairs two couches ago. It formed part of a last-resort seating area in the center of my concrete floor. There was a ragged, braided rope rug woven with colors of gold and rust, together with a vinyl recliner that didn't recline anymore.

"I remember when you bought that couch new," Jane said. "Now it looks more like one I fooled around on in a run-down Victorian—a house in the Haight-Ashbury at a party with the Grateful Dead." She snickered.

"Ah, yes, the glory days of your trip—in all senses of the word—to San Francisco," Kelsey said. "Your whole sex, drugs, and rock-and-roll thing. Doing deeds you later forbade me to do." The two of them cracked up.

To me, this particular memory hadn't quite risen to the point of being funny yet.

"LSD was practically still legal in California then," Jane said now.

"Practically," I said with great emphasis. "You were one year late for that party."

"Hey, now," Jane said, pretending to be put off. "It's not like you were Miss Goody-Goody Two-Shoes all your life. What with the barbies you popped back in the day."

What? I was completely taken aback, my body ablaze.

"Barbies?" I said. Where had that come from?

Jane laughed. "Barbs. Downers. Dolls. Whatever y'all called 'em in the fifties. I'm not judging. Barbiturates were legal then. I'm just glad you didn't die."

"Lots of women took those then, and amphetamines, too," Kelsey said. "No wonder housewives had waists the size of bread loaves."

"Who in the world told you I took barbies?" I wouldn't let it go.

"Oops," Kelsey said.

"Linda Jo mentioned it eons ago," Jane said of her cousin. "Aunt Abbie had apparently let it slip."

I was livid. Abbie Glenn had been six feet under for going on twenty years, but her careless mouth could still slay me. In all the time we were sisters-in-law, we had never gotten on well. We had "too much baggage," to borrow a modern term. But I had to push these thoughts away. I had to keep faith that Abbie hadn't let anything else "slip." As soon as the thought entered my mind, another one struck me: Had

Abbie also broken her promise about Kathleen? Was this why Jane had punished us by not sharing how she'd given birth to Kelsey? And had Jane's knowing of my taking pills led her to experimenting with drugs on her own? Then I had to wonder, had Jane also told Kelsey?

I felt empty. No, not empty. Filled. Filled with wrath. And frigid cold. But I couldn't let these negative feelings disrupt more precious minutes with my girls. I would learn soon enough the extent of the damage Abbie had wreaked. I had to calm down.

Thankfully, it seemed my girls were already on to the next thing.

"What's this?" Kelsey asked. She'd picked up something stuffed in an old wicker clothes basket.

"Oh," I said. I was still cold and could barely think straight to answer, despite how I tried to shove Abbie Glenn's big mouth out of my head. "It's a plaque your grandfather was awarded from Gunnison Homes." I'd always wished my name were engraved on it, too. But I refrained from saying that.

"Hey, let me see," Jane said. Her fingertips traced the letters of her father's name engraved on the brass plate.

Jane told Kelsey, "Your papaw used to lift me onto his back and lug me all over his building sites. He taught me about blueprints. They were like paint-by-numbers for constructing a house." She paused, looked at me. "He taught me a lot about the building trade. That's largely why I pursued the work I did. Mind if I keep the plaque?"

"It's yours," I said, not wanting to linger on it. "So over here," I said, swooping my arm in the direction of a fairly open space on one far end of the basement. "You can have the boys shift a few things around if you need to. But I suggest you each keep all your belongings in a designated area."

"Gotcha," Kelsey said, and gave a thumbs-up.

⌐

"Look here, Jane," I said, drawing her attention to a box I'd kept filled with mementos from her youth. Report cards, spelling bee ribbons, elementary school yearbooks. This was exactly what I needed to get back on track—happy memories to settle my nerves.

"What fun!" Kelsey said. The movers were almost done with their part, and both girls began digging into the box. Jane pulled out a hand-drawn picture of three people—a mommy, a daddy, and a girl standing beside a Christmas tree colored with green and red crayons. It was signed *Janie*, and I had made note in ink that the year was 1955.

"I didn't realize you'd kept all these things," Jane said. "I love them." She looked genuinely pleased.

"Of course I kept them," I said. My chest puffed up.

"Aww, check this out," Kelsey said. "A dried clay figure of a baby in a basket."

The sight of that handmade gift from Janie stilled me. The clay figure fit in the palm of a hand. I'd not thought of that thing in years. I regretted getting out the box now.

Jane was equally solemn. What was she thinking? If Abbie had told Jane my secret, did Jane know the significance of the figure in a way she hadn't when she made it?

"I remember making this," she said after what felt like ten minutes. "I was maybe seven? I gave it to you, and I thought you loved it at first. But then I thought you hated it. You had put it away the next day and I never saw it again. I'm surprised you kept it."

Janie had come home from Sunday school with her grandma and told me how she'd rolled the clay into baby Jesus's body, rolled a little ball for a head, patted a piece of clay flat for a blanket. I had oohed and aahed, delighted at her skill and creativity. And then she pointed her index finger just so and said she'd placed the tiniest little fist by the baby's mouth. "It's sucking its thumb," she said, her thickly lashed eyes gazing up at me so proud. I'd drifted into my room and silently wept.

Rebounding now and wanting to smooth things over, I said, "It's wonderful that we found this box, then, huh? Now you know. I treasured everything you ever gave me."

Jane smiled, and our eyes held for a moment. I never wanted to hurt her again. I would say what needed to be said when the packing boys were gone.

Jane headed upstairs to use the bathroom and to get a drink.

"Grandma," Kelsey said, "what's in this box over here?"

"Let me look."

"See? This one says **SAVE** in big, black letters," she said from the other end of the basement. The decades-old wrapping tape had warped and loosened, and Kelsey began to lift the box flaps. "There's a random shipping mark in the corner. Dated 1951. The historian in me is dying to know what's in here."

"Don't open that box," I ordered. Had I spoken too harshly? I was trembling. The anchor of guilt shifted inside of me. "I mean, don't waste your time, honey." I gave her a fixed stare. "We'll get to it later." I hadn't thought of bringing that box out with my story, but it would be a natural thing to do. If I could bear to lay eyes on its contents again.

"Okay. Mind if I just slide it over here? I've got a couple of pieces that I don't want getting mixed in with Mom's stuff. I need a teensy-weensy bit more space."

"Fine," I said. "Push it over there."

Jane called down the staircase from above, "Kels, the guys need your sage advice on one last thing in the den."

"Coming," Kelsey said.

Jane returned from upstairs with bottled waters. She handed me one and smiled. She'd already broken the seal and twisted the cap open on mine. Thoughtful. "Thank you, sweetie."

The boys' tramping feet on the steps signaled the last load on its way. I had forgotten to set out the money. I headed back up.

Kelsey was in the kitchen on her cell phone, presumably with Aaron. "Yup, they're finishing now. Going to be close, but it'll fit."

I laid out the money for the boys with a nice tip and went to the bathroom. When I returned, Kelsey was still on the phone. I had to sit. My knee joints screamed at me that one trip, let alone three, up and down those steps was enough for one day.

I needed reserves of energy, too. The time was drawing near, and I found myself leery. Telling this story would be harder than I thought. But I'd do it.

"Mrs. Glenn," the taller boy said as the two reemerged from the basement, "your daughter needs you."

"Is she hurt?" My heart skipped a beat.

"No. I think she just said it's important," he said.

Kelsey signed off her call and said, "She needs the Master General's approval on where to put her Jane Fonda exercise mat or her sacred lava lamp." We said goodbye to the boys, and she helped me descend the steps.

Jane sat on the ratty couch, hovered over a large open cardboard packing box. Wads of airy, crisp, browned tissue paper floated like seafoam at her feet.

She didn't look up. Was Jane ignoring me? I didn't want to return to those cold shoulder days. I saw then that the box she had was the one marked **SAVE**. I froze.

Kelsey saw it, too. "Eek," she said, thinking Jane was in trouble. She joined her mother on the couch.

Jane held the old pink-and-blue baby album open in her lap. Whether or not she knew yet that it was her sister's, I had no idea. The world went dark, and the cement floor seemed to slant. I felt a loss of balance. Yet I felt like a mummy, too, petrified and unable to move.

"Yay, another box of keepsakes," Kelsey said. She dangled tiny yellow booties that her great-grandma Glenn had made. "Were these

Mom's when she was a baby?" Kelsey asked, dipping back into the box. "Look at all these little baby clothes; they're so cute."

My lips were too numb to respond right away. Then: "Jane, I was going to tell you about this. Today."

Kelsey's head craned from her red-faced mother to me. "You were going to tell Mom what?"

"I've tried to tell you many times," I said, still unclear about how much Jane knew.

Kelsey said, "Guys, what did I miss?"

I lifted my chin, and somehow, though my legs were wobbly from exertion and fear, I managed to stride across the concrete without my cane to the braided cord rug. I lowered myself into the recliner.

"Who is Kathleen?" Jane asked at last. Goose bumps swarmed the backs of my arms. Abbie hadn't told her after all.

"Oh, it's a baby book," Kelsey said. "Let me look?"

"Who is Kathleen?" Jane repeated.

"She's your baby sister." My throat ached from the strain of these foreign words on my voice box.

Jane and Kelsey gaped. This wasn't how my daughter was supposed to find out. I was to have lovingly told her my story and led her by the hand to the truth.

"I'm totally confused," Kelsey said.

Jane just sat there, in shock, I supposed. I got up and joined them on the couch, Kelsey scooting to one end, giving me the middle.

Jane had turned no further than to the album's first page. It read "My Name Is," and the name filled in the blank was Kathleen Sylvia Glenn. The middle name she would recognize as my mother's first. Dennis's and my names and the baby's birthdate were just as I'd hand-written them in ink, wobbly, more than sixty years before. My mind was frantic with what to say next.

"Mom?" Kelsey said, straining to see Jane, concern creeping into her face.

Jane closed the album. She ran her fingertips over the padded cover of satin in baby-girl pink with whimsical letters in baby-boy blue and pictures of frolicking little white lambs. The corners of the cover were frayed, and the underlying cardboard poked out at their tips. The book's title was embossed: *The Story of Our Baby*. She opened the cover back up, and the book spread to the center pages, which emitted scents of another age. Old, weathered paper from the early 1950s.

"But, Grandma, I don't get it. You gave birth to two babies?"

"Yes. Another daughter, sixteen months younger than Jane. She only lived about three hours." There. I'd told them one of the hardest parts, and my heart tapped a beat in awaiting a response.

Kelsey's hand came to her neck. "I'm so sorry this happened to you. And to poor Papaw."

"I don't believe this," Jane said. Her lips were dry and gray.

"Why don't you believe it?" Kelsey said.

Jane was eyeing me as she spoke about me in third person. "I just don't believe Mom and Daddy never told me."

I didn't know how to respond. Kelsey was speechless, too, and that was unheard of.

"Is this why you hated my clay baby in a basket?" Jane said.

"Oh, Jane, honey. I didn't hate it. I, I—"

"This is the last thing I expected to learn today," Jane said with a mirthless laugh and threw up her hands. "Huh. First of all, this week I learn I may have cancer. And now, I learn my parents kept something so fundamental from me? I had a sister. I mean, I'm . . . well, I'm . . ." She struggled to find the right word. "I'm flabbergasted. And to think, all the way back from Georgia in the car, driving for eleven hours, the things primary in my mind were how I was going to be a grandmother—and how I would first try to reconcile with you."

She had hugged me on the sidewalk in front of my house on the day she'd returned, awkward but long. She'd brought me oranges. We'd come so close . . .

180

"Why on earth did you not tell me I had a sister?"

Jane's face was red. Mine felt hot, too. My fear was coming to fruition. My secrets were coming out. They'd soon know what I'd done. Kelsey got up and went over to put her arms around her mom. I felt cruel. Abandoned.

I couldn't lose Jane over this; if I did, I'd lose them both.

"I hate that you had to learn about your sister this way," I said. "I was going to tell you today, I promise I was." I clasped my ancient hands together. "I'm sorry. In the past I was always too weak to go through with telling you. Losing a child was the worst thing that ever happened to me. The longer time went on, the harder it was to bring it up to you."

Kelsey said, "More babies died back then. It wasn't unusual for families never to speak of great loss."

Jane shook her head. "Thank you for that historical footnote. But I just can't believe I had a sister. *I* had a sister who died." She looked utterly forlorn—the slump of her shoulders, the large blackness of her pupils, the limpness of her lips. "I'm sad for you and Daddy," she said. "I'm sad for me."

"I'm sad for you, too, honey," I said in barely more than a whisper, for my throat ached so badly. "More than anything."

I couldn't decipher what else was swimming through my daughter's head. How had I thought for one stupid second that this revelation would bring us closer?

Jane tossed the album on the couch and stood up. "I have to go. I can't deal with this now."

"Mom?" Kelsey stood, too. "I can see how hard this is for you. Can you begin to imagine how hard the loss was for Grandma? Can't you stay, just a bit longer?" She held Jane's arm tenderly.

Jane sighed with the full weight of her world. "I have to go. We'll talk later."

"There's more to this, Jane," I said abruptly, and I caught a pleading lilt in my voice. "Much more. Please let me explain."

She looked at me as if considering, her gaze as intense as that of an executioner assessing a convict strapped in an electric chair. Then her eyes shifted. Jane kissed her daughter, crossed the room, and ascended the stairs without as much as a backward glance my way.

There was no taking back what I'd said today. She'd already found the album.

"Grandma," Kelsey said softly. I'd forgotten she was still there. "You know Mom. She'll work this out. She'll be back."

Sweet, sweet Kelsey. She'd said the precise words she knew I craved to hear. Too bad I doubted the truth of them.

"There's more," I told her. "If only Jane would listen to me."

"I'll go to her," Kelsey said.

I'd have to tell them both the rest. I'd have to tell them what came next.

If I could.

CHAPTER FIFTEEN

May 1951

It was a lovely spring morning, the finest kind with sunshine and bird-song and air thick with lilac. The "good ol' Kentucky bluegrass," as Dennis called it, lay like wall-to-wall carpeting on the ground between our house and a small copse of oaks in our backyard. He liked to mow the grass on the diagonal. The roots of the sod had taken to the soil, and its seams were no longer visible.

The Glenns thought we'd made progress. In the two months since our baby died, Dennis had put up more houses, sold more lots. We visited the farm. But the family must've overlooked the bags beneath my eyes. I often slept with fitful dreams. I'd managed to get dressed, do most chores, though. Dennis would kiss my cheek when he came home each night to a warm meal. We would talk about the news . . . the Rosenbergs' sentencing, President Truman, or the Lassie movie that we hadn't seen. I cried less. And I continued caring for Janie—the bright spot in my life. That and knowing Dennis and I would try again for another baby once my body healed enough to be intimate again.

But today was my first Mother's Day since losing my daughter. I could hardly savor the glorious springtime.

Dennis handed me a card as we sat in the backyard. He smiled. I slipped my thumbnail under the envelope's sealed flap and removed a pretty pink card laced with purple butterflies and white doves. "For My Beloved Wife . . ."

I kissed him. He smiled again. He was so considerate. "Thank you," I said. I was grateful he was trying.

Then he got Janie to hand me a second envelope. Her card read, "For the Best Mommy in the World," and my eyes welled up. I didn't think I deserved that. Not after what I'd done or hadn't done in carrying Kathleen. Dennis had held Janie's hand while she traced in blue crayon inside, "I love you."

The two cooked me breakfast—oatmeal and eggs sunny-side up. "Delicious," I mumbled, nibbling on a bite of toast with blackberry jam. Though I tried to hide it from Dennis, because he'd been so thoughtful, it was one of the hardest meals I'd ever eaten. Thank goodness, at a year and a half old, Janie was too young to understand what this day meant or my reaction to it.

Neither Dennis nor I mentioned Kathleen the entire day. I wished he would have. Until now he would settle into dark, quiet periods, but he'd never even said her name.

⌐

The Thursday following, Pauline and I had planned a quiet day. Raggsie was chasing squirrels, and Janie and Pauline's Tommy were cackling as they watched. The toddlers were best friends like Pauline and me. The four of us whiled away the morning in the peacefulness of our quarter-acre lots. The Irvings had bought the lot beside ours and built a larger Gunnison model.

"Neighbors forever, whether you like it or not." That was Pauline. I did like it.

The children set to playing in Janie's sandbox, the one with two benches her daddy had built. A gate with a metal latch connected the parklike setting of our backyard, which Raggsie thought was doggie paradise, and the Irving backyard, which would soon become a resort. Bob had drawn up plans for a pool—the only pool I'd heard of to belong to real people, not movie stars. We Glenns were adding a bonfire pit. Pauline had it all planned out. I'd bring the suntan lotion in the summer. She'd bring the marshmallows come fall.

"Janie, no, no, be careful," I said, popping up from my lounge chair as if I'd never had surgery and sloshing iced tea on my lap.

"Tommy, slow down, sweetie," Pauline said. "Janie can't go as fast as you."

At eighteen months old, my tomboy daughter had ridden her first pony at the farm with her grandpa hanging on. She'd performed crooked somersaults with her cousins. And whatever Tommy Irving did, she tried it, too. But he was two months older. Now he was walking the bench of the sandbox as if it were a tightrope. Janie tried to stand on the bench, perilously.

"Be careful," I yelled, and Janie tumbled to the ground six inches below. I ran to her side and lifted her to her feet. "Are you okay, are you okay?" My mind raced, and I imagined how, if she were injured, there would be an ambulance with lights and sirens to come steal her away to a hospital. My heart was pounding, pounding. "You could've broken your leg." But Janie wasn't even crying. She was laughing. She was squirming to get loose and play with her friend again.

"She's fine, Millie. She's fine." Pauline's soothing voice was reassuring, but her face showed concern at my reaction.

The children were soon playing again as if nothing were amiss. My primal instinct to save Janie was undeniable. But I had overreacted as usual. Who could blame me after what I'd been through?

My pulse was still in high gear when Pauline said, "You just wait. By the time these kids are twelve, Janie will shoot up and be taller than Tommy. She'll kick his hind end and never look back."

This was her attempt to make me smile. I couldn't get through a day without smiling if Pauline had anything to do with it. The day before, she'd said, "Just think, our two kids can get married one day, and you and I will be in-laws. I won't even hold it against you for being mother of the bride and getting your pick of dress color first." The day before that, she related the latest antics of Abbott and Costello, since I hadn't made it to the theater in months. Years before, I hadn't foreseen what a wonder Pauline was beneath all her pizzazz. Or until two months ago I hadn't looked. If she cooked a pot of stew, she made enough to share with my family. If she ran to the grocery, she picked up Prell shampoo for me. And the best thing she did was listen—whether it was to my bemoaning how my stretch marks and scar itched or how I would wake up at three in the morning thinking I'd heard an infant crying but it had not been Janie. Venting to Pauline meant Dennis got less of an earful.

"Bob's coming home early," Pauline said now. "Gonna meet with the pool guy."

I was still shaken over Janie's tumble but had to act as if all were well. "That means you serve dinner early?"

"That means I go out for a while, *sans* my son. Want to come? Bob can watch over them both."

Allow Janie out of my sight for an hour, two? In the care of cowboy Bob Irving? No way.

"You need a break," Pauline said. "We'll tucker the kids out before we go. They'll camp out on a blanket on the floor."

"But—"

"You pick the destination. Shillito's for dresses? Selby Grao's for shoes?" She fingered her hair, strawberry blonde from the beauty parlor—unlike mine, which had a cold wave perm but no added color.

"No, I couldn't." I would worry too much about Janie's safety while I was out being frivolous. I couldn't let her out of my sight.

"Millicent," Pauline said, taking on her drill sergeant manner. "I'm a firm believer that if you do what's best for yourself, you'll be better able to care for your daughter."

She was a smart cookie. If we went, I'd become a better mother. Truth was, for days I'd been pining inside to go somewhere particular. I hadn't told anyone, not even Dennis.

"Well. My pick?" I sucked in a big breath. "The cemetery."

The look that crossed Pauline's face was sad, but she consented. Anything I needed, anything at all, she was there for me.

In the hospital after the tragedy, no one but immediate family had been allowed to visit, but I'd insisted Pauline could come. My recovery room—a room at the end of a long hall, far away from new mothers having their infants brought to them every four hours for feedings—was filled with vases of flowers, all white roses. Mother Glenn had told me the meaning of those: purity, innocence, sympathy. After Janie's birth, by contrast, the bouquets had burst with pink carnations. Pauline had come into my room after my loss and gently lowered herself onto the bed beside me. She'd brought a box of Brach's chocolate-covered cherries. She'd smelled of spring rain and lavender soap, and she'd held my hand. A tear trailed down her cheek as she said, "If I were going to live only one day, I would thank God if you were my mother." This was the unforgettable loyalty of a true friend.

Today Pauline would drive me to the gravesite. She would know to stay in the car so I could be alone.

I needed to tell my younger daughter goodbye—without Dennis present. He'd had his turn, his solitude. He'd found the plot. He'd selected the tiny casket. He'd presided over the family memorial while I lay in a bed with plastic sheets beneath the linens and tubes pumping morphine through holes in my arms. He'd overseen the burial, too, with the steadfast determination of a man who knew his contractors, knew his soil, and knew his tools. He'd done what he must; he'd had no choice. But he'd gotten to say goodbye.

He had saved something for me, though, and for that I loved him dearly. I'd had the honor of choosing Kathleen's headstone.

A week after my discharge—the week after I'd forced Dennis to remove the red womb chair—I selected granite at the Schott Monument Company. The stone was sparkly gray, a tiny slab with flush-pink undertones. I'd wrestled with the final wording. How could I express on so small a stone our enduring love for this child? The child I'd never had the privilege of seeing, let alone holding? Today would be the first time I steeled myself enough to view the stone in its forever place.

I climbed out of Pauline's car, and rays of light warmed my face, a blessing from the skies. I was glad I'd taken a pill to calm my nerves. It was a comfort to me to have them handy; I took one pill just a day or two a week. The trees and the grass and the sky were pretty here today.

One thing was true, what they say: the sun does rise every day.

Pauline said, "Just wave if you need me."

I took small steps at first, slowly through the grass, afraid to look too far ahead. I walked between large stones and modest ones that marked where women had lost loved ones since long before I was born. A dog barked in the distance. The tires of another car crunched over gravel in the lane behind me. As I came nearer to the knoll where I knew Kathleen to rest—in the section of the cemetery where children were buried—my pace grew more determined.

Her marker appeared smaller in the ground than it had in the mason's shop, so tiny compared to adult headstones—flat and flush on the ground, a fringe of green grass framing it. The sun had gone behind a cloud, and when it peeped back out, the pink undertones of the stone I had picked sparkled even more than I'd hoped they would. I smiled. Then a wail escaped my throat so swiftly and with such force I hadn't felt it coming.

I fell to my knees before my daughter's grave and brushed my fingers across the granite, smooth but for where each letter was etched:

KATHLEEN SYLVIA GLENN

B. MARCH 23, 1951 D.
OUR PRECIOUS BABY

Was it all my doing that this child was buried? That her condition, the one that started with an *E*, had taken root in my womb while I carried her? Was it that I'd selfishly insisted on spreading myself too thin, as my sister-in-law warned? "This is a wonderful time in a woman's life," Abbie had said during one of my pregnancies. "Children and home-making should be your only priorities."

Whatever I'd done or not done in carrying my baby to term, one thing was certain: I would never forgive myself for the outcome.

As I treaded back to Pauline's car, a wind blew and the high tops of the oak trees rustled. I climbed into the sedan, beaten.

"You mustn't take responsibility for losing her," Pauline said quietly before starting the engine. "You told me once how when you were young, your opa explained that in German, your name Millicent means strength. He was right, you know."

How had I forgotten that? Had I remembered it lately, I'd have thought he was wrong.

CHAPTER SIXTEEN

September 1951

It was the Labor Day holiday, the official end of summer, and Janie bounced in her stroller with her stuffed Donald Duck toy. Older children at the festival smiled and waved at her as they passed. Janie waved back. Dennis's whole family had her spoiled, but I was glad of it.

It'd been five months since our loss, and I was getting better now—at least I was sleeping through most nights and being more productive during the day, though I hadn't resumed my beloved paperwork for the business. I wasn't ready for that, especially if it were to mean a battle to convince Dennis. I still didn't get out much either, but I'd not had a single pill since the weekend before. I was counting the months till my body was recovered enough so Dennis and I could "try again." My husband was anxious to make love, but I was more anxious to make a baby. He was cautious with my emotions across the board, not wanting to set me off, I supposed. Or else he continued to guard his own feelings the way Fort Knox guarded gold. He went to work. He came home for dinner. He manicured the yard. He played with Janie. He helped out around the house. He told me he loved me, said I was the prettiest girl a guy ever got; I said he was the most charming guy a girl ever snagged.

I believed it, too, but I knew there was less enthusiasm in our voices than there'd been in the carefree days.

Yet today promised to be a fun family outing. At close to two years old, Janie was excited because she recognized the words *ice cream*. We were headed to Graeter's.

Dennis had said it was a nice day for a jaunt—and he'd urged me to make a go of it. He had chosen Cincinnati's Hyde Park, where the ice cream shop was decades old. Shop owners on the square had hung red, white, and blue banners and bunting. Small flags on sticks lined the green grass along the walks. Hyde Park's convertibles were out in droves, their chrome bumpers glistening in the sun. The aromas from vendors ranged from Belgian waffles to chocolate fudge, while many people milled about with their children and pedigreed dogs in every breed from German shepherds to Great Danes. No one had mutts like our Raggsie at home, so named for how he looked like a pile of old rags. In the cutest sort of way.

Everything was beautiful and lively and gay. It'd been a good decision to come.

Our little family stood beside the historic fountain, where droplets of water caught Janie's face and she laughed. Dennis twisted the stroller and headed to the other side of the square while making silly sounds with his cheeks. Janie giggled. How I loved her giggles.

She was so innocent. She had no idea what had befallen her parents—neither the tragic loss nor how we walked on eggshells, each in our own subtle way . . . Dennis never saying Kathleen's name. My feeling intrusive when asking about the business. His acting as if all were well. My protecting Janie as if my life depended on it—my guilt for how I'd carried Kathleen making me vigilant: tying Janie's shoestrings in double knots so she wouldn't trip if they loosened, not letting her have lollipops for fear she'd choke and die.

We would tell her one day, of course, that she'd had a sister. But that wouldn't come until after she had another sibling. I was glad she got to experience her young life carefree, without knowing the bruise of loss. Except for Pauline, none of our family or friends spoke of Kathleen, at least not in our presence. Not even the Glenns. If tragedy existed, it might come too close to them. It might rub off. I thought they feared becoming targets when nature's ax made its next random slice through the world. Or they knew they too could stumble, make a heinous mistake, and suffer the consequences. Dennis, on the other hand, thought they were all merely being nice, didn't want to be nosy, didn't want to upset me again, didn't want to make me cry.

Thank God for Pauline. She let me be me.

"There's a bee, Mil," Dennis said. "Don't move." His grandad had taught him how to avoid being stung: stand like a statue, even if the bee lands on you. I'd learned the hard way on the farm. I'd flailed my arms and got stung on my elbow. Mother Glenn had stirred up a poultice of water and baking soda to draw the poison from my sting. I'd stood still around bees ever since.

Yet when this one started buzzing too close to my precious daughter's tender head with her crop of downy-fine hair, I started swatting at it. What species of bee was that anyway? It looked monstrous to me, like a prehistoric creature in furry black and yellow.

"Stop, Millie, you're going to agitate—"

"I can't just stand here and let Janie get stung, can I?"

My voice was much higher than Dennis's, and other families turned our way. But caring mothers like me couldn't just stand around doing nothing. Bad things happened to children. Children needed protecting. That's what mothers were for.

The bee flew off, and I breathed heavily with relief. I thought I'd saved Janie, but Dennis said it had flown off of its own accord. But all the fuss had made Janie wail. Dennis frowned. *See what you did?*

"But Janie was—"

"She's fine," Dennis said flatly.

If I had a dime for every time someone said those two words to me, *she's fine*, I'd have been a rich woman. As justified as I felt in my response with the bee attack, I knew intellectually there was only one thing for me to do. This day could slide into the abyss, or we could pick back up where we began and have fun. It was my responsibility as wife to see that we rallied.

"Daddy says it's time for ice cream." I tried to rein them both back in. "You scream, I scream, we all scream for ice cream."

Dennis stared at me, mystified. How could I be cheerful one minute and a wreck the next? And then cheerful again?

I tried teasing Janie with the ducky, making quacking noises and bringing his rubber beak to her cheeks, and going on and on about "banilla" ice cream, as she called it. But she was having none of it. She whined and looked at me like I was the danger instead of the bee. I had pangs of guilt, feeling like a failure as a mother. Had I packed my pills?

We walked the length of both sides of Erie Avenue, the three of us. We offered polite hellos to passersby. Peeped into windows of shops mindlessly. Commented on how hungry we were getting, whether it was true or not. The only change after a time was that Janie quieted, distracted by a clown and balloons and boys laughing.

At Graeter's we settled into the parlor chairs atop the tiny octagonal black-and-white tiles. Dennis spooned nibbles of vanilla ice cream into Janie's mouth. He was good with her. Minutes before, she'd twisted her head back and forth and pursed her lips when I'd tried to feed her. Now as Dennis extended a bite, she swallowed it and then bobbed up and down and opened her mouth again like a hatchling awaiting a worm. Perhaps Janie had come to prefer Daddy more often. I wasn't sure what to think of that. Did she sense my grieving more than she did his? Of course, she would. She spent many more hours with me. Dennis sipped on his malted milk through a straw, for it was easier than holding a cone the way I was doing with my melting black raspberry chocolate chip, the flavor that'd made Graeter's famous.

I had just reached the edge of the cone and was biting around its soft, chewy rim to get to the crunchy part when someone at a table in the middle of the shop caught my eye. The place was bustling with families, so I had to lean left and narrow my eyes to view her better.

Yes. It was her. That beauty mark above her lip.

My face flushed. Nurse Breck rose and made her way toward the restroom.

"I need to use the ladies' room." I grabbed my purse and told Dennis I'd be right back.

Nurse Breck was washing her hands, alone, in the small restroom with two stalls and one sink. She smiled at my image in the mirror.

"Nurse Breck?"

She spun, and the full circular cotton skirt of her red-and-white checked dress swished into place beneath her knees. How tiny her waist was, accentuated by a slim red plastic belt. She had the air of one who'd been born here in Hyde Park, not down in the city's basin like me, and not on a farm. How different she looked without her pressed white uniform and nurse's cap.

"Nurse Breck," I said again. Then she recognized me. Color rose in her neck.

This woman had seen my Kathleen alive. She had covered my hand with hers. *Mrs. Glenn, these are the most difficult words I've ever had to speak. Your baby, your daughter, hasn't survived.*

"Please, call me Carolyn," she said. But there was distance.

"Carolyn." I found it hard to call her by her given name anyway. She'd been my nurse. I wadded the napkin from my cone in my fist. I'd carried it with me.

"How are you, Mrs. Glenn?"

"Please." I bit my lip, feeling a tad out of place. "I'm sorry to intrude on your day, but—but I have to ask. Did you hear about the conclusion regarding our daughter's death?"

She looked away to toss her paper towel. "Investigations are standard procedure," she said.

Another patron entered and squeezed past us, into a stall.

"Do you by chance know anything more?" I said quickly. I told her how I'd read the description of the baby's condition in the book at the library. Nurse Breck might suspect the specific cause—such as inflammation from a virus when I carried the baby. I had to know how to prevent the condition from occurring again. She could help me.

"How can I improve my prenatal care so my next baby is healthy?"

She started. There was something in the manner in which the nurse looked away that suggested there was indeed something she knew, but she didn't answer. Dennis was waiting with Janie. I had to get back, but first I had to know.

"Anything? At all?" My eyes implored her.

"Mrs. Glenn, I don't think—"

"Please," I said more softly. "Sometimes I lie awake unable to stop thinking it was my fault." A toilet flushed. "I need to know before I try again to have a baby."

"Well, perhaps you could call me." Her cheeks looked feverish, as though the instant the words came from her lips, she regretted having released them. Before she could change her mind, I'd shuffled around for a pen in my pocketbook and pushed it into her hand. Nurse Breck jotted her number on my napkin. I slipped it into my purse.

2015

Today I was alone. I was in the back seat of a taxi with my purse in my lap. Tiny heat vents put out little warmth for all the racket they made. I hated not driving myself—hated going to the cemetery at all—but I couldn't be behind a wheel. Not today. It was supposed to be the day of Jane's biopsy. We hadn't spoken since she learned she had a sister and walked out of my house without saying goodbye. I had telephoned her twice and left messages, but she'd not called back.

I'd spent three days fretting, distressed that I had thrust Jane and me back into our near estrangement, just when we'd been getting close.

Kelsey and I had both been set to go to Jane's appointment today no matter what. Forty-five minutes before she was to pick Jane up, and then come by for me, she got a call from Jane. The electric company had been working on lines in the vicinity of the breast center, a tree had gone down, and service was disrupted in the surrounding area. By the time the crew expected service to be restored, Jane would miss her appointment. If the center was able to operate at all the rest of the afternoon, remaining slots were already booked. Jane was forced to reschedule for four days later.

Another long, agonizing wait for us all.

There I'd been, all ready to go, anxious to see Jane, ready a half hour early, my heart and my head and my gut tied in knots, unsure of Jane's future, unsure of ours. When the appointment was canceled, I threw my cane crashing to the kitchen floor.

I had let my temper subside and touched Jane's speed-dial number. It rang. Once. Twice. It rang five times in total and went straight to her voice mail. I hung up. She'd see a missed call and reach out if she wanted. But she'd made it clear she didn't.

This was what I had coming. What I deserved. I hadn't slept. I thought: *I should have said this, I should have said that. I shouldn't have said this, I shouldn't have said that.* Every scenario of the day in my basement plagued my waking hours. The only variance from that was: *How would Jane's biopsy turn out? What would we say when we finally encountered each other? How would I fix us?*

I had to visit Dennis.

"Ma'am, where should I let you out?" said the cabbie.

I was here. I'd been in a daze as we passed through the cemetery's ornamental wrought-iron gates. "This is good." I paid the man an extra twenty dollars to wait.

I secured my head scarf around my neck and slipped on my gloves. The man helped me climb out. He supported my elbow while I got my bearings with my cane on the gravel path.

"Thank you, young man," I said.

"I had a grandma once," he said, kindly. He trudged back to the yellow car, already entranced by the cell phone in his hand.

Clouds shifted in front of the sun's face, throwing shadows and light all around me. I looked from the bend in the gravel path to the gardener's brick house, the oaks and black birches and blue ashes— trees spreading their wings along the knoll. I looked down now to my husband's marker, to the dates of Dennis's birth and death—life's two most notable events—though the stone was silent, giving no hint of all that'd happened in between. On this stone was also engraved my name, Millicent Marion Glenn, and my birthdate. There was a blank spot, as well, for the future date of my death. The space had been there many years. Only now did seeing this blank space scare me.

I wasn't ready. I had much left to do.

The autumn breeze tugged at the sleeves of my car coat and the cuffs of my slacks. I couldn't smell the honeysuckles this time of year. The graveyard was quiet but for squirrels shimmying through leaves and sparrows singing. Not even the groundkeepers were out this morning. Good.

"Dennis," I said as if he were still here. "Jane's come home. We've been trying to patch things up. But now she knows—she knows about Kathleen." My throat seized. I had to wait until its cords let go of their grip. I pulled a pack of tissues from my purse.

"Jane's hurting. She doesn't know the rest yet, about what Nurse Breck said. What I've realized in these last days is I can't go on keeping it all bottled up anymore." Tears dribbled down my cheeks. "I can't hold it in, especially without you here." Especially, I thought, with Pauline gone, too.

"And now Jane's sick." I choked out my words between sobs. No matter what transpired beyond or within our control, Dennis and I had stayed together. We'd made a life. We'd loved each other to the end. "And we're to have a great-grandchild. I wish you were here. I miss you so badly."

I cried and heaved, leaving tissue upon tissue in ruins, shuddering, until I stopped.

"I don't know how, but I'm going to see this through, Dennis. I'm going to bring this family together for good. I won't be back here until I do."

I kissed the pads of my damp fingers and then pushed their tips to the cold granite, letting them remain for a time. It was the way I could be closest to Dennis.

Next, I went up the knoll to where my baby had been buried in the children's section, six decades before. And I told her she had an older sister who loved her.

Kelsey FaceTimed me from work the next day.

It'd taken three tries last summer for me to learn how that mobile app thing worked on my iPhone. But Kelsey had been a patient teacher. Soon I'd enjoyed watching her as if she were on TV. Now I still wore my flannel gown, my robe, and furry slippers. My eyes were puffy, and my joints ached something awful. I would do some stretching, but I was too tired to attend water aerobics.

On the screen of my cell phone, Kelsey talked between bites. She was eating a salad for lunch in her office. It looked to me like she had dark rings beneath her eyes. She was tired, too. Tired from watching her mother and grandmother have a world war on top of her mother's health scare. Not to mention being pregnant.

Fear struck my heart: What if, while Jane and I were busy alienating each other, we caused something bad to happen to Kelsey? I could not under any circumstances shoulder the guilt of something happening to that girl. Or her baby.

"I tore this lettuce just the way you taught me, Grandma—first bang the core end of the head one time on the counter, as hard as I can, and then remove the core." She was determined to go on through this call as if nothing were happening around her.

I'd humor her for a while. "That's exactly how your great-grandma Glenn taught me the first time I came to the farm. Except that she added that removing the core was like extracting a tooth from a child's gum."

"I've thought a lot about what happened to you losing the baby," Kelsey said suddenly.

"We need to focus on yours," I said with a knee-jerk reaction. I had enjoyed our conversation being light. "How is the baby?"

"Kicking. A lot," she said. She stood to model her tummy for the phone. "Might have an athlete on my hands here." We should have giggled there but couldn't. "I want you to know, your story is helping me put things in perspective." She returned to the topic being me.

"Oh?"

"I'm leaning more and more toward a midwife, because I want you and Mom to be present at the birth, with Aaron and me."

Knowing Kelsey, this was her way of being a peacemaker, of trying to bring us back together. Did they even do that these days, have a roomful?

"Are you sure?" I said.

"Yes, and Aaron has come around to the idea of a midwife. He's all in."

"What'd he say?"

"At first, he said maybe there's a reason that babies don't die as often as they did two centuries ago. Because there is better medical care." Kelsey held my gaze; we both knew that was debatable. "He asked if I was going to hire a wet nurse, too."

"He was kidding, right?"

"Yeah, being sarcastic. But he did some research on the whole thing himself, and it's raised questions on hospital maternity care in his mind as well. Finally, he said that my comfort level was the number one priority in our birth going well. So I'll decide."

I smiled into my cell phone screen. "You got a good one. And I'm honored that you would ask me to be present at the birth."

I would make sure nothing bad happened to that baby, even if Jane and I didn't speak a word through every contraction.

"You and Mom mean the world to me." Did her voice crack?

"You're a good girl," I said, and my heart fluttered.

I was dying to ask about Jane, but it'd gotten me nowhere with Kelsey the last few days. She'd just say, "You know Mom." Poor Kelsey, always stuck in the middle.

"And how are you feeling?" I asked. "Any cravings?"

"Thankfully, no. I have another checkup next week. But I have put on a couple more pounds." Kelsey pinched her nonexistent love handles.

"I can't see it on you," I said. I became more sober. "How's your mom?" I'd asked anyway. I couldn't help it.

"Three more days until we know something on her breast. Given the circumstances, I think she's doing okay. She's coming to terms about Kathleen, too. You'll see, Grandma."

If that were the case, why hadn't Kelsey begun this call with that headline? Why hadn't Jane answered her phone?

Kelsey blew me kisses, and despite my reservations, my spirits couldn't help but lift as I caught each one.

I needed to reach out to Jane. Texting was a challenge—holding the phone at the same time I typed with one crooked, shaky finger—but I'd try that instead of calling.

I texted: Hi, how are you doing today?

I waited. I did light stretches for my arms, back, and legs, the same moves I'd done with Jack LaLanne during his exercise show in the 1950s. I poured a cup of coffee. I tuned into my favorite TV cooking programs, which I couldn't pay attention to. By the time they were over, an hour had passed.

How long would Jane's silent treatment last? Surely she didn't think we'd go the rest of our lives without hashing everything out. Should I text again? Try calling? Should I just settle down because she was probably taking a bath? I lowered the volume on the TV, reclined on the couch, and rested my head on a plump, fringed pillow. When I roused from a catnap another hour later, I saw that Jane had responded.

Jane: I went for a walk in the park.

Eight little words. I'd never been so relieved to read a message in all my life. There was hope.

Me: Good, good.

Jane: We'll get together soon.

I wanted to print and frame this message and tape it to my fridge. I wanted to ask when, where? But I dared not push Jane. We'd made progress. I might even get two hours' sleep that night.

Me: You're going to get through this.

Maybe we both would get through this. I would do everything in my power to make it so.

CHAPTER SEVENTEEN

September 1951

I should have kept my trap shut about Nurse Breck.

"Mil, you aren't seriously considering calling her?" Dennis said between drags off his cigarette. He'd laid out his clothes for the day on our bed. "You've got to put this to rest."

"But—"

"Don't you think I suffer too? My God, I've never been through anything so wrenching as these last months. But I know that you and Janie have to eat. It's my responsibility to earn a living. Put food on the table. So I keep my lips zipped, and earn I do."

I was shocked into silence. He'd called his experience "wrenching." So it wasn't just my agony alone.

Yet his further meaning was clear: I had my responsibilities, too. I needed to move forward, avoid going backward. He trailed me to the kitchen.

"You're right," I said to be amenable. "I don't know that I can bear to hear whatever the nurse says anyway."

"This nurse—Breck, is it?" Dennis said, spotting her number on the napkin on the counter. "I remember her. She was nice to me on the ward. But here's the thing: no matter what, it can't bring Kathy back."

I started. This was the first time he'd spoken our daughter's name since she died. The nickname I'd given her, at that. It bowled me over: he'd said her name I'd longed to hear. That was forward progress for him. I wouldn't go backward. I was a good mother to Janie. A good wife. I wasn't perfect after all, but I'd work harder to show Dennis Glenn how well I performed my duties. And I didn't even need a pill to prove it.

"You're right," I said. "It won't bring Kathy back." I exhaled, realizing I'd been holding my breath.

He wadded up the napkin with its black raspberry ice cream stains and Nurse Breck's number and threw it into the kitchen trash bin.

The next morning I arose early and served pancakes for breakfast. For Janie's, I made a smiley-face pancake. I dolloped batter, a teaspoonful at a time, onto the hot buttered griddle, placing the dollops in the position where two eyes and a curved mouth would be. Once those bits cooked to a toasty brown, I poured a ladle of more batter carefully over top in the shape of a nice, round flapjack. When I flipped it over, the face was visible on top as the underside batter sizzled. Janie adored smiley-face pancakes, and if she was a good girl and wore her bib without fussing, she got her own tiny pitcher to drizzle Aunt Jemima over the bites that she'd eat with her fingers—although Janie's drizzle was more like a downpour.

When she beckoned, working her fingers for me to bend over and give her kisses, I did, with bliss, and I didn't mind that she got sticky maple syrup in my hair.

~

It was ten a.m. and I held my pad and pencil, trying to scratch out a grocery list: bread, spinach, feminine toiletries. Another monthly period had arrived. I wanted to go nine months without one—I could hardly wait to try again to have another child. After the course of this cycle was past, it was time. I'd have clearance to be sexually active again.

That was one of two thoughts interrupting every hour of my day. That and the thought of calling Nurse Breck. I couldn't help it, no matter what I'd told Dennis; no matter how I'd thought I'd let the idea of calling the nurse pass, I was wrong.

Noon. Janie was in her high chair, and I fed her some Gerber baby peaches from a jar. She kept grabbing for the spoon. Mother Glenn had said that meant Janie was about ready to feed herself. So I poured the peaches into a small bowl.

"Here, sweetie-pie," I said, handing her the stubby, baby-size silver spoon. "Mommy's going to let you feed yourself."

In minutes her chubby cheeks were smeared orange, sticky clear to her hair—and runny peaches were splattered on her tray, on her bib, and on the floor—but she was living it up, and I was happy to let her. I usually had a damp rag in hand mopping every drop. Today I'd clean it later.

All I could think about was calling Nurse Breck.

By one thirty, when *Young Doctor Malone* came on the radio and Janie was entranced with her Buzzy Bee toy, my reminder of the day before when Janie almost got stung—the day I also discovered Nurse Breck—I couldn't stand it any longer. I had to know. I had to know what the nurse could tell me. I'd taken one pill, but it had little effect.

I imagined myself ancient—maybe ninety years old—in a semi-private room in a nursing home, wondering what had happened that March 23. Might I be lying listless on a disinfected mattress all alone, looking back on my life and asking: Why hadn't I placed the call?

No matter what I would learn by asking, I reasoned, surely knowing would be better than not knowing.

Nurse Breck might know what I'd done wrong when I was pregnant. Maybe I had overexerted myself with Janie, ingested too much salt, or not taken enough vitamins. And I continued to be plagued: What if Abbie had been right? What if my work with Gunnison Homes had impaired my child's health in my womb? If Nurse Breck told me that any of my actions had affected the baby—anything leading to brain damage, to the big word that started with an *E*—I would be racked by more guilt.

But I would know better how to go through my next pregnancy. I'd find out on behalf of the next child.

I jerked open the cabinet door under the sink to get the trash. I had to have that Graeter's ice cream napkin. Damn. Dennis had taken the wastebasket out while I was getting Janie dressed. Janie was toddling around the living room now, but she'd be okay for a minute. I ran in my house slippers out the back door, letting the screen door slam behind me. I charged through the breezeway to the garage and attacked the large metal bin. I threw off the lid, letting it clang on the concrete floor. The garbage crew was due the next day, so the container was rank with week-old chicken scraps and days-old spilt milk. I opened the bag, the one recently deposited on top, and was greeted with a sticky mess— remnants of our scraped-off breakfast plates with syrup and pancakes and fried sausage grease.

I dug deeper into the next-to-last layer of refuse. I hoped I'd find that wadded-up Graeter's napkin, and if I did, that Nurse Breck's number would be legible. I dug and I dug. There, there it was, between the clean side of butcher's paper and a strip of aluminum foil.

I yanked the small wad out, gingerly unfolded it, held up my thigh, and flattened the napkin against it. Yes, I could read it. Was the second number a one or a seven? The last digit was faded (a three? an eight?). I'd try every numerical combination.

Oh my gosh, Janie. I crammed the trash back into its bin, slammed the lid on, and ran.

~

When I returned to Janie, she was sitting on her knees on the floor in her bedroom, flipping the pages of *Goodnight Moon*, mumbling, pretending to read it to herself. What a good little girl. She was fine. My heartbeat evened out. In recent days she had started tugging on her own socks. Now she was feeding herself with a spoon. Brushing her own hair, sort of. She would be grown before we knew it.

I tried calling Nurse Breck twice—at least I'd concluded I had her number after getting it wrong a couple of times—and when no one answered, I took it as a warning that I was not to know the truth.

But something grabbed my heart and pushed it up my throat, urging me to try again the next day, when it was Pauline's morning to keep the babies.

One last try. I spun the rotary dial and crossed my fingers.

"Hello?" It sounded like her. The moment had arrived, but I couldn't speak.

"Hello? Anyone there?" she said.

"Nurse Breck? Carolyn?"

"Mrs. Glenn, is that you?"

"Yes," I said. Had I heard hesitation in her voice?

"I imagine you've called to learn more about that day in the hospital, but I'm afraid I'm having misgivings."

"I, well, but I must know, to help my next baby."

Silence.

"Please?"

"All right, all right. We can talk," she said, and my shoulders rose and fell. "But we should meet somewhere. Somewhere quiet."

Relief overtook me. "Eden Park, tomorrow?" It was the first place that popped into my head: public, but not crowded like a restaurant. No waitresses butting in. Nurse Breck or I could leave at any time. The art museum in the park was under renovations, and kids were back in school, so park visitors wouldn't overwhelm.

"Yes," she said. "Noon, at the gazebo." A hint in her voice made me fear she'd back out.

CHAPTER EIGHTEEN

September 1951

Eden Park overlooked the city and the Ohio River Valley from high atop Cincinnati's Mount Adams. The day was mildly breezy and warm. Pauline completely understood my plan and reasons for it, kept Janie with her, and dropped me off a few minutes before noon. I stood alone in the turn-of-the-century Spring House Gazebo, though a couple of bicyclists rode nearby. The gazebo had arches and scallops and ornamental spheres brought to life with paint of pale green and antique white. Inside I leaned against one of the pillars, remembering what had happened under this clay tile roof seven years before. Dennis Glenn had gotten down on one knee and proposed. It had been blistering cold that early December, but fluffy white flakes fell all around us, as if we were in a magical snow globe of our own making.

That day seemed forever ago. But there was a tiny, hidden piece of me that remembered that day, remembered what it was to be carefree. I reveled in it until reality came hurtling back.

After I'd changed my mind yesterday about meeting with Nurse Breck, I couldn't look Dennis in the eye during dinner, and I retired to bed early by claiming a headache. Deceiving him was not in my nature.

But meeting the nurse was something I had to do for myself—and for my next baby.

I checked my wristwatch every few seconds. Two minutes past twelve, three minutes past. No sign of Carolyn Breck. Would the maternity nurse leave me hanging?

"Mrs. Glenn?" I snapped to the sound of her voice behind me.

"Nurse Breck." We were both back to formalities. Perhaps it was easier that way. "Shall we walk?" I asked shyly. I would reserve this gazebo for only my happiest memories.

We headed out past Mirror Lake, the sun warming us.

"I love your outfit," she said.

"Thank you. And I yours."

I was casual in straight-legged cigarette pants with a large black-and-beige plaid. Tucked into my waist was a lightweight mock-turtleneck sweater. Nurse Breck looked like a debutante, attired in a double-breasted coat dress with French cuffs halfway to her elbows. Her red lipstick was accentuated by her beauty mark. To a few preschool-age children running races across the way or their mothers pushing babies in buggies, Nurse Breck and I must look like two old friends out for a stroll. But I was anxious to begin. I slid on some sunglasses. "Please," I said. "Don't keep me in suspense."

"Are you sure? This isn't going to be easy."

So it was worse than I'd thought. I'd done something unpardonable.

"Yes," I said. "Please tell me."

"All right. Part of the reason I'm here is because I want to disabuse you of any misconceptions you have. Put things straight. I genuinely care about your family."

I could feel the tension cross my brow.

She took a breath. "On the day of your daughter's birth, I'd come on shift at half past four. Nurses were in short supply, and I'd never seen the ward in such a bustle. The beds were full. A friend who worked the nursery said she'd fed more than twenty babies the night before, every four hours. But as my supervisor had said when I checked in, 'What are we supposed to do? Turn women away? They can't give birth in the streets.'"

"I recall I had to wait for a wheelchair to free up."

Nurse Breck turned to me and shielded the sun from her eyes with her hand. "It's best for you to understand, if there was one thing nursing students had drilled into their heads, it's that if they expect to be nurses and stay employed, they must comply with doctors' orders."

I nodded. I'd been privy to more than one nurse's deference to doctors.

"Nurses like Nurse Tibbers and I manage childbirth, from sedating patients to sorting instruments for deliveries. That doesn't count the few difficult cases, the operations. In all our work we're carrying out doctors' orders. We do not offer opinion. We do not question. We do not disobey."

I strode along, wondering why she was making such a point of this. The breeze caught a whiff of Nurse Breck's perfume then, sending citrus and floral notes my way. We continued to walk in our own little world. Young girls in pigtails played off in the distance; older men threw horseshoes, too far away to hear us.

"Nurse Tibbers prepared you for surgery. I started the IV and attached your monitors.

"Dr. Reynolds had been on call that night, and because the ward was so crowded, he had gotten the summons from Dr. Collins, your original OB. Dr. Reynolds didn't show until six o'clock, later than normal. His hair was mussed, his tie loose." Her steps picked up pace—I assumed they matched the rate of her heart or her need to have this tale over with. "He wasn't slurring his words, but I could tell before he masked up."

"You could tell what?"

After a runner went by, Nurse Breck said: "I could smell the alcohol on him from two feet away."

My body shook. "The doctor had been drinking?"

"Yes. Quite a bit, I think."

This was nothing I could have expected to hear. Doctors healed people. My mind felt frenzied. Was this why Nurse Breck had been reluctant to talk at first? Bile inched its way up my throat.

She pointed to a green-painted bench that had just freed up. "Shall we?" We proceeded to the shady spot, which was remote enough from other park guests. It felt good to sit down—to have something to catch me. And I could face Nurse Breck better as she spoke.

"Dr. Reynolds was moving slower than normal," she said. "I'd seen him this way on two prior occasions. Nurse Tibbers looked at me and without speaking, we both knew that we'd have to stay on our toes.

"He wasn't shaky when he made the vertical incision. He went in for your uterus and made that cut fine, too. I was relieved. But then he stalled. Sweat beaded on his forehead. He belched. I thought he might vomit. I didn't think he'd be able to finish."

She looked out over the vast expanse of lawn, now active with more young children in shorts and sneakers. What had the doctor done to me while I slept?

"What else?" I said, sounding more agitated than I intended.

"Your heartbeat was fine. All your vitals were normal. The doctor recovered and reached in. We were almost home. As he lifted your infant out, I could see it was a girl. She had her sweet little thumb in her mouth," Nurse Breck said, and then she hesitated, fidgeting with her purse strap. "You know, it's difficult for me to tell you this."

My daughter had sucked her thumb while she lived. If only I could smile at the picture this evoked. But I tasted the metal flint of blood in my mouth, unaware until then of how I'd been biting the insides of my cheeks. Perspiration had dampened my top, too.

I had to get through this. "Continue."

"Dr. Reynolds lifted the baby fully out, clamped and cut the umbilical cord, and held her up. And the baby slipped," Nurse Breck said. She looked straight at my frozen face. "She slipped from one of the doctor's hands, and he barely hung on with the other. But then he dropped the baby to the floor as he tightened his grip on her ankles."

I gasped, my hand at my mouth. I lost vision for several seconds, seeing only red and yellow spots propelling in front of my sunglasses.

"It was too late for us to do anything. Her little head hit the tiles, and then he pulled her back up by her ankles. He thought she was fine. He held her close to his chest like one of his own. Then he saw what I saw."

"He dropped her?" I said in scarcely a whisper. "You're saying he dropped her." Nurse Breck nodded. The doctor had done this to my baby. Had my baby's lungs let out a blood-curdling wail?

I bent over and retched in the grass with a hot, uncontrollable force. My glasses fell to the ground. I sat back up and smeared my mouth with the back of my hand—and then I bent over again, lower this time, and vomited until I choked only spit.

"Oh dear. What have I done?" Nurse Breck said all the while. She handed me a hanky now, and I wiped my mouth and cheeks on it, red lipstick marring its colorful embroidered butterflies, the taste of acid sharp on my tongue. "I should never have told you," she said.

She opened her large handbag and pulled out a short thermos of iced water and two small cups. She poured and handed one to me.

In the distance, old men continued playing horseshoes, and I shivered at the clang of iron on the stakes, their heavy thrust of metal on metal, the unrelenting ringing of it though far away from me, and the men's laughter, their joy, oblivious to my whole world crumbling.

Why had I selected this public place? But then, where was the right place to learn about the day your baby died? To learn of how a worthless drunkard of a doctor had killed her?

I needed my pills. And for the first time I needed more than one.

What the nurse and doctor had seen was what Dennis had later seen, what my husband had called an inflamed, swollen spot on Kathy's head. So the spot had not been part of a soft, misshapen head that occurred naturally as with other babies—our baby hadn't even squeezed through the birth canal. Nor was Kathy's spot the result of forceps.

"Tell me," I said. "Tell me the rest, and then I'll go." I would find my way back to the gazebo somehow, in time to meet Pauline. I needed to hold Janie. I really needed pills.

Nurse Breck drank from her thermos cup, her hand shaking. "I took her," she said, "the baby. Nurse Tibbers helped Dr. Reynolds get you back together. He seemed sober again, maybe from the shock. He finished the operation fine."

"My baby was still alive."

"Yes. She was beautiful. I washed her with the softest terry cloth and patted her tiny belly and arms and legs dry."

This woman got to do what I never got to do—wash my baby's skin, pat her dry. Hearing this was as hard as learning of the drop. I'd been robbed of my maternal rights over and over. But oddly, I didn't begrudge this woman. It gave me comfort that Kathy had received a kind touch. If only it had been mine.

"I wrapped her in one receiving blanket and then another," Nurse Breck said. "She wasn't hurting. She didn't cry for long."

Not for long?

"I let your husband hold her, you know, though it was against hospital rules. It was after I told you the baby was gone, and you'd been sedated in order to sleep."

No, no, no, I did not know that. Dennis hadn't told me he'd held her. My anguish was palpable, but I wouldn't humiliate myself by admitting I hadn't known.

"Afterward," she went on, "I went to the head nurse and said that Dr. Reynolds had been drunk. It didn't matter if I lost my job. I was riddled with guilt over not stopping him when he first arrived on shift. I hoped my supervisor would take it to the administration. But she called in Nurse Tibbers, who denied everything. Denied the alcohol, the drop, denied everything. She had her own children to support. She needed the job. She backed the doctor entirely."

I was incapable of speech. The pulsing red and yellow spots reappeared and blinded me for a moment.

Nurse Breck straightened her back, made her voice firm, and said, "In the medical profession, doctors are gods."

"It was all Dr. Reynolds's fault." My voice was little more than a squeak. "It was all Dr. Reynolds's fault."

Nurse Breck replaced the lid on the thermos and said, "I'm sorry. You requested I tell you everything."

"Yes," I said, my ears pricking. I now knew what she'd meant about "disabusing me of my misconceptions."

She'd known Kathleen's condition wasn't my fault and had felt compelled to tell me. Much as this woman hated coming here and reliving it all herself, she wouldn't let me go the rest of my life thinking it had been me—thinking it had been my fault. How could I thank her? Under different circumstances, I could see we might've been friends.

Why, then, did I suspect she was holding something back?

"There's one more thing," she said, as a breeze blew the blades of grass at our feet.

2015

Kelsey and I wore our jackets and wandered into the grassy rear yard among the dwindling sprays of fall wildflowers—white and yellow asters, dainty white snakeroots, and prickly purple thistles. The goldenrods were already gone. Jane's rescheduled biopsy was two days off, and she was finally ready to get together. Kelsey had banked a bunch of vacation days, and while she hated being away from her work at the moment, she'd said we were more important. My level of apprehension in waiting for Jane to arrive was equal to that of awaiting Nurse Breck in the Eden Park gazebo years before.

It was my time to pass my story down.

Nurse Breck had had the advantage of knowing fairly well how I'd react. Not so with me and my audience. It was the great unknown that sent a rush through my legs when the screen door to the enclosed rear porch squeaked open and clapped shut.

Jane was here. Kelsey and I turned from the flowerbeds and waved tentatively.

Could I gauge from this distance—a distance of about as far as from a handicap parking space to the entrance of a grocery—my daughter's demeanor? Her strides were long but slow, her hands stuffed into the pockets of her jeans. Cane in hand, I began the trek to meet her in the middle, and Kelsey was one step behind. Jane wore a plaid flannel shirt and navy Nordic vest and looked from side to side as she strode, directing a glance at Kelsey and me only once. She might not have been as nervous as I, but this was no cakewalk for her either.

Kelsey welcomed Jane with open arms first. I believed it was her way of breaking the ice—and her way of establishing for her elders how this gathering would go. I was cognizant of the mix of smile and worry clouding my face as Jane turned to me. I reached my lonely arms out, and she leaned into a loose hug with two pats on my back. It brought a memory of when she'd granted me a long embrace the day she returned to Ohio. I hadn't foreseen how I would come to miss that.

"I see you've still got the old tire swing," Jane said, tilting her head toward the sugar maple.

"Yes," I said. "Kelsey and I were just reminiscing about that."

"My all-time fave tree," Kelsey said.

"Should we go in? Get some tea?" I said. It was filler. Space-and-time filler talk.

"Nah," Jane said. "I'm getting used to crisp air again. I think I'd rather talk. Or listen, I should say."

The phrase *eat and run* popped into my head. She wanted to *hear* and run. I would rather have not been rushed.

"Grandma," Kelsey said, "that day in your basement, you said there was more. More we should hear." She laughed. "I guess I speak for both of us when I say we're ready to hear it now."

It sounded scripted and rehearsed. I motioned for them to join me in the garden chairs back out by the flowers at the rear.

"Ooh! That's cold on the butt," Jane said. The chairs were painted white, ornamental cast iron.

"And hard and pointy," Kelsey said.

"Not too late to go in," I said. They shook their heads as if to say, "Get on with it."

I began with the letter from the hospital and what I'd learned at the library. How I believed I'd done something wrong—caught a virus, not eaten well, worked too hard—to cause the baby's problem. Kelsey listened with the attentive ear of a historian. I thought she would've loved her laptop to take notes. And Jane listened with the stern brow and keen ear of a legal prosecutor. Though interestingly, neither asked a question. It was as if Kelsey had given Jane marching orders before they arrived: *Hear her out. She's your mother. She deserves it.* That would be just like her.

I touched on the strain that the loss had put on Jane's father and me, but how we had cared for Janie throughout. "I was glad you got to enjoy your childhood without remembering the tragedy." That'd been my view when Jane was a toddler, and that view was the same now.

Jane said, "But I spent a lot of time with Pauline and Tommy, didn't I? A lot of time with Grandma Glenn, growing up, too. Not sure how normal that was."

I felt a jab. Did she think I'd pawned her off? Did she resent that? Or was I being paranoid? I preferred to believe her time spent with friends and family enriched her life.

My story continued to the Labor Day outing at Graeter's. I held the collar of my jacket closed with one hand at my neck as a damp fall wind blew through.

"That's when I encountered the labor-and-delivery nurse. The woman with a beauty mark above her top lip . . ."

Kelsey said, "I can see where this is going. You would meet her on the side."

"Though Daddy was dead set against it," Jane said.

"Sometimes we do what we must," I said firmly. Jane looked down and back up. "If it makes you feel any better," I said, "I eventually told him. We didn't keep things from each other, your father and I, at least not for long."

Jane scooted back in her chair. I'd mollified her.

Kelsey said, "Sorry, but I need to stretch my back."

We walked the perimeter of the yard. I might have felt overtaxed, but no, I was up for this. The adrenaline in my body pushed me forward—and so did the fact that no one had gone running, screaming away from me yet. I took one step at a time, my cane ahead of each foot. I picked Nurse Breck's story back up.

"'I could smell the alcohol on him from two feet away.'"

Kelsey gasped. "Your OB was drunk?" I nodded.

We three girls had settled our walk near the center of the yard by then. "Mom," Jane said. "This is hard on me to hear. Worse than I thought. No matter what happens next, we know it's not good. I can't imagine how hard it was for you, sitting there, waiting."

"Right," I said, feeling vindicated. "Every minute I was waiting to hear how my child had died."

We stood in a huddle, immune to the cold or to children playing in yards down the way or someone outside the neighborhood burning leaves. I was getting to the worst part.

"The doctor dropped her. Dropped your sister, and she hit her head. She was perfect until that. Nurse Breck saw it all."

"That's horrible," Jane said. "This is absolutely horrible." Her contorted face matched her words.

Looking at her, I now knew how my face appeared when Nurse Breck told me. I hadn't realized how badly I'd needed Jane to know. We had this experience in common now: the hearing of these words.

"It is horrible," Kelsey said. "I don't know how you and Papaw survived it."

"So unfair." Jane spoke again.

Kelsey put her arms around me. She whispered, "I'm sorry, I'm sorry. I hate this for you."

I suddenly recalled again the time a boy had pushed me down in the street. Gravel and dirt got in my scrapes, but I didn't cry. I ran home and up the stairs to the third floor and barged into the flat and there was my opa. "What happened?" he'd asked. And as the story of the mean boy poured out, so did my tears. It wasn't until I shared my pain with someone who loved me that I let it out.

I cried softly on Kelsey's shoulder, not hard the way I'd wept on Mother Glenn's the day I returned from the hospital with empty arms. But I cried for having told her. I felt another hand stroking my back. It felt warm. I lifted my wet face and turned. Jane was there for me, too. *Thank you, God.*

Kelsey and I dislodged, and Jane and I embraced—a true embrace. "That's what happened to your sister," I said. "See why it was inconceivable for me to tell you when you were five? Or nine?"

She pulled back. "Yes."

We were all quiet for the longest time, listening only to the mounting wail of a siren in the distance. Jane squatted down to pick up some large twigs that had fallen from a tree.

After a spell, she spoke. "I've been trying to get my brain to sort through all this since the day in the basement. I understand the tragedy more now. I get the reasons you held off telling me when I was a kid. But I can't figure out one thing." She straightened.

"What?" I said.

"Why didn't you tell me before now? That I had a sister, I mean, even if you didn't reveal this part about how she'd died? Why did you wait so long? You could have told me standing there in Ashbury Street in San Francisco. Or when I had a toddler of my own toddling around. Why did you wait?"

She assumed the story ended here. That it was over. But it wasn't. There were more reasons why it was harder on her father and me. Reasons that made it harder to tell.

"Mom," Kelsey said to Jane, picking up on my distress. "Maybe Grandma just couldn't."

"But I feel kinda like I've been lied to all my life," Jane said, tossing aside the twigs she'd been carrying. Her voice rose. "Remember, Mom, how you almost washed my mouth out with soap one time for lying?"

I hung my head. I was ashamed for my granddaughter to witness me being accused. To make a point that day, I had threatened to swish a wet bar of Ivory around in Janie's mouth to wash out a child's lie—just as my mother had done to me. Had *really* done to me, that is. But I had abstained with Janie.

But Jane was right about one thing: I'd lied. Or, at least I'd lived a lie, and let her live a lie, too. Or I had committed the sin of a lie of omission.

Jane pressed on. "Grandma Glenn never mentioned it. No one in the entire family ever talked about it? And here I was left with the fallout."

What fallout did she mean? My taking pills? My coddling her?

We girls had stopped walking now. We stood in the center of my yard. If only life could be as carefree as when Kelsey swung on the tire with Dennis pushing her. Now Kelsey's eyes shot between her mother and me. I needed to prevent this day from spiraling out of control.

"I do understand how you suffered," Jane said. Her eyes were big and sad. "It's the most horrific thing I've ever heard. No woman should go through that. What I don't get, though, is how or why you kept this covered—"

"Mom," Kelsey said in a low voice, "I think you need to chill."

"I just don't get it," Jane said loudly.

I scanned the neighbors' yards on either side, concerned that others might hear us. Concerned that others might know my shame—the shame of my secret, the shame of my family disintegrating.

"Janie—I'm sorry—I mean, Jane," I said. "You have every right to be disappointed in me. I tried telling you years ago, back during *Roe v. Wade*." She jerked. Did she remember? "I tried telling you and Kelsey a week ago at our sleepover. But something always stopped me. I was going to tell you when we got done in the basement the other day, but I was too late. You'd found the album by then. I'm so sorry." I motioned for us to move back toward the house, but not one of them budged.

Jane glared.

Did she blame me for something specific? Was her childhood less idyllic than my biased eyes remembered? Yes, there was something in her teen years. It had driven her to run away. What had it been? Or maybe Jane was going through the early stages of grief right now, even though she'd never met the sister she lost. First denial, followed by anger. Anger with the doctors. Anger with me.

Or the stress over her own health was making her snap. Of course it would.

"And Daddy," she said, her palms up and her fingers spread wide. "I can't believe he deceived me. He of all people."

What had we done to poor Jane? Was it irreversible?

"Mom, really," Kelsey said before I could ask. She pushed up her fake blue eyeglasses. "I get why you're upset. I mean, circumstances deprived you of your only sibling. It's effing unreal." Jane glared at Kelsey now, too, though it was clear from Kelsey's demeanor that she was coming from a place of sympathy and unity. "But you don't get to freak out on Grandma. I mean, look at her. Do you think she kept this all bottled up her entire life just to hurt you? I don't think so."

Poor Kelsey. She'd always had to be the go-between.

"Girls, girls, let's take this inside." I stamped with my cane through the lawn in the direction of my house.

I turned back to see Jane had stood firm with the corners of her tight lips tucked in, the way Dennis's used to when he got upset. I had to do something. I had to bring us together. But I was flummoxed. The stress of everything had mounted in me, too. I didn't know how to fix us.

"Can't we go inside? Please?" I said. Kelsey followed.

"Mom, it's a simple question," Jane persisted, trailing us with an exaggerated, mock-calm tone. "Why was this all a big secret?"

Inside my screened-in porch, Kelsey must have snapped, too, or else her hormones came clawing out, because she said something as I closed the door I never dreamed I'd hear.

"Seriously, Mom. Like you're any better? Try looking in the mirror."

Jane's head swiveled toward Kelsey in the manner of a knight drawing his sword.

Kelsey went on anyway. "Why, you ask, didn't Grandma tell you something so terrible she could scarcely think or speak of it? Let me ask you. Why did it take you so long to tell me about my father?"

"Girls," I said, "let's—"

Jane raised a halting hand. "Kels. I did tell you everything. I waited only until you were old enough to understand."

"I was twenty-effing-five."

"Yes. But I'd tried hard to be a good single mom and to provide—"

"Don't be a martyr. This isn't about the plentiful love you gave me, nor all the inspiration," Kelsey said. "Asking who fathered me was one. Simple. Question. And how did you respond?" She paused dramatically and leaned in. "You didn't even know who he was."

That was true. I envisioned Jane's hippie commune outside of Phoenix. Everyone going around barefoot. Eating organic greens grown in a garden. Clothes hanging on a line. Guys with thick beards and girls who didn't shave their legs. An acoustic guitar and folk songs being sung around a fire. Years later, Jane told me she had ditched LSD, weed, all of it before she got pregnant.

Jane said now, "How I came to conceive you, Kels, is not a book-length novel. It's a short story."

We all knew that short story. Jane had been candid in telling me months after she first brought baby Kelsey home. Jane had stood right in my knotty pine kitchen and said she'd "had a thing" with two brothers—not at the same time. Communes in the seventies were tamer than The Haight of the sixties. The two encounters were spaced a couple of weeks apart. One encounter was wild, clothes half-off, half-on, up against the outside wall of the dormitory before dawn. The other went on for hours, tender, naked, and moon-soaked atop two layers of sleeping bags in a meadow. The next week both brothers left for places unknown. Jane had never learned their last name. I hadn't been scandalized when Jane told me the truth; she'd already had the baby, so I'd felt closure more than shock. I had inwardly hoped Kelsey's father was the brother under the light of the moon. I had hoped Jane had felt the overpowering rush of love, had experienced that pinnacle of closeness when she conceived.

In time Jane had loved another man in Georgia. But a few years into their relationship, she'd asked him to leave. Without warning.

Had Jane been unable to commit? Was this part of what she called the *fallout* from her childhood? Had she detected angst between her father and me in those early years after all? But in time Dennis and I had bonded back together in a way even I hadn't foreseen. Had it been something else with her then? Either way, until now I hadn't realized what a mess I'd made of what should have been the best years of her youth.

It was deeper than that, though.

Now Jane might have breast cancer. She might die. And I'd fretted over that with every blink and breath for days. What I hadn't the common sense enough to see was that after I'd lost one daughter long ago, somewhere along the line I'd lost the other one, too. I'd lost Jane, by manner of speaking, years before now.

Without meeting the eyes of my girls, I surveyed the screened-in porch. Everything was in its place: the wicker love seat in the corner, the glass-top end table beside it, the tall leafy plants by the windows that I'd soon have to move inside. Yet it felt as if a tornado had whipped through, wreaking its destruction everywhere. Our spirits had collapsed. Memories were shattered. Pieces of our hearts were strewn or missing.

I'd kept something from Jane. She'd kept something from Kelsey. The pain had passed down along with the German blue of our eyes—and with equal permanence.

Had I been the one, then, to set this all in motion? This friction? This act of secrets being handed down from mother to daughter?

Yes.

I was accountable for ruining their lives in fundamental ways. It was the worst mockery for me, because I had intended—had spent so many years and energy in good faith trying—to effect the opposite.

Opa once told me how insignificant he felt when the brewery closed. He was "a particle of dust in a big political machine." How was it that today I felt fully responsible and wholly insignificant at the same time?

All the good I'd done in life "didn't matter a rat's ass," as Papa Glenn might've termed it. In the final analysis I was a *bad mother*.

They could add that to my tombstone when they carved the date I died.

"So, Mom," Kelsey said to Jane, less flushed than before. "You're not so different from Grandma. There are secrets corroding us inside, truths that affect others we love but that can only come out when our hearts are ready to release them. It's not the end of the world."

My granddaughter was wise beyond her age. Would Jane see it too? Time ticked by as she pondered and clouds rolled in, casting shadows through the sunporch.

"I honestly didn't know who your father was," Jane said. "So I couldn't answer the question with precision." She waved her hand in my direction. "That's far different from this scenario with your grandma. She knew everything."

I mulled over her words.

"You're wrong," I said. "It's not so different here. There were things I honestly didn't know in my time either."

"But you have known those things for years now, right?" she said. She glared at me some more. Kelsey scowled at her.

"I have." I felt my eyebrows lift. "But there are things you still don't know about me, Jane."

Her cell phone rang, and we all jumped. Jane looked at the caller ID and said, "It's the breast center."

~

Jane lay in a hospital gown, facedown on a special table connected to a big machine. Kelsey and I sat erect in small chairs lining the wall that held prints of flower paintings that, according to her, were in the manner of Georgia O'Keeffe. The breast center had received a last-minute cancellation, and they said if Jane could arrive within forty minutes, they could perform her biopsy today. We'd all piled into Jane's four-door and arrived within half an hour.

My daughter had driven with the patience of Job. She was strong. But I was her mother. I knew her insides were roiling. When she'd been in seventh grade, she'd tried out for cheerleader. Her best friend made it, but she did not. I had felt her disappointment as if it were my own. When Jane graduated with her bachelor's in sociology—she was already in her thirties, living here in an apartment, and Kelsey was young—I felt Jane's sense of accomplishment as if I'd walked the stage wearing honor cords myself. So when we'd pulled into the crowded parking lot at the breast center, I felt in my bones her invisible fear and vulnerability as if it were alive under my own skin.

"The weird thing about waiting," Jane had said that first day in the doctor's office—back when she was glad I was there—"is how every minute you think: this could be it. This could be the day, the hour, the very minute I learn I'm going to die." Here we were again. This time she wasn't glad I was here. But I still wished I could take her place.

Now my daughter's left breast was numbed and hung down through a large hole in the table, isolating it for the stereotactic biopsy. Jane had asked special permission for Kelsey and me to be present. Kelsey whispered to me, "The table is like a massage bed at a spa—only instead of a cradle for one's face, the hole here is chest-level." And there was no feeling relaxed. Then the table rose mechanically, as if levitating Jane in a séance, and a technician prepared to target the flesh where a special needle would make one tiny incision and remove a few samples of tissue.

Were they hurting her? What would they find? How did she feel? What went through her mind? These questions buzzed around me like bees, and I sat still as a statue.

Afterward as we slowly walked back to the parking lot—my cane in hand—Jane said, "That was not the most comfortable experience of my life." She snorted. "But those people treated me so kindly." I thanked God for that.

"They said you'd have some discomfort for a few days," I said. "Be sure to follow their instructions so you don't get infected."

"Mom. They gave me one stitch and a bandage."

"Looking on the bright side, you two," Kelsey said, "the pathologist will assess the results, and we'll all be out of limbo in three to five days."

"Three to five business days, that is," Jane said. "How am I supposed to get through those without going crazy?" She opened the car door for me, a glint in her eyes. "I know how, Mom," she said. "You can fill us in on whatever it is you said I still don't know."

She surprised me, given the breakdown between us earlier. She wanted to hear more? Could I take her lashing back out if she didn't like what I said? Was she already lost?

But I'd do it. I'd try anything to save us. If there was the thinnest string connecting us, I'd take the chance. I'd give the next chapter to her.

"Yes," I said. "That's what I'll do."

CHAPTER NINETEEN

September 1951

The shower spray hit my bare skin with a chill. I adjusted the temperature. Warmer, warmer. I let the stream massage my face. The back of my neck. My spine. Nurse Breck's story preyed on my mind. At the end of our meeting in the park she had said, "There's one more thing."

"What is it?" I'd asked. I'd felt there was more, and then knew I was right.

"After I took my stance with the nurse supervisor," she'd gone on, "accusing the doctor of being drunk while Nurse Tibbers denied it, my administrator said, 'I'm afraid this means your employment is terminated.' 'But you can't fire me,' I said. 'Because I quit.'"

She had taken a stand. Nurse Breck had taken that stand for me.

I lathered a cloth with a bar of soap and washed my arms and legs. I squirted shampoo into my hand and worked the creamy liquid through my hair and then rinsed. These steps came automatically to me. I didn't think about them. My body knew what to do from habit—even to the point of avoiding the tender scar running up my belly, washing only on either side. As I climbed out of the pink-tiled shower my husband had built, I thought consciously of only one thing: I had carried a healthy baby to term. I had loved Kathleen inside of me for nine months. I had nourished her, guarded her, caressed my tummy when she kicked, and hummed lullabies to her. Into our lives, mine and Dennis's, I had brought a second robust baby girl. My actions—my diet, my prenatal care, my work with the business and the house, my dedication to Janie and Dennis—had not rendered me the mother of a dead child. No.

Dr. Reynolds had dropped—had killed—my child. An inferno of fiery hate swept through me, up and down like a blaze in the stairwell of a building. Hot, relentless, unyielding.

Dr. Collins had called in a physician known among the staff to be tipsy at work. There'd later been arrogant men sitting in their walnut boardrooms, wearing their crisp white coats that their wives or maids had ironed for them—those men who hadn't given my plight a moment's passing thought. To these men, these administrators, my loss represented a single letter on one afternoon. A page with a word beginning with *E*. Signed, licked, stamped, posted. They knew nothing would come of it. Complaints were unheard of. Their official letters with their golden imprinted insignia bore the final word.

No one could go up against them. No one had proof if they did.

Except the nurses. And that proved futile.

"In the medical profession, doctors are gods," Nurse Breck had said.

It was all the doctor's fault.

⌐

The following day Pauline had come for Janie in the afternoon while Dennis worked the weekend. "I have to be alone," I'd said when I'd called. "Not for long." My best friend didn't ask questions.

For an hour now I'd been sprawled on the floor of my living room, flat on my back, unable to lie still in a bed or recline in a chair. I couldn't eat, couldn't talk. I was stiff with rage—my limbs rigid, but my mind warped like a hunk of clay on a potter's wheel spinning out of control.

I'd performed my part. I'd carried her well. Kathleen had entered this world safely. Then came the hands of the man who took his role— his Godlike role in a mortal life—for granted.

Then a new thought whirled its way through the soft matter of my mind like a worm to an apple, a thought I could not escape: I was the one who had changed doctors.

It *had* been me.

I had snubbed the doctor who'd delivered all the beautiful Glenn grandchildren and Janie. I'd done it because I wanted to show Dennis, and maybe even Abbie, who was in charge.

I rolled on my side on the hard, carpeted floor beside Raggsie, where he slept. I convulsed with sobs and curled myself into a ball next to him.

It was all *my* fault.

I'd shown my husband whose domain this was, all right. Months had passed since I'd selected the doctor—and since our daughter died. I hadn't let Dennis know I'd called the nurse. He'd been adamant that I shouldn't. Did this mean I'd disobeyed him? Broken my wedding vows? My head was splitting. Wait, he hadn't formally forbidden it. I didn't like keeping a secret from him, yet he wouldn't want to know, I reasoned. He didn't want to know half of what torment plagued me. He wanted me "to be happy." We went through the motions of every day of waking up, going to bed. Taking care of Janie in between.

What I had learned was too much to unload on a person. Too much to unload on him.

Anyway, he had held Kathleen in his arms and hadn't let *me* know. Hearing that tidbit of news had hurt. But he hadn't thought I was strong enough to stomach it.

Some truths were too hard to bear before their time. Or too hard to state.

I couldn't abide all the things that'd gone wrong. My mind was cruel to remind me of them. I hated myself for my own part.

I scavenged for another pill—in my pocketbook, the bathroom vanity, the bedside table drawer, the coffee cupboard. I had run out. I couldn't get away from my own head. Couldn't escape.

Ah, there, the liquor cabinet. I could drown my miseries in booze. There would be gin. I dug in for a bottle. Oh, Scotch. Or Kahlúa? A fifth of vodka. Yes. I slid my palm up and down the cool glass bottle, feeling its label catch on my skin. I unscrewed the brand-new cap and took a swig. *Ack, ack.* Hot. Bitter. Then another. *Ah, ah.* I twisted my face and held my breath as if I were jumping into the river. And I slugged another gulp. *Whooo.* The fluid burned my tongue and burned my throat and burned all the way down to my belly. Would I guzzle the bottle's whole contents? I turned the bottle up again and then gagged for a bit of air.

Then a vision of Opa appeared before me. An apparition. My beloved opa was holding my hand, as when I was girl. He'd taught me about the three kinds of people: he was the good kind. Even during Prohibition, during the height of his poverty and despair, when the bootleg king George Remus offered him a sack full of cash to run his booze, my opa had declined. He'd hated the Eighteenth Amendment and the Volstead Act, but Opa would not manufacture liquor, distribute liquor, nor sell liquor. And he refused to drink it if thrust in his face. "My own grandfather," Opa had told me, "didn't immigrate to this country only to defile it by breaking its laws. I would not dishonor his memory."

Until today I used to think I was the good person, too, the kind who only sometimes did something wrong. But now, I realized, I was the bad person who sometimes got things right. Opa should never have called me Millicent the Strong. I was Millicent the Weak.

Then another vision appeared: Dr. Reynolds with his gloved hands and masked face, his bloodshot eyes, and disheveled hair as he sliced my body open . . . and as he held my infant by her delicate newborn ankles.

Janie cried from her bed. I jarred. No, no. She was still with Pauline.

I poured the rest of the vodka onto our linoleum floor like an idiot—the only sane thought in my head being how I recoiled to think I was becoming a drunk like Dr. Reynolds. I recoiled to think I would dishonor my opa. The liquid gurgled and splattered and sounded like a cow pissing on flat rocks in a field at the farm. I didn't care. I emptied it to the last drop. I didn't know if I could be the mother my Janie deserved anymore. I doubted I could. But liquor—the accessory to my Kathleen's murder—would not be my downfall.

⌐

I had avoided Dennis's gaze for days. I didn't even think he'd noticed. But I had. Guilt. I'd cleaned up my mess and made my excuses for the house smelling of booze, a supposed accident while cooking with wine. But the scent lingered in the membranes of my nostrils, an unwelcome reminder. Guilt.

By the third day I could no longer pretend to Dennis that I hadn't called Nurse Breck. I had to come clean.

I had made bad decisions—within the realm of my home's domain—and for these decisions I had to take responsibility. I had to let Dennis know. Every time he looked at me, I felt shame. I'd let him down. I'd deceived him. This was guilt. Yet how ironic that he'd driven me to it; he had excluded me from the business. I'd fought to reclaim my power.

Now I had to do the right thing. I had to do what Opa would do.

Dennis arrived home early. Rain had set construction back. I waited on pins and needles all evening—while he changed his clothes, romped with Janie in her room, ate a tomato-and-mayonnaise sandwich, and then turned on the television set. I put Janie to bed. All the while my stomach grew more ill, as if I were afraid I'd get in trouble. But I was not a child. He was not my parent.

Dennis had the newspaper open when I came back to the living room. I sat beside him and cleared my throat. He twisted his head my way behind the paper, shot me an inquisitive smile.

"I have something to tell you," I said. I'd gotten more pills and had taken only one. One pill tonight, that was. One pill that morning. One at midday. The newspaper rustled as he folded it in half, folded it in half again, and laid it on the table.

"I thought you seemed off tonight," he said. He hadn't questioned it up front, I surmised, because I was "off" so often these days. "Are you relying too much on medication?" he asked, and I jerked. "Maybe you should cut back."

Was he counting the missing tablets in the bottle? He surely didn't think anyone else in my situation could manage any better. Did he? Look at all that'd happened to me!

My head sank between my shoulders.

"I telephoned the nurse." My voice was shaky. Maybe I slurred.

Dennis lowered his own head, stroked the curve of his ear. He raised his head and faced me again with a tolerant expression, soundless. His calm frightened me more than if he'd yelled. But I had to go on. I told him everything from the beginning, from my wavering about calling the nurse to my dialing her number, to our baby sucking her thumb, to the doctor drunk with booze.

Then I spoke the words: "The doctor dropped her."

Anguish and disbelief crushed in on Dennis's face. A guttural groan came from deep inside his core.

"I'm so sorry," I said, and I cupped my hands to my face. I cried, letting out my pain and my guilt, my anger and remorse.

Dennis rose and paced the floor. He couldn't stop shaking his head no, nor rubbing his face. I should have kept this all inside. I should have spared him this pain.

"I'm so sorry," I said again and again. He sat back beside me.

"Look at me," he said, tilting my tearstained face up by my chin. "Nothing's changed. You didn't do anything wrong."

"I did. It's all my fault," I said. I was a horrible mother.

"No, no. It's not your fault. Nothing you do or say or think will ever make this your fault." He took me into his muscular arms. I didn't recall the last time he'd held me so tight. It gave me life—I breathed freer in his hold—but I was undeserving.

"But it is my fault, all my fault," I said again, meaning it.

"It's not. But if it were your fault," he said, his eyes meeting mine, "I would forgive you."

Those were the sweetest words I'd ever heard—sweeter than Opa telling me I was his favorite girl, more than Dennis saying I was the prettiest girl a guy ever got. His forgiveness filled my soul with sugar. He truly was his mother's son. So kind and fair and loyal.

He would forgive me. Perhaps I had judged too harshly his stoic manner in the past.

I bawled, deep, wrenching sobs. Then I considered: Did he feel the anger I felt, a corrosion in the belly like acid, the anger aimed at the doctor to the degree I did? Would I ever know?

I asked him to tell me about Kathy. "I'm ready."

He reached into his shirt pocket for his cigarettes. His face looked more aged, more like his father's, and there was a slump to his shoulders that I didn't recall. He tapped one cigarette a few times on his silver metal lighter. It took him three times to get the Zippo's flint to catch, trembling as he was. He took a long, deep drag and blew smoke toward the ceiling.

⁓

"I came into your surgical room just after the nurse told you we lost her, the baby. You were only awake for the shortest time. You were on serious painkillers. I'd already been told Kathy was gone.

"At that point, Kathy was in your room on a metal tray with wheels, fully covered in a white sheet. When the nurse raised the sheet, I thought Kathy looked like a papoose wound in blankets.

"She had the longest lashes and perfect lips like her sister's. Her head was swollen on one side. Purple. Earlier, when I'd first picked her out in the viewing window, I'd seen a bruise there, a bump. I assumed it was done by the forceps. But by the end, in your room, the spot had doubled in size." Dennis's voice cracked.

"I told the nurse, 'I have to hold her.' She looked around and said, 'It's against the rules of the ward.' But then she agreed. So I picked Kathleen up. Her skin was cold, but she smelled like a perfect little baby, like Janie. I said into her ear, 'We love you.'"

I whimpered at Dennis's words. I hadn't had the honor of seeing or holding our daughter, and I was jealous. But I thanked God for letting her be held by her father. Even if she was already gone.

Dennis cleared his throat. His nostrils quivered as he fought hard not to cry. "After I went to the men's room and splashed my face, I came back, and Kathy had already been wheeled away."

Dennis and I held each other. Never had I needed to be embraced by the arms of this man so badly.

~

We made love that night for the first time since our loss six months before.

By the time it was done, I could see that our act was not driven by lust or love or tenderness, nor was it fueled by power or control or someone being right and the other being wrong. It wasn't a means of making up. It was driven by our unspoken, single-minded mission to bring hope back into our lives. Another child.

Hope.

CHAPTER TWENTY

October 1951

I sat stiffly in a worn brown leather chair with bent metal arms in old Dr. Welch's tidy little office, he on the swiveling stool by my knees. I didn't think he and his nurses begrudged me for having snubbed them with my last baby. The desk nurse asked about all the Glenns and their kiddies. My charts and records had been sent back to this practice by Dr. Collins.

Dr. Welch performed my six-month post-op checkup with ease. After I got dressed, he said, "You've healed remarkably well. Your incisions show no signs of infection."

No matter how this doctor had condescended to me at times, our next baby would come into this world with the trusty hands of this man who'd safely delivered my Janie. He closed the chart, propped his glasses up on his nose, and said, "You won't need an appointment for another six months."

I smiled. "I'm hoping to return sooner than that."

He shook his head. Here it came. He was going to warn me again of how another birth would be "hazardous to the mother."

"You and Mr. Glenn are having relations again?"

I blushed and stammered.

"As well you should," the doctor said kindly. Dennis and I had experienced more than a physical act. Our days had found a peace as well. Togetherness.

"And," I said, "we hope to be expecting again right away."

"Mrs. Glenn," he said sternly. "You'll recall what we discussed after your first baby was born. Two cesareans is the limit I advise." He rubbed his scalp. "But it's a moot point, isn't it?"

"I know what you'd said before. But it's not a hard-and-fast rule, is it?"

"I'd gathered from your medical records that authorization forms had been signed for a tubal ligation. Consistent with having had two surgeries, I thought that was wise."

"Check my records again." I kept my voice modulated, but I didn't want to deal with his old-fogey runaround. "I didn't have the procedure."

"That's quite irregular." He opened my file back up, looking confused.

The doctor switched on a green glass lamp on his desk. I watched, beginning to perspire as his finger traced the front and back of sheets one after another. Yet I was certain Dr. Welch would look up from his study and conclude I was right. I saw his brows knit.

"You are correct, Mrs. Glenn." He didn't look up at me. "Dr. Collins inked in a notation on the bottom of this page. It says that in December of last year he'd advised you to have the procedure after the birth, but that you and Mr. Glenn would not sign the forms."

I sighed with audible relief, though I'd known I was right all along.

"But there must have been some misunderstanding," Dr. Welch said, licking his thumb and rapidly paging through my file. He slid out another sheet, one with a red ink stamp in the top corner.

"You see here," he said, pointing. "I'm afraid the procedure did go through. Dr. Reynolds severed your fallopian tubes."

My heart stopped beating. Then it spiked hot blood from my scalp to the arches of my feet. Dr. Welch handed me this new page with the red ink stamp. I pinched it between my fingers and thumb, and with the paper shaking in my grasp, I heard it rattling.

"There's been a mistake," I said. I tossed the paper back at him. I jolted to my feet, shaking my hands. I couldn't believe it.

"No mistake, Mrs. Glenn," he said, stuffing the papers away as if to signal my appointment was nearing its end. "I'm sorry to be the bearer of bad news."

My mind raced to find a logical explanation. "But, but. I still get my periods," I said.

"You're normal." Dr. Welch sounded exasperated. "Women's monthly courses are not curtailed by the tubal ligation procedure."

"This can't be," I said. It was as if a furnace had been stoked inside of me. "This simply cannot be right." I leaned my face into his. "I am going to have another baby, Doctor, I assure you of that."

He pushed up the bifocals on his ruddy nose. "I think you should sit down," he said. "Here is another sheet where your husband authorized the tubal procedure himself, on the day the baby was born."

"Are you crazy? My husband would never do that." I plopped into the chair. My knees started bouncing up and down. "Never."

Dr. Welch insisted I read the page, but I batted it away. "Get that thing away from me. It's lies," I said. "All lies."

The cubic space of the room seemed to compress and suck the air out with it. My mind must have been playing tricks on me. I started to weep.

Then the image of Nurse Breck came into focus. Was the tubal procedure the real "one more thing" she had referred to back at the park? Had she wheeled out of giving me the full picture when she'd merely said she'd been fired? Perhaps Nurse Breck had come close to telling me the truth but then became concerned with how I'd receive it—with how I'd react to learning of my husband's duplicity.

The doctor still held out the page. Reluctantly I accepted it. I was determined to find him wrong. I studied the page. I didn't want to believe it. My eyes were blurry with tears. But it was Dennis's signature all right—with his trademark large capital *D*.

How could my husband have betrayed me?

I was sterile. Barren. Spayed. And he'd never told me. No one had.

"It's not fair," I said. "It's not fair."

I flung the page on the floor and stamped on it with my shoe. "Dr. Reynolds butchered me," I said. Dr. Welch's mouth gaped.

"No need to get hysterical," he said.

"I'm not hysterical," I shouted in a tone that could only be labeled hysterical. The doctor's head jerked as if my voice had smacked his face. No one spoke to doctors, gods, in this manner. Then a new fear hit me: What if the nurses in the outer office heard me? I didn't want anyone to know. I couldn't let anyone—Abbie Glenn and all the others—get wind of my causing a ruckus. I had to get my wits about me.

I scowled at the doctor. "And please tell your staff not to say anything of my affairs to anyone. Keep these facts to yourselves. No one is to know," I told him. "This is a private medical matter and—"

"Again, I'm sorry to be the unwitting messenger of disturbing news—news about a procedure your other doctor performed, may I remind you." His voice was hard. "I assure you I operate a practice that's held in the highest regard. Given the unfortunate circumstances and your state of mind, shall we telephone a member of your family to drive you safely home?"

Had he not listened to a word I'd said? We'd not be sharing this news with them. I wouldn't let others know of my loss or my frenzy.

I wouldn't let them know of Dennis's deceit.

"I have my own car." Like the Irvings, we were a two-car family by then. "I'll see myself home." The way my knees were buckling as I stood, I had no idea how I'd manage. But I would.

He rose and opened one of his glass-doored cupboards and shuffled about inside until he removed a medicine bottle. He handed the bottle to me and described the remedy's calming effects for anxiety.

More barbiturates. These pills apparently cured ailments as simply as sticking a pacifier in a baby's mouth. The doctor advised plenty of bedrest. Bedrest and more pills—as if they could cure my disintegrating life.

～

Outside, the skies were gray going to black. Thunder clapped and lightning struck, scaring me half to death. I yanked the car's gearshift into reverse and backed out with a jerk, praying I didn't run into someone. I maneuvered the vehicle onto the street. There weren't many cars. *Where do I go?* I asked myself, disoriented. *Oh, oh, yes, I see the turn-off ahead.* The tires screeched as I slammed on the brakes and cranked the wheel right. Then I drove straight for, I don't know, a mile, two? Then my car slid off the road onto a berm, kicking up gravel and pelting the chassis underneath. I gripped the steering wheel tighter to regain control, to maneuver the vehicle back onto the pavement. I swerved as an oncoming car blinked its headlights and blared its horn at me. I was frantic. I was lost. I wanted to claw my nails down someone's face.

I pulled into the parking lot of a five-and-dime, and out front there was a telephone booth. Big, fat drops of water splashed on the windshield, and I feared the roads would turn slick. I stopped the car. I yanked a scarf out of my purse, covered my head, and ran to the louvered door of the clear glass telephone booth, my purse tucked under my chin. More thunder. I quaked.

I struggled to open my pocketbook. I rifled inside for my change purse. I squeezed it open, and my coins spilled, pinging as they dropped to the metal floor. I crouched to pick up one dime and managed to slip it into the telephone slot. Pauline's number was engraved in my head, as deep as my own middle name. I cranked the rotary dial one numeral at time. The rain was now a bucketing downpour. *Answer, answer. Please answer.* My friend was the only one I trusted. I didn't know how I'd cope with this—another tragedy. And my husband's disloyalty. I didn't understand. He'd been so open when he'd told me of how he'd held Kathy. This was as bad as my baby being dropped. No . . . it was worse. This was my Dennis. Hate rose up and tasted bitter in my mouth. I spit on the floor. As I sat on the round metal stool in the phone booth, waiting for Pauline to rescue me, the skies opened up so loud, so dark, but I was hidden.

No one could see me banging the telephone receiver into the machine when Pauline didn't answer, nor see my wailing through the deluge of rainwater. No one could hear my screams of pain and outrage.

—

"I still can't believe it," Pauline said. Her voice was low and revolted.

"Believe it."

I'd managed to make it back to her house and changed out of sopping wet clothes. Janie and Tommy were napping at Pauline's. I had called Pauline again when the rain let up, and she'd answered; she had begged me to let her come for me with the children, but I'd been incapable of telling her exactly where I was. I'd floundered and found my way back.

"What are you going to do?" she said.

"Do?" I said, so furious I could speak only in clipped words. "Suffer."

But I'd leave him. I'd pack my bags, take my jug money, drain my savings, take a cash withdrawal from *our* business, load up Janie, and leave him as soon as I figured out where to go. I'd get a job. I'd tell Mother Glenn what her son had done—tell Papa Glenn, too. Tell how their son had betrayed me even as he was granting me forgiveness and shooting his seed between my legs. One betrayal was as bad as the other. He wasn't the man I married.

I was in bed, thankfully, by the time Dennis returned late from Dayton, where he'd been to bid two homes. I wasn't ready to confront him yet. I had to plan. I couldn't sleep, but I was exhausted. Janie was tucked in and dozing. It took all my willpower to pretend that I slept—to relax my shoulders, keep my breathing in check, and keep my eyelids from fluttering, given the scenes that raced through my mind. He tiptoed into our room and kissed me softly on the cheek. I inwardly recoiled.

I wasn't ready to face him. I had to be alert. I would wait until morning.

At some point the first of the doctor's pills must have kicked in, for when I awoke well after the break of day I had to scramble to cook breakfast. I flipped Dennis's pancakes with such force the batter splattered onto the backsplash behind the stove. I didn't make smiley faces. I didn't warm the syrup and transfer it to tiny pitchers. Dennis got cold syrup served straight from the bottle.

When he came in from his shower and asked how my appointment had gone with Dr. Welch, I was wiping syrup off Janie's face, and I gave a direct quote from the doctor: "He says my body has healed remarkably well." I smiled, baring my teeth.

"That's great," Dennis said. He needed to rush out in a flurry. He was to receive some commendation at Gunnison headquarters. In Indiana. An award.

I threw the spatula in the sink. "If only you hadn't consented for me to be sterilized, I'd be pregnant by now."

He gawped at me. "What the hell are you talking about?"

Janie started to cry. Our nasty voices had scared her. But I couldn't stop.

"Don't you play dumb with me, Dennis Glenn," I said. "Don't lie. From the very beginning you thought the procedure should go through. I guess having a bigger family wasn't as important to you as it was to me. You'd already had that growing up. So *you* decided. There I was, lying helpless in a bed with morphine pumping into my veins, and you just had to scrawl your big old John Hancock all over the dotted line. Now I'm barren. It's all your fault. You showed me who's boss, didn't you?"

A fat blue vein had protruded on his forehead like I'd never seen. His face and neck were wildly inflamed.

"For crying out loud, Millie, I don't know what you think you heard or saw or read, and I don't know what kind of shit is going on in that head of yours." He looked completely boggled. "But I'm going to take it that you're still grieving and concerned that you're not pregnant again. Or that all the pills you pop are, I don't know, getting to be too much, maybe, huh?"

His words gave me whiplash.

"I'm barren, I tell you."

"Just hear this: I did not sign any papers. I thought we were still trying to have a baby, despite the advice of two physicians. Because you wanted it so badly. Don't you ever—ever, you got that?—don't you ever accuse me of doing something that dishonorable to you. And do not bring this up again. I'm serious. When I come home, I'd better find the girl I married."

Janie was bawling. The framed picture of our family fell from the wall as her father slammed the door on his way out.

⌐

As soon as Dennis left, I changed Janie out of her pj's and fastened her into her bouncy seat. I gave her the sippy cup. None of the bad things were my precious baby's fault. I would protect her.

I took another pill. I had to think, think.

Dennis had stunned me with his repudiations. He actually looked righteous. Sounded offended. But every time I recalled his signature, I wanted to pound his chest with both fists and scream.

And beneath all my anger I was the saddest I'd ever been.

I took another pill.

It was Wednesday. Dusting day. I would pretend my time here was not through until Pauline came and left and I decided where to go. I scribbled the words *why, why* with my fingertip in the dust on the coffee table. Then I sprayed furniture polish and wiped it so clean with a cloth, I could see my face like on a TV commercial. But mine was not a happy-homemaker face.

Dennis and I had never had a fight this bad. I'd never known couples could slide this far. I never knew he could betray me. Didn't know I could resent him so much.

By afternoon my jitters had eased. Pauline dropped by with Tommy as I knew she would. She was my best friend. While our children played with their wooden puzzles and barnyard set in the living room, tussling over the occasional cow or horse, we mothers spoke in low tones in the kitchen.

"Horrible. Just horrible," Pauline said of what I'd learned. She was pale and wide-eyed. She shook her head. "You poor thing."

"Pauline, do you know what kills me most?"

"Dennis betraying you? And then denying it?" She paused, the steam of her coffee curling in front of her lips. "Or else somewhere deep inside . . . you think he's telling you the truth? That despite the evidence, you believe him?"

What? "The thing that kills me most is I'll never have another baby," I said. "I'll never hold a sleeping newborn of my own again. I'll never get to dress Janie up in matching outfits with a little brother or sister. I'll never walk down the sidewalk with one child at my side and another in a buggy. I always wanted more children. I still do."

It was so unfair. A waste. My choice over my own body: obliterated.

"I wish there were something I could say or do to help," Pauline said, her face filled with agony. "I'm so sorry."

"I'm going to leave him."

Pauline's mouth fell open. "No one we know has ever gotten divorced. But if Dennis did that, I can't say I blame you for feeling this way."

I didn't think I'd ever met a divorced person.

Raggsie jumped into my lap and licked my chin as if he sensed I was hurting. I held him close and nuzzled him. "I need another pill," I said.

"Honey," Pauline said, "I'm only saying this because I love you like the sister I never had. And I can't imagine anything worse than what you're going through. But I can't help but think—that is, I'm unsure whether the pills help you."

First Dennis, now her?

I'd let her comments pass. I saw no need to curb my pills. They helped me get through the day.

"Whether you stay with Dennis or whether you leave, you've got to have a clear head. These pills—"

"What I put in my mouth is none of your business," I retorted. I covered my lips as soon as I saw rejection glint in her eyes.

"You don't mean that," she said, tears welling.

The telephone rang, and we jumped. We stared each other down, and on the third ring Pauline said, "Aren't you going to answer it?"

"No. Don't you bother either. There's no one I wish to speak to."

Finally the shrill sound of the ring waned. For several long moments Pauline and I sat quiet. "I'm sorry," I said. "I didn't mean it. Everything about me is your business."

"I know." She covered my hand with hers. She was the friend I didn't deserve.

I said, "You think it's possible Dennis isn't lying?"

Pauline gave an ever so faint shrug of one shoulder. "If you're having doubts," she said, drumming her nails on the side of her cup, "there's one person who knows for sure."

The phone rang again and scared the wits out of us. By the fourth ring Pauline couldn't stand it and hopped up to answer. But it was too late. There was no one there.

2015

I was abruptly aware—in the way we awaken from nightmares and find ourselves safely in bed—that the three of us, Jane, Kelsey, and me, formed a quasi-circle beside a bonfire out back at night after the biopsy that day. Our hands were clasped in a chain. My granddaughter had been in a patio chair on the opposite side of the raised steel pit. The fire had been her idea. At some point, though, Kelsey had come to kneel in front of me, her gently bent elbows resting atop my thighs, the light of the flames flickering in her face.

The girls knew what the doctor had done. With the baby. And with the procedure that I hadn't authorized. After all this time I'd had to let that out, and it felt liberating, therapeutic.

But I didn't tell them about the paper bearing Dennis's signature nor of its aftermath, our fight—and what happened next. He was Jane's father. I was her mother. What was the purpose of letting her know our personal betrayals?

Weren't there some things a parent did that a child need never learn?

"I can't believe a doctor did that to you," Kelsey said. "Taking away your ability to have a baby, without permission, is too terrible." Her voice was pitched high as if it took all her mettle to speak without breaking down. She was trying to stay strong for me.

"Did you sue the sons-o'-bitches?" That was my daughter.

"No," I said, my back straightening and voice firm. "You have to understand. Doctors were gods in those days."

Kelsey said, "I don't think medical malpractice suits were a thing until the sixties. Aaron would know."

"It's so unfair," Jane said.

In my left hand was Jane's dry hand, her pinkie finger kinked at a knuckle. It was a precursor of what was to come—that's how my arthritis began. And in my other hand was Kelsey's petite, youthful hand of satiny-supple skin. My hands had once been smooth and clear like hers, and then age spots had appeared here and there until one day I saw my skin darkly mottled. It'd all happened so fast—as quickly as bananas get spots and then blacken and rot in a basket. To the girls my hands must have felt like a first step toward my grave . . . bony, veiny, skin papery thin and brittle.

"I remember," Jane said warily, "being at a big Glenn family shindig at the farm. I was around six. All my cousins were running around having fun, and I said, 'Mommy, I want a sister. I want one right now.' You looked stricken with panic and didn't utter a sound. Aunt Abbie jumped in and said, 'Sweetheart, maybe instead you could get a new kitty.' I guess she knew and tried to help. A moment of grace for her?"

I remembered that day, too. It wasn't Abbie's grace. It was another example of words spilling out of her mouth that sounded considerate on the surface but that grated on my nerves, or rather, hurt my feelings. When Abbie had said the word *kitty*, memories had spilled back to my wedding reception. I'd always wondered if Abbie had overheard what Mama said. *Not all women have babies the way alley cats squirt out kittens.* I suspected Abbie had heard it and was throwing up a subtle dig.

As the fire died Kelsey said, "It's been a long day."

It had.

"Thank you for listening," I said. *Thank you for not deserting me when I finished.*

I walked them to the driveway. Jane hugged me, and it was good. I thought I would sleep.

⌐

I folded myself into my cavernous king-size bed that night, covered in a sheet and two quilts. My mother-in-law had fashioned them with scraps of old dresses and swatches of fabrics. Nothing kept me warmer when I lay all alone. As I drifted in and out, the peace of slumber beckoning but eluding me, a memory pounded, pounded, pounded—it would not be dismissed until I'd suffered its images again.

"Nurse Breck," I had said on the phone decades before—right after Pauline left my kitchen when I was reeling from Dennis's betrayal. I had kept the napkin bearing the nurse's number. "I have one more question."

"I've been trying to reach you, Mrs. Glenn."

"You have?"

"Yes," she said. "I'm afraid there's more I haven't told you."

Was it she who'd been phoning that day in my kitchen when I'd let it ring? I'd thwarted Pauline from answering too?

"Why didn't you tell me that I was barren?" I said. "Why didn't you tell me that my husband had signed the tubal ligation consent form?"

I heard her ragged exhale. "That's why I've tried phoning you. Because I couldn't live with myself," she began. "I couldn't sleep knowing how you would wait every month for the next ten years, hoping you'd conceived."

I felt grateful and fitful all at once, my head throbbing.

"But let's be clear," she said. "Your husband didn't sign that paper."

Goose bumps swarmed my arms. "I saw his signature with my own two eyes," I said. His big *D* had been as legible as could be. But now I felt sickened to the marrow of my bones. Had I misjudged him?

"I came back to your room after taking the baby to the nursery for viewing," Nurse Breck said. "This was before you awoke. The doctor was washing his hands. Nurse Tibbers indicated he'd finished the tubal procedure. Alarmed, I said, 'But there was a notation of record. No tubal was to be performed.' When the doctor was done drying his hands, he swiveled and looked at me, a mix of confusion and accusation. He said Dr. Collins's patients always had their tubes severed if they'd had two cesareans. Nurse Tibbers concurred. 'But the documentation,' I said. Dr. Reynolds barked at me: 'Bring me a consent form.' I balked. 'That's an order,' he said. I refused. He nodded his head at Nurse Tibbers. He rifled through other papers while she stepped away, studying one in particular. I believe it was the admissions document your husband had signed earlier. What I'm getting at is this: I was three feet away from the man who signed your husband's name. Dr. Reynolds forged an updated consent form for the files."

Sweat broke out at my hairline. I thought I might faint. "It's so unfair!" It was not a whisper. It was a bellow. "He forged my husband's name. He took away my womanhood!"

And because of that, my lack of faith was on the brink of ruining my marriage.

"I almost told you that day in the park," she said, her words filled with sympathy. "But you were suffering so badly already."

"I understand," I told her. I quietly placed the phone receiver back in its cradle without saying goodbye. I had to lie down quickly.

She had explained before how she'd been fired for questioning the doctor's drunkenness, but she hadn't told me the extent of her insubordination to him in that ward. Again this woman had taken a stand on my behalf. She was a good person.

I curled up in the fetal position on the couch. Had I possessed Nurse Breck's strength of character and conviction, I might not have destroyed Dennis. I might not have thrown our marriage away. Was it too late to save us?

He wouldn't return from corporate Gunnison for two days. I had forty-eight hours to let my remorse fester. To think: I'd almost left him. Well, he might throw me out now.

I had to atone. And I had to do it in person. I had two days until my act of contrition.

That was good, because I was boiling over with anger, too. But not at him. I slid out the kitchen drawer where we kept the telephone book. I opened the pages of the weighty volume, so thick that Pauline had used it as a booster seat when she came, since Tommy had outgrown the high chair.

I flipped on a light and thumbed through, madly searching for names beginning with *R*.

PART THREE

PART TWELVE

CHAPTER TWENTY-ONE

October 1951

The next day I took a train to the northern suburbs and then walked more than a mile. I did not drive my car. I did not have someone drive me. I wanted anonymity.

We'd had our first frost the week before, but a sunny warm spell had arrived that morning. Indian summer. The air would hit seventy by midafternoon, and by the time it all passed, we'd know winter was coming to stay.

I owed Pauline two mommy times in future weeks, but I'd said I had to get out of the house. Dennis would return the next day. I would face him then. But I couldn't stay cooped up watching the teapot clock tick. Pauline understood. I'd told her how wrong I'd been—how my husband hadn't lied. I was teeming with pent-up energy. Rage. I couldn't fix things with him yet. But I couldn't sit around waiting for what was coming: my confession . . . my fight to save our marriage. I had to escape for a couple of hours; there were other things I had to do. Pauline didn't know where I was headed. Could be the cemetery. The library. The church. It was my time. She wished that I could be downtown trying on new dresses, getting a pedicure, and stopping for a malted milk at Newberry's lunch counter. But even she knew that was a pipe dream.

Instead I was in Mariemont, Ohio, an upper-crust suburb of Cincinnati. It was close enough that corporate barons commuted to their skyscrapers, but far enough out that a town crier still wandered its square—yes, a town crier in the 1950s, calling out news of the day. He wore a tricorn hat and a red waistcoat; visiting Mariemont was like stepping back in time. Taking one last glance at the memo sheet in my purse, I confirmed that I was within two blocks of the house: the home of Dr. Lawrence T. Reynolds, OB.

The occasional orange and brown and bloodred leaves dotted the manicured yards on Dr. Reynolds's street. The homes had been erected in the 1920s. Lots of Tudors in brick and white stucco. I might have been traversing an old English village.

I wore my ballet flats, a casual skirt, and a lightweight cinnamon-brown sweater tucked in. I might have been a homemaker out for a stroll. A neighbor. I waved to old men and said hello to some teens. I tipped my head at the postman. I dodged the hobbyhorse that a child had left on the walk.

I regarded the right side of the street with apparent nonchalance but kept an eye on the even-numbered addresses opposite. Eighteen fifty-four, eighteen fifty-two, eighteen fifty. Ahead, children were playing in a yard. I was close now, looking for eighteen thirty-six.

All last night I had envisioned this moment. I'd go to the door, bang its brass knocker, ask for Mrs. Reynolds. That was what doctors' wives were called, wasn't it? *Mrs.?* If doctors were gods, did that make her a goddess? Mrs. Reynolds the goddess would come sashaying through her grand foyer carrying an old-fashioned in the middle of the day, wearing her ruffled apron, her hair freshly coifed from the salon. She'd have handsome young rascals in cowboy hats and tutu-clad princesses—a whole blissful, healthy brood of them. Enough for a birthday party.

I would see that Mrs. Lawrence T. Reynolds knew what her husband had done. I would pitch a rock at her Rockwell-esque life. Hadn't that man's actions ruined my own life and led to my marriage's downfall? Eighteen forty-two. Eighteen-forty.

Then came the doctor's house. On the lawn, two little girls with barrettes in their hair were playing. One older, one younger. Squealing with their wagon and their trikes. Calling, "Mommy, Mommy." The front door was ajar. I was certain the woman of the house was not far.

I'd come to the prettiest home on the street. Eighteen thirty-six. The doctor had two daughters. Beautiful, angelic creatures with blonde, bouncy curls. They must have been about three years apart.

The doctor's home was traditional Tudor with its peaks and roof pitches, stucco with diagonal exposed-wood beams. There was field-stone on one face with its mullioned window up high where the girls probably slept in canopied beds; an arched opening onto the porch and light glinting off the panes. It was as if the family had uprooted these trees from the Old World and replanted them, so charmingly did they frame this house in its setting. And the sun: sunlight glistened behind the small manse, throwing it in relief against a golden sky.

The girls waved at me and called hello. They had their dollies and played on the yard's tiny slope, wearing their matching smocked dresses and anklets.

Two precious daughters. One. Two.

Mrs. Reynolds possessed what rightfully belonged to me: the perfect family. It wasn't fair that her husband had stolen that from me. I wanted to hurt him the only way I could. I'd strip him from his godlike throne. His wife would see the real man.

I took the first step up. It was the hardest one, I found—no turning back. The second step invited me to ascend toward the private sidewalk, the next of four large flagstone steps. I accepted the invitation without hesitation. Kathleen deserved for me to advance.

"Girls," a woman called.

I stood still as a statue—the way Dennis would have me do if being attacked by a bee. I smiled. I lifted my right hand, my fingers loose and friendly.

"Hello," I said.

The woman I presumed to be Mrs. Reynolds had the expression we might all have—all of us mothers. One that was at once approachable, as if perhaps she knew me but couldn't place my face, and on guard in case I meant her children harm. I pushed the thought away. I didn't want to relate to this woman. Her girls dropped their toys and ran to their mother.

"Mrs. Reynolds?" I said. We were on equal levels of the yard now, on the main flagstone walk between the lamppost and house.

"Yes, that's me. I'm sorry," she said, looking perplexed. "But you're . . ."

Her face was radiant. The woman had iridescent skin like Grace Kelly. She wore a pleated skirt, a white blouse, and a robin's-egg-blue sweater tied casually about her shoulders.

She extended her hand to shake mine. It was cold, and I felt her bones.

"Are you a friend from the hospital?" she said.

No.

Again that movie star smile, but now I saw the faintest puff of circles beneath her bloodshot eyes. A pinkness in her cheeks that seemed not from the sun or cosmetics.

Her older daughter clung onto her legs. The younger one said, "Mommy, can we have a Popsicle?" while hopping on one foot and then the other.

"I'm Millicent Glenn." I could not help but notice my heartbeat picking up. Again I tried to exude the warm manner of a neighbor.

But Mrs. Reynolds's face shadowed. She glanced quickly across her shoulder to the door.

"Girls, run along into the house. Nana will be waiting for you."

The younger one ran around the Radio Flyer wagon and on to the door. The older stayed latched to her mother's thigh.

Mrs. Reynolds took a deep breath. "Mrs. Glenn, I was going to send you a note."

She knew me?

"It's just, well, with Lawrence's mother here, and with the children, I—" she said. "I'm sorry for what happened to you."

"What happened to me?" I said, anger spiking. "You must mean what happened to me *and my daughter*."

The child at the woman's side twisted her head toward me. My tone had startled her. Yet I felt a snarl coming from somewhere deep inside me where my babies had grown.

The woman shooed her daughter inside to Nana, keeping her eyes on me.

"Nothing 'happened' to me," I said. "Nothing 'happened' to my baby. Your arrogant, unethical drunkard of a husband killed my daughter. He destroyed my family in every way imaginable. That is what *happened*, Mrs. Reynolds."

She drew back. "I know," she said softly with a slight shake of her head and her limp and upturned hands. "I know everything."

My lips parted, and my neck prickled with surprise. I saw her eyes fill with water.

"I'm going back inside now, Mrs. Glenn. But first, please know that my husband was tormented by what he'd done. You see, he left me a letter. That was before he . . . went away. Your family has my sincerest apologies. And now I must make calls. I need to complete the funeral arrangements. And I've yet to tell the girls."

She turned and strode to the arched stone entry of her storybook home, the pleats of her skirt swaying, her shoulders squared, and her head held high.

I heard the door's latch from where I stood. I watched the doctor's wife float from one window to the next to the next, drawing the draperies in the midafternoon light.

CHAPTER TWENTY-TWO

October 1951

The headlights from Dennis's car beamed through the front picture window as he pulled into the drive. A wave of nausea overtook me. He was back from the Gunnison meeting in Indiana, where he was to have received a commendation. I lifted Janie out of her high chair. We would greet Daddy tonight, together, at the kitchen door. When he came in, he'd be enamored with her big smile and a new tooth she had just cut. That wouldn't help smooth over his and my first encounter since our big fight—since I'd blamed him for hurting me. But it would give me a second to breathe. There was much to tell him. Dennis didn't know of the doctor's forgery. He didn't know the doctor had committed suicide. And I was sick with the burden of having to admit to him my mistake, to repent for all the hateful words I'd said. *There I was, lying helpless in a bed with morphine pumping into my veins, and you just had to scrawl your big old John Hancock all over the dotted line. Now I'm barren. It's all your fault.*

How could the words *I'm sorry* ever mean enough?

Were there things said in a marriage that could never be taken back? If I could take back the words I'd said, I'd cram them into my mouth with a shovel bite after bite until I gagged in the pit of my throat—but I'd swallow every last crumb. Yet would that be enough for me to be pardoned?

When I'd returned home from berating Mrs. Reynolds—where I'd left a wounded woman who would raise her children alone—I in my selfishness thought only of myself. I thought only of my own devastation. My own lost family. Lashing out at her in my need for revenge hadn't helped me. I still hated that doctor even in his death. He'd taken everything I had. He'd led me down the path to condemning my own husband.

After old Dr. Welch had shown me the signed form in his office—and after Dennis proclaimed he'd not consented—how had I not considered my husband might be loyal? I'd lain awake all last night asking myself: What'd caused me to doubt him?

I was not myself these days, I reasoned. I had suffered the two greatest tragedies of my life.

First, I'd lost a daughter at the hands of a drunkard. One noble nurse had stood up for me; another had caved to the power of her godlike superior. It wasn't fair.

Second, I'd lost my ability to bear children. The drunkard had struck again, snipping my insides with the blades of his scissors. It wasn't fair.

It wasn't fair what this man had done.

And that's when it came to me. I bolted upright in my bed, the light of the night's sky slicing through a crack in the curtains. I hadn't thought for a moment that Dennis didn't sign the form because somewhere deep inside me—buried beneath the pain of my belly's scar, the ache of my empty arms, the agony of hearing the words that my baby was dropped, the devastation of seeing a big letter *D* scrawled on the page, and the load of my buckets of tears—I remembered: I remembered a hint of how my husband had taken things away from me before, too. My work, my professional value, my sense of worth in the business. It wasn't fair.

Yet I was suffocating in this terrible time and blinded to all the good.

Indeed, I was so utterly bereft I'd forgotten how Dennis had once held me blameless of the condition that started with an *E*. I'd dismissed how he'd said he'd forgive me if our loss was my fault for choosing the doctor—which he'd insisted it wasn't. I'd ignored how he'd put me above all others on the day that we wed. He was an imperfect man; he'd made mistakes. But I, with my inner terrors and rabid drive to lash out, had overlooked his love.

It was a Friday, but that morning I crawled out of bed and went to the Presbyterian church with Janie in my arms. While we'd never been an every-Sunday family, today I'd needed to be in a holy place. Janie and I had sat alone in the sanctuary with her little-girl voice rising to echoes as she looked up, pointing to the vast high ceiling. How would Dennis and I get through our problems? Over the course of time since we'd said "I do," we'd known them all: diminishing the other's value, retaliation, being closed off or unbearably open with our feelings, mistrust and spite, suffering loss and grief and fear and fury.

How could we make our wedding vows last? "For better, for worse, till death do us part?" Was it too late?

Even Mama couldn't have warned me of how bad the worst parts would be. I had closed my eyes in the church, bowed my head, folded my hands, and prayed: *Dear God, please help us through this. Help Dennis and me to heal. Help us to unite, face our losses together. Help him to accept my contrition. And, please, if You can, forgive me my sins. In Your holy name I pray, Amen.*

"Daddy, Daddy," Janie called now as Dennis came through the kitchen door from the garage.

"How's my love bug," Dennis said, his smile bright for his precious girl. Her arms stretched out to him and he took her—and he looked right through me. He didn't kiss me. He didn't say, "Something smells good," like he usually did. He didn't ask, "What's for dinner?"

His air was so cool that I shivered. He carried our daughter into the living room as though I were not present.

"Janie got a new toothy?" he said. Janie let him rub his finger along her swollen gum, the way she hadn't let me. Dennis had not needed me to point out her new tooth. Would he ever need me again?

I retreated to the kitchen like a mechanical metal robot and tested the pasta on the stove. With a long-tined fork I pulled a spaghetti noodle from boiling water, pinched it in half with my thumbnail, and studied the inside. Seeing no hard center, I tested the strand between my teeth. Perfect al dente. I had planned Italian night for my husband's homecoming, complete with homemade marinara and meatballs I had stocked in the freezer. And Janie would get one of her favorites, too: garlic toast. Now I felt like throwing everything in the sink and washing it all down the drain. I was too late. I feared I'd lost everything dear to me.

"How was the meeting at the factory?" I asked, desperate, grasping. I served Dennis his plate and took my place at the side of the table.

"Fine," he said as he twirled a bite of spaghetti onto his fork. Silence.

I cut Janie's pasta into bite-size bits while she tore her toast in two. "Here," I said. "It's going to be yummy." I set the bowl on her high chair tray.

"Was the traffic all right driving home from Indiana?"

Dennis shrugged and handed a cup of milk to Janie. "Here, honey, have a sip," he said. "That's a good girl."

I hated being closed out. "And the Gunnison award?" I said. "You brought it home?"

He nodded.

Any shred of hope I'd had was sinking. My husband did not offer a word to me through the whole meal. He spoke only to our daughter. I felt like a leper at my own table.

I was watching the good part of my life slip away. I might never enjoy a family dinner around our table again.

After the meal Dennis wiped Janie's face of the red, sticky sauce and carried her away, her voice gurgling in delight, her dimpled hand at his nape. Once she was down for the night, it would be just Dennis and me. Butterflies flew through my belly, flapping their wings.

I heard water running in the bathtub. I heard Dennis playing with Janie's tiny tugboat and her splashing as he bathed her. I heard him singing her his silly barbershop ditty as he vigorously dried her hair with a towel: "Go to the bobb-ie, get a massag-ie." Janie squealed with joy. I cleared the dishes and wrestled with whether to take a pill. If I resisted, my anxiety would only worsen. If I gave in, there was some chance I'd get a little sleep. I'd limit it to one pill—to stay balanced, to give me a boost when I finally got Dennis's attention. If I got it.

Dennis was telling Janie a bedtime story when I padded down the hall without making a sound. "And he huffed, and he puffed," Dennis said to her, "and he blewwww the house down." She giggled as he tickled her ribs.

I missed being part of their fun.

I came out of the bathroom to find Dennis turning on the television. He squatted before it and rotated the channel knob to all three stations in turn. He landed on *Man Against Crime*, a program about private eyes.

"Dennis," I said, as he scuffed to the sofa. I turned the volume down on the television as he lit a cigarette. The corners of his lips were tucked in.

"I shouldn't have mistrusted you," I said. His eyebrows rose.

I had rehearsed what I'd say in my head so many times that even now, as tranquility set in from the pill, the words spilled out just the way I wanted them to. I had not started with what I had learned from the nurse nor from the doctor's wife. I began with where I was wrong.

"I accused you of doing something you'd never do," I said, taking the chair opposite him with my fear settling inside like a brick. "You wouldn't have gone behind my back and signed those papers."

"I'm glad you finally recognize that," he said, his tone flat. I hung on his words, his voice aimed toward me, however monotone. I was that needy. I yearned to be relevant. To not be cast away.

"I realize how badly I hurt you," I said. "I know you were telling the truth. You hadn't conspired to make me barren."

"Right," he said. "I've made mistakes. Big ones." His stare was penetrating, making me quiver. "But I wouldn't have done that to you."

"I know. I'm very sorry." I had turned on my ally. There was a buzz in my ears to fill the dead silence.

He sighed and lit a cigarette.

"I called Nurse Breck again," I said, lowering my head in shame. Not because of calling her, but because I hadn't come to her conclusion on my own: Dennis's innocence. "She told me something she hadn't revealed before. Dr. Reynolds forged the papers. He wrote your name on the authorization form after he'd carried out the procedure by mistake."

"Fuck," Dennis said under his breath. With his cigarette pinched between two fingers of one hand, he rubbed his free fingers up and down his forehead as if he were in pain. Smoke swirled in front of his face and over his head. "Fuck," he said again, jarring me.

He took a drag. When he blew the smoke out, it came as a rumble from his throat. "I wish I felt vindicated," he said. "But I feel like shit."

"There's more," I said, remembering the letter left to Mrs. Reynolds. He shook his head no, fervently. "No more. I can't take it."

"But—"

He rose. "Not tonight. I have to get some sleep."

What did this mean? Had he accepted my apology? Or did he need more time? Or was this the first step toward him walking out the door and my life forever? I didn't want him to go. I wanted to save us.

A glint of light on metal caught my eye. On the table beside him. "What's that?" I asked, pointing.

He snuffed out his cigarette in the ashtray. "The Gunnison award."

I went to retrieve the walnut plaque with its engraved metal inset. Gunnison manufacturing headquarters had honored him:

FASTEST GROWING DEALERSHIP IN A FIVE-STATE REGION
GUNNISON HOMES BY GLENN
DENNIS GLENN, PROPRIETOR AND AUTHORIZED DEALER

I couldn't help a genuine smile. I wished I'd have been there, but wives never attended those meetings. My hard work would go unrecognized. And my resentment for that—for Dennis keeping my contribution contained—had blinded me to his virtue when our family crisis struck.

But he'd worked hard to build the business. He deserved this. "I'm proud of you."

There was an ever so faint, reluctant dip of one dimple. "They've asked me to do a new dealer training in the spring. Imagine, this old country boy in front of recruits."

A rush of hope surged. He'd spoken in future terms. Might we survive, Dennis and me?

"Don't teach them too well," I said, risking a small smile.

"I won't give away all my secrets," he said.

⁓

The obituary appeared in the morning's paper. I seldom read the *Cincinnati Enquirer* before Dennis scanned it over breakfast. But now

I had reason. I ran warm water over my fingertips to erase the paper's black print. I'd left the page turned up for when Dennis came out of the bedroom. We'd slept the whole night without touching. But he hadn't slept with his back facing me. He'd wished me good night.

"Good morning," I said. Our eyes connected.

"Morning." He wasn't as cold as he'd been the night before, but he was still on edge. He sat down to his scrambled eggs and toast. "Thank you."

"Remember last night, after I explained about the forged papers, I told you there was something else, but you wanted to wait?" I said. "May I tell you now?"

"What is it?" He spread a pat of butter on his toast.

I gestured to the newspaper. "Dr. Reynolds committed suicide. Authorities found him in the ravine below Grandin Bridge."

Blood rushed to Dennis's face as if he'd been hanging upside down on the swing set with Janie for a long time. I expected to hear him say that the man—the one who had killed our baby, sterilized me, and forged his name—had gotten what he deserved.

I slid the newspaper closer. He picked it up and scanned the obit.

He said nothing. Had I ruined a reconciliation before it was cemented?

"His poor family," Dennis said then, sounding strangled. "He had kids."

That's all he had to say? The man who killed our child was dead.

"Have you anything else to say?" I tried to keep my tone contained. Our marriage was balancing on a tightrope.

"How do you know he killed himself?" he said. The obit hadn't indicated that, had it? "Did you call your nurse friend again?"

"No."

I didn't want to tell Dennis of the two beautiful girls in twin smocked dresses, one older, one younger. I didn't want to tell him of their beautiful mother, who revealed to me her grief on the flagstone steps after I'd badgered her. But I had to.

So I told him.

Dennis's lips tightened. This was it. He'd leave me. He'd take all his worldly goods and go. Mama's sad, weathered face came to me, frightening with its picture of destitution and loneliness. And unlike her, I had contributed to my own marriage's downfall.

He pushed away from the table and stood. I could see from his eyes—by the way the blackness of his pupils had overtaken the blue—he had but one thing to say, so I'd better listen.

"I might have done the same thing if I were in your shoes," Dennis said, and I felt relief. "Now forget about it. Forget about what the doctor did, too. What you don't seem to get is that his being gone doesn't fix a damn thing. Nothing we do will bring Kathy back. Just take care of Janie. Take care of yourself. And take care of us." He kissed my cheek and left the room.

The greatest danger had passed—there was hope we'd survive. I closed my eyes and rejoiced.

But unlike Dennis, I couldn't forget the doctor so easily. And I was troubled by this helpless feeling I got when my husband gave a directive and ended our conversation before I was through.

⁓

I heard Dennis in the bathroom lathering his face with cream, letting Janie watch him shave. Daddy-daughter time couldn't be forgotten, no matter how shocking the news I'd given him.

When he came out, I was still sitting at the table, my coffee cup empty. Dennis had his old jeans on and said, "I have to mow the grass one more time before winter." That man had always loved the smell of fresh-cut grass. It reminded him of the country.

Janie cried, and I swiftly made for her room. I settled her in the playpen in front of the television: *Cartoons and Coco* would amuse her for a time. I carried a stuffed wicker clothes basket to the couch. I'd gotten behind on folding Dennis's whites. *Forget about what the doctor did*, he'd said at the table. I separated his cotton undershirts from his jockey shorts and then tackled one pile at a time. How could I forget about everything? I couldn't just say *Snap! It's over.*

In our bedroom I set two neat stacks of folded whites on the bed. Darn. I couldn't fit all his whites in the drawers anymore. I'd been putting off rearranging his dresser, but it couldn't wait any longer. I slid open the drawer with his casual shorts and removed two pairs at a time. These could go in a box in the cedar closet until summer came again—when the forget-me-nots would bloom in the color of Dennis's eyes. The lawn mower buzzed outside.

What was this? As I reached in for the last pair of shorts, I felt something like paper pushed to the back of the drawer.

I slipped out an envelope in the shadows of the drawer. It was a large manila envelope addressed to our home, to the attention of Mr. and Mrs. Dennis Glenn. Something containing my name he hadn't shared? That rattled me. I bit the inside of my jaw. My fingers grazed the back side of the envelope. The wide lip was loose, its dry sticky-gummed seal having been ripped, its metal clip released. In the top right corner of this front side, the envelope's postal mark noted it had been sent in early April, when I was still hospitalized. Now it was fall. I scanned the return address.

The parcel was from the funeral home.

The lawn mower continued its roar, louder as Dennis ambled toward the house, fainter as he walked away. I lifted the flap and peered inside.

Enclosed were two sheets. I slipped them out, my hands moist. Laughter from the cartoon characters on the television set mocked me. Janie giggled along with them. I read the two documents.

One was a birth certificate. One was a death certificate.

The same name was typed into the blanks on each page: Kathleen Sylvia Glenn. Like a gravestone, these pages captured a life's two most notable events. Birth. Death. But the paper, like the stone, was silent, giving no hint of all that'd happened in between. Seeing the tragedy spelled out so plainly on two official forms made my shoulders hunch forward; it was worse than reading the hospital administration's letter weeks after our baby died. Kathleen had been born at 7:45 p.m. and died at 10:55 p.m. My daughter's life had lasted exactly three hours, ten minutes.

Trembling, I returned the documents to their envelope. I put the envelope carefully back where I'd found it, and I replaced the summer shorts in the drawer, too.

Seeing the contents of the envelope Dennis had secreted—this symbol of his own torment, of something he'd hidden to try to protect me from pain—humbled me. He hurt, too. And he cared.

I went to the bathroom, washed, and repaired my face. Neatened my hair. I was sitting with Janie, watching the children's show, when the back screen door slapped against its frame and Dennis tramped in.

"Care for some apple cider?" I asked.

"Sure," he said, and his dimples almost flashed.

I had a feeling God was answering my prayer.

2015

I'd asked the girls to meet me at the St. Thomas Episcopal Church in the village. It wasn't a Sunday—and even when it was, I didn't attend regularly. But I needed to be in this sacred place now. Being closer to the presence of God had helped me years before with Dennis. It might work again in my present church with the girls. Jane and Kelsey would soon arrive, each on the precipice of a significant moment in their lives.

And so was I, for I had something more of import to tell them—a confession I'd come to since last night by the fire.

I sat alone for now in the quiet of the church's nave. No sermon, no choir singing, no parishioners coughing. The reverend had waved as I passed and would not disturb me. The traditional pews had a sheen and smelled faintly of lemon oil. I'd selected the pew nearest the stained-glass window of Mary overlooking her baby in his manger. A golden glow shone from Jesus's head. The nave's lanterns—suspended from the tall, beamed ceiling planked with dark wood—were not illuminated. But midmorning sun shone through the window, setting its scene aglow in crimson reds and royal blues, leafy greens and shimmery yellows.

I bowed my head, closed my eyes, and folded my gnarled hands together. *Dear Lord,* I prayed silently. *Give me strength to bring my story to conclusion. And for the girls to accept me, no matter my weaknesses. I pray, oh Lord, for two other things, greater things beyond any hope I have for myself. I ask that You watch over my Janie—heal her. And I pray for Kelsey and the baby she will have, too: please bring that child into this world safely. In Your holy name, I ask, Amen.*

⌒

Kelsey arrived first, her windswept hair smelling of herbal shampoo. She wore maternity jeans and her poncho that looked Southwestern with its hues of turquoise, brown, and orange. She slid into the pew beside me.

"Hi, Grandma," she whispered. She hugged me and said, "The baby's kicking."

Hearing that took my breath away. "May I?" I asked, reaching my hand over. Kelsey pulled her poncho aside. Tears welled in my eyes. My great-grandchild was shifting around inside Kelsey, and the baby's faint movement—movement that I could foresee growing more pronounced, more visible in months to come—tickled the palm of my hand like feathers.

"Isn't it wonderful, Grandma?"

"The best sensation in the world," I said. I would never forget the feeling of my own babies leaning their rumps to my side on the right, or their elbows rippling back and forth beneath the taut skin of my tummy for Dennis and me to watch.

Now one of those babies, Jane, appeared in the pew. She was pink in the cheeks. Kelsey moved out to let her mother sit in between us. We all had a cursory embrace. Nothing more and nothing less had happened since the night before at the bonfire. The imaginary thin string connecting Jane and me had not been cut. Not yet. But it remained stretched taut.

"I'd almost forgotten," Jane said, letting her gaze take in the stained glass, the ceiling, "how pretty this church is." Her expression shifted. "But why are we here?"

Did she mean, why had I chosen this place? Or why were we together at all?

"Girls, thank you for coming," I said. "There's something from my heart I need you to hear." Kelsey leaned forward in the pew to see me better over her mother, her elbow resting on her thigh, her jaw propped on her bent-back hand.

"No matter what went on in that hospital on the night Kathleen passed—no matter what the doctors or anyone else did or did not do—losing the baby was really all *my* fault," I said.

They had to know this much, if not how the near-collapse of my marriage was also my fault.

"I had changed doctors midstream. I put pride before my child."

Grief and alarm filled their faces in turns. "Mom," Jane said, shaking her head left and right, "don't you ever blame yourself for what that man did."

"You didn't do anything wrong," Kelsey said, reaching over Jane to pat my leg. "I mean, from everything you could see, you chose a fine physician. Dr. Collins had amazing credentials. Pauline had used him herself. Then he delegated someone else to you on an overcrowded night in the ward. And that guy was drunk." Kelsey's eyes pleaded with me. "I agree with Mom. You can't possibly blame yourself."

"I decided on that doctor who Pauline had used because I wanted control. Pure and simple." I tugged a tissue from my purse and blew my nose.

"If there's anything I've learned in the last month," Jane said, "it's that nobody has control. Not doctors. Not women. Nobody."

A silence settled over us. I could almost hear the girls' heartbeats as shadows from clouds dimmed the glow of the stained glass. Kelsey took out a bottled water, passed it around for us to sip in the way of a communion chalice. Could it be true that they didn't find me culpable?

At last someone spoke. Kelsey.

"So you made that decision. You've gotta know, though, that I'm sitting here this whole time thinking that if women like you hadn't taken risks and asked for more, women like me wouldn't have any choices." She folded her arms to her belly.

"She's right," Jane said, her eyes connecting with mine in a way I'd forever cherish.

But it was my fault. Pride had gotten in my way just as sure as Mama's had when she pitched those oranges out the window, one piece of fruit at a time. I too had cut off my nose to spite my own face. "But my pride—"

"Grandma, did you ever think that maybe pride had gotten in Papaw's way first?" Kelsey said, thoughtfully.

That stung. I wouldn't have expected it to, but it did. By necessity this story revealed not only my flaws, but Kelsey's grandfather's as well. It struck me then: I wanted Dennis to remain a hero in her eyes, even if I fell from grace. Perhaps I would tell the girls of how I'd doubted him—and of the forged papers—after all. But then, I thought, where would I stop this story? Would I continue with my candor? I would not lie. But moving forward after that, would I omit other things that happened, to protect his legacy?

But Dennis had let me choose the doctor. I bore the ultimate responsibility.

As the sun brightened again, and the abundant stained-glass windows of the nave were awash with colorful arch-shaped light, Jane looked at me, solemn and determined. And in that instant, I thought perhaps that here in this house of God, I was not only to have a promise of prayers being answered, but I was to get my last wish—one I'd wished way back when Jane first came home. Forgiveness. Forgiveness for having kept from her the truth about her family.

"Ladies," Jane said soberly, rubbing the scar at her brow. "I've been wrestling with when to tell you this, but now is as good a time as any." The hair on my arms stood on end as I suddenly felt very cold. "Just as I arrived outside a bit ago," she said, "the breast doctor phoned me personally. The pathologist's report is already in."

CHAPTER TWENTY-THREE

January 1952

I had always known bitter, slicing winds in the city every winter. Nothing, though, had prepared me for the harsh winters at the farm— and it seemed worse today, here, on the far other side of the acreage, a quarter mile away, where Nathan and Abbie lived. Thank heavens the snow and gusts that whipped out of the west and charged across the sallow fields had yielded, but Nathan had thigh-high drifts against fence posts and one end of his house.

"Here you go, Margaret," Nathan said. He tossed the wood-and-metal Flexible Flyer into the snow at the feet of our eight-year-old niece. Margaret climbed atop the sled—not an easy task with the snow up to her knees. Making matters worse, the surface layer was frozen crisp in spots.

But off she went down the short slope, while we all cheered her on. *"Wheeee!"*

Janie was two now, and I'd bundled her up in boots and a blue snowsuit that Dennis's sister had passed down from the boys. Our daughter looked like an imp who'd grown up in an igloo. She was getting so big—she'd even taken to climbing out of her crib at home.

"You want a turn, love bug?" Dennis asked Janie, pointing to the sled. My heart lurched. I let loose of the lapels of my coat with which I'd guarded my face from the cold. Janie was excited, snow spraying off her mittens as she clapped her hands. I would step back and let her enjoy. She was in her father's care. He wouldn't let her get hurt.

In the three months since my apology and our reconciliation, we had focused on our family. With winter snows came fewer house builds. Every morning after I served breakfast, Dennis played with Janie before going into the office. From her rocking horse to puzzles to tea parties for bears, he had his daddy time. I was unable to follow Dennis's advice and "forget" what the late doctor had done, to put memories in little boxes in compartments of my mind, but I had learned better to count my blessings. I thought that come summer, maybe I'd take on some business duties. But certain things would trigger my guilt or grief—babies in buggies, articles on pregnancy, news of medical calamity of any sort. A daily pill or two helped contain that. Dennis and I had returned to our marital bed, and he still called me the prettiest girl a guy ever got, not to mention the smartest. That man had a way of not holding a grudge.

Our youngest niece—Nathan and Abbie's girl who'd been born two months before Kathleen—turned one today. Following the sledding, the Glenns would celebrate. Mother Glenn and Papa Glenn and all four Glenn siblings were here together with their spouses and children. Eighteen people in all.

I'd taken one pill and would work hard to savor the best parts of today: Dennis, Janie, and me. My small family.

Dennis didn't let Janie go down the hill alone. He didn't let go of the rope at all. He steadied her with one hand on her back and led the sled by the rope with the other. Dennis was no dummy. He'd figured out how to head off my overprotective response before it could strike.

"*Wheee!*" Janie screamed. The other children jumped up and down, rooting for their cousin on her first downhill slide. Mother Glenn had her camera—a newer Canon where she looked through a fancy three-mode optical viewfinder—and snapped all the children's pictures on their turns. I laughed despite myself.

The kids—the little kids and the big kids, otherwise known as adults—started a snowball fight. Even Papa Glenn joined in. I bent, picked up two handfuls of snow, packed a ball the size of a grapefruit, and threw it at Nathan, who ducked just in time.

Unfortunately, it smacked Abbie in the side of the head. She was fine, but I couldn't help myself—I fell into a giggling spell the likes of which I hadn't had in ages. I couldn't make it stop.

⁓

Inside Abbie's house was a different affair. My spirits sank. It was as if every day she stepped out of *Ladies' Home Journal* and swept through her rooms, a feather duster in one hand, and cream and sugar in the other. Abbie had transformed her stylish house into a one-year-old child's paradise. Yellow crêpe paper and party streamers dangled from the living room ceiling. I had to spread them apart with my hands while walking through, the way a person on safari might do in a jungle. The colors complemented her striking walls—two of which were painted in dark Adirondack green, the other two in calabash yellow. Abbie had borrowed long folding tables from the fellowship hall at their church, and though the kiddies would dine in her kitchen, space was still tight. Nathan had moved all the living room furniture to the perimeter— a modern orange sofa, armless with its backrest button-tufted into squares, dark-green chairs, and accessory pieces in blond wood. White tablecloths covered the makeshift dining tables, and running down their centers, Abbie had twisted and taped more yellow streamers. Balloons in every color of the rainbow were tied on one chair at each table. As centerpieces, Abbie had arranged framed snapshots of the birthday girl over the course of her first year. I couldn't bear to look at them.

I hadn't been in that festive room for three minutes when I had to get out. It was all too much. I would catch my breath, I thought, and return when better prepared.

I navigated the kitchen, squeezing between Mother Glenn carrying a tray of roast beef sandwiches and Dennis's sister clutching a stack full of plates. This room was no different. Its jolly air stifled me.

Would the bathroom be free? I darted down the hall. I closed the door, pulled the pills from the pocket of my slacks, and popped one with two handfuls of water. Then I swallowed another pill. I dried my hands and face with a sage-green towel monogrammed in gold with a scrolling *G*. I returned to the kitchen to find Abbie flitting about as if she were mother of the bride, not mother of the one-year-old. She'd set her baked masterpiece on a cake stand in the center of her rectangular table. The birthday cake stood tall and proud, three layers high, and had white seven-minute frosting that she'd boiled and whipped until it was as peaked as meringue. There were lollipops on sticks with colorful swirls stuck about the cake's top, and gumdrops running up and down the sides like the twine on a drum. One pink candle graced the cake's center. I counted to ten in my head, so I wouldn't break down.

I would make a beautiful cake this year, too. For Janie.

When time came to sing to the birthday girl in her high chair, I stood beside Dennis, one arm entwined in his and holding his hand tightly. Over the years I had held hands with this man through Coney Island and the zoo and the park—but today his hand was as clammy and needy as mine. Our eyes met, and though he let it show so infrequently, his eyes harbored his own grief. It was good that I wasn't alone in that moment. Abbie lit the candle and everyone's voices rang out, and the children's eyes and smiles were wide all around—including Janie's. No one cast a sympathetic glance at us. No one had spoken that day of what they must know to be true: Dennis and I were heartbroken beneath our gay facades. In fact, no one talked about our loss at all. Ever. Not even Mother Glenn. They didn't want to bring it up, I supposed, for fear of peeling the scabs off our wounds. They didn't appreciate how pretending nothing had happened hurt my feelings just as much. More.

Yet in their defense, the family didn't know the worst. They didn't know *how* Kathleen had died. They didn't know about my becoming barren. Dennis and I had agreed to keep that to ourselves.

Baby Linda Jo smeared the devil's-food cake and fluffy white frosting all over her nose and eyelids and through her hair, which had finally started to grow. She licked her fingers and dropped chunks of cake on the floor. Nathan's dogs lapped up the crumbs. We ate, and for a few moments the merriment was almost contagious because Janie and the kids were having such fun.

Janie wiggled her fingers. "Moe cake."

Soon the women cleared the mess in the kitchen. I'd survived the birthday party. Papa Glenn and the Glenn sisters' husbands took the kids back out to sled. Dennis and I would pack Janie up and leave as soon as he checked out his brother's bomb shelter plans in the basement. Nathan was considering putting a bomb shelter underground, to house his family in case of Soviet attack. It was the latest thing. I'd read that schools had started having drills where children huddled beneath their desks, too. Nathan would be the first one we knew to build such a shelter. But I was ready to leave.

As I heard the women laughing, I escaped to the bathroom and scrounged in my pocket for another pill.

I stumbled my way back to the kitchen. Abbie cornered me. She wiggled one index finger at me. We stood near her pantry while the Glenn women chatted and the dishes rattled and metal pans jangled in the porcelain sink. "Millie, I've been so busy today," Abbie said in a whisper, a sympathetic expression on her face. "I just want to tell you I'm sorry about everything."

Abbie actually empathized. It surprised and warmed me. "Yes, this is a hard day on us. We miss Kathleen."

Abbie's face wrinkled with confusion. Had I spoken indistinctly? Slurred my words?

"No, no, dear," she said. "I mean about how you can't have more children. Poor Janie will never have siblings."

Now I was confused—and outraged. My body went rigid. How had Abbie known? I was 100 percent certain that Dennis had told no one.

"What's going on over there?" said one of Dennis's sisters. "Are we missing some juicy gossip?"

I wanted to drag Abbie by her hair to the bathroom and have it out in private. I waved my other sister-in-law off.

"Did you hear me?" Abbie said, eyes sorrowful and boring into mine. "I said it's a pity that Janie won't have any brothers or sisters."

"I heard you," I said, not moderating my tone. "Did Dr. Welch's nurse, your friend, tell you?"

Abbie nodded. The women had all gone quiet and were staring at us now.

"What's wrong?" Mother Glenn said, her face registering concern.

Abbie said, "I believe I've just stuck my foot in my mouth. I think I've upset Millie."

Mother Glenn's arm was around my shoulders by now. "Abbie, what did you say?"

"I merely offered my concern," Abbie said to the curious faces gathering around as if I were an animal in the circus.

I wiggled out of Mother Glenn's arm. "Abbie, why do you insist on being such a busybody?" I said, with every word becoming more pointed, louder. "Why do you insist on sticking your nose in my private affairs?"

Someone said, "Millie dear, calm down."

"Don't ask me to calm down," I said. "I have every right to be anything but calm." It was a shout. "Hear ye, hear ye, you Glenns one and all," I yelled. "I am sterile. Janie is doomed to be an only child just as I was. The doctor—no, no, not good old Dr. Welch—but the new doctor I'd handpicked, just so you know, pawned me off on another OB. An SOB. Yes, it was that doctor who had severed my tubes like a Nazi. I can't have more babies," I screamed.

I resisted Mother's Glenn's attempts at comfort. I pushed back. "Please don't," I said. I looked to her and to our horror-stricken hostess and the rest of the stunned faces, and I yelled, "No one. No one." I thrust my finger into Abbie's face, so she'd know that meant her, too. "No one will ever speak of my loss again. Not to my face, not behind my back. From this point forward, as far as the world knows, the two tragedies Dennis and I suffered didn't happen."

"Millie."

I turned to the voice. It was Dennis.

He stood in the corner of the kitchen near the basement door, beside his brother. They'd returned from their talk of bomb shelters. Every head in the room craned from me to my husband.

Dennis was still across the room, but he said for all to hear: "I stand by my wife. What Millie wants, I want." He stared directly at Abbie. "Millie has asked that no one repeat the fact that she can no longer conceive. And that no one speaks of the baby we lost. That shouldn't be so difficult, should it? Given that not one of you offered a word of sympathy as she and I quietly suffered through this day."

He stood by me, and I felt important. I recalled him plunking a cheese cube in his mouth eons ago at a party where husbands taunted me. This time Dennis put me first.

His gaze scanned the room. "Promise us," Dennis said as the last of the day's sunshine streamed through the window over the sink. He looked to each of the women in his family, and to Nathan, too.

"We promise," they said, each and every one. Including Abbie.

And if I could read the lines on Mother Glenn's face, they said she'd do everything in her power to ensure no one broke that promise.

2015

Sunlight shone through the church's stained glass, casting colorful prisms on Jane's face. My daughter said: "I got the all-clear sign from the doctor. I'm going to live."

"Praise the Lord!" I said. Janie was fine. She was fine. My little girl was fine.

Kelsey said, "I'm so, so, so relieved."

We were joyous. We hugged and we cried and we gave thanks. Together.

⁓

"I gotta go find a bathroom," Kelsey said. "Be right back."

Once Jane and I were alone in the pew, I told her about the fateful winter day at the farm, of her sledding with her father, of Linda Jo's first birthday party. Of the family confrontation.

Jane said, "Now I finally understand why Kathleen was a secret. You had forbidden anyone to speak of her—or to speak of what else the doctor had done to you. You felt it was your personal right to keep it private. I love how Daddy extracted the family promise. But—" She stopped midsentence and looked at her lap.

"But?"

"But. But I wish I'd known everything much sooner." She pulled some breath mints from her purse, and we each took one. They were like little strips of tape that tasted as if I'd swallowed sprigs of mint. "I might have understood where you and Daddy were coming from while I was growing up. Like I might have appreciated why you were overprotective or distant in turns."

It was clear she had more to say to me. I let Jane keep talking. She had listened to me these last couple of days whether she'd liked what I had to say or not.

"Do you know, I remember how sad you got every Mother's Day? I get it now. But back then, I thought it was my fault. The breakfasts Daddy and I cooked didn't measure up to yours. The gift I made or bought wasn't something you wanted. The card we gave you was not 'whatever' enough. You were the only mom I knew who was sad on Mother's Day."

"Jane, that's terrible," I said, pressing my fingers to my forehead. How could I have hurt her that way? I'd not realized the extent to which she'd internalized my actions. "I'm so sorry. You and your father did everything to make Mother's Days special for me. Everything. I mean, I wouldn't have survived that holiday without you." How had I not conveyed that?

People at times describe their experience as "an emotional roller coaster." That's what this day was for me. The low of confessing my fault in Kathy's tragedy. The high of all highs in learning that my eldest was out of harm's way. Followed by the careening low of hearing how I, myself, had caused Jane so much pain. When would we get to the coaster's flat track, to the smooth-coasting part where it slowed to a stop?

Kelsey returned from the restroom. "I feel better." Then she stared at us, sensing the tension between her mother and me. "You guys. I need you two to be good. You do realize that, don't you?" Her voice cracked. "I mean, what can possibly dampen the great news we got?"

"Ladies," a voice called, and we all startled. The church secretary. "Sorry to disturb your private worship and fellowship, but I'm afraid we'll soon be locking up for the afternoon."

"No problem," said Kelsey, eager to leave.

We thanked the woman and scooted out of the pew, and Kelsey opened the heavy doors of the church. I prayed again silently, thanking the Lord for giving me more time with Jane. We stepped out into the bright, pretty day of God's green earth. Even the chilly air smelled better, somehow, now that my girl was safe. The breeze carried a spark of hope for us.

Then Jane rubbed at the scar at her brow, and I slid down, down into another rabbit hole of memory.

CHAPTER TWENTY-FOUR

August 1952

Janie. She was shouting, crying, "Mommy, Mommy." Was I dreaming? I forced my eyes open and listened. Daylight. It was the middle of the day. I'd drifted off to sleep while Janie was napping. But she wasn't sleeping now. Her shrill screams were getting louder. I shot out of my bed.

She wasn't in her crib. She wasn't in her room at all.

I found her in the bathroom, her face covered in blood. Her hands covered in blood. She had climbed out of her bed—and climbed atop the toilet seat.

My heart was in my throat. I'd never felt such thumping panic. She was bleeding from her forehead. "What happened?"

"Have, have," she said, but it rhymed with *behave*. Have, have. I didn't understand what she meant. I felt groggy. I wanted to call Pauline to help, but I couldn't let go of Janie long enough to get to the kitchen phone.

I snatched a dry washrag from the towel bar and gently patted the area over her eye, blood soaking it. She was cut—a nick of skin dug out and half of her left eyebrow gone. I pressed the cloth to try to stop the bleeding. I lifted the rag. The brilliant scarlet blood kept seeping out. I switched the rag to a clean part and pressed it in again. I glanced down. Her father's razor was in the sink, not standing in its usual cup.

I understood now: Janie had tried to shave herself. "Shave, shave," she'd said.

I swept her into my left arm, keeping the pressure on her eye with my right hand, and I ran with her to the kitchen phone. I was heartsick. Dennis shouldn't have left the razor lying out. He had to be careful now that Janie was mobile. But he had trusted me—and Janie had depended on me—to keep her safe while in my care.

I'd failed her. Just as I'd failed her sister.

Frantic, I held the telephone receiver between my jaw and shoulder. In one arm I held my Janie, too, and with my free hand I let go of her wound just long enough to dial.

Pauline's phone rang. One ring. Two rings. Three rings. "Answer, please answer." Five rings.

"Hello," she said after the fifth ring.

"Janie's hurt," I said, and Janie wailed. "I need help."

"Oh my gosh," Pauline said, and I heard my panic echoing back through my friend's voice. "Coming."

She and Tommy soon charged through the kitchen door. Janie and I were both bawling by now. Pauline saw that the rag pressed against my precious girl's face was soaked red with blood.

"What happened?" she asked. Her face expressed how scared she was—but her voice was soothing as she set her son on the floor with his yellow metal dump truck.

"Janie got Dennis's razor," I said. "I only had one pill, and I'd lain down when she was napping."

"Oh dear God," Pauline said. "His razor?" She gently took my fingers and lifted them and the rag up a tiny bit.

"What should I do?" I said, feeling more and more jittery.

"We may have to take her to the hospital. For stitches," Pauline said. In a whirlwind, she yanked open three kitchen drawers, one at a time—silverware, potholders, towels—hunting for dish rags. She pulled out a clean one and replaced the one in my hand. Pauline spoke steadily, having let her alarm turn to complete composure for me. "I remember when my brother fell off his bike," she said, "and he scraped his forehead near his temple. My mother said it took longer for facial wounds to clot. So let's take Janie and we'll all sit down on the couch and we'll keep the pressure on her brow for a little while longer." Her soft rhythmic voice brought me hope. She was one sharp cookie.

Pauline switched out the rags over the next half an hour, so we could gauge the amount of fresh blood. The stream was slowing. Janie was calm. "Should we call Dennis?" Pauline said.

"No," I said too quickly. I was jumpy. "Not yet."

I needed to see how this all ended, to know Janie was okay first. I was ashamed to think that I wanted more pills even as we sat there. But I did. Dennis and I had been in a good place since the party at the farm. He had proved that day what I meant to him, and it'd anchored me. He knew I used medications still, too. Just because we had moved forward together and were content didn't mean I didn't still grieve. I took the pills daily to keep ahead of things. And I was doing my job with our home and family.

Until today.

I was itchy. I craved a pill, maybe a whole handful right then so I might not feel the shame. But I had emptied a bottle that morning.

"I'll be back," I said to Pauline. She kept the pressure of the rag on Janie's eye.

I dashed to the bathroom and threw open the medical chest. I scavenged for a new bottle. I searched behind the aspirin and ointments and rubbing alcohol. Nothing. Frantic, I turned to the cabinet beneath the sink, batting away boxes of Kotex and Kleenex. Desperation pulsed through me.

I'd run out of pills.

What was I going to do? I couldn't believe how strong my desire was. I felt it everywhere from my throat to my toes.

Maybe, I thought for the first time, I couldn't stop. Maybe I needed pills the way flowers needed sun.

I returned to Janie and Pauline, wringing my hands.

Pauline said, "I think Janie's going to be okay."

Relief cascaded over me like warm rainwater, and in that instant the pills suddenly meant nothing. Janie was going to be fine. She was fine.

"Will the tip of her little brow grow back?" I asked, my finger trembling as I pointed.

"Probably. She's going to be a great beauty just like her mama," Pauline said, but serious concern still riddled her face.

We didn't talk as we adhered two bandages above Janie's eye in crisscrossed fashion. "Let Mommy kiss your boo-boo," I said. "It will make it feel better." And then I lifted her into my arms and got her into bed. She was tuckered out and slipped quickly to sleep.

Tommy had fallen asleep, too, in the middle of the floor. Maybe Pauline would run out to get me more pills. My jitters were returning.

"I'll fix us some coffee," Pauline said. "We need to talk." Her serious gaze eyed me again. I looked the other way.

"Honey," she said from across the kitchen table as we sat. It had begun to pour down rain outside, and my kitchen was dark for an afternoon. "You can't go on like this."

"Like what?" I was on edge. "Can't go on still mourning the needless death of my baby?"

"Of course you're still grieving. I don't know if that'll ever stop." She stood and flipped on a light. "I do think, though, that you need to stop depending on pills. You need your full faculties to care for Janie."

I slumped. Pauline's words weren't words I wanted to hear. I doubted she wanted to say them either. I had wanted to think I could recover from the tragedies and get back to living a halfway normal life—that I only needed a little boost to tide me over.

"Janie didn't end up needing hospital care," Pauline continued. "But you may have to go to the hospital yourself."

What was she talking about? "Absolutely not. I'm not going back there, Pauline." I stood. She had crossed a line. I could smell the shiny hospital floors now, hear the rattling of the instruments. "So what if I've taken a few pills, for Pete's sake? It's not like I'm doing anything illegal."

But I knew that I'd taken a risk. With Janie. I gnawed on a hangnail at my thumb. Had I not taken a pill, maybe I wouldn't have slept as soundly while Janie napped. I would've heard her rousing, getting up, and messing about. I would've heard Raggsie wanting to play, which he no doubt did.

"Can you stop on your own accord then?" Pauline asked. She wasn't going to let this drop. "For good?"

"I don't know."

"I'm going to help you," Pauline said. She insisted on telephoning Dennis, and I didn't balk.

"Millicent needs you to come home."

I could just imagine how he responded. "In the middle of the day? Is everything okay?"

"Not an emergency," she said. "Just come home soon."

I was surprised at how quickly she hung up. It was the first time Dennis had ever had such a request, and given the pitch of my friend's voice, Dennis apparently didn't debate it. He'd told her it would be half an hour, and Pauline promised she wouldn't leave until he came.

I scrubbed myself in the shower and shampooed my hair with force, needing to rid my skin of my guilt and my filth. I slinked into our bed after making sure my daughter was still fast asleep. Pauline was there, and Dennis would be home soon. I couldn't face him. He had never blamed me for what happened to our second daughter. But he would blame me for this. Rightfully so. My actions, or inactions as they were, were indisputable. Without pardon. He *should* blame me.

I blamed me.

I may stay in this bed forever, I thought, *and never get up again.* As I lay there twitching and yearning for the pill I didn't have, I concluded that here was where I had arrived in my life: if shame were a sauce, I'd be spaghetti—I'd be the hot, tangled mess piled in a mound and smothered in homemade shame the color of red that stained everything it touched.

"I need to be left alone," I mumbled to my husband when he came into the room with Pauline not far behind. Bafflement showed clear on both of their faces.

Then I hid my own face in the sheet while Pauline explained what had happened with the razor—speaking in journalistic terms, objective. Not laying blame at his feet. Not laying blame at mine. Dennis was disturbed by the negligence on both of our parts. But he said he'd grown up on a farm. He'd seen blood and broken bones and people needing stitches, slings, and casts. He didn't overreact. He said it was no one's fault. "That Janie, she's a climber now. It's gonna serve her well one day."

On Opa's good-bad-evil scale, Dennis scored high. One would think I'd have been happy with his reaction today. Relieved. Yet his lack of pointing fingers made me feel all the more defective.

I was skittish. My tongue was thick. No matter how badly I craved a pill now, Pauline was right. I had to stop.

I alone had let Janie get hurt.

"Take care of her," I said to Dennis. I was so ashamed I couldn't do anything. I couldn't show my face. "Just please leave me alone."

Pauline said, "Dennis, if you need anything, you can call on me or Bob. You know that, right? Anytime day or night."

He thanked her. Then I overheard him phoning his mother.

⌐

I have no idea how long I'd lain there before Mother Glenn knocked on the door and tiptoed in. Hours? A day? I did know she wasn't supposed to be here. It was dark out. She had late-summer work at the farm, corn to shuck and freeze for the winter. She closed the blinds. My blankets and cover sheet and bedspread were scattered in heaps as if I'd been fighting a bull in my dreams. But I didn't think I'd slept at all. Mother Glenn brushed my forehead with a feather touch of the backs of her fingers.

"You have a fever. You've got to drink something, eat," she said softly. "You're shaking. Are you cold?"

I was, I was freezing, but I hadn't realized it until she asked. She straightened the covers, tucked me in as if I were Janie's age.

She returned a few minutes later. "Sit up a bit, honey. Sip this soda. Take this aspirin."

I complied. "Just take care of Janie, please. Leave me be."

A better woman than me would've hated the idea of her mother-in-law thinking less of her—which Mother Glenn was sure to do—but I didn't care. I was incapable of caring. I needed to heal.

"Dennis wants to talk to you. Pauline's concerned, too."

"No." I was too ashamed to let him see me. Or Pauline.

Then my body racked with some kind of seizure. "Oh, dear girl," Mother Glenn said. "Hang on."

I would look back on that moment and wonder if I'd really heard fear in her voice, or if it had been an effect of my altered mind. The only mother I had left in the world put her arms around me, holding me tight until the tremor subsided.

"Drink. I've brought you a banana, too. Potassium." She unpeeled it and broke off a bite. "And some warm Cream of Wheat."

I slumped back into the bed after swallowing a few bites and guzzling a quarter of the soda, my breathing erratic. "I have to use the bathroom."

She let me lean on her as I staggered across the hall, my elastic knees almost giving out, and she helped lift my nightgown so I could get to my underpants. My energy had drained with my confidence. As I sat on the stool, she unspooled the roll of toilet tissue and handed me a fistful. She stroked my hair. It must have felt like a giant bird's nest resting atop my head. A mess. Then she stepped out and closed the door to wait.

As we scuffed back into the bedroom, Dennis stood in the hall. He flipped on the light. He watched me as one might view an injured driver crawling out of a wrecked car.

"I love you," he said. His face was sad, sad as it had been when I'd told him Kathleen had been dropped.

I didn't remember anything else until the venetian blinds were open again and the sunlight peeked through.

"You're still here?" I asked Mother Glenn.

"For as long as you need."

But what about her chores? The chickens. The vegetables that needed pulling.

I was shaking again, shivering. Thirsty. I wanted one little pill. Just one. Just *one*.

It was a new day.

—

"Mommy, Mommy," Janie cried from somewhere in the house. "I want my mommyyyy." There were times my daughter wanted her daddy. But she still wanted me. Guilt spiked in my heart because I wanted to comfort her, to hold her, but I knew I wasn't good for her.

Mother Glenn's voice tried to soothe her, *"Shh, shh."*

Janie's cut—and the bright-red blood—took over my mind's eye. The memory of her screaming made me roll over and yank the pillow around my head, cramming it to my ears, trying to deafen the voice. Trying to forget. Trying to forget so much.

I was unaware of how long it'd been. "I fixed you some Jell-O. Raspberry," Mother Glenn said. She fed it to me, one slow bite at a time.

"I told you once," she said, "that I'd bear all your burdens of pain for all you lost, if only I could." In went another bite. I met her eyes. "But I can't."

Silence. A long, thick silence. My legs jerked convulsively. Silence still.

"You're the only one who can bear it, sweetie," she said. "You have a little girl who needs you, never mind your husband at the moment. Janie needs her mama."

Over the hours Dennis's mother prayed with me. She told me stories of the Glenn family matriarchs the century before, of their struggles and fortitude. "And then there was my own aunt Agnes," Mother Glenn said. Dennis's great-aunt Agnes had played "I'll Be Home for Christmas" on the piano at our wedding. "She had an awful ordeal during the great Flood of '37," Mother Glenn said.

I remembered that flood from when I was twelve, how the streets at Third and Vine had been like a canal. Electricity had gone down across the city. People had died. It was the worst natural disaster in Cincinnati history—and the Ohio River's flood had wreaked havoc from Pittsburgh to Illinois.

"Aunt Agnes," Mother Glenn said, "was a young widow living near the river with her four-year-old boy. Her home flooded so badly, she and her son escaped in a rowboat out the window of her second-floor bedroom, oaring with a broom between the limbs of their treetops. It was January—and record rains and melting snow had caused the flood. Her little boy got hypothermia, and but for the Red Cross set up at a school, his shivering body would never have survived. Aunt Agnes had gotten him there in time."

My eyelids weighed heavy as Mother Glenn spoke. I said, "I didn't know Great-Aunt Agnes had gone through that." I drifted off to sleep, dreaming of mothers who were strong for their children against all odds.

Two days passed. Now four. A visiting doctor came once. I was addicted, and he couldn't do any more for me than my mother-in-law already had. I'd have to ride this out.

⁓

I got up to use the toilet. Alone this time. I combed my hair by myself, too, and washed the sleep from my face. I climbed back into my bed. I still hadn't spoken to Dennis. I hadn't seen my daughter. She called for me, but I didn't deserve it.

Opa's marble was on the nightstand, in the cherrywood box my husband had made to display it. I took the glass sphere into my hand and squeezed. And with that squeeze my tears broke through, as if they'd been all dammed up like the yellow and orange swirls frozen inside the marble's glass.

Janie getting hurt had been tantamount to my losing the baby all over again. It'd been as if I'd lost Opa and my mother at the same time as Kathy: all one horrific catastrophe. It reminded me, too, of losing my goodness on a flagstone walk before a Tudor house when a widow apologized to me. Janie's injury symbolized my losing one more precious thing—like losing my childbearing womb—gone. Carved out of me. Or forsaken through my own stupidity and pride. I'd neglected my duties. Harm had come to my girl. Mother Glenn, hovering somewhere in the hall, gave me comfort—but she also added to my shame for the mother I'd become.

I took the cool glass marble between my hands again, rolled it around and around and around in the pit of my palms until the German glass turned hot. I thought of all the times my opa had held this marble in his hands, too. How he'd been young once, like I had, and he'd knelt to a circle in the dirt with the other boys, competing for bragging rights.

I would not swallow another pill. There were three kinds of people in the world, Opa had taught me. I would be the *good* girl my opa always saw in me. *You're Millicent the Strong. Don't you ever forget it.*

"Dennis," I called out. My voice was weak, but he stood inside our room in less than a minute, his expression every bit the little boy he'd been once, and it was as if he awaited news of getting a new pony. He was eager for me to be back in his life.

"I love you," I said. "Please bring our Janie and come sit with me."

He stretched out his arm to take my hand. "I'll always be here for you."

2015

The girls and I still stood outside the church. Clouds had overtaken the sun, and the breeze was more of a wind.

"So your episodes with the barbies," Jane said, "were more harrowing than I realized."

I felt a quick rise and fall of my brows.

"Grandma, good for you for persevering." My darling Kelsey gave me what she called a high-five hand smack.

I reached to touch Jane's scar then with the tip of my index finger, gently, and she let me. "You were little more than two and a half years old. I hope you'll accept my apologies."

"The day I got cut is my earliest memory," she said. "All I recall is bleeding and crying and you pressing things to my face. But you know what? It was worth reliving the bad parts so I could come out on the other side." She kicked at a pebble in the crack of the sidewalk. "If only I could get past my invisible scars as easily."

I didn't recoil. I didn't get struck with a lightning bolt. I held amazingly calm. I would soon learn of her invisible scars as she had learned of mine.

As if Kelsey intuited my thoughts, she said, "Mom, Grandma, this is where I leave you two for some much-needed one-on-one time. I'm parched. I need another bottled water. I need to eat. Baby Glenn-Goldberg is hungry, too. I expect to hear a date to celebrate. Soon." She kissed us goodbye. "Mom, I'm beyond thrilled that you're not sick."

Neither Jane nor I tried to convince Kelsey to stay. Thank heavens I had my cane. I couldn't stand much longer. And the afternoon chill had begun to snake its way through my jacket and the yarns of my sweater to my skin.

"Let's hop in my car," Jane said. Her white four-door was parked in front of the church near mine.

"We should've climbed in here twenty minutes ago," I said as she opened the passenger door for me.

There we sat, the console and gear shift feeling like a barricade between us. I cupped my hands in my lap. Jane turned on the car's heat. I wasn't sure how much of Jane's "troubled childhood" I could stand to hear.

But she deserved for me to try.

Mother Glenn once said there was no sense in beating around the bush. It was high time I learned.

"Tell me, Jane. Tell me about your invisible scars."

She patted the top of her thigh nervously. Had she played in her mind a film reel over the years, about how one day she'd tell me her story? And now the moment had come? I suspected she'd learn it wasn't as easy to do as it sounded.

She blew out air in the way of exhaling a cigarette's smoke. "In 1963," she started, "spring break was not good for me."

My insides contracted.

The days leading up to Kathy's spring birthday had always been hardest on Dennis and me. I moistened my lips with my tongue.

"I was thirteen," Jane continued, "and back then, I logged a day's activities in my diary. You'll recall the small white one bound in faux leather I got one Christmas. Its pages had shiny fake gold on the edges, and there was a lock and key the size of a penny.

"I attended my first slumber party with the cousins and their friends in the basement at Carrie Ann's house. We played forty-fives on the record player—the Beach Boys, Chubby Checker, and the Shirelles. We told our fortunes with the Ouija board, and you know what? That damn thing knew I'd never get married." Jane sniggered while I went rigid.

"The older girls played Truth or Dare, and we younger ones tagged along," she went on. "When they got bored and left to read *Seventeen* magazine or to talk about boys, Linda Jo and I continued the game.

"'Truth or Dare,' I said. She responded Truth. 'What's the worst thing your perfect mother ever said?' I asked her. Linda Jo scratched her head and hemmed and hawed.

"Then she told me how she had walked into the kitchen one morning while Aunt Abbie was on the phone with her own sister. The words Linda Jo overheard—and those I later wrote down in my diary—were: 'I tried to stop her, but that Millie Glenn went to a doctor who butchered her. No more babies for her.'"

I choked. It took me a few seconds to recover. Abbie had broken her promise? She'd told someone about my unauthorized procedure? My skin seemed to bubble up on my bones. I was furious. And shocked. But . . . Jane hadn't known about my sterility until I told her this week. That much had been clear. So I was confused.

A school must have let out close by, because long yellow buses tracked past the church and Jane's car one after another, shadowing the interior of the car.

"You know what we teenage girls thought about that?" Jane said. "The butcher doctor and no more babies? Linda Jo said you had an illegal abortion after I was born. It was then that I began to absorb how deeply I'd disappointed you. So much so you couldn't stand the thought of raising another child—"

"No—" I reached across the car's center barricade, but Jane pulled back. I was mortified.

"Let me finish," she said curtly with her hand to her heart. "I might've given you the benefit of the doubt, but in the days that followed, my memories reinforced Linda Jo's conclusion." She paused. "Such as the clay baby you didn't like. And sad Mother's Days. And Daddy burning french toast for supper because you couldn't get out of bed and cook or even to sit by me. Other times you smothered me and protected me like I was a pet project—one that suited your social appearance in the world."

I shrank back into my seat. Could I make myself invisible? Dread hovered over me like an enemy helicopter in a war-torn field. I might not survive this battle.

In life, did we remember the bad things more prominently than the good?

"Of course," Jane went on, her tone softening, "I now know the impetus for all these things and more. I know I grossly misconstrued them. But you see, on that day, all I knew was I felt unwanted."

"Is that why you later punished me by not letting me know you had Kelsey?" I said. "That's why you withheld her until she was three months old?"

"Partly that. There were times when I was feeling especially sorry for myself, where I assumed you wouldn't want my baby any more than you wanted me."

"Oh, Janie. Oh my gosh, that cannot possibly be true. Please tell me it's not so." My jaw and teeth ached from their clamping through the stress of all this.

"Okay, okay, let's not overstate it," Jane said quickly. "I mean, I'm a complex, fucked-up human being, like the rest of us."

Like the rest of us. Then something else hit me.

Suddenly Jane's and my argument from years before Kelsey was born made sense, too: it was 1973, the day after *Roe v. Wade* came down. Jane was home for a week for Tommy's wedding. She was twenty-three, and we'd just finished the breakfast dishes.

"There's something I must discuss with you," I'd said, my tummy queasy, my heart thumping. I was ready to tell her about Kathy for the first time. "You might want to sit down."

"Don't worry," she said, her voice raised and sounding like a smart aleck. "Abortions are legal now, but I won't be running out to get one.

I'm glad for women everywhere; they get *to choose*. It's the best thing to come out of Washington since the signing of the Civil Rights Act. But it's not my bag. If ever I conceive, I'll have the baby and love it."

"That's good," I'd said, completely thrown for a loop. Was Jane building up to letting me know she was pregnant? "Why are you telling me this?" I said. "It's not remotely connected to what I had to say."

"Don't pretend with me, Mother," she said. "I know you had one done in some seedy back-alley bed."

"I never," I said, the pitch of my voice as low and loud as hers was high. What had made her think I'd had an abortion? She was frightening me. Was she on psychedelic drugs? Hallucinating? "I think you—"

"What? What do you think about me, Mother?"

"Forget it, Jane," I said. No matter what her problem was, she was a twenty-three-year-old woman, and I wasn't going to stand there and be abused. She had no earthly idea what she was talking about, and I couldn't tell her my life's worst nightmare under these conditions. "I won't trouble you with what I was going to say after all," I said. "You're obviously much smarter than me."

And there it lay.

She'd gone back out west after Tommy's wedding and would not have a child until several years later. My family secret remained buried. And the rift between my daughter and me widened.

I realized now that Jane had indeed had a cancer growing all these years after all: it was a tumor born of misinterpretation and doubt and blame.

How had she not considered for one second that what she'd heard about me was false? My head pounded. The answer was easy: because she was no better than her own mother. I had thought the worst of her father once, too.

Jane reached over the car's console to nudge me. "Mom? You listening? We were talking about the day I brought Kelsey home."

"Sorry. Say again?"

"Honestly, I saw your face when you beheld your granddaughter for the first time, and I felt deep remorse for what I'd done." Jane looked full of repentance, and my heart soaked it in like a hug. "It was clear that you accepted my baby," she said, "from the instant you reached out your arms. I never withheld Kelsey from you again." This much was true.

Jane dabbed tears at the bags beneath her eyes. "But the unresolved problems you and I had, well, they remained."

"The words 'I'm sorry' will never be enough," I said. The degree of compunction I felt was surely more than a human was intended to bear. I felt bludgeoned. "How do I make it up to you? How do I fix us?"

"Don't you see?" she said earnestly. "No matter how old we get, no matter the pent-up resentment or how wronged or injured we've felt all our lives, we all want our parents' approval. We strive to be granted their love."

"I do love you. Unconditionally," I said without pause. "And not 'in my own way' either. I love you in the way you love Kelsey."

She nodded once. Bowed her head. "We have many blessings. Thank you for bringing me to church so I could be reminded of that fact." She raised her head and looked at me. "I'm healthy, as much as any old, reformed stoner can be. And somehow I did something right in raising Kels. Part of your good mothering wore off on me after all. Tell you what, let's go toast to your birthday at a fancy-ass restaurant—your official celebration, not with carry-out food. Real cake and candles and all. We'll celebrate my nondiagnosis as well. Tomorrow night?"

We embraced goodbye. A nice, long, warm, real mother-daughter hug.

As I drove along the streets I'd known since I was a young woman, streets with a few more stop signs and lights, I realized what a journey I had taken in the last two weeks. I'd set out to have Jane understand me—to understand why I am the way I am. And I'd held hopes of understanding her better, too.

I pulled into my drive and grasped that I had arrived there: at the beginning of our healing.

CHAPTER
TWENTY-FIVE

December 1953

It was almost time for the holidays, more than a year since I'd weaned myself off the pills, and Pauline and I would soon head out for our first-ever Tupperware party. It would be fun to shop for canisters, salt and pepper shakers, and tumblers in the home of a friend in the neighborhood—I could buy Christmas gifts for all the Glenn women. And Dennis liked that I was getting out with Pauline more these days.

I bathed four-year-old Janie and put her to bed early—not that my husband was incapable, but I needed to ensure no soap trickled into her eyes and that she had her Muffie doll in case she awoke while I was gone. And I couldn't possibly leave without reading to her a few pages from *The Velveteen Rabbit*. Dennis flipped on the front porch light and wrapped me up in my red woolen coat—ever the gentleman, even with our ninth anniversary just around the corner.

The golden glow of the light shone through the door's two half-moon-shaped windows as he gave me a bear hug goodbye. "You're the prettiest girl a guy ever got," he said. "Not to mention the smartest." He had been with me every step of my recovery; he'd never given up on me.

"And you're the most charming guy a girl ever snagged," I said.

Dennis kissed my cheek. "You girlies have fun."

Pauline arrived and off we walked, attired in gloves, hats, slim dresses, earrings, and heels. Thankfully, no snow had fallen in two weeks. Soon we sat in Dorothy's living room before piles of plastic containers in all manner of pastel colors, artfully arranged on a six-foot table set up in front of the dormant fireplace. The hit song "Come On-A My House"—sung by Rosemary Clooney, a gal from just over the river—played in the background.

We still lived in Mount Auburn, where another cluster of midsize Gunnison homes had recently sprouted. The neighborhood had grown so much. Last summer, Bob Irving had been the first to buy a Weber kettle grill, and Pauline had invited our newest neighbors to what she called a "backyard patio party" so we could all get acquainted around their pool. She'd had a picnic table with benches, red-and-white checkered linens, Kahn's wieners. The works.

Although Pauline had had another son by then, she bounced from one social event to the next. I was busy decorating. Trying new recipes. I took time for myself twice a week to relax while Ruth Lyons hosted *The 50/50 Club* on TV. My schedule was filled to the brim. I sewed corduroy drop-seat overalls for Janie. Taught her to count to one hundred. Read to her every day. Played with her in the yard. Cuddled and kissed her. Sang songs to her. Prepared her favorite foods.

I suffered moments, of course—those triggered by memories or dates or words people said—where I'd lapse into spells of great sadness. But I was good to Janie.

One thing that was hard on me was card club with the girls. I was held captive every four weeks, rotating among portable tables with mothers obsessing over everything from trouble with teething to whether the polio vaccine worked. Eventually someone would lay down her trump card, perhaps a jack of spades, and then turn to me and innocently ask, "How many children do you have?" Or, "Are you planning to have more? I'll bet Janie would love a little brother or sister." It was hard to hear. But I'd learned how to say I had one. I'd learned to pretend I might have more.

The most difficult part of making Abbie and the rest of the family promise not to talk about Kathleen was that sometimes I needed so badly to talk about her. Not often. But I needed for someone besides Dennis, someone who remembered what I'd been through, to let me speak of our loss freely. Thank God Pauline was that friend.

Tonight neighbors from two blocks over and ladies from church squeezed into folding chairs our hostess's husband had dragged up from the basement. These women were giddy as kids gathering to go trick-or-treating.

"Bingo!" someone shouted. The Tupperware lady warmed up the guests with games before demonstrating the benefits of her food storage products. So we all matched tokens to square cards in our laps that bore the names of famous people. President Eisenhower. Ricky Nelson. Lucille Ball. The bingo winners took home sets of Tupperware wagon-wheel coasters.

Dorothy, ever the model hostess, jumped up to pour hot coffee and asked that we help ourselves to her pineapple upside-down cake. It was set on her dining room table strewn with candles, smartly displayed in a Tupperware piece she called her bake-and-take cake carrier.

Word spread like wildfire that the Tupperware dealer had bought a new car with her own money. I was pleased that I had come tonight to support a modern, industrious woman. Being there prodded the yearning I already felt for getting back into our own business.

For the first time in my marriage I could even foresee the day I might break out and do something else beyond the business, too—something big on my own.

"Ladies," the dealer said, "to keep your food's freshness locked inside, let the air out, and then 'burp' the lid." With much fanfare, the Tupperware lady revealed the secret to a container's airtight seal.

"Burp, burp, burp," the women all chanted amid bursts of laughter. The dealer passed around a pale-green, six-piece bowl set with lids, so we could all have a try. The more products we bought, the better Dorothy's chances of earning a special hostess gift—a rose-patterned set of silverware. It was good marketing. So we all scribbled away on little pink forms with stubby pencils without erasers. I was having a swell time.

Ideas bubbled up in my head. To get my job duties back, I would not appeal to Dennis with a dinner of Swiss steak and hope for the best. Taking a cue from the Tupperware lady, I would go to him with a means to increase sales. We could host a pizza party for past customers to encourage referrals. I could launch an ad campaign with testimonials—people loved to see their pictures in the paper. I might establish a program with local vendors to give our customers a discount for appliances and furniture and more. It would get more traffic through their doors and be a win-win for everyone. A whole plan for the business was taking form in my head. I would present the plan to Dennis as his partner with a fully fleshed-out case. I would follow through on the plan *without asking permission.*

I was beginning to be excited again. I could contribute. If Mama were alive, she'd be proud of where I'd come after falling so far. I had new purpose.

That's when I saw our neighbor from over on Oakbrook Lane, tucked behind two others beside an antique armoire. The pregnant neighbor. She rose steadily from her seat as if she were the newly crowned Queen Elizabeth of England, and as she spun to her right to greet her many admirers, the hems of her generous, bell-shaped top swished happily to and fro about the tops of her thighs.

None of these women doubted that when a nurse wheeled the new mother out of the hospital come discharge day, she would be cradling a bundle in her arms. Not a soul could possibly doubt that a bit. Except me.

I would be strong, though, not letting the pregnant neighbor sink my spirits. "When are you due?" I asked like any other one of the girls, smiling.

She rubbed circles on her tummy. "I'm six months along. I'll have a spring baby. My due date is March 23." She beamed.

I grasped hold of the arm of Pauline's chair beside me. Pauline touched my hand, and her soothing voice echoed as if from miles afar. "Oh, honey. That date. You going to be all right?"

Kathleen would have turned three on the following March 23. I shifted my eyes to where our hostess was extolling the benefits of her Wonderlier bowl. The bowl was perfect for leftovers. Spillproof, too. And so durable. It saved time. Saved money. Nearby, three neighbors huddled, gossiping all the while they crammed celery sticks stuffed with Cheez Whiz into their faces. The room began to spin, and I pinched the bridge of my nose, the noise around me becoming louder and louder.

"You look wonderful, my dear. Any names picked out yet? You say little Jimmy learned to ride his bike last summer? *Shh*, don't repeat this, but Maryellen found that new magazine, *Playboy*, in her husband's desk drawer. The one with Marilyn Monroe? I suppose he's stashed away the Kinsey report on women too? Burp, burp, burp. Bill's whole clan is coming for the holidays. Did you hear? Lynn is expecting again too!"

I longed to dip into my pocketbook, slip out a bottle of pills, and make my way to the powder room. So easy. But I had none. My hands fisted, my nails making dents in the life lines of my palms. I would not backslide.

"Excuse me, aren't you Mrs. Glenn?"

I twisted to see a young woman with wavy hair the color of mayonnaise, juggling some Tupperware bowls. I should have been able to place her. Grocery store? Church? But in my current state I could not.

"I'm Valerie Percy. Your husband built our house." She was bubbly with round cheeks, full and sweet as cinnamon buns.

"Of course," I said. "The Percy home, over on Birch, isn't it?" The importance of Dennis's sales, of clients and referrals, of our security, rocked me back to attention. In this moment I had to do my part, however slight it was. An upwardly mobile, satisfied homeowner could be a builder's customer for life. She could send droves of referrals our way, too.

"We love our home," she said. "It's so convenient and cute. You know, you were a big help in our making a decision."

I was taken aback. "Me?"

"Yes. I remember the first time I met you and your husband at an open house. My Joe and I were so nervous. Picking out house plans and a mortgage and all. But you and Mr. Glenn were so patient. We felt we were in the best possible hands when it came to signing the papers. I'll never forget how you told me on the side, woman-to-woman, that a house was more than a home. It might fall under our domain, but it was a beginning. It was there for us to prove what else we could do." She glowed. "I'm going to the university now. Training to be a pediatric nurse."

That woman brought hot tears to my eyes. "You're so sweet," I said. Pauline had a broad smile. This past customer, Mrs. Percy, would have a job helping children. "I'm humbled," I said. "Truly."

Another idea for the business came to me. I could start up a morning program, a women's group for Gunnison homeowners' wives. We could meet and have speakers or test new products. Maybe we all had something of import to share.

I had Janie. I had Dennis. And I had much work left to do.

2015

Having been given my choice of restaurants to celebrate, I picked the Precinct, one of Jeff Ruby's steakhouses. Beef was a bit hard to chew, but these old teeth had gotten me this far, and red meat hadn't killed me yet. Jane had said she'd choose a salad. And besides, I liked to get all dolled up in a dress and earrings every once in a while, brush a little rouge on my cheeks. This place reminded me of going out on the town with Dennis and Pauline and Bob when we'd come to the Precinct when I turned fifty-eight—the fall before Dennis first got sick.

Jane played chauffeur. The restaurant was in a former police patrol house built in 1901. We climbed out at the corner of Delta and Columbia and let the car be valeted. The building had a high foundation of large rectangular stones, while old red bricks ran up the rest, including a turret on one end. Jane took my arm, and we ascended the few steps under a large purple awning bearing a big and elegant *P*.

We were greeted with Sinatra music. The foyer was warm with rich wood floors, a red button-tufted circular bench, and two vintage barber chairs to sit in for fun.

"Let's take a selfie," Kelsey said. "You two act as if you like each other." Jane and I rolled our eyes, laughed, and posed.

I pressed my lips together to add sheen to my lipstick and perk up my face. As if that would do any good. Men's hairlines may recede, but so did women's lips. Such were the perils of becoming *elderly*, a word I despised, though I didn't mind *old*.

Kelsey snapped our picture as we snuggled before the wall of celebrities' photos; the Precinct had welcomed everyone from Sylvester Stallone to Pete Rose. We checked our coats, and my girls looked pretty—Kelsey had painted her nails blue and wore black leggings, black Tory Burch flats, and a sleek black maternity top with a tangle of long blue beads around her neck. Her shoulder bag was large enough to tote a dozen diapers. Jane was in slacks, boots, and a flowing kimono in paisley and fringe. I was relieved to see her looking radiant.

The hostess led us through the swinging saloon doors of wood and leaded glass. "I never tire of this cool, quirky place," Kelsey said. "Good choice, Grandma." I patted her back.

I wanted to breeze by the ornate Brunswick bar as we went to our table. I loved hearing the shaking of martinis—that rigorous sound of ice cubes on metal, a sound from my younger days and now back in fashion. Soon we were seated in the main dining room, where giant images of turn-of-the-century policemen hung in relief against exposed brick walls. This contrasted with chandeliers of both brass and crystal and paintings of nudes.

Jane said, with her index finger poised on her jawbone and tilting her chin left and right, "How do I look? This dim, flattering light would make even Norma Desmond appear decades younger." She laughed. "Grandma Glenn and I stayed up late one night watching *Sunset Boulevard*. She loved that movie."

"I had no idea," I said.

"I miss Great-Grandma Glenn," Kelsey said. "No more stories about her taking a cow's udder and squirting milk in Papaw's face when he was a toddler."

"No more ice-box cake," Jane said. "Goodness gracious, I loved that woman. Has it really been twenty-five years since we lost her?"

"She was a good egg," I said. Mother Glenn had been a second mother to me. Loyal and kind and true. She had outlived Dennis. She'd lost her own child, and I'd held her as she wept. It was a twisted fate of the world that as mothers we'd been forced to do that for each other.

"I'm gonna watch *Sunset Boulevard* this week just for shits and giggles," Jane said. "Unless Tommy Irving asks me out on a date."

"Whaaaat?" That was Kelsey, her eyes big as cow patties and surely matching mine. Tommy was recently retired from Procter & Gamble and had been divorced for years.

"Just kidding," Jane said. "Got you. But he heard I was back, and he's going to pull some old friends together soon."

"Wonderful," I said. Might those two end up together? I smiled at the possibilities. Yes, my Janie was in a great mood tonight. She didn't have cancer. And neither of us could get the smiles off our faces.

A server set down two kinds of bread: sourdough and salted rye. These were accompanied by two kinds of butter, one a velvety sweet cream and the other dotted with minced black truffles.

"The bread service alone makes this place worth coming to," Jane said, grinning. Perhaps only in Cincinnati would fine dining feature rye bread, a nod to the city's German heritage.

The server brought Jane a glass of Riesling and me a cabernet. Kelsey lifted her goblet of sparkling water and said, "To my two favorite women in the whole wide world—two women who've survived everything life has thrown at them." Her voice was sentimental and joyous and young. "May there be many more birthdays for each of you . . . our birthday girl and for my mother, who escaped a close call."

"Cheers!" We clinked glasses. Life presented these moments of unexpected beauty to balance out all the rest.

"Jane," I said, "I am over the moon happy for you. A prayer answered."

"Thank you," she said warmly. "Now I can concentrate on my grand-child." Jane asked Kelsey, "Any update on midwife versus hospital?"

"Midwife," Kelsey said.

Jane said, "I assume that means no labor meds."

"Well, yeah. I have friends who view vaginal births as barbaric, who don't need to 'prove their womanhood' by going through all that pain. That's what makes them feel in control. Not so for me."

It always came down to yearning for control. But as Jane had said in the church, how much could any of us be in total control?

"Remember our talk about C-sections?" Kelsey went on. "They're vital for some women and babies. But Aaron says his buddy, a medical malpractice attorney, told him that women aren't seen as mothers-to-be by hospitals anymore. They're litigants-to-be. Therefore, doctors are more apt to operate, and that way if they get sued, they can claim they tried everything they could."

"Scary," Jane said.

I slathered sweet cream butter on rye bread and said nothing. Over the course of sixty years, then, society had gone from no one getting to question a physician to everyone questioning physicians. In my view there were good doctors and bad. More good than bad, I thought. Why couldn't there be a fair balance—a clear recourse for patients who'd been wronged, but not everyone jumping on the bandwagon?

Sometimes society took things too far. Sometimes it cut off its nose to spite its own face.

Kelsey fondled one of her loop earrings. "C-sections are the most common surgery in the country now. That's a lot of knives."

The waiter was coming our way. "Mind if we shift the topic to the kind of knife I'm going to use for my steak?" I said.

By the time we placed our orders, diners had filled more tables. The room wafted with scents of lemony-buttery Dover sole as it was filleted right in front of one couple. The thirty-something lovebirds at the table a few arms' lengths away appeared to be marking an anniversary. A bottle

307

of champagne chilled in a silver bucket. Their fingers—hers bearing a rock so big it could carve bulletproof glass—were interlaced across the table's wide stretch of white linen. I wondered, as I often had over the years when observing strangers, whether their blissful existence might one day shatter. Would this sunny, unsuspecting couple suffer great loss, as Dennis and I had? I sent over silent vibes for them, that they'd be strong, that they'd last. That they'd keep their vows for better, for worse; for richer, for poorer; in sickness and in health till death did they part.

This had been the only way for Dennis Glenn and me. Our vows and our love had held us together. And I felt a swell of wholesome pride in that.

"I brought something fun," Kelsey said. "A few pictures."

She'd taken a shoebox of old photographs home from my basement. For tonight she'd hand-selected the black-and-white studio shot of my young, happy parents. And a picture Dennis had snapped of me in the Eden Park gazebo after he'd proposed. There was also Janie and me rolling out Christmas cookie dough—her with flour and sprinkles all over her face.

Mother Glenn had once said that our good memories were there for us when we needed them; they're there to sustain us. How wise that woman was.

"Grandma, look at this one of you at Kroger. You're so official." She passed it around.

"I was quite a bit younger then," I said. But it wasn't a pose at my first Kroger job, the one before I'd married. It was me when I retired.

When Jane was in high school, I'd left Gunnison Homes, gone to college, and earned a degree in accounting. On the evening before my first day of class, Dennis had come home with a bouquet of fall flowers . . . and a note attached:

To the prettiest girl a guy ever got, not to mention the smartest. Go get 'em, Mil. Can't wait to see how high you soar. Love, D

I'd kept that note. How heartwarming it'd been to see how far he'd come. He'd watched how I'd stepped back into the home-building business without waiting for his consent, worked by day while Janie was in school, and by the time she reached high school, revenue had grown by 15 percent.

After earning my college degree, I got a job fulfilling my first passion, crunching numbers—as an accounts payable specialist for the largest grocery chain in the country, Cincinnati-based Kroger. I'd started out at the very first Kroger Super Market when I was seventeen, and years later I got the gold watch from the company headquarters.

"Grandma," Kelsey said, "you're such an inspiration."

Sweet Kelsey. "The day I'd gone to interview for that job Pauline said I was a shoo-in, because I had tons of experience with numbers and groceries."

Kelsey and Jane chuckled—but it brought a pang to my heart. It was less than two years ago that my best friend had phoned me, saying, "Millie, it's me." I'd known right then and there that something was terribly wrong, because Pauline had always called me Millicent, not Millie. In the end, I was holding her hand when she died of kidney disease in hospice.

Jane said, "I agree with Kels, you're inspiring. I remember you talking to me about *The Feminine Mystique*. You even quoted to Daddy from the book. And when we watched the March on Washington, you served sloppy joes on TV trays—I still ate meat then, ha, ha—and after Martin Luther King Jr. gave his now-famous speech, you asked me if I had a dream of my own."

"I vividly recall what you said," I told her now. I hoped I wouldn't get choked up by repeating it. "You said, 'I want to grow up and help people.'" We'd had good times along with all the bad, she and I.

"And that's exactly what you did," Kelsey said. "I'm proud of you, too, Mom."

"I took a few detours before landing at Habitat," Jane said. "But we should never say never."

No, never say never. I should never have counted Jane and me out. I'd lost one daughter. But Jane wasn't lost after all.

Kelsey handed another photo to her mom. "Here's you and Papaw, wearing your hard hats."

"Daddy built houses for *a* living. I built houses *for living*," Jane said. The nonprofit at which she'd first volunteered, and then spent her career, helped families in need around the globe. "But Daddy," she said, remorse tinging her voice, "was a man who offered his little girl what other men left only their sons. And I turned it down."

In the eighties, Dennis had asked Jane if she wanted to take over the home-building business when he retired. He'd been disappointed that she'd said no, and he'd later sold it.

"Don't fret about that decision," Kelsey said. "The whole point of the women's movement meant you got to choose, right?"

How that dear child warmed my heart.

Two servers arrived at our table. "Petite filet with cognac-peppercorn sauce?" That was mine. I'd ordered the steakhouse hash browns, too. I'd never eat it all, but it would warm up well the next day. "Wedge salad with extra blue—hold the bacon—with a side of mac and cheese? Sea bass with carrot purée?" The stiff-collared server pressed his palms together. "Ladies, will there be anything else?"

"We're all set," Kelsey said.

"I know you have a career choice ahead, too," I said to her. "Have you given more consideration to what you'll tell your boss?"

"I have," she said. "You two are an amazing pair of role models, you know? Career women. And wonderfully imperfect, loving mothers. I want to be both. It doesn't have to be either/or."

"So what are you going to do?" Jane asked.

"My job will let me go part-time after six weeks of maternity leave." Kelsey's face was a mix of hope, satisfaction, and distress. "I love my work. But I want to be home with my son or daughter, too. I don't know if this plan will last forever. I may end up going back to work full-time—or I may change my mind and become a stay-at-home mom. Playdates and carpools to soccer practice. I don't know. But I think part-time will be a good balance for starters."

"Best of both worlds?" I said, cutting my steak. It was tender as could be, and delicious. Worth the pain in my hands to slice off another bite. I considered Kelsey's pending decision: Why couldn't my granddaughter be happy at home—even if one day she stayed home full-time—no matter what Mama had drilled into me? Kelsey had earned a reputation in her field, and whatever she chose moving forward would be good enough for me.

"We've got the best of all worlds right here. The three of us," Jane said.

I remembered again how I'd felt on Janie's first night home from the hospital as an infant. And my heart overflowed again with that abundance of love.

~

"Dessert, madams?" said the server.

"What kind of cake do you want?" Jane asked.

I scanned the menu. "Three-layer carrot cake sounds good."

"Can you put ninety-one candles on her piece, please?" Jane said. Had she let a stronger Southern accent seep out on purpose? "Or one candle would do," she said. Then she pointed to her menu and added, "And bring us one of these, too. The warm skillet chocolate chip cookie. Don't skimp on the ice cream."

"Three plates. Three spoons," Kelsey said.

The whole meal and conversation were what I'd long hoped for: harmony, closeness, love, and respect. My purse, a large one, was hanging on the arm of my chair. I pulled out a framed keepsake, one that I'd removed from the shelves Dennis had built.

"It's my turn." I handed the frame to my daughter while Kelsey looked on.

"What's this?" Jane said. "Your collage?"

"Take the collage out of its frame," I said. "Go on."

Jane raised her brows but complied. She slid her glass of water aside. When she got the frame's backing and the muslin and the yellowed slip of paper removed, the message was as clear as the day I'd written it in cursive. She read it aloud: "Made with love, in memory of our happiest day yet, a day that will only be surpassed by the glorious moment that our first baby is born. Millicent Glenn. April 13, 1949." That was several months before Janie was born.

"Oh, Grandma," Kelsey said. She gave me a big smile.

Jane wiped her eyes. "It's a preserved moment in time. It's over the top."

"I wanted you more than I'd ever wanted anything my whole entire life," I said. She blushed. It felt good for my throat to hurt when saying words that actually made her happy.

Kelsey excused herself to head to the ladies' room, but not without kissing the top of my head first.

"Mom," Jane said. "Have you ever regretted making that call to Nurse Breck? Learning what happened?"

"Never. Kathleen had been forced to suffer it. As her mother, she deserved for me to be strong enough to hear it and never forget it."

A few minutes later I emboldened myself and asked my daughter, "Not long ago, you said you'd wished I'd told you about Kathy much sooner. But now that you know everything you know, would you rather have never been told?"

"No regrets," she said. Kelsey was walking back toward our table. "And you know what? Maybe I needed this health scare, too. I needed to experience some hint of personal trauma. I can't begin to imagine the crisis if it'd been my child at risk instead of me." She took my hand in hers as Kelsey took her seat. "Kelsey's right. You're a survivor."

Something in me fluttered. If the sensation had a name, it might be affirmation. I'd made the right decision in telling Jane most everything after all. *Surely knowing would be better than not knowing.*

I had no regrets.

"I love you, Mom," Jane said, surprising me with these three beautiful words and her eyes glistening. "Don't ever worry again about what you told me or what you didn't. You hear? You did what you had to do to survive something no mother should ever have to endure. I'll be okay. Promise." She had a warm bend to her lips. "All is forgiven."

Forgiven. My heart leaped and did a flip. I'd gotten my last wish.

"I love you, my daughter," I said. Jane leaned over the table and embraced me with one arm. I breathed in her scent of sandalwood. Her hair tickled my face. Kelsey actually got back up and joined in, and we had a family bear hug right there in public.

Kelsey said as our arms slipped aside, "It's like you both always needed to know the other was there and you were loved, but you were both too hurt and vulnerable to ask." Out of the mouths of babes.

Our desserts arrived, and I blew out my candle, my heart full. Birthday parties, it turned out, need not be big to be special.

As we shared the cake and the melty skillet cookie, my mind slipped backward again—far, far back this time toward a day I would not share with my girls. Indeed, I would forever hold private this one last memory.

My storytelling was done.

CHAPTER
TWENTY-SIX

December 1957

Pauline and I poured out of the theater with the rest of the throng. It'd been a Saturday matinee, and we had just seen *Peyton Place*. The year before, Pauline and I had both devoured the *New York Times* bestseller by the same title. A housewife whom no one had ever heard of had written it. The story boasted well-heeled characters with loose morals—New Englanders who'd committed everything from adultery to murder. The film wasn't without controversy. But it starred Lana Turner and Hope Lange. Pauline said as we filed through the lot to my car, "My lands, that Hope Lange should win an Oscar for that performance." I had to agree. Her character had been raped by her stepfather, whom she subsequently killed in self-defense.

Dennis and Bob had expressed no desire to see that film. I think my husband wondered why we women were so keen on peeking into other people's problems. Hadn't we had seen enough of our own? I could appreciate that.

We had lost a child.

Pauline said as we climbed into the front seat, "You're not gonna believe this."

"What am I not gonna believe?" I inserted my key in the ignition.

"My head is throbbing," she said. "And I've got cramps. I think I'll take a rain check on shopping."

I craned my head her way. "You? Turning down a shopping spree?"

"I know," she said. "It's a rotten shame, isn't it?" We burst out laughing.

It wasn't a problem for me, though. Janie was at the farm for the weekend, baking gingerbread with her grandma, and I could spend more time with my husband. Just us two.

Pauline crossed the lawn, and I waved and headed into the house. Because I was home early, I expected to find Dennis watching basketball on TV. Or reading *Popular Science*.

"Honey?" I said from the kitchen. "I'm home." No answer. His car was in the garage. But there was no sign that he'd eaten a thing. No soup bowl and spoon. No Oreo crumbs or graham cracker wrappers.

I made my way to the living room. "Dennis?" All was still.

Where was he?

The hall bathroom was open and dark. As I went toward our bedroom, I removed my clip earrings, which had started to pinch. I thought I heard something. Was that moaning? Dennis moaning?

There was no sign of him in our room. The bedspread was perfectly neat, just as I'd left it that morning. But again I heard him moan.

I scurried to Janie's room. Nothing.

I ran across the hall and burst into our spare room, the messy one with all my sewing stuff and his home files for the business. There Dennis was, wriggling on the twin guest bed, bunched up in yellow-striped linens. His feet stuck out at the foot of the bed, his shoes still on. His face was in agony.

"What are you doing?" I said, trembling. I spoke loudly so there'd be no mistake.

His head popped up. His eyes wide. I could see from where I was that his pupils were dilated. His shirt collar was crooked. His hair was in disarray.

"What in the world are you doing in here?" I said, coming closer. I smelled the alcohol before I noticed the bottle on the cabinet of my sewing machine—the bottle was beside wadded-up packs of cigarettes and an ashtray bulging with butts. Bourbon. Almost empty.

He was sloshed. My husband of almost thirteen years—we would celebrate our anniversary the day after Christmas—was sloppy drunk. Of course, he imbibed with our friends and at parties, just like I did. But I couldn't recall a time I'd seen him soused.

He tried to sit up. He flopped back down.

Besides the alcohol and the smoke, there was another odor, too. I sat next to him on the bed, and beneath the cover sheet on his other side was a stinky patch where he'd barfed. Not a big patch, thank goodness.

"Can you get up? So I can clean in here?"

"I may never get up again," he mumbled.

"Dennis Glenn," I said. I was so frightened I was angry. "What's this about?"

I hopped up and looked around the room for a clue. He had house plans on his drafting board. A stack of paint chips. Nothing unusual. That's when my foot slid on a crumpled-up pile of newspapers. I bent to the floor and picked up the top page.

"We should have discussed this years ago," Dennis said. Discussed what? Now he had me even more mystified.

Dennis had folded the newspaper page in such a way as to highlight one section. I glanced at the date in the corner. This morning's edition. The society section.

He repeated, "We should have talked about this years ago." He rubbed his whiskered cheeks roughly with both hands.

Talked about what?

I faced the window to scan the page without him watching. What could these photos of pretty women with wedding announcements mean? Then I saw her: Mrs. Reynolds.

The doctor's wife had married a second husband. She looked elegant—a more mature Grace Kelly, perhaps. But happy. Her fiancé had also been widowed, the article said. An engineer.

I lowered my head. Ashamed to think of her. I recalled vividly her flagstone steps. The toys scattered in the yard, the Tudor lines of her house. Two darling girls—and their mother closing the draperies one at a time in the daylight.

Dennis blocked his eyes with his arm as if too much sun streamed in. But it did not. The sun was setting.

He said, "I lied to you."

~

"That time I went to the builders' conference for the award," he said. I started. "I didn't really go. They shipped the plaque to me the next day, on a truck with a kit."

Was this to be some sort of confession for sins of the heart? An affair? I had doubted Dennis once before—when I thought he'd signed consent papers. I'd been wrong then. Now I knew that trust must be stronger than doubt.

"If you weren't at the conference, then where were you?"

"Dr. Reynolds came to see me," he said. "At my office, when I was gathering up things for the conference."

I winced. "What?"

"He came to apologize. For his negligence that led to the death of our daughter. Nothing more."

My hand flew to my mouth.

"When the doctor had gone, I decided I'd let him off too easy. I hadn't yelled or cursed enough. I hadn't punched him in his face or broken his surgical fingers. I couldn't forget ripping up my box of cigars—the ones I'd bought to pass out to the guys—or the tobacco leaves I'd crumbled into the trash. I couldn't shake the memory of holding Kathy. I couldn't get the picture of her purple wound, her tiny lips, out of my head. And I couldn't forgive what he'd done to you, too."

"Dennis." My heart was thudding so hard, so fast, I thought it might explode. "What exactly are you saying?"

"It was past ten o'clock that night. After Reynolds had left that afternoon, I looked up the doctor's address and went to his house."

I gasped. I pictured the Reynoldses' lamppost aglow, the mullioned windows.

"As I came close to his place, his Buick pulled out of the drive. He was alone. I followed him. I figured he was on the way to the hospital for a night shift, and I'd have it out with him in the parking lot. Wasn't long after, as I trailed him west on US 50, that I realized he was going somewhere else. I held back but stayed on his tail."

"Dennis," I said, taking his hand. "Honey, you don't have to tell me this, you know." I wasn't sure I could bear to hear it. His head quivered left and right as if to say, *I've got to get this out.* I let him go on. I was too rattled to think what this might mean.

"Soon, we were on old Grandin Road. His headlights. My headlights. We barely passed a car. He stopped at the bridge. I shut off my lights but let the car creep on a piece farther. There was a full moon. I saw him open the driver's door, climb out. He looked around in a cursory way. And he headed on foot to the center of the bridge.

"I parked my old Chevy off the side of the road. Climbed out. I was nervous as a whore in church. So many things were whizzing through my head. But one of them was—"

What? What was whizzing through his head? He coughed. Coughed again.

"The doctor climbed up the fencing that bordered the bridge, about four feet? One thing kept spiraling through my mind: *Jump, you son of a bitch. Let me see you jump. Let me watch you smash to the ground down below. Let me see you rot in the ravine with the maggots and the snakes."* Dennis's face had gone from sickly white to hell-bent red. He didn't kill the doctor, did he? My husband was the man who contained his feelings, who never held a grudge, at least not against me. Yet I had a sinking feeling of trepidation.

"I wanted to push him over," he said.

"Dennis—" What had my husband done? My teeth clamped together. I prepared myself for the answer, aware that I'd know this the rest of my life.

"That's when I waffled," he said. "I thought of you and Janie, and Mother and Father. I'd been taught to do what was right. What if I landed myself in prison? What good would I be to you then? It was like a thunderbolt. I had my family to take care of. And so help me, I thought of the asshole doctor's family, too. I started running. Reynolds had climbed over now. His feet were on the metal base, his hands still connected to a rail. He was leaning out . . .

"I went into a full-on sprint, shouting, 'Stop, don't jump. Stop!' I came within ten or so feet of him and yelled, 'Stop.'"

I pictured the scene in my mind's eye. Had I not known how the story would end, my wicked, vengeful heart would be wishing the man would jump. Die. But I'd be worrying in this instant that he'd turn on my husband first and hurt him . . .

"He looked over at me," Dennis said. "I knew without a doubt Reynolds recognized who I was. 'Don't do it,' I said.

"He lifted a leg to swing it back over, as if he would save himself. I was relieved. I'd stopped him." Dennis started to weep as he spoke. "Then his other foot slipped. Just like that. He fell. He *dropped*, all the way down to the ravine."

My stomach fell, too, a sensation of tumbling. I covered my mouth.

Had Dennis not caused the doctor to pause, he might not have slipped. Who knew how differently things might have turned out?

I looked away and saw the newspaper. The former Mrs. Reynolds.

That doctor's name infuriated me all over again. I couldn't help it. But Dennis had witnessed his fall.

"You lived these last few years believing a man, a father, might not have died had you taken different action?"

All Dennis could do was nod and let his eyes shutter. Then: "I couldn't face you that night. I took a room at a motel. Didn't budge the next day. I came home that Friday as if I'd been at the conference all along."

I visualized him curled up on a musty motel bed, agonizing over what'd happened. Perhaps one day he'd explain to me how it had really felt.

Hmm. Of that I had my doubts.

I grabbed tissues from the box beside the bed, dabbed one to Dennis's eyes, and another to his lips and his whiskered chin. Silver hairs had crept in over the years when I hadn't been looking. Silent tears were streaming down my cheeks now, too. I felt their hotness slip from my face and watched them splash onto his, one tear at a time.

So many secrets.

"I'm sorry," he said.

The secrets Dennis and I'd kept were as much to protect each other as to shield ourselves. That's what love and loss had done to us. We'd gone through something horrible *together* that had almost torn us apart. For as long as we would live, there would be things that would dredge up a memory or invoke our rage or grief. But now I knew, we had each gone through something horrible *apart*, too, and that had bound us back together today, stronger than before.

"Dennis, I'm going to say something I should have said a long time ago."

I lay down next to him. I lowered my head onto his shoulder, brushed my wet hand across his rough cheek, and then wove my fingers through his like the branches of our sugar maple.

"You did nothing wrong," I whispered.

I remembered the story of the boy who'd gone to fight the war, but Uncle Sam had turned him away. I remembered the husband who had hidden the birth and death certificates to shield me from more pain. I remembered the man who had stood by me in front of his family. And I would not forget my beloved who'd stuck by my side, even after I'd made decisions out of pettiness and pride.

"Even if you had done something wrong," I said to him now, "I would forgive you."

EPILOGUE

April 2016

The girls—all three of them: Jane, Kelsey, and the baby—came for a Saturday visit. Joy Millicent Glenn-Goldberg was now two months old. I'd added new photos to the shelves Dennis had built. The first was of Kelsey and Aaron and Joy in the private, soft-sided tub where Joy had been born. A water birth. The couple had decided on a birthing center instead of home or a hospital. To them it was a happy medium. Kelsey was still immersed to her waist, wearing her tank top and resting back against the new daddy, who sat behind her wearing his swim trunks. Their sweet baby, photographed at only two minutes old, had looked right up at her mama and reached her tiny, wet fingertips up to Kelsey's chin.

And there was the shot of Aaron giving Kelsey a sterling-silver charm bracelet, a bangle engraved with the words *Family Forever* and a silver heart closure. "It's a push present," he'd said, all bashful-like, "for everything you've done in delivering our baby."

I'd never heard of a push present before, of course, but Kelsey had nearly swooned. On the bracelet hung one silver charm, a tiny ring with three dangling letters: *M.O.M.*

In the birthing room that day, after Aaron held Joy, he'd lifted her out of the water and presented her to the midwife, who wrapped her in a pink-and-white-striped receiving blanket. Soon the midwife brought the baby to Jane. My daughter's face was filled with such wonderment, such extraordinary gratitude, and a kind of delight filtered down through the hearts and tears of many generations who'd come before her.

Yet without taking Joy from the midwife, Jane said, "No, let Great-Grandmama hold her first."

Tears stung my eyes as I looked to Kelsey, who nodded. It was as if these two had it planned all along.

I hadn't gotten to hold my second daughter all those years ago. I hadn't gotten to hold my Kelsey as a newborn either. Now, I reached out to receive this precious child. I was honored that they all trusted me with these old, decrepit hands of mine.

I took her into my arms and brought her snug to my chest.

In that moment—a moment I cherished beyond all the moments of my days—I was holding Joy, the weight of her a precious gift in my arms. And I had my daughter with one arm around me, and my granddaughter smiling at me with a lustrous shimmer on her dewy, young skin.

How had I come to be so blessed?

I touched my lips to the damp, satiny top of Joy Millicent's head, closed my eyes, and thanked the Lord for her safe passage. I knew she'd grow up to face challenges—of that there could be no doubt. But she could make a difference. And more than anything, she'd grow up loved.

Kelsey's doula, the birth advocate who'd helped the midwife, took my picture using Jane's iPhone. And so on my shelves that Dennis had built, there now was a picture of me with Joy—but there was also another new picture of me. Well, not a new one, but an old one that I'd pulled out of Kathy's old album. I was eight months pregnant with Kathy in the photo and had fifteen-month-old Janie on my lap. Mother Glenn had snapped that pose of us in the parlor at the farm—with Dennis leaning over my shoulder, and he and Janie and me all radiant.

Kathy was part of our family story at last, never to be forgotten.

The doorbell rang at my house, and Jane went to answer. The disarmed door tinkled its friendly hello. "Welcome," Jane said to our guest—and Jane's seven-week-old pug yapped in her arms. The pup was all black, and she'd named him Blackie.

"Hi, I'm Kelsey," I heard my granddaughter say. "It's an honor to meet you."

The woman with the beauty mark above her top lip followed the girls into my den, carrying a bag stuffed with tissue in white and baby-girl pink.

"Millie."

"Carolyn," I said, grinning—no more calling her Nurse Breck.

We'd reunited at the ice cream parlor a couple of weeks before. I would've known that woman anywhere, no matter her having a few years on me and despite the ravages of age. Kelsey had found Carolyn on the internet.

Now my friend took a turn holding my precious great-granddaughter, whose hair was as dark and thick as her grandmother's had been, with some curls from her daddy, too.

Carolyn said, "This little girl is my dream come true for you."

"Mine, too."

When we had met recently, we had talked of the time in the maternity ward and of how neither of us was ever the same. And though she knew nothing of my opa—of what he'd called me when I was small nor of lessons he'd taught me—she said, "You're a good person, Millicent Glenn. You're strong."

Our eyes held each other's gaze, and a realization dawned in my mind. I *was* good. I *was* strong. It was as if two enormous cymbals came crashing together, each one gripped by the gloved hand of a musician in a marching band, the arched metal discs letting out a loud and musical clang that reverberated in sound wave after sound wave around us.

It's time that you forgave yourself, I thought. And when the imagined echoes of sound waves had subsided, I realized I was free.

If I were to be granted my life's last wish, it would be that my daughter—and her daughter, and her daughter, and the daughters who come after—would not wait until they were ninety-one years old to accept this truth: the whole of one's life need not be defined on the grounds of one decision. While good may come when others support you and affirm you and even forgive you, you will never be complete unless these things you provide for yourself.

Yes, I had forgiven myself. Though I would never forget.

Who knew how long I had left to live . . . a day, a month, a year? Or more? The date of my death wouldn't be carved on the headstone near the perfumed honeysuckles anytime soon—not if I had my say. For I had a new purpose in life to enrich the lives of the women in my line. To teach them all I'd learned. And each time I was handed that special baby girl, and each time my eyes drifted across a room and caught Jane's gaze, and each time my phone chimed with a text from my lovely granddaughter, I was also given a new chance at happiness.

And I took it.

AUTHOR'S NOTE

This story and its characters are fictional, though the maternity ward scene draws from a long-ago tragedy in my family. Among the many sources I researched, the following stand out most in my mind: *The Fifties: A Women's Oral History* by Brett Harvey; an interview with Randy Shipp, an expert on the prefab homes industry and author of the white paper "Gunnison Homes: A Brief History"; a tour of the Gorman Heritage Farm, which is open to the public outside of Cincinnati; an interview with Anne Delano Steinert, director of the board for the Over-the-Rhine Museum in Cincinnati; a walking tour of OTR and its brewery heritage led by John Funcheon of American Legacy Tours; an interview with Debbie Schutz, nurse practitioner, on testing for breast cancer; an interview with Jacqueline H. Wolf, PhD, author of *Cesarean Section: An American History of Risk, Technology, and Consequence*; a pregnancy manual from 1940, *Expectant Motherhood* by Nicholson J. Eastman; and the *Ladies' Home Journal* magazine, May 1958 cover story: "Cruelty in Maternity Wards."

ACKNOWLEDGMENTS

I am so appreciative for my editor, Chris Werner, and agent, Katie Shea-Boutillier, for falling in love with Millicent's story and giving me a chance—and to Tiffany Yates Martin for helping me dig into the story's emotional layers. I've been blown away by the process and amazing support from the whole Lake Union Publishing team. Thank you all for making my book better, and for making it available to readers!

My heartfelt thanks go to gifted writers Betsy Crosby, Joy Kniskern, and Kay Heath, who form my historical fiction critique group (and who are also my friends and psychiatrists and confidantes and devil's advocates and cheerleaders). What would I do without you girls? Many thanks to our novel-writing classmates, too—and to our wonderful instructor, author Joshilyn Jackson, who first brought us together and shared her time and writerly wisdom.

This novel would not have been published without the sage developmental advice I received from author and teacher Jenna Blum, and editors Liv Radue and Laura Chasen. I also learned so much through the Yale Writers' Workshop. A shout-out goes especially to Terra Elan McVoy.

I am also incredibly grateful to the writing community at large—to the gracious, supportive authors who've inspired me with their work and who have endorsed mine. Thank you, thank you. And hats off to the excellent Atlanta Writers Conference and my friends at FoxTale Book Shoppe.

Thank you to this novel's brave early readers: Carla Gunnin, Amy Anderson, Linda Berthold, Renee Bissell-Cole, Katie Woodruff, and Kathy Schroeder—and also to beta readers Carole Jay (who answered questions about Cincinnati) and therapist April Mojica Whitaker (who advised on my character's addiction). I am indebted to you all for your years of support.

Throughout my long writing journey, several people offered encouraging words, often when I needed them most: Andrea Bailey Powers, Sylvia and John Smith, Ken Isaacson, Ranen Abdallah, Pansy Whitaker, Shelley Vallier, Mary Sutton, Robin Gauthey, Anne Glenn, Melodee Hand, Kim Lister, Leandra Lederman, Susan Daugherty, Michelle Gilliam, Evey Gaither, Wynette Stewart, Jane Ashmore, Hollie Whitaker, Mary Beth Chappell Lyles, and my Facebook friends everywhere. I also wish to thank Kian Cheng, Rebecca Pugh, and countless other Constangy colleagues for their insights and kindnesses. I haven't forgotten.

I feel blessed that my mother, Sheila Cole, has been by my side over the course of my writing endeavors, having pored over the manuscript for this book alone at least three times. Thank you for having dreamed the dream where you'd seen my book be published, and for writing "hooked!" or "tears!" in the margins of my pages. I've kept those pages. And while my father, Ron, is now sadly gone, I also cherish him telling me when I was sixteen that I could write.

Thank you to my beloved sons, Justin and Brolin, for unwavering support as I've worked toward my goal of holding this book in my hands. I'm honored that you've believed in me and thrilled beyond words to have you celebrate this moment with me. And to John, my dear husband of more than forty years: Thank you for all the vacations you've spent in museums instead of at the beach, for never minding that my clothes pile up on the floor at home, and for always being okay with watching movies like *Road House* (again) while I write past midnight on weekends. Most of all, thank you for reminding me that I'd only fail if I didn't try.

And finally, thank you to my grandchildren, Lane and Evie—and to my own grandparents who came before them—for the joy you've brought into my life. I hope you see that a hint of that grandparent kind of love seeped into the pages of this novel.

BOOK CLUB QUESTIONS

1. Millie is ninety years old when the book opens, and readers soon learn that she carries a long-held secret. Do you believe that most people who've lived that long have a buried secret or regret? Has anyone in your family (or other families you know of) harbored secrets that eventually came out?

2. Which character did you relate to the most?

3. In what ways was Millie's life shaped by her mother? By her mother-in-law, Mother Glenn?

4. How do you assess America in the 1950s—that slice of time between the victory of World War II in the 1940s and the era of protest and the civil rights movement of the 1960s? Was the baby boom era generally a time of happy, carefree days? How has your opinion of the era been reinforced or changed after reading this novel?

5. Millie believed that her own pride led to her family's tragedy. Do you agree? At one point Kelsey says, "Grandma, did you ever think that maybe pride had gotten in Papaw's way first?" Discuss the nature of pride in this story, including Millie's and Dennis's—and that of Millie's mother. Are other characters prideful?

6. Millie never knew her father. Kelsey never knew her own father either. Discuss the extent to which Jane, who had a close relationship with her father (Dennis), really knew him. How well can any child truly know a parent?

7. Opa taught Millie that sometimes good people make mistakes, and sometimes bad people get something right. In your opinion, is Dennis a "good guy"? Did your views of Dennis change over the course of the novel? Why or why not? What about Abbie? Is she a good person?

8. How are maternity wards of today similar to or different from maternity wards of the 1950s? How has the treatment of expectant mothers changed, if at all? Are doctors still seen as gods?

9. Were you aware that one in three women who give birth in US hospitals have cesarean sections? What factors contribute to this trend? How do you feel about it?

10. Which do you believe Millie longed for more: to be a wife and mother and raise a large family? Or to make a professional contribution to business and earn her own money? Do you consider Millie a feminist?

11. Describe the role of friendship in Millie's circle. Did her lifelong friendship with Pauline resonate with you? Was Abbie Glenn ever Millie's friend? Was Nurse Breck?

12. What were Millie's motivations for keeping the truth from Jane for so long? How might their mother-daughter relationship have been different had Millie been open about Kathleen early on?

13. How do you feel about the book's ending? Did Millie's story resolve in a way that you expected or hoped? What will Millie's family look like five years from now?

14. Discuss the grandparent relationships in this novel: that of Opa and Millie, and of Millie and Kelsey. Share a special memory of one of your own grandparents. Do you have a photograph of when this grandparent was young?

ABOUT THE AUTHOR

Tori Whitaker grew up in the Midwest. She now resides outside Atlanta, Georgia, where she and her husband of more than forty years live near their two sons. When Tori was born, she marked the fifth living generation in her family, and when her grandchildren came along, her family had five generations again—this experience might've influenced her love of stories that shift between the past and present. Tori belongs to the Historical Novel Society, and her feature article, "Multi-Period Novels: The Keys to Weaving Together Two Stories from Different Time Periods," appeared in the *Historical Novels Review*. Tori graduated from Indiana University and is chief marketing officer for a national law firm. She is also an alum of the Yale Writers' Workshop. *Millicent Glenn's Last Wish* is her first novel.

Connect with Tori at www.ToriWhitaker.com; on Instagram at tori.whitaker.37; on Facebook at Tori Whitaker, Author; and on Twitter @ToriLWhitaker.